Praise for Mary Daheim and her Emma Lord mysteries

THE ALPINE ADVOCATE

"The lively ferment of life in a small Pacific Northwest town, with its convoluted genealogies and loyalties [and] its authentically quirky characters, combines with a baffling murder for an intriguing mystery novel."

—M. K. Wren

THE ALPINE BETRAYAL

"Editor-publisher Emma Lord finds out that running a small-town newspaper is worse than nutty—it's downright dangerous. Readers will take great pleasure in Mary Daheim's new mystery."

—Carolyn G. Hart

THE ALPINE CHRISTMAS

"If you like cozy mysteries, you need to try Daheim's Alpine series. . . . Recommended."

—*The Snooper*

THE ALPINE DECOY

"[A] fabulous series . . . Fine examples of the traditional, domestic mystery."

—*Mystery Lovers Bookshop News*

By Mary Daheim
Published by Ballantine Books:

THE ALPINE ADVOCATE
THE ALPINE BETRAYAL
THE ALPINE CHRISTMAS
THE ALPINE DECOY
THE ALPINE ESCAPE
THE ALPINE FURY
THE ALPINE GAMBLE

THE ALPINE GAMBLE

Mary Daheim

BALLANTINE BOOKS • NEW YORK

 Published in the United States by Ballantine Books, a division of Random House, Inc., New York, and simultaneously in Canada by Random House of Canada Limited, Toronto.

http://www.randomhouse.com

Library of Congress Catalog Card Number: 95-96149

ISBN 0-345-39641-3

Manufactured in the United States of America

First Edition: August 1996

10 9 8 7 6 5 4 3 2 1

Chapter One

MY SON ADAM had started a war. He hadn't meant to, but he's always been a bit rash. Indeed, animosities between the combatants were long-standing. All it took was a careless remark to Lydia Twofeathers about Jacinto de Mayo's spotted dog.

"It's like this," Adam said to me over the phone from Tuba City, Arizona. "The Navajos and the Hopis usually hate each other. There's this big argument about who should live where, and the government really screwed up. Has Uncle Ben ever told you what a mess they made of the Native Americans around here? It's better now, I guess, but dumping the Hopi reservation into the middle of Navajo lands was a bummer. That's what really caused the problem when I went into the Tuba City Truck Stop to get a taco."

"Uh-huh," I remarked, somewhat vaguely. My attention had been distracted by Ginny Burmeister, my business manager at *The Alpine Advocate*. She had just dropped off the first group of classified ads for the newspaper's premiere personals page. "So you mentioned you'd seen Jacinto de Mayo's dog digging in Lydia Twofeathers's garden. Why bother bringing it up?"

Given my son's penchant for convoluted explanations and harebrained motivations, the question was ill-advised. Naturally, I got what I deserved:

"It was when I got arrested. My hubcap fell off. Well, Uncle Ben's hubcap, from his truck. After the cop drove away, I had to—"

"Whoa!" Maternal sharpness cut into my voice. "You got arrested? What for?" Suddenly *SWM seeking free-wheeling SWF for bed-and-not-bored* didn't look like much of a crisis.

Adam's impatient sigh reverberated in my ear. "I *told* you, Mom. For speeding. You can only go about ten miles an hour on the reservation. It's really dumb, but they watch everybody like a hawk."

"You got picked up for speeding when you visited Ben at Easter. This is Memorial Day weekend. Or was. Why are you still yakking about Jacinto de Mayo's dog?" I tried to ignore *SWF wants SWM with big rig*. Alpine, Washington, is a logging community. Perhaps the woman wanted a man with a truck. Perhaps not. "And why," I persisted, "are you still in Tuba City, instead of back at school in Tempe?"

"I'm going tonight," Adam replied, sounding as if he were gritting his teeth. "I don't have class on Tuesdays."

The sudden silence indicated that my previous question was being dismissed. I refused to let Adam off the hook.

"Okay, okay," Adam said in a testy tone, "I got picked up again. Which is why I need a hundred and fifty dollars. They doubled the fine on me this time. These Navajos really know how to stick it to the white man. I don't blame them, of course," he added in his youthfully broad-minded manner.

I held my head, closing my eyes to *DWF wants Same*.

"The war, Adam—what about Ben's hubcap and the Navajo-Hopi war?"

"Oh, that." Adam now sounded breezy. "The hubcap

rolled into Lydia Twofeathers's yard where the dog was digging up her flowers. She came out and yelled at both of us. I ran back to the truck and drove off. Then I saw her later when I was getting my taco. I felt sort of bad, you know. I didn't want her to think I'd ruined her garden. So I mentioned this spotted dog, and she knew he belonged to Jacinto de Mayo. He's a Hopi and she's a Navajo, and that's how it all started. Now everybody's mad because they say there's been a lot of trespassing and stuff. Uncle Ben's trying to keep the peace, but he won't have time because he'll be coming with me to Alpine in a couple of weeks."

"Three weeks," I clarified. "Nobody's shot anybody, I hope?"

"Not yet, but they're threatening to." Adam's voice was alarmingly cheerful. "Hey, got to go. Uncle Ben just came in with somebody from the Navajo council. See you. Oh, send that money to—"

I hung up. Adam could cope with his own stupid speeding tickets. But of course he wouldn't. If I didn't send the money, he'd borrow it from Ben, who, as a mission priest, was in even more straitened financial circumstances than I was as a small-town weekly editor and publisher. Immediately, I was filled with remorse. I'd call my brother and tell him to refuse my son's request. Adam was twenty-two. He should learn some responsibility.

I was still mulling over my family problems when Vida Runkel, *The Advocate*'s House & Home editor, stomped into my tiny office. With disgust, Vida indicated the cigarette I'd just picked up.

"You said you'd quit." Vida's gray eyes were hard behind the big glasses with their tortoiseshell rims. "I'm very disappointed in you, Emma Lord."

"This is only my second cigarette today," I protested, guiltily putting it back in the pack.

"It's not yet ten o'clock." Vida's majestic figure radiated virtue, indignation, and disapproval all at once. "You didn't smoke for a week after New Year's. You stopped for eighteen days during Lent. Where's your willpower?"

I scanned my cluttered desk as if I could find my willpower somewhere under the personal ads or the first draft of my editorial on the Iron Goat Trail. It was pointless to defend myself: Vida was right. I'd gone for years without a cigarette, weakening only when our new ad manager, the nicotine-stained Leo Walsh, came aboard in September; I'd succumbed completely when Sheriff Milo Dodge lighted up during an ugly murder investigation the previous November. I gave Vida a sheepish smile.

With a sigh, she lowered herself into one of my visitor's chairs. "Remember the Californians?"

I frowned. "Which ones?" Alpine gets its share of out-of-state tourists, at least during the summer. Winter visitors are usually skiers who come from within Washington.

Vida was adjusting the many ties that were intended to form a bow on her bright pink blouse. It was a complicated task, and while Vida has a multitude of skills, artistic coordination isn't one of them. The result looked like a wad of bubble gum.

"Last November," Vida said, impatient as usual when I was slow to recall specific names, places, and events. "They stayed at the ski lodge. They're developers from Los Angeles, and they're back. Henry Bardeen called this morning."

Henry manages the ski lodge. Humorless and efficient, he usually isn't prone to disclose his visitors' names unless there's a self-serving reason involved. Naturally, my curiosity was piqued.

Naturally, Vida was pleased to show off her knowledge. "You know the mineral springs by Scenic—these developers want to buy up the property and build a hotel. A spa, as it were."

I regarded Vida with interest. During my five years in Alpine, I'd never visited the so-called hot springs, which I understood to be a series of muddy holes where hardy health-seekers wallowed for various reasons. They were located near the whistle-stop of Scenic, a couple of miles east of Alpine. Many years ago there had been a hotel, but it wasn't directly connected to the hot springs and had long since been abandoned.

"Aren't the springs on state timberland?" I inquired, discovering that my fingers were straying to the cigarette pack.

Vida shot me a warning glance. "No. That particular parcel is owned by Leonard Hollenberg, one of the county commissioners. I've heard he intended to build a chalet so his children could come up from Seattle to ski. Henry Bardeen figures that Leonard would prefer to sell it to the Californians for a big price and build the chalet at his other property east of town. Naturally, Henry's wild."

The image of the sober-sided Henry Bardeen going wild and flipping his toupee provoked a giggle. "You mean he's afraid of competition with the ski lodge?"

Vida nodded, causing her jumble of gray curls to bob up and down. Her hair might be unruly, but at least it was her own. "It's no laughing matter, Emma. These Los Angeles people have no respect for the environment. Henry is entitled to be upset. My father-in-law, Rufus Runkel, helped build the lodge in 1930, after the original mill was shut down. It saved Alpine."

I knew all about the town's rickety history. It had started out before the turn of the century as Nippon, with Japanese immigrants working on the railroad and mining the mountain cliffs. Circa 1911, Carl Clemans had come from Snohomish to build a lumber mill. He renamed the town, hired logging crews, and created a fledgling community. But in 1929 a variety of factors led to the mill's closure. The town itself was to be abandoned unless residents found a new economic source. Rufus Runkel and Olav the Obese—as local lore fondly called the big Norwegian—sunk money into the rocky slopes of Alpine, thus becoming pioneers in the ski business. Over sixty years later the lodge still flourished, though other mills had come and gone.

I pointed out this well-known fact to Vida. "The only ongoing industry that isn't endangered by the spotted owl is tourism," I said, keeping my hands folded in my lap. "Skiers, hikers, campers, fishermen—they're Alpine's mainstay. Logging is increasingly unstable. Look at all the out-of-work people around town."

Vida harrumphed. "It would be different if somebody local was interested in creating a resort spa. Or even someone from Seattle. But these developers are *Californians*." Vida made their state origin sound obscene.

Cigarette smoke wafted into my office. It was followed by Leo Walsh, who was a California native. "Hey," Leo said with a grin, "do I hear my homeland's name being taken in vain?" He poked Vida's shoulder as he sat down in the other visitor's chair. "What's wrong, Duchess? You afraid that Alpine is attracting Californicators?"

Having recoiled from Leo's poke, Vida curled her lip at the nickname she despised. "There's no need to be crude, Leo. I'm merely offering my opinion on out-of-state developers who have an eye on easy money and no moral or ethical responsibility. You carpetbaggers have brought a great deal of trouble in your wake."

Leo waved his cigarette in a dismissive gesture. "Hell, I've seen the bumper stickers. 'Don't Californicate Washington' or whatever. I saw one at the Venison

Inn the other day that said 'Keep Montana Clean—Put Californians Back on the Bus.' Oregon and Idaho are just as bad. Is that any way to treat people just because they want a fresh start?"

Though his voice was serious, the twinkle in Leo's brown eyes indicated he was teasing. Vida, however, had temporarily lost her sense of humor. She often did when she was in Leo's company. She also often coped by ignoring him, which she did on this occasion.

"Here, Emma," she said in her primmest tone as she handed me a piece of paper. "These are the names Henry gave me. Blake Fannucci and Stan Levine. Obviously, there's a story in it. You may want to handle it, rather than turning it over to Carla."

I acknowledged the unspoken criticism of my youthful, if dizzy, reporter with a slight nod. "I'll call the lodge and try to arrange an interview for today. This is a short week, so we're up against deadline."

Wordlessly, Vida left my office. Leo leaned across the desk and handed me his cigarette. I took the last puff, then hastily extinguished the butt in a Trader Vic's ashtray I'd swiped from the Benson Hotel in Portland during my tenure as a reporter for *The Oregonian*.

"How was your three-day weekend?" Leo asked, putting his feet on the chair Vida had vacated. "Full of adventure and romance?"

I wanted to pretend that it was, but instead I made a face. "I got out the lawn furniture and put in bedding plants. What about you?"

Leo shrugged. At just over fifty, he occasionally exhibited a boyish air that didn't quite go with his usual world-weary attitude. His wavy auburn hair was flecked with gray and there were deep lines in his pleasant face. Obviously, Leo had laughed and worried and drunk a lot. But most of all, he exuded an aura of frustration.

"I drove down to Seattle with Delphine Corson," Leo

replied, referring to the buxom local florist. "We stayed at the Edgewater and screwed most of the time." He stretched and yawned, though whether from exhaustion or boredom, I couldn't tell.

"How nice," I said, aware that I sounded like a waspish vestal virgin. "I think we'd better go over this first set of personals. I'm not sure we want to run some of them as is. In fact, I'm not sure this was a good idea in the first place." I shoved the proof sheet at Leo. "We're only going to do this once a month. That way, if it gets to be a real nightmare, we can drop it without too much flak."

The idea to run personals had come from Ginny Burmeister last fall. I often felt that Ginny had little imagination, but sometimes she surprised me. She was also pressing for a Summer Solstice Festival to replace the outmoded Loggerama.

Leo's smile was quirky as he read through the ads. "Some of these are a little raw," he allowed. "If you take them that way." He wiggled his bushy eyebrows at me. "But these people are prepaying by the word. That's what I've got against so-called obscenity. One word is the same as another when you count them up for an invoice. What difference does it make if you say *fuck* or *intercourse*? Either way, it's fifty cents."

"If you can get a fuck for fifty cents, you've got a real bargain," I said, refusing to be drawn into a moralistic debate with Leo. Then I fluttered my lashes, just to annoy him. "Of course, maybe Delphine works for free."

Leo reddened, bristled, and started to get up. "Emma, that's a bitchy thing to say!" With effort, he got his temper under control. "Delphine's a decent woman. She's just lonesome. Like the rest of us." The last few words were muttered into his chest.

I had the grace to be embarrassed. "Sorry. I like Delphine. Really. She does wonderful arrangements."

The comment made Leo grin, if wryly. "She leaves her artistry in the shop. Trust me. If Delphine's an exotic orchid at work, she's a shrinking violet in the bedroom. Now let's see what we can do about these ads. What I like is the deception. Take this one—'DWM, cuddly, fun loving, big spender seeks sympathetic DWF homeowner with no strings attached.' The guy's probably been married three times, he's fat as a hog, can't pay his bills, and is looking for some sappy female who'll put a roof over his head and give him three squares a day. Plus boudoir benefits, if he's still awake. He doesn't want anybody with kids, either. Personals are like real estate ads—you know, *fixer-upper* translates as 'falling down, complete with stalker from former residents.' Let the *big rig* and the Lesbian DWF go. Change the 'bed-and-not-bored' to 'no boredom.' You'll preserve the tone of the paper and save the guy a buck. The rest of them look okay to me, babe." He ignored my cringing at his breezy term of endearment, then chuckled. "You see this one? 'SWM, mature, financially secure, gourmet cook, varied interests from baseball to Beethoven; desires companionable relationship with sixty-plus woman; prefers intelligence, adventuresome spirit, ample figure, roots in community, yen for travel.' " Leo arched his eyebrows again, but this time in inquiry. "Jesus, who does the ideal woman sound like, Emma?"

Involuntarily, my glance darted to the outer office. I could see half of Vida, typing away on her battered upright. "Wild," I breathed. "Who is this guy? At fifty cents a word, he spent a small bundle on the ad. Maybe he really is financially secure."

Leo tapped the page proof. "Has Vida seen this?"

I shook my head. "Ginny brought the ads in while I was on the phone."

Leo grinned again. "After you edit these, let the Duchess read proof. Maybe she'll find her duke."

I started to demur. Then I, too, grinned. "Okay, Leo. Why not?" After all, everybody needed romance in their life. Except me. I had a phantom, and his name was Tom Cavanaugh.

Blake Fannucci sounded very agreeable on the telephone. It took a four-call game of telephone tag to reach him at the ski lodge, but by eleven-thirty we had set a lunch date. He and his partner, Stan Levine, would treat me at King Olav's. Since almost nobody in Alpine is ever willing to pick up the tab in exchange for an interview, I leaped at the opportunity.

The Iron Goat Trail editorial was in the pipeline. It was one of those noncontroversial pieces, praising the innovative and adventuresome souls who had spent more than two years re-creating the former passage of the Great Northern Railroad through the Cascade Mountains. The accolade was overdue, well earned, and therefore easy to write. The editorial of the previous week had also featured goats, but they'd been the real thing. National Park officials had proposed reducing the burgeoning mountain goat population by using helicopters, spotters, and marksmen. The situation was an environmentalist's nightmare: The animals gulped down various delicate plants and caused serious erosion. Attempts to capture the goats and sterilize them had not proved practical. I had urged park personnel to come up with a third alternative. My suggestion had provoked anger from several factions. The goats were probably on my side, but they didn't write letters.

The spa story might prove equally tricky. Under fitful clouds, I drove up to the ski lodge for my lunch date.

While the lodge is old, if well maintained, the restaurant is relatively new. Until about two years ago there was only a coffee shop, which still exists in a refurbished state. But King Olav's itself features handsome Scandinavian decor and, for lunch, an eclectic menu. I was thinking about a crab omelette as I pulled into the parking lot.

In the high-beamed lobby with its knotty pine and gray stone decor, I spotted my hosts without difficulty. Their casual but expensive attire, the deep suntans and their easy manner, stamped them as Californians. Blake Fannucci was stocky, with wavy brown hair and deep-set blue eyes. His partner, Stan Levine, was tall, lean, and sharp-featured, with a receding hairline. They greeted me as if we were old high school chums, which was mathematically possible, since they both appeared to be in their early forties.

"Excuse me if I don't shake hands," Blake apologized, holding his right arm at an angle. "I took a spill at poolside last month and I've got gamekeeper's thumb."

Deciding that was a subject we could tackle later, I smiled with sympathy. Stan Levine's handshake was firm and friendly. His manner was somewhat more reserved than Blake's, however, and I figured he was the less outgoing of the pair.

"This restaurant isn't half bad for being in such an out-of-the-way place," Blake remarked as we sat down at what I assumed was the power table. I'd never considered that King Olav's possessed such a thing, but Blake had made a point of indicating where he wanted to sit. The hostess, Angie Patricelli, had regarded him with mild curiosity. Even Mayor Fuzzy Baugh didn't seem to mind which table he was given, as long as the chair legs didn't collapse under him.

Stan Levine was nodding agreement with Blake

Fannucci. "The wine list features some reputable California vintages. I can't speak for the Washington vintners. What do you think, Ms. Lord?"

I blinked at the wine list. "I'm no connoisseur," I admitted. "My favorite drink is Pepsi."

Blake and Stan chuckled as if I'd said something genuinely droll. Maybe I had and didn't know it.

"You've hit on something," Blake said, carefully placing his injured right hand on the blue and white linen tablecloth. "Whether it's soda pop or mineral water or Dos Equis beer, we'll offer it at the spa. People are tired of being told what to eat and drink. They're going right off the edge of the envelope. We intend to give them choices."

I, however, was not given any. Our waitress, who was one of the Bjornsons, was told to bring a bottle of chenin blanc from the Napa Valley.

"Nice," Blake commented, waving his left hand at the room in general. "Very integrated with the environment. Native American in the lobby, Vikings in the restaurant. But too narrow a purview. How many people know Odin?"

Odin was represented by a Fogelberg replica perched on high between the tall windows at the far end of the dining room. "Odin's big around here," I noted. "We have a large percentage of Scandinavians." I wasn't one of them, but suddenly I was feeling defensive.

Blake nodded. "My point exactly. That's insular thinking. We want to attract people from all over the Pacific Northwest—Washington, Oregon, British Columbia. We're thinking global. What're hot springs about, really? Using high tech to get back to basics, right? In touch with their bodies, in touch with the earth itself, but with state-of-the-art convenience. This is alternative medicine in a luxury setting. What's more therapeutic than minerals coming right out of the ground? What we're talking here with our Windy Mountain spa concept is Marienbad Goes Digital." He leaned back in his chair wearing a self-satisfied smile.

"Wonderful," I said lamely. "But isn't Windy Mountain on the other side of the highway?"

Blake wagged a finger at me. "Sharp, very sharp. Yes, but the view from the spa will be of Windy Mountain. Unfortunately, the peak nearest the springs is called Spark Plug. We can't name a five-star resort after something like that. Unless," he added, frowning up at the open-beam ceiling, "we have the state or whoever change the mountain's name."

I tried not to look askance. "Is your plan to build the facility on top of the hot springs?" I had already taken out my notebook and was prepared to write.

Stan Levine, who had been gazing out the window at a sassy flock of crows in a cedar tree, nodded gravely. "That's right. If the architect considers it structurally feasible. We've hired one of your people."

I regarded Stan quizzically. Until the first of the year, Alpine had no architects. But Scott Melville and his wife Beverly had moved to town in early February. Scott's first job was the renovation of the Skykomish County Sheriff's headquarters on Front Street.

Stan was nodding again, still solemn. "Melville's from California, originally."

I knew that, courtesy of Vida's feature story on Scott and Beverly. They were an attractive young couple who had been frightened by the recent earthquakes in the Los Angeles area. Scott had been quoted as saying he didn't want to design or live in buildings that could be demolished every time the ground shifted.

"Good," I said, making a note. "Have you actually acquired the property yet?"

Stan and Blake exchanged quick glances. Melissa

Bjornson arrived with the chenin blanc and went through the presentation ritual, which clearly bored her.

It did not have the same effect on Blake Fannucci, however. "That's the wrong year," he said in a pleasant yet assertive voice. "I asked for a Ninety-one. This is Ninety-two."

Melissa, who was barely of legal age to serve liquor, narrowed her blue eyes at Blake. "So? It's wine, isn't it?"

Blake assumed an avuncular air. "My dear . . . Melissa," he said after a quick glance at her name tag, "let me give you a short course on wine. Every year brings change. Climate conditions create differences in grapes. In Ninety-two, the Napa Valley was subject to . . ."

Blake went on. And on. I turned to Stan. "Leonard Hollenberg owns that property. It covers a large parcel of land, mostly uphill. Has he put a price on it?"

"We're negotiating," Stan replied. "This Hollenberg is trying to hold us up, of course. But who else would want it?" His expression was ingenuous.

"Right," Blake chimed in, having concluded his sermon on grape-raising. Melissa had taken away the offending bottle. "VineFan, cap V, cap F—that's the corporation's official name, half Levine, half Fannucci—VineFan's willing to purchase all or part of what Hollenberg owns. Our big bargaining chip—besides money—is that he can keep the acreage by the highway. The springs are actually two miles up into the mountains."

I considered the site, trying to draw a mental map in my head. A washed-out gravel road led to the steep hot springs trail, or so Vida had informed me before I'd left for lunch. The land must be very rugged. I posed the obvious question:

"You'll have to buy the right-of-way to build a road, though. Won't this be an expensive project?"

Blake and Stan both nodded, with varying degrees of certitude. "You bet," Blake replied. "Offhand, we're figuring fifteen million, total. But if you want the best, you have to pay for it."

I couldn't help but be impressed. As far as I knew, no one had ever spent that kind of money to build anything in Skykomish County.

"Where do you get your financing?" I inquired, making another note.

Melissa returned, bearing the proper vintage. Blake sniffed the cork, took a sip, and pronounced the chenin blanc acceptable. Despite his approval, Melissa seemed sulky as she left the table.

"Ah, financing." Blake savored the term, along with the wine. "Naturally, we'd like to use your local bank. But we met with their people Friday right after we got here, and frankly, the Bank of Alpine doesn't have the resources for a project of this magnitude. We'll deal with our usual contacts in L.A."

I nodded, wondering if Blake was right or merely tactful. It was true that the Bank of Alpine was small. It was also true that the Petersen family, which had run the local financial institution for years, wasn't inclined to take on risky ventures.

"What projects have you been involved in recently?" I asked, after sipping my wine and wondering if I could have distinguished this particular year from any other, or, say, from a glass of 7UP.

Blake responded with a list, featuring names such as Leisure Palace, Indoorsport, and Innertainment. They all seemed to be in places such as Long Beach, Newport, and Rancho Mirage.

My next question had to wait until after Melissa had returned to take our orders. This exercise lasted several minutes, with Blake going over the menu item by item, and Stan asking about various substitutions.

"Very odd menu," Blake said when Melissa finally trudged off. "So many beets and potatoes and fish. Haven't you people learned how to graze?"

I was beginning to feel as if my hosts and I weren't merely from different states, but different cultures. "Graze?" I echoed a bit numbly.

"Right," Blake said. "It's not a new concept in southern California. Not at all. It refers to small portions of food that can be eaten on the move, as at a party or a gallery showing or even in a restaurant."

"But the selections have cohesion," Stan put in. "That's essential."

"Right," Blake agreed. "Interactive cuisine, that's the concept."

I tried to envision the Burl Creek Thimble Club grazing its way through a monthly meeting or Vida's fellow Presbyterians devising a mobile John Knox menu. Somehow, the concept didn't work for me. Or for Alpine, either.

"What brought you up here?" I inquired, refocusing on my story.

"New worlds to conquer," Blake answered easily. "People in California are backing off from big construction projects right now. Too many earthquakes, fires, floods—all the rest of it. We thought about Alaska, but that's too remote. British Columbia gets complicated, though the exchange rate is very favorable with Canada at present. Oregon's environmental laws are tougher than just about any other state. Washington seemed promising. It offers natural irony—the wilderness is still close to the cities. You know, Nature Meets Microsoft." He turned to Stan. "By the way, did you call Bill?"

Stan inclined his head. "He's out of town. He'll get back to us next week. I'll send an E-mail reminder."

My pen was poised over the notepad. "Bill? Bill Gates of Microsoft?"

Blake nodded. "Right. It's always smart to touch base with the local movers and shakers. Who knows? Bill might want to get involved. We'd consider it—wouldn't we, Stan?"

Stan's high forehead creased. "Probably. But these self-made software billionaires can be a pain. I've always felt it's better to keep the decision making in our hands."

The mention of *hands* recalled Blake's accident. "What happened?" I pointed to Blake's right arm. "Did you break something?"

"Chipped, actually," he answered as a glum Melissa brought our salads. "Right at the base of the thumb where the ligament's attached. I just got out of the cast last week. There's some permanent damage to the ligament, which causes lax or gamekeeper's thumb. It's named after a condition gamekeepers in England used to get from strangling rabbits." Blake grinned at me. "You know—D. H. Lawrence Does Hollywood."

I tried to appear amused and sympathetic at the same time. The attempt felt as awkward as it must have looked. "Will it go away?"

Blake shrugged. "Maybe. Maybe not. Oh, it's annoying. I can't write. That's the obvious loss. But you'd be amazed at how many things you do with your thumb that you take for granted."

Steering the conversation back to the proposed project, we spent the next hour talking about the development's possible directions. While many of the Pacific Northwest's mineral springs had been left in their natural state, others already had been converted into modest spas, retreat centers, or destination-style resorts.

"This is where Scott Melville comes in," Blake declared, critically eyeing his veal cutlet. "There's not much level ground. Form will determine function, in this case. We're open."

It had occurred to me that I should talk to Scott Melville before I wrote the story. My watch indicated it was after one o'clock. A call to Leonard Hollenberg was also in order. I was beginning to feel the pressure of deadline.

Consequently, when Melissa asked us if we wanted dessert—though her hostile tone dared us to do so—I declined, saying I had to get back to work. I thanked Blake and Stan for their generous hospitality and prepared to leave.

"Let me walk you to your car," Stan offered as Blake scanned the bill that Melissa had slapped down in front of him. "We appreciate the coverage you're giving us."

"It's news," I said, nodding to Henry Bardeen, who was standing behind the front desk, looking grim. "If you go ahead with this, it'll be the biggest thing to hit Skykomish County since the railroad."

As usual, Stan was wearing a serious expression. "It's reassuring to have you on our side. I sense that not everybody around here welcomes Californians. But we're not all greedy opportunists."

We had stepped outside, into the parking lot. On the last day of May, there were only about two dozen occupied spaces. The ski season was over, and the summer tourists hadn't yet started to arrive.

"Alpine's been going through a recession," I admitted. "The timber industry, you know. The downturn in jobs started in the late Seventies, with the technological revolution. Then came the spotted owl ruling in Ninety-one. Sometimes it feels as if the town's at war with the environmentalists."

Stan's dark eyes studied the patches of snow on Mount Baldy. "Oh, yes. I know all about those environmentalists. But they have a point. Personally, we'll do everything we can to avoid causing problems. It's essential. If we harm the environment, we could ruin the hot springs. We'd certainly harm the natural setting."

Somewhat to my surprise, Stan seemed awestruck by his surroundings. When he finally stopped staring at the second-growth timber that marched up the mountainsides, he broke into a smile and pointed.

"See the chipmunk? The only wildlife we have in L.A. carries handguns."

I smiled back. Stan Levine might not be quite as relaxed as Blake Fannucci, but his company was more relaxing. The ninety-minute concept lunch had worn me out.

"It's quiet up here," I remarked. "And it usually smells good. Damp earth. Evergreens. Wood smoke, from the cedar mills."

Stan took a deep breath, appreciating my litany. "And just plain fresh air." Abruptly, he turned to me, exhibiting almost boyish excitement. "Do you know I saw a MacGillivray's warbler this morning?"

I must have looked blank. "You did?"

Again he nodded, this time with enthusiasm. "They breed in all the western mountains, from Vancouver Island to Arizona. Townsend's, the hermit, and the black-throated gray warbler all nest around here, too. I haven't seen them yet. I hear the cedar waxwing winters here. Now there's a handsome bird! I'd love to sight one of those."

I wouldn't know one warbler from another, but I recognized the cedar waxwing. In fact, a pair of them were frequent visitors to my backyard. A bit shyly, I asked Stan if he'd like to drop by on Saturday.

"If you and Blake are still in town," I added.

Stan considered the invitation. "We may be. It'll depend on how things go with Hollenberg. Have you got fruit trees in your yard?"

I didn't. My cozy log house was virtually built into

the forest. The waxwings perched among the Douglas firs and western hemlock.

"Waxwings usually nest in orchards," Stan said, once again very serious.

"The neighbors have a couple of apple trees," I said, edging toward my aging Jaguar XJE. "Stop by, if you can. I've got binoculars."

"So do I," Stan replied, his smile returning. "I take them everywhere. You never know when you're going to find something startling."

How true. How prophetic. How sad.

Chapter Two

I WAS FORCED to hang up on Leonard Hollenberg. Not that the old windbag was telling me anything, but Ginny Burmeister had shoved a note onto my desk saying that my brother Ben was on the phone from Tuba City, Arizona. I interrupted Leonard's coy evasions about the proposed hot springs sale and pressed line two.

"Hey, Sluggly," said Ben in his crackling voice, "you owe me two hundred bucks."

"Like hell," I retorted. "Listen, Stench, if you were dumb enough to fork over Adam's speeding fine, that's your problem. Besides, it was only one fifty. And stop calling me Sluggly. We're not ten years old anymore."

"Then stop calling me Stench," Ben ordered, though I knew neither of us was inclined to surrender our childhood nicknames. Maybe, in our forties, it was a way to hold on to our youth. "Has Adam left for Tempe?"

"About two hours ago," Ben replied, now sounding slightly disgruntled. "I know the ticket wasn't two hundred. I took the extra fifty out of the poor box so he could buy beer."

I ran a hand through my shaggy brown hair. "Great. You shouldn't have given him anything. The boy—the *man*—has got to grow up."

"Why?" Ben shot back. "So we can feel *really* old? Hell, Emma, I was forty-six on my last birthday. Besides, I wanted to get him out of here. Things are a bit ticklish in Tuba City just now."

"The war?" I wasn't sure whether to take it seriously. "What's happening?"

Ben sighed. "Some Navajo sheep got their throats cut. There was a fire at a Hopi cornfield early this morning. I'm trying to get everybody to talk it through, but let's face it, I'm an outsider. You know what that's like."

I certainly did. After five years in Alpine I still hadn't been completely accepted into the community. Probably I never would be, unless I died. Non-natives can only expiate the sin of being born elsewhere by getting buried in Alpine's cemetery. The locals will embrace a headstone before they take another human being to their collective bosom.

"Are you going to be able to get away for a couple of weeks?" I asked, beginning to sense that Ben wasn't talking about a tempest in a teapot.

"I hope so," my brother answered. "Most of my flock is Navajo or Hispanic or both. The Hopi are more inclined to keep to the old ways. But some of them are willing to listen to the Christian concept of God and can reconcile it with Maasaw, their deity of life. I try to offer a rallying point for mutual understanding, but the more rigid Hopi view me as a Navajo dupe."

Had I never lived in Alpine, I might have wondered why people with so much in common couldn't get along. But small-town life had taught me about feuds. I knew members of the same families who not only wouldn't speak to each other, but who spelled their last names differently just for the sake of spite.

"I still wish you hadn't given Adam that two hundred dollars," I said, for lack of any cogent advice on intertribal warfare. "It'd serve him right if he got his driver's license revoked. He's been nagging me about buying him a car."

"Don't worry, Emma," Ben reassured me. "I'll make him work it off on the dig this summer."

The previous year, Adam had been a novice at the Kayenta Anasazi archaeological excavation. He had performed menial tasks for his room and board at the parish rectory. But because my son had shown an aptitude as well as an interest in the dig, Ben had promised to pay him this coming summer. I congratulated my brother on his solution, but issued a warning:

"I know you weren't going to pay him much," I said, aware that line one had lighted up again. "Adam will try to finagle money out of you after the first week. If there were any spare jobs in Alpine, I'd insist he spend the summer here."

"We'll work it out," Ben said. "Our flight gets in around noon on the eighteenth. I'll probably talk to you before then, unless I end up as cannon fodder."

On that disturbing note, Ben rang off. I picked up line one and heard an unfamiliar male voice.

". . . called while I was with Sheriff Dodge," said the voice, even as my mind tried to cope with recognition. "Construction should start June tenth. Is that what you were calling about, Ms. Lord?"

"Oh!" It dawned on me that I had Scott Melville, architect, on the line. "Yes—and no. Milo Dodge hadn't confirmed the start-up date. What I really wanted was to know how far you've come with the Windy Mountain plans."

Scott chuckled, a pleasant yet reserved sound. "Not far. Have you hiked up to the pools?"

I confessed that I hadn't. Scott's tone became businesslike. "That's really rugged terrain. If Fannucci and Levine buy that property, I'm envisioning terraces, maybe built right into the mountainside. It's going to jack up the price by another two mil."

"May I quote you?"

"No," Scott replied. "Not the numbers. This is for publication? Let's just say that if it's done right—if it can be done at all—it's going to be more than the earlier estimates."

"I suppose," I said in a ruminative voice, "I ought to see the site for myself."

"Wear boots. There's still snow around the pools. Hollenberg says it doesn't melt until mid-June. We're talking serious elevation here, like maybe four thousand feet."

"Then what's the point?" I asked. "Can they keep a road open more than four months of the year?"

Scott's laugh sounded forced. "They're talking helipad, maybe a tram. It's their money. I'm just the talent."

Vaguely, I recalled articles I'd read over the years in *Variety*. Hollywood people could talk a great line. The Second Coming was not only imminent, it would be shot in Panavision with Dolby sound. Or so the reader would believe by the end of the story. I thanked Scott for his call and hung up.

With a sigh, I turned back to my word processor. Vida stood in the doorway, her nose wrinkled, as if she could smell a story. In this case, she wasn't quite on target.

"Damn," I said, looking up from my screen, "without Hollenberg's okay, all I've got is speculation."

"Leonard's an old fool," Vida declared, removing her glasses, breathing on the lenses, and then wiping them on her pink sleeve. "He worked as an engineer for the railroad, you know. His trains always ran late."

"Will he sell?"

Vida shrugged her broad shoulders. "If the price is

right. He's tight as a drum. These Californians won't get the best of Leonard." As much as she might criticize a Skykomish County commissioner, Vida would take his part against any outsiders.

"Okay, I've got an *if* story. I hate them. 'If Leonard Hollenberg agrees to sell' . . . 'If the California developers can raise the financial backing' . . . 'If architect Scott Melville comes up with a feasible design' . . ." I lifted both eyebrows at Vida.

"We should have a look," she said. "I haven't been to the hot springs since 1969."

I glanced at the stock photo we were going to run on the front page. It showed somebody's bare legs immersed in a small plastic-lined pool. "Who took this picture?"

"Leonard. He's been generous about letting people use the springs. I'll say that for him."

I gave a faint nod, then turned back to my keyboard. Vida, however, lingered in the doorway. It was rare that I ever exhibited impatience toward my House & Home editor. But the clock was advancing on four P.M. I had to write the article and finish making up the front page.

"What is it?" I asked, hoping I didn't sound annoyed.

Vida frowned, adjusted her glasses again, and glanced over her shoulder to make sure nobody was eavesdropping. Nobody was. Ginny was at her post in the front office, Carla was picking up some photos at Buddy Bayard's studio, and Leo had gone over to the Grocery Basket to make last minute changes in their Break Out the Barbecues ad.

"I proofed those personals," Vida said, almost in a whisper. "Interesting, aren't they?" She looked not at me, but somewhere in the direction of my filing cabinet.

"I guess," I said noncommittally. "Some of them are kind of weird."

"Not all, though," Vida said. "I wonder how much you can believe?"

I tried to concentrate on Vida instead of letting my brain write the story without my fingers. "That depends. How much advertising in general can anyone believe?"

Vida fingered her chin. "That's the problem. So much of it is blind faith. Oh, well." She turned and walked back into the news office.

For about ten seconds I considered Vida's conundrum. Obviously, she had read the personals ad that seemed to be directed at her. Or someone like her. She was intrigued. I was surprised. And touched. Vida always seemed so self-sufficient. She'd been a widow for almost twenty years. She'd finished raising three daughters on her own. I'd never been aware of Vida expressing interest in any man, let alone going out with one. She knew everyone in Alpine, including the eligible widowers and bachelors. That was the problem, it seemed to me—she knew them *too* well. And vice versa. Bemused, I turned my attention back to my highly conjectural story. *If,* I wrote. *If* . . .

But part of my brain was still thinking of Vida. "If," it said. "If Vida answers that ad . . ."

Then what if . . . ? I couldn't help but smile.

Sheriff Milo Dodge was plying me with cheap drink. Beer, to be exact, at Mugs Ahoy. His motives weren't nefarious. They never were, a fact that usually pleased me. Milo was celebrating the start of renovations to the Skykomish County Sheriff's office. I had used the information from Scott Melville in a small front-page story, along with a quote from Milo, who had said he was "pleased and gratified that the voters had passed a bond issue that would allow their local agency to update and improve facilities while also adding much-needed personnel."

A new deputy had joined the force in early May. Dustin Fong was from Seattle, a graduate of Shoreline Community College's law enforcement program, and of Chinese-American descent. He was one of a half-dozen non-Caucasians now living in Alpine, and as such, was considered strange, exotic, and, in extreme cases, a likely candidate to start a Tong War.

"The new software's being installed next week," Milo said, lifting his beer glass in a semitoast. "Maybe Carla can take a picture of Dustin or Jack Mullins or one of the other deputies using it."

"Sounds exciting," I said, hoping I meant it. "How many jail cells will you have when the renovation's done?"

"Six, instead of two." Milo lighted a cigarette. I did the same. Somehow, I'd gotten through the day without smoking, but I couldn't refrain in the darkened, derelict interior of Mugs Ahoy. It seemed wrong *not* to smoke. "Let's hope we don't need them," Milo continued, exhaling a blue cloud. "The main thing is the technology, and the space for it. Scott Melville's bill is paid, but if Nyquist Construction comes in over budget, we're screwed."

I sipped my beer, wishing I liked it better. If Mugs Ahoy or the Icicle Creek Tavern would import a brew that came from beyond the Canadian border or the Idaho state line, I might not have to wince every time I took a drink.

"Nyquist is dependable," I said, hoping to soothe the sheriff's fears.

Milo lifted one shoulder. "True. I wonder if they'll get the contract for the spa thing."

"Hey," I cautioned, "you're jumping the gun. Leonard Hollenberg is still sitting tight. Wait until tomorrow—you'll read all about it in *The Advocate.*"

But Milo shook his head. "Leonard is seventy-six years old. His big thing in life is walking out his back door and trying to coax a steelhead out of the Skykomish River. Not that I blame him. I intend to do the same when I retire. If his kids want him to build a chalet—and bear in mind that those *kids* are in their thirties and forties—then they can let him put it on the same property where he's got his house. Hell, he owns two acres, and it's only eight more miles to the summit. Big deal."

"Why did he buy up all that land with the hot springs in the first place?" I asked, waving politely to a couple I recognized from St. Mildred's Church.

"Damned if I know," Milo replied. "Some out-of-town doctors used to own it. I guess they lost interest. Maybe Leonard thought he could sell it off piece by piece to the loggers. But that idea went down the drain with the spotted owl. They've been sighted up there, along with a lot of other birds. Those guys from L.A. better watch it, or they'll have all the tree-huggers on their necks."

I mentioned that Stan Levine seemed concerned about the environment. And that he was a bird lover. Milo wasn't impressed.

"California bullshit," he remarked, giving Cal Vickers a high sign. "Hey, Cal—you got time to check out my Cherokee Chief tomorrow?"

Cal Vickers, owner of Cal's Texaco Station and Auto Repair, paused on his way out of the tavern. Apparently, he and a couple of his employees had stopped for a beer after work. Cal tugged at the bill of his stained Texaco cap and grinned.

"Sure, Sheriff. Bring it in, first thing. What's the problem?"

There ensued a discussion of things mechanical in

which I had neither interest nor understanding. My mind wandered, leaping from the spa project to Vida's single status to why Mugs Ahoy's decor still featured Easter bunnies almost two months after the fact. My attention returned only when I caught a fragment of Cal's conversation with Milo:

"They must have rented it in Seattle," Cal was saying, his weathered face registering disapproval. "You won't find any of those Range Rovers around here. That's what kills me about Californians—they have to show off."

Milo was nodding. "They're spoiled. Nuts about cars, too. I went to L.A. once, when Mulehide and I took the kids to Disneyland. In Beverly Hills we counted ten Rolls-Royces in ten minutes."

Cal looked suitably disgusted. "Charlene and the boys and I went to Disneyland twice, but we skipped L.A. All those freeways and all that smog—bah! They can have it. The Rolls-Royces, too. What's wrong with a good old Ford?"

Milo poked me. "You interviewed these guys, Emma. Tell Cal what you thought of them."

I gave Cal a semihelpless look. "They're hustlers, especially Fannucci. Levine seems more serious. But hustling doesn't make them crooks." I turned back to Milo. "Why don't you run them through your data base? If nothing else, we could squelch any rumors that they're wanted in several states."

But Milo shook his head. "I can't. The old software was pulled this afternoon. I'd have to go through Snohomish County, and I don't like bothering them unless it's important."

My inclination wasn't to push, but Cal Vickers felt otherwise: "Hey, Milo, this *is* important! Even if they're not con artists, do you want these L.A. types running Skykomish County? Let the first two in the door, and the next thing you know, we'll have newcomers behind every tree, condos up our butts, traffic jammed on Front Street, and gangs shooting it out at the high school!"

Though Milo laughed, he gave Cal a reassuring slap on the shoulder. "Come on, Cal, relax. Alpine and the rest of the county need a boost. I'm hoping these guys move ahead with the project. Think of all the jobs it'll create, right from the get-go."

Cal, however, wasn't assuaged. He yanked at the rumpled collar of his grimy coverall and glowered at the sheriff. "You're nuts, Milo. These L.A. guys are nuts, too. Think about it—two miles up, a switchback to accommodate all those fancy cars, a great big old *building* stuck on the side of Spark Plug—and the environmentalist bozos talk about clear-cutting being an eyesore! Shit!" Cal glanced at me. "Sorry, Emma. This deal's got me riled up. You can bet that most folks here in Alpine aren't for it, either." He tipped his battered cap and left.

Milo's long face was mildly perturbed. "Cal doesn't rile that easy," he remarked, signaling for Abe Loomis to bring another round. "As a rule, he's pretty easygoing."

I agreed. Cal was a bit of a redneck, in his way, as are so many Alpiners. His wife Charlene had always struck me as reasonable. She and I played bridge together; Charlene almost never tried to kill her partner over egregious mistakes. That fact spoke well for Charlene Vickers's equanimity.

Mugs Ahoy's owner and resident bartender, Abe Loomis, skulked to our table with more beer. Because of his funereal mien, I secretly referred to him as Abe Gloomis. Indeed, his attitude was more sepulchral than ever.

"Cal's upset," Abe said, setting the schooners before us. "I don't blame him. Have you heard that these Californians are going to allow *nude* bathing?"

I tried to look ingenuous. "You mean in the resort's bathrooms? My! I've been taking nude baths for years."

In the dim, smoky atmosphere, I could have sworn that Abe's sallow face blushed. "Of course not. I mean in the spa, or whatever they call it. Skinny-dipping, plain and simple. God only knows what else will go on."

Milo ran his fingers through his sandy hair. "Don't worry about it," he said. "It's supposed to be a classy operation. Ignore the rumors, Abe, and give these guys a chance."

"A chance!" Abe was aghast. "Do you realize what's going to happen? All these rich people will come up here from Seattle and Bellevue, and they'll want those fancy imported beers and little appetizer things instead of peanuts, and the next thing you know, I'll have to hire a gay waiter! And wine—what's wrong with Gallo and Yosemite Sam? They may even want to eat something besides my frozen sandwiches! I'll have to take delivery more than once a month!"

"Perish the thought," I murmured. "Just think, Abe," I went on more loudly, "you might actually make money."

Abe was regarding me with a dark, almost sinister expression. "Very funny, Emma. You don't know diddly about running a tavern. The money is in the *beer*. The rest is just a headache." Abe put a long, awkward hand to his temple, as if he were already suffering from migraine. "Don't try to cheer me up. This resort idea is too much. Everybody says so. Mark my words, it'll never happen. Those two Angelenos will be lucky to get out of Alpine alive."

Milo and I both laughed. Our host did not.

Later, it would be hard to admit that Abe Loomis was right.

Chapter Three

"WHAT HAS THREE legs and no hair?" asked Vida, blowing a stray curl off her forehead.

I glanced up from the current edition of *The Advocate*, which had just arrived from the printer in Monroe. "Durwood Parker on a cane?" I suggested in a joking manner.

"That's right." Vida eyed me crossly. "How did you know?"

"I didn't." Relieved not to find any glaring typos or factual errors, I set my copy of the paper down on Leo's messy desk. "What happened to Durwood?"

Vida sighed. "He got his driver's license back, heaven help us. He parked up on the curb by Itsa Bitsa Pizza and fell into one of the civic beautification planters. He pulled something or other in his leg and smashed the sweet alyssum that had just been set out the day before. He also hurt the ageratum. Not only can't Durwood drive properly, it appears he can't even walk."

Durwood Parker, retired pharmacist, was the worst driver in Alpine. I made appropriate noises, then inquired if Vida was getting a head start on "Scene Around Town," *The Advocate*'s version of a gossip column.

"Yes," she answered on a long-suffering note. "This week's is deadly dull. Have you read it yet?"

I had. Along with my presence at King Olav's—"*Advocate* editor-publisher Emma Lord making the ski lodge lunch scene with L.A. developers Blake Fannucci and Stan Levine"—were such other nonstartling items as "Donna Wickstrom hauling a wagonload of her day care clients to Old Mill Park for a romp on the jungle gym," "Stella Magruder featuring breezy summer cuts at her styling salon," and "Doc Dewey bragging about his new grandson at Fuzzy and Irene Baugh's Memorial Day picnic." The only unusual bit was "Crazy Eights Neffel leading a Jersey cow into the public library." But even that wasn't unusual by Alpine standards. Crazy Eights was our resident loony, and his peculiar antics were the norm.

"We could use more titillating items," I said as Ginny Burmeister and Carla Steinmetz came into the news office. It was the first of June, and therefore payday. Ginny and Carla had obviously taken some time off to shop. Both were carrying bags from the sportswear store at the Alpine Mall.

"I got new sweats," Carla announced, pulling out matching green pants and top.

"I got a windbreaker," Ginny said, waving a royal-blue garment at me. "They were having a sale. We ran the ad."

I nodded, commenting favorably. Ginny, however, swiftly changed the subject. "Are we going to the Chamber meeting next week? You promised to push them about my Summer Solstice idea."

I avoided Ginny's probing gaze. I'd been making the same promise for a year. To be fair, I'd done my best to gain the Chamber of Commerce's approval. But most of the merchants still clung to Loggerama. It was familiar, it was traditional, it was Alpine. Never mind that the concept was becoming increasingly outdated, even melancholy in its nostalgic celebration of the macho timber industry past. The only Chamber member I had on my side was Francine Wells, owner of Francine's Fine Apparel. Maybe she thought her upscale clothing would reach a wider audience if Alpine's annual civic festival improved its image.

With an apologetic air, I gave Ginny a sickly smile. "It won't happen this year. These things take time. A lot of planning is involved. The town has an investment in the Loggerama props."

Ginny's green eyes were wide. "Props? You call some rusty old saws and a couple of ugly axes *props*? Or are you talking about the parade floats? They're just logging trucks and pickups and Mayor Baugh's Chrysler with some crepe paper streamers and Richie Magruder wearing long underwear pretending he's Paul Bunyan. It's totally stupid."

There had been loggers and millworkers in Ginny's family, but if her scornful attitude was typical of the younger generation, maybe it was time for a change. Thoughtfully, I regarded her plain face with its crown of amazing red hair.

"Loggerama is in August," I said at last. "The Summer Solstice is in June."

"So?" Ginny's manner was hostile, which was very unlike her. My office manager was normally even-tempered, even stoic. "Why is that bad? It would be like a kickoff for the summer tourist season. By the time August rolls around, people are thinking about back-to-school."

Ginny had a point. "Okay," I said. "You can come with me to the Chamber lunch meeting next week."

Ginny lifted her round chin. "I will." Still pugnacious, she sashayed out of the news office.

"What's with her?" I asked my two remaining staff members. "Are she and Rick on the outs again?" Ginny had been going with Rick Erlandson, one of the tellers at the Bank of Alpine, off and on for over a year.

Carla and Vida exchanged conspiratorial looks. "No way," Carla said, snickering behind a fall of raven hair.

"Really, Emma," Vida said somewhat disparagingly, "don't you keep up?"

"With what?" I felt at sea.

Carla and Vida both leaned forward on their respective desks. "Ginny and Rick are getting engaged," Carla whispered.

"Oh!" I beamed at my female staffers, then suddenly sobered. "So why is Ginny belligerent?"

"Because," Carla replied, still whispering, "Ginny doesn't know it yet."

Dumbfounded, I stared at Carla. "Then how do you . . . ?" The question trailed off as my eyes roamed in Vida's direction. Lynette Blatt, one of Vida's numerous kinfolk, worked at Tonga Gems, the jewelry shop in the Alpine Mall. "Lynette?" I inquired, also whispering.

Vida nodded once. "Rick was in over the weekend. He's buying on time, a diamond solitaire in white gold, ten carats, twelve hundred dollars, with a wedding band for another two fifty. Rick's birthday is June fourth, which is Saturday, so Lynette figures he'll pop the question then. Ginny has bought him a very nice gold watchband for sixty dollars. She paid cash."

Having long since gotten over Vida's remarkable pipeline, I merely nodded. "So Ginny is off her feed because she doesn't know that Rick has the ring?"

"Right," Carla responded, fiddling with her Nikon thirty-five millimeter camera. "She thought he'd propose over Memorial Day. But he didn't, and now she thinks he never will." Carla's grin was infectious.

"Well, well," I remarked cheerfully, "that's great! Rick's a nice young man." At twenty-three and twenty-five respectively, Ginny and Rick seemed rather young to be married. But in Alpine the average age for matrimony is much lower than in the city. At least for the first time around. I refrained from saying so, however. I had no right to criticize. What did I know? I'd never been married at all.

Leonard Hollenberg was short, stocky, and almost bald, with a seamed face like tree bark. Still, he was vigorous for his age, and somehow reminded me of a bulldog. I'd never known Leonard during his railroading career, but I'd often watched him in action as a county commissioner. Or, in lack of action, since the three men who sat on the Skykomish board spent more time talking than doing. On this drizzly Thursday afternoon in early June, Leonard was talking to me.

"You got to see the hot springs, Erma," he declared. In the five years that I had been in Alpine, Leonard had never figured out that my name was Emma. I'd long since stopped trying to correct him. The bulldog quality prevented Leonard from changing his mind about anything.

"I'm thinking about hiking up there over the weekend," I admitted. "Vida wants to go, too."

"Vida?" Leonard made a face. "She'll never make it. Too damned flat-footed. Big woman, too. Not like you, Erma. You're almost puny."

At five-foot-four and 120-some pounds, I didn't consider myself puny. However, I often felt insubstantial next to Vida—for many reasons.

"We'll see," I replied enigmatically. "Now tell me, Leonard"—I repressed my perverse urge to call him Leopold or Leroy—"what is the final figure?"

Leonard patted the desk with his pudgy fingers. "Six bits. That's seventy-five *thousand* dollars." His thick lips curled in a smile of self-satisfaction. "Those Los Angel-ease fellas were offering sixty. I fixed 'em, huh,

Erma? No fast-talking Cal-eye-forn-eye-ans are going to get the better of Leonard Hollenberg."

I gave Leonard a half smile of congratulations. "That includes the right-of-way through the property you're keeping?"

Leonard nodded, both chins bouncing. "It's a good deal for me. I'll have a free road to the ski chalet. Maybe I'll get that Milldew fella to design it for me."

"Melville," I said faintly, not quite giving up completely on straightening out Leonard. "So Doukas Realty will handle the sale here, and the developers are getting their financing from L.A."

"You got it." Abruptly, Leonard's round face darkened. "Listen here, Erma—you know what they say about strange bedfellas. I'm no dummy, I'm a politician. I know there'll be some backlash. Yeah, that's the word—backlash. Some of the voters are going to think Leonard Hollenberg sold out. But let's face it—what Skykomish County needs more than anything else is *jobs*. And that's what I'm giving 'em. Hell, I wouldn't care if I sold the property to Hitler for two bits. If it means putting food on the table for all these out-of-work families, then swell. Come November, they'll thank me. You wait and see."

Leonard had a point. I'd forgotten that he was up for reelection in the fall. "May I quote you?" My smile was benign.

"Huh?" Leonard's small blue eyes narrowed. "Yeah, sure. Not about Hitler, though. He doesn't get votes."

"Okay," I agreed, somewhat reluctantly. I liked the quote. I wasn't sure I liked Leonard Hollenberg.

"Good," said Leonard, rising from the chair. "Now let's put Alpiners to work." Suddenly, he was running for election, puffing himself up, holding out his hand and grinning at me.

I shook Leonard's hand, subjecting myself to a professional squeeze job. The self-important county commissioner had barely left my office when Ed Bronsky thundered through the door. The former advertising manager of *The Advocate* and current millionaire-by-inheritance wore a stormy expression.

"Hollenberg!" cried Ed, dumping his bulky body into the chair Leonard had just vacated. "That traitor! Is it true he's sold out to the Californians?"

My manner was unperturbed. "He's sold to them, period. How've you been, Ed? I haven't seen you since the last Chamber meeting."

Ed whipped out a rumpled handkerchief and lustily blew his nose. "I got a cold attending the Memorial Day services at the cemetery. It was raining, remember?"

I did remember, though I hadn't been at the cemetery. My own dead were buried in Seattle, at Holyrood. My memorial had been in the form of Masses offered up at St. Mildred's by our pastor, Father Dennis Kelly. Ben, of course, had said Masses for our parents' souls at his mission church in Tuba City.

"Something's got to be done," Ed announced, stuffing the handkerchief back into the pocket of his raincoat. Before Ed inherited his fortune from an aunt in Cedar Falls, Iowa, his clothes were always old and wrinkled. Now they were new and wrinkled. But Ed had changed in other ways. No longer was he negative, pessimistic, or lethargic. The inheritance had charged Ed Bronsky's batteries. Money had given Ed power, and a heady dose of self-importance. It was not for me to point out that Ed was still Ed, no matter how high the limit on his Visa card. He wouldn't have understood.

"Got to be done about what?" I asked, trying to sound interested.

Ed waved a hand, the raincoat falling open to reveal the newly acquired cellular phone he kept hooked to his very large belt. "Hollenberg. The L.A. guys. The hot springs. I've been taking a straw poll around town. People talk to me. They trust me. I'm telling you, Emma, this Windy Mountain spa idea is a disaster. Haven't you been getting outraged calls and letters?"

I had, but no more than usual. My inconclusive article in Wednesday's paper had rung no loud alarm bells. A half-dozen subscribers had phoned so far, damning California influence. The letters that had arrived in the morning mail contained only two protesting the Windy Mountain project. One was from Darla Puckett, who was old enough to recall the original hotel at Scenic, and who lamented the possibility of "a modernistic monstrosity which would deface the natural beauty of Skykomish County." The other was anonymous, rambling, and addressed me as Dear Poop-Head. The response would heat up next week when we ran the story about the pending sale.

I fought the urge to light a cigarette. "The project means jobs, Ed. Have you got something against people working? *Other* people, that is?" I kept a straight face.

Ed took me seriously, which is more than he ever did when I was his boss. "No, of course not. In fact . . ." He lowered his big, balding head, snuffled a bit, and cleared his throat. "You and I don't always see eye-to-eye." Ed's brown spaniel eyes were fraught with meaning. Or so I supposed, since they were also watery and bloodshot. "Last fall, the Chamber vote, the murder hunt idea. You were on the other side."

Ed's harebrained scheme to turn a homicide investigation into a commercial game for gain had appalled me, as well as several other members of the Chamber of Commerce. I'd spoken out against the wacky, tasteless plan, which subsequently had been voted down. Obviously, Ed hadn't quite forgiven me for my alleged betrayal.

"The killer was caught and convicted, as you know,"

I said calmly. "Let's forget all that. What's on your mind?"

Ed rubbed at his reddened nose. "Well—it's like this: the basic idea about the hot springs is fine. It's been real nice of Leonard and those doctors before him to let people use the pools for free. Of course I never knew the doctors—they weren't from around here—and Leonard does it to help get votes. But now we've got these Californians with their big bucks and big ideas. It's not Alpine, Emma, and you know it."

"Which doesn't mean it's bad," I pointed out, still staying calm.

Ed's expression said otherwise. "It's not appropriate. Now, I've never hiked up to the springs myself," he admitted while I bit my lip to keep from laughing out loud at the mental image of tubby old Ed clambering up the side of Spark Plug Mountain, "but I've got a good idea of where they're located on the map. Building a big resort up there is going to be impossible. Look here." The chair groaned as Ed struggled to his feet and went over to the U.S. Forest Service map I kept on the wall. "See, here's Scenic on Highway 2, the Burlington Northern railroad bridge, then the old dirt drive into what used to be a hotel, and here's the washed-out gravel road that goes as far as the power lines." Ed ground his thumbnail into the map. Up close he smelled like Vicks VapoRub and cherry cough drops. "From there, you start a steep two-mile hike that's mostly uphill. Look how that baby climbs!"

While the trail wasn't marked on the map, I could get a general idea of what Ed meant. The terrain rose steadily, from the three-thousand-foot level, which was the approximate altitude of Alpine, to well over four thousand feet.

Ed smacked the map with his fist. "That's mountain goat country—literally. There isn't enough flat land to build a parking lot, let alone tennis courts and a golf course. What do these guys think this is—Palm Springs?"

Ed, Shirley, and the five little Bronskys had been to Palm Springs in January. *The Advocate* had carried an account of their trip, which had centered around Ed's sighting of various aging celebrities and Shirley's shopping exploits. It was only later, after the Bronskys returned to Alpine, that we had heard the *real* news: Ed had been mugged on route to a local convenience store to get a couple dozen burritos. Maybe Palm Springs was losing some of its luster, at least for Ed.

"Now cabins are another matter," Ed was saying in a musing voice. "You could build cabins, maybe a small restaurant. But that's about it." His bloodshot eyes took on a bit of sparkle.

I cocked my head to one side. "Ed—are you thinking about a contingency plan?"

Ed gave a self-conscious shrug, making the Aquascutum raincoat quiver around his bulk. "It's an idea. These L.A. guys are going to bail out. I could get some local investors together, maybe even go as far afield as Everett, and we'd come up with something realistic. Talk about jobs—Alpine could look to Ed Bronsky for them."

I tried to ignore Ed's pompous stance. If he wanted to play lord of the manor, why not? Ed had rarely earned his salary at *The Advocate*; maybe it was only fitting that he should help other people earn theirs.

"But," I pointed out, "Fannucci and Levine have struck a deal with Hollenberg."

"It's not a done deal yet," Ed reminded me. "At best it'll take—what? Thirty days? At worst—which is my prediction—it'll never happen. They won't get the financing, they'll back out, Leonard'll get cold feet, the whole thing will blow away. Then I'll step in, offer

Leonard say fifty grand, and we're airborne. What do you think?"

To be fair, it wasn't an implausible scenario. If, for some reason, Fannucci and Levine couldn't come up with the money, Leonard Hollenberg probably would be just as happy selling to a local, even at a lesser price. Certainly he wouldn't be as open to criticism from the electorate.

"Okay, Ed, you're making sense. We'll have to see what happens." I gave my ex-employee a genuine smile. "Just let me be the first to hear about it. I don't want the story broken in *The Everett Herald* or *The Seattle Times*."

I was kidding, but Ed didn't think so. "You got it, Emma," he said, very seriously. "I wouldn't bother with *The Herald* or *The Times* anyway. I'd go straight to *The Wall Street Journal*. I subscribe now, you know."

"Good for you," I said, allowing Ed to shake my hand. He waddled away, leaving me in peace. Or so it seemed, until Vida showed up less than five minutes later. She was wearing her version of a business suit, which was a collarless beige linen jacket over a matching straight skirt. The chartreuse polyester blouse and the brown broad-brimmed felt hat with its garnet roses didn't enhance the illusion. However, I couldn't help but be intrigued when Vida closed the door behind her. My staff members rarely did such a thing unless they were going to talk about sex or money. While *The Advocate*'s employees had little of either commodity in their lives, it was usually the latter, rather than the former.

But I was wrong about Vida. She had let the brown hat slip down so that her eyes, as well as her glasses, were all but hidden. I was reminded of a spy from a World War II B-movie.

"That ad," she began in a hushed voice that did nothing to destroy my little fantasy. "I answered it."

Maintaining what I hoped was a sober, yet sympathetic expression, I leaned closer. "You did? You mean the one about a mature . . ." Offhand, I couldn't recall the rest of the lengthy wording. But Vida was nodding, causing the garnet roses to bob. "Have you heard anything?" I inquired.

Pushing the brim of her hat off her forehead, Vida regarded me with her gimlet eye. "Of course not. I only wrote to the P.O. box number today. I shouldn't expect any reply until Saturday, at least. Do you think I'm foolish?"

The anxiety in Vida's voice moved me. "Goodness, no! Whoever wrote that sounds . . . *sincere*."

"I haven't told my girls," Vida murmured, referring to her three married daughters, only one of whom lived in Alpine. "I should, though. They've been nagging me for years to . . . to find a companion." Before I could comment, Vida gave me a withering stare. "I chose the word carefully. That's precisely what I mean. It would be pleasant to have a man around for social occasions, even trips to Seattle for the ballet or symphony."

While I knew Vida enjoyed classical music, she had never attended any Big City cultural events since I'd known her. But maybe that was because she felt the need for a male escort. In many ways, Vida was very old-fashioned.

I remained openly sympathetic. "Ginny has set up a special box at the post office," I noted, though Vida was aware of the fact. "She'll be checking it every day, except Saturdays."

Vida shrugged. "I can wait until Monday."

"Why didn't you just give your letter to Ginny?" I asked, and then realized the answer before I could retrieve the question.

Vida had turned very severe. "Do you think I want everybody and his brother to know? Ginny would tell Carla who would tell Leo who would tell the whole town. Really, Emma, this is a very private matter."

Of course it was. I allowed as much. Vida retaliated by invading my privacy:

"What have you heard from Tommy?"

Nobody but Vida referred to Tom Cavanaugh as *Tommy*. The great love of my life and the father of my son was finally getting a divorce. I had confided only in Vida—and Ben, of course—that Tom's mentally unbalanced wife, Sandra, had left him. Given Sandra's erratic, even criminal, behavior over a quarter of a century, Tom had far more provocation to call it quits. But Tom also had an enormous sense of responsibility, as well as a few tons of guilt. Thus, when Sandra fell for Zorro, a stand-up comedian half her age, she was the one who had decided to end the marriage.

"I spoke with Tom Saturday morning," I answered carefully. "It's getting complicated. Sandra's been living with Zorro in a cabin near Big Sur, but suddenly she's decided she wants the house in San Francisco. She says it's impracticable for Zorro to be so far away from the city, because of his comedy gigs. He's also, I gather, too far from his drug supplier."

"Oh, dear." Vida took off her hat and fanned herself, despite the cool, rainy weather. "Sandra wants the house as well as half of Tom's newspaper holdings? My my—that doesn't seem fair, given the circumstances."

Maybe not, though it was Sandra's inherited money that had given Tom the stake in building his empire of weeklies throughout the West. For the first time in my life I grudgingly allowed a point scored for Sandra Cavanaugh. As for the house, it didn't seem to me that either would want it. Sandra and Tom's two children were in college, and while I'd never seen the place, I'd gathered it was of mansion proportions. Perhaps Zorro wanted some room for his horse. The double entendre made me smile.

"What is it?" Vida demanded. "How on earth can you find Tommy's problems funny?"

"I don't," I readily admitted. "I was thinking about Zorro."

"Well, don't. He's not worth the mental effort. Nor is Sandra." Vida radiated disapproval, though she had never met Sandra and knew Tom only from his brief visit to Alpine three years earlier. "When are you going to tell Adam?"

Nervously, I ruffled my shaggy hair with both hands. "When he gets here," I said, without much confidence. "It will be better to have Ben with us."

"Oh, good grief!" Vida rolled her eyes. "Since when did you require moral support? Hasn't your whole life been lived as though you didn't need Tommy or anyone else?"

Vida's comment stung. It was true. Having discovered that the man I loved had gotten both his wife and me pregnant at about the same time, I'd spurned Tom's offers of help. I'd kept him out of my life—and Adam's—for the first twenty years. Then, with reluctance, I'd permitted Tom to meet his illegitimate son. The two had gotten along quite well. Better late than never for Adam to realize that being a bastard didn't mean he was also fatherless.

"Ben and Adam have become very close," I explained. "Besides, one of the things I've learned in the last few years is that you can't always do everything by yourself."

In a painstaking manner that was uncharacteristic, Vida rose from her chair. "Yes," she said in an odd voice. "That's so, isn't it?"

* * *

Friday was relatively uneventful, if busy. I'd called Adam in Tempe around eight o'clock and managed to catch him just as he was going out. To study, he said, but being a Friday night, I suspected otherwise. I inquired into his most recent speeding ticket. He mumbled a bit, something about Uncle Ben advancing him the money and how he planned to pay it back by doing something or other.

"Have you talked to Ben since you got back to Tempe?" I asked.

Adam hadn't, which didn't surprise me. "I've been in deep stuff here, Mom. I've got a term paper due and finals are coming up. You've forgotten how hard college is. And it's a lot tougher these days, with all the competition. You wouldn't believe the kind of stress I'm under."

If Adam thought I would swallow that line of tripe, the only thing he was under was a delusion. But it cost money to argue long distance. "Just make sure you pay Ben back," I warned my son.

Adam's tone became indignant. "Oh, yeah, sure, as if . . . you think I'd pull some dumb stunt on Uncle Ben? I'm not a kid anymore, Mom."

Well, he wasn't. Maybe I should start treating him like a man, I thought. My glance fell on a framed photograph of Adam and Ben at the Anasazi dig the previous summer. In their sweaty exuberance, both son and brother looked happy and fit. I'd liked the picture so much that I'd had it enlarged. The play of sunshine and shadow emphasized Adam's increasingly chiseled features, and heightened his likeness to Tom. Ben, on the other hand, looked playful, like the big brother I'd always known. If I tried very hard, I could imagine they were here with me, all the time. "I'm not sending you any of the things you asked for," I said, fighting off maternal guilt. "You can wait until you get to Alpine."

"Mom!" The outraged whine indicated that Adam was feeling about twelve. But to my surprise, he regrouped. "Okay, fine." The pout in his voice was minimal. "It's only a couple of weeks. But I'm almost out of socks."

"It's hot in Tempe. You can go barefoot." I laughed evilly.

"Sure, and get my toes chewed off by scorpions."

"I thought they were iguanas."

"Whatever. Hey, got to go. My buddies are here with the . . . study guides. See you."

Funny, I could have sworn the word he'd intended to say rhymed with "here." Maybe I was mistaken. After all, Adam was trying to be a man.

By Saturday the rain had stopped, though the clouds still hung low over the mountains. About ten o'clock I called Vida to ask if she really wanted to hike up to the hot springs site. She did, but her grandson Roger was staying with her. The steep trail might tucker out the poor little tyke.

Since the ten-year-old terror couldn't be stopped by a SCUD missile, I was surprised. On the other hand, I certainly didn't want Roger tagging along. After hanging up, I debated the wisdom of making the trek on my own. I was still mulling when Stan Levine called at ten-fifteen. He wanted to come over and bird-watch.

I'd forgotten my casual invitation. Caught off guard, I told Stan that would be fine, though the sooner the better. I didn't want to spend my entire Saturday sitting around waiting for a boy and his binoculars.

Fortunately, Stan showed up in the next ten minutes. I watched him park the black Range Rover in my driveway and then pause to admire the contours of my log house. Or so I assumed.

"Very nice," Stan said, stepping back on the small

front porch. "This style is hot in L.A. these days. Several stars have built log houses."

Inviting Stan to come into the living room, I accepted the compliment. "I didn't build it, I just bought it," I said. "They require quite a bit of upkeep. Mine needs to be stained again. The exterior wood gets very gray with all the rain and snow. It's probably time to rechink, too."

Stan was now studying my inner walls. The kitchen, hall, and bath had been finished with gypsum board, but the logs in the living room, dining nook, and bedrooms had been left exposed.

"Lodgepole pine?" Stan ventured.

"No. Douglas fir. Speaking of which," I continued, "would you like to come outsidc? The birds usually congregate in the evergreens behind the house."

With his binoculars slung around his neck and a small three-ring binder clutched in one hand, Stan followed me out the back door. I offered him a cup of coffee, but he declined. "Yesterday I saw a varied thrush by the ski lodge. You probably call them Alaskan robins. We don't usually get them in southern California."

"They look like a robin," I remarked, glancing up at the tall trees that stood at the edge of my backyard. Only a couple of crows were hopping among the branches at present. "Last year I had a pair of goldfinches hanging out for almost a week. I've never understood why they're the state bird. You hardly ever see them, at least in western Washington."

"Ah!" Stan's thin features became animated. "Otherwise known as the wild canary. They're great birds, wonderful birds." He whipped through the pages of his small binder. "See—I've made a note about them. They nest later than any other bird, any time from the last week of June to Labor Day. Very compact nests, usually lined with dandelion or some other kind of down."

I gazed at the cramped, yet artistic handwriting. Stan had noted that the goldfinch often built in saplings or blackberry bushes. "Darn," I murmured. "My backyard was overgrown with blackberries when I moved in. I got rid of them."

Stan took the binder back, then tore out the page I'd just been perusing. "I didn't realize the goldfinch was Washington's state bird. Take this, I've made notes about what a special character it is. Their song is absolutely delightful. It's not just their yellow color that makes people call them canaries."

Thanking Stan for the notes, I slipped the sheet of lined paper into my slacks. "By the way, congratulations on the pending sale," I said, hoping to sound enthused. "I'll be checking in with you and Blake before we go to press."

Stan pocketed the binder. "Oh—yes, by all means. We intend to stay here until Tuesday afternoon. Then we fly back to L.A. to firm up the financing." He was moving slowly around on the grass, peering through his binoculars. His own manner was rather birdlike.

While Stan Levine might have the leisure to wait for the arrival of a rara avis, I didn't. Insisting that he make himself at home, I started back inside.

"Say," Stan called after me, "have you been up to the hot springs yet?"

I confessed that I hadn't. Stan ankled closer. "Blake and I are going up this afternoon. Would you like to join us?"

The suggestion sounded good. Somebody from *The Advocate* should get a firsthand look at the site. It didn't seem likely that Carla could be coerced into making the climb.

"That's fine," I said, smiling in what I hoped was a gracious manner. "I'll drive down to the office to get my camera first." With that as my exit line, I went into the house. Stan didn't seem to mind; he had his binoculars in place and was following the flight of what appeared to be an ordinary English sparrow. He seemed content.

Later, I would remember his pleasure with sadness.

Chapter Four

ALMOST NOBODY IN Alpine comes by *The Advocate* over a weekend, which is why I was surprised to see a small beat-up car parked in my usual place. I was even more astonished when I heard someone call to me as I approached the office door.

A young woman in jeans and a plaid shirt had emerged from the old car. Her slightly freckled face needed no makeup. Its classic bone structure and natural contours were sufficient for beauty. She moved effortlessly, though her voice had a slightly reedy quality.

"Do you work here?" she asked, gesturing toward the newspaper's unprepossessing one-story building.

"I'm the editor-publisher," I said with a wary smile. "Emma Lord. Are you looking for me?"

The young woman, who looked to be about thirty, put out a slim, freckled hand. "I'm Skye Piersall. I'm looking for *somebody*." She pushed a stray strawberry-blonde lock off her high forehead. "Can you tell me about the hot springs project?"

Since Skye Piersall appeared to be neither armed nor dangerous, I invited her inside. "I can give you a copy of this week's paper," I said, stepping behind Ginny's reception counter.

"I've seen it," Skye replied. "Frankly, it doesn't give much in the way of details."

That was an understatement. "There've been some developments since we went to press. Where are you from?"

Skye Piersall leaned against the counter. Up close, there were fine lines around her eyes and mouth. Perhaps she was closer to forty than thirty. Or maybe she'd spent too much time in the sun. "Seattle—more or less," she answered with studied vagueness. "I move around a lot. I'm with CATE—Citizens Against Trashing the Environment. We deal more with aesthetics than ecology. This is a fact-finding tour."

"I see." I'd never heard of CATE, or if I had, it had slipped through the cracks in my mind. *The Advocate* received a weekly barrage of information from so many groups and organizations that I tended to deep-six all but the most pertinent. "What facts are you looking for?"

Ginny had a desk and two chairs behind the counter which she used when helping customers lay out complicated classifieds, or when she occasionally pitched in on the regular advertising copy. I indicated the extra chair and sat down. With a faint show of reluctance, Skye joined me.

She pointed to my hot springs piece on page one. "Have Blake and Stan made some progress since this came out?"

I regarded Skye curiously. "You know the developers?"

Skye laughed, a heartier sound than I expected after the reedy voice. "Of course. CATE members get to know all of these people. We have offices up and down the West Coast, so we often cross paths with the same soldiers from the opposing army. Last year, these two were trying to start a retreat center in the San Juan Islands. CATE rallied the local residents and put an end to that idea."

Congratulations were probably in order, but I refrained. I was a journalist, and therefore trying to keep an open mind. I explained that Blake and Stan had made an offer that had been accepted. I elaborated on as much as I knew of their ambitious plans. I also pointed out the topographical problems involved. And I added that while the locals didn't favor out-of-state intrusions, they badly needed jobs.

Skye listened attentively. "I'd like to see the site. Can you show me a map?"

I hesitated. "Are you on speaking terms with Blake and Stan?"

Skye laughed again. This time the sound wasn't quite as pleasant. "Oh, definitely! What we say to each other varies wildly." Her green eyes were unreadable.

I explained my own minor involvement. "You'd probably run into us somewhere along the trail this afternoon anyway, so you might as well join us. If Blake and Stan share your tolerance, they won't mind."

But Skye had turned thoughtful. When she finally spoke, there was a defensive note in her voice. "Okay, why not? If it's a steep climb, Blake will have to shut up or he'll get winded."

"True. And Stan doesn't talk as much."

The enigmatic expression had returned to Skye's face. "But he says more when he does."

I shrugged. We agreed to meet at the Burger Barn around one. There would be room for all four of us in the Range Rover. Blake and Stan might not be thrilled at hauling along the enemy, but I'd been put on the spot.

By the time I got home with my camera and a couple of rolls of film, Stan was just leaving. He had seen blue jays, a downy woodpecker, several robins, a pair of purple finches, and countless sparrows. Even Stan didn't seem much interested in the noisy, contentious crows that flapped among the trees and often frightened the smaller birds away.

"Maybe I'll sight the cedar waxwings next time," he said optimistically.

Somewhat awkwardly, I told him about Skye Piersall. His thin features changed dramatically, and I thought there was alarm in his dark eyes.

"Skye Piersall is *here*? Oh, God!" He turned around on his long, thin legs, a hand to his balding head. Then slowly, almost shyly, he looked at me from over his shoulder. "Skye's a terror when it comes to preserving the natural environment. This rock, that tree, those ferns—everything is sacred. She hates anything man-made. If Skye had her way, she'd live naked under the stars."

Strangely, the idea seemed to calm him. He was now smiling and looking back off into the evergreens. I wondered if he'd seen another bird. Or maybe the image of Skye Piersall. Naked.

Whatever I imagined about Stan Levine's reaction to Skye Piersall, the initial encounter was uneventful. He and Blake greeted Skye politely, but with reserve. On the way up to the turnoff, I was left to make small talk. I filled the Range Rover's empty air with an account of the Iron Goat Trail and the enthusiasts who spent their spare time preserving the Great Northern Railroad's old route.

"They come from all over," I pointed out, "though they're restricted by the weather. Some of them use their vacations and camp out along the way."

None of my listeners, with the possible exception of Stan, seemed to give a damn. I switched to the topic of mountain goats and the National Park Service proposal to blast them off the ridges. Blake was indifferent, Stan reacted with a frown, and, to my surprise, Skye endorsed the idea with enthusiasm.

"That's where CATE differs from other organizations," she declared, setting her jaw. "It isn't only humans who harm the environment. Animals cause great damage, too. The worst of it is, you can't reason with them. Of course some people are just as bad." Her green eyes flashed at Blake and Stan. Neither responded, though I thought there was a faint smile on Blake's lips and Stan seemed to stiffen a bit.

Fortunately, the drive was brief. The Californians obviously knew their way, which was more than I did. After we'd bumped along for a short distance on a rough washboard of a road, Stan pulled into what passed for a parking area under the huge power lines that cut across the Cascade Mountains.

The trail began nearby, a narrow, steep incline almost immediately swallowed up by trees and underbrush. Standing next to Blake, I hesitated. Despite living amid raw nature, I wasn't exactly the hearty outdoor type. My so-called hiking shoes were a pair of sturdy Rockports. Fortunately, my companions pretended not to notice. The two Californians and Skye Piersall were properly attired in laced-up boots that looked as if they could have scaled K2.

The ascent was taxing. Except for safety ropes tied to trees, Leonard Hollenberg obviously hadn't bothered to maintain the trail. Despite the sun, which occasionally filtered through the evergreens, the air turned chilly as we gained altitude. Upon reaching the last quarter mile, the ground itself grew muddy. I was about to remark on a patch of dirty snow between two rotting logs when the trail took a sudden dip and we saw a wooden sign that read: HOT SPRINGS—USE AT OWN RISK.

"Here they are," Blake announced, his expansiveness

held in check by a shortness of breath. "What do you think?"

I thought that the series of three small pools with their blue plastic linings were ugly. The nearby ground was discolored from the minerals, the corrugated tubing that carried the water out of the rocks was strictly utilitarian, and the pockets of old snow were pockmarked with debris. Worse yet, the mountain air was tainted with the smell of sulfur. The only saving grace was the view of Windy Mountain and the surrounding foothills.

"It's . . . rugged," I said finally, sitting down on a streaked boulder and panting.

"It's relatively unspoiled," Skye remarked, taking in the vista between the western cedars. "I'd like to see it stay that way."

At the moment, I didn't care if Blake and Stan put up a Ferris wheel. I was hot, tired, and vaguely disappointed. Somehow, I'd expected rippling waterfalls, sylvan pools, and a shady glen that hinted of primeval romance. The only bit of charm was a birdhouse made of cedar shakes which sat on a sturdy vine maple pole about six feet off the ground. Maybe Stan had put it up to encourage nesting. I was too beat to ask.

Fists on hips, Skye was studying her surroundings. "Second-growth timber," she noted. "From when? The Twenties?"

Stan nodded. "Most of this area was logged in the first quarter of the century." He looked past Skye to where I was sitting. "Right, Emma?"

"Right." Carl Clemans had been ahead of his time, reforesting the land. The timber after the 1929 harvest had been limited to isolated parcels, mainly beyond the summit and to the north of Stevens Pass.

Skye gestured at the pools. "Who did this? The seller?"

Blake regarded the plastic-lined holes in the ground.

"No. The people who use the springs fixed them up. Or so we were told by Mr. Hollenberg."

It figured. Leonard wouldn't bother himself. Maybe he wanted to get rid of the property before somebody took a tumble and sued his broad butt off.

Skye was laughing, somewhat derisively. "I think you two are crazy. Even crazier than usual. Look at this terrain—it'd take a mountain goat to get around here. Why did you pick this place? There are mineral springs all over the Pacific Northwest in more feasible locales."

Stan, who had been eyeing the birdhouse, now turned to frown at Skye. "You know the answer to that. Most of the others are already tied in with some kind of resort or are on government-owned property. Scenic was available. We'll have to make the best of it."

"How?" Skye snapped. "By bulldozing and blasting?" Now her laugh was scornful. "That's the only way you *can* create a building site. And CATE won't stand for it. We're prepared to fight you every inch of the way."

Though Stan was frowning, Blake appeared unperturbed. "Right, we're as seasoned at litigation as you are. Our Suits versus your Suits. We're prepared to put this on the ballot and let the locals decide. We can offer jobs. What will CATE give these poor out-of-work bastards? Spotted owl crap and a free dip in the springs?"

Skye was glaring at Blake. "We have the law on our side, Fannucci. The environment is protected."

"This is private property, sweetheart," Blake retorted. "Check your Washington State laws. You're blowing smoke. Go save a whale or some other worthless animal."

"Like you?" Skye shot Blake a withering look, then started back toward the trail. I finally got up and began snapping a few pictures. I could get a shot of Skye in the so-called parking lot, unless she decided to walk back to Alpine. I wouldn't have put it past her.

But she hadn't. By the time we had put the sulfuric stink behind us and arrived at the bottom of the trail, Skye was leaning against the Range Rover, wearing a stern expression. Approaching her gingerly, I asked if I could take a photo.

She shrugged. "Why not? It's good publicity for CATE."

I got her to pose at the trailhead. As a rule, my photographs are never as good as Carla's. Or Vida's, for that matter. But the sun was behind me, the shadows weren't overwhelming, and I was careful about framing and focus. The only distraction was caused by Blake and Stan, who were posting a sign that they had removed from the Range Rover. Signaling to Skye that I had finished, I turned to read the message on what appeared to be professionally printed tagboard:

HOT SPRINGS CLOSED FOR RENOVATION. PRIVATE PROPERTY—PLEASE DO NOT USE TRAIL. THANK YOU.

"Great," Skye muttered. "VineFan not only wants to screw up the environment, it wants to prevent other people from enjoying the natural wonders."

Ever the fence-straddler, I tried to keep the peace. "But the intention is to let everybody have access to the springs. There are plenty of people who could never hike that trail."

Skye sniffed in derision. "Sure, everybody who can afford their price. You call that magnanimity?" She paused, but didn't wait for my response, which would have been lame at best. "Have you shot those two yet?"

I explained that I had, up at the hot springs.

Skye gave me an ironic half smile. "Good. It's a wonder somebody else doesn't shoot that big-mouthed Fannucci. With a gun. He's tempting Fate."

As it turned out, both Blake and Stan were tempting much more.

The Californians dropped Skye off at the Burger Barn, then drove me up to my house on Fir Street. The short ride back to Alpine had been quiet, though the tension in the car was palpable. After Skye got out, Blake had made a remark about her narrow-minded tenacity. Stan had merely shaken his head. I kept my mouth shut.

It was going on four o'clock when I returned home, too late to start any major weekend projects. I got out the new laptop I'd bought recently and wrote a letter to my old friend from *The Oregonian*, Mavis Marley Fulkerston. The laptop had maxed out one of my two major credit cards, but I hoped the expense would be tax deductible.

Except for the anticipated arrival of Adam and Ben, the news from my end was thin. A retired journalist, Mavis always appreciated anecdotes about life on a small-town weekly. Or so she assured me. But Mavis is basically a very kind person.

I was recounting our first batch of personals when the phone rang. It was Leo, sounding vaguely sheepish.

"I screwed up, babe," he said without preface. "Delphine and I are supposed to go to a cocktail party tonight at the Melvilles'. I guess Scott asked me because I'm a fellow California exile. Plus, he liked the ad I put together for him when he first came to town. Anyway, I got the dates mixed up and told Delphine it was next Saturday. She can't go tonight because she's giving a wedding shower for her niece. Could you fill in?"

Coming off the bench for Delphine Corson didn't strike me as very appealing. On the other hand, my Saturday night was open. "What's the occasion?" I thought I might as well hedge a bit before succumbing.

Leo's voice brightened somewhat. "The Melvilles bought a split-level in the Icicle Creek development. Pretty mundane, typical tract housing. Naturally, Scott wants to remodel. This is the kickoff. Once they start tearing the place apart, he and Beverly won't be able to entertain for a while."

I knew the house; it was three doors down from Milo Dodge's uninspired but comfortable residence. Maybe Scott would drink a lot of white wine and reveal juicy tidbits about the hot springs project. It was shaping up into the year's biggest news story. I'd be foolish to ignore an opportunity to elicit some usable quotes from the resort's architect.

Leo sounded more relieved than elated when I agreed to go with him. "It's sort of a buffet," he explained, "so you'll be able to stuff yourself."

My ad manager knew me well enough to recognize that I had a hearty appetite. Luckily, I also had metabolism that kept me relatively slim. I might not be physically fit, but at least I didn't resemble a butter tub.

Cocktail parties, as opposed to keggers and roll-up-your-shirtsleeves drinking bouts, are rare in Alpine. The occasion sent me scurrying to my closet. I decided on a gauzy wraparound blouse and striped skirt with a side slit, an outfit I'd carefully chosen for my meeting with Tom Cavanaugh at Lake Chelan the previous June. The ensemble had given me confidence, though I suspected that Tom wouldn't have remembered if I'd been wearing designer sportswear or a Seahawks uniform. Not that Tom couldn't be observant when it came to clothes—but so overcome were we both by our long-awaited reunion that removing garments had been far more important than admiring them.

A year later the separates looked a bit shopworn. Maybe I did, too. But when Leo picked me up shortly after seven, he actually complimented my appearance.

"You look sharp, babe. Too sophisticated for the yokels. Won't they be wearing their bowling team shirts and those pants with shiny butts?"

"Not all of them," I said lightly. "Not Scott and Beverly Melville. Not you." My tight little smile was intended to flatter Leo's summer-weight sports coat and neatly pressed slacks. He didn't wear a tie, of course, but his yellow shirt suited his coloring. As I got into his secondhand Toyota, it occurred to me that we made a very presentable couple. At least for Alpine.

The Icicle Creek development is on the east side of town, between the railroad tracks, the golf course, and the older, grander homes of First Hill. The more expensive residences sit between Icicle Creek and the fairway. The houses closer to the train tracks are more modest. Like Milo Dodge, the Melvilles were somewhere in the middle, on the opposite side of the creek from the golf course, but sufficiently removed from the Burlington Northern route so that their foundation wouldn't wobble when a big freight rumbled through town.

The house itself had a temporary look, no doubt due to its imminent renovation. The Melvilles also seemed transitory. Maybe it was Beverly's cliché Malibu blonde appearance or Scott's practiced charm. They struck me as people who were passing through, checking out the ambience, poised to move on to the next sensation. It was possible that I was being unfair. First impressions are often inaccurate.

The assembled guests, most of whom I already knew, were gathered in the dining and living rooms. They were a curious crew, seemingly chosen to represent segments of Alpine life: Mayor Fuzzy Baugh and his wife Irene; high school coach Rip Ridley and his spouse Dixie; Cal and Charlene Vickers; Harvey and Darlene Adcock, who owned the hardware and sporting goods store; the Episcopal vicar, Regis Bartleby, and Mrs.

Bartleby, whose first name eluded me; and the local undertaker, Al Driggers, with his ribald wife, Janet. Last but not least were Ed and Shirley Bronsky. Ed wore a cummerbund, and given his girth, all he needed was a fez to look like Sydney Greenstreet in *Casablanca*. Shirley, in blue and green chiffon edged with matching feathers, resembled Greenstreet's parrot.

"Great spread," Leo remarked, forking up seafood beignets, tartar sauce, and an onion tart.

"The food? Or Shirley Bronsky's behind? Now that she's rich, why doesn't she join a health club and work out?" Feeling mean-minded, I shoved a chunk of mozzarella-covered bruschetta into my mouth.

Leo, however, ignored my snide comment. "I wonder," he said, trying to juggle his wine in one hand and his appetizer plate in the other, "if Windy Mountain will offer exercise equipment? Have you asked?"

"No," I retorted, vaguely irked that Leo should remind me how to do my job, "but I'm going to right now."

I had caught Scott Melville's eye over Charlene Vickers's padded periwinkle-blue shoulder. My host met me halfway, by a pair of armless damask chairs that probably would cost me a month's take-home wages. Scott smiled, revealing dimples in both cheeks and chin, more dimples than the law allowed, even in southern California.

He answered my question directly, but with what I assumed was professional detachment. "That's the tentative plan," he said, pushing an unruly lock of dark blond hair off his forehead. "Full services for mind and body. Herbal wraps, aromatherapy, massage, mud soaks, waxing, swimming pool, full gym—the works. There'll be diet and exercise consultants, dermatologists, hair restoration, maybe even physical *and* behavioral therapists. Blake and Stan are going first-class." Scott's tone remained matter-of-fact.

Judging from my host's own muscular build, he was already keeping fit, at least in body. Still, I couldn't help but be impressed by the plans for Windy Mountain. I also couldn't help but wonder where all the money was coming from. "They're flying to L.A. Tuesday to arrange the financing," I noted. "Suddenly that fifteen-million-dollar price tag doesn't sound so high after all. Do you think they can swing it?"

Scott shrugged. "They've put together big projects in the past. They're major players."

They were also absent. I asked Scott if he expected them to drop by.

"Not tonight," he answered in what I was getting to know as his studied detachment. Scott's manner didn't gibe with his boyish good looks. "They're doing dinner with somebody."

I made a guess. "Leonard Hollenberg?"

Scott shrugged again. "Could be. I'm the architect, not the social secretary."

The response seemed to dismiss me, but the awkward moment was broken by Scott's wife, Beverly, who held out her hand. "I don't believe we've met officially. I'm Bev Melville."

I shook her hand, vaguely in awe of her long, straight blonde hair, tall, trim figure, and astonishing big blue eyes. If the hair was bleached, it was recently done, and while the cut was simple, I knew it was deceptively expensive. Somehow, I didn't think she'd gotten it locally at Stella's Styling Salon.

"I hear you have a log house," Beverly began as her husband drifted away to join Ed Bronsky and Harvey Adcock. "I'm envious. But logs wouldn't work in this setting. Scott says we're going to have to blend in."

"Blending in is required in a small town," I said, putting my empty hors d'oeuvres plate down on a small drum table. "At least it is if you want to get along with the locals."

Briefly, Beverly's expression was rueful. But when she spoke, her voice was enthusiastic. "We do, definitely. Why else move to a remote area? Except to avoid all the Big City problems, of course."

"Small towns have problems of their own," I pointed out. "Blending in is just one of them. But you're right, there are advantages."

Again there was a brief pause before Beverly responded. "Ironic, isn't it? People like us move to get away from urban ills, then try to make over our new backwater into what forced us to leave in the first place. Is that progress, Ms. Lord?"

Since I was probably no more than eight or ten years older than Beverly, I insisted that she call me Emma. Otherwise, I was starting to feel like Grandma Moses. "Don't ask me what progress is," I said, noting Janet Driggers zeroing in on us. "What's important for Alpine is putting food on the table. Given the timber industry crisis, the town's in danger of dying."

"Dying?" Janet's voice was perky. "Anybody doing it here? Tell Al—we could use the money. There hasn't been a funeral in Alpine since the first week of May."

I smiled at Janet's comment, but Beverly didn't. "This party may be dying. I feel a lot of negative energy. What about you?"

Janet blinked her false eyelashes at Beverly. "I tried to feel your husband, but he backed into the garlic dip. I thought Californians were more adventurous."

Obviously, Beverly didn't know Janet well enough to realize that she was teasing. Maybe. After almost five years, I wasn't sure I knew Janet that well, either.

"I mean," Beverly said, clearing her throat and looking vaguely uncomfortable, "that some of our guests don't seem very pleased to be here. I have the distinct impression that we may have invited some foxes into the henhouse."

"No foxes here, except your old man," Janet declared. "Fuzzy Baugh's a jackal, Ed Bronsky is a hog, and the vicar's some kind of rare but homely bird. As for—"

"I think," I interrupted in what I hoped was a polite voice, "Beverly means that some of the guests are sort of . . . at odds with the spa project." Noting my hostess's grateful look, I continued. "Ed's pissed because he didn't think of it first. Cal Vickers is anti–outside intervention. So is Harvey Adcock, I imagine, though he's too well-mannered to say so out loud. Fuzzy Baugh has to straddle the fence, but he's very good at that or he wouldn't keep getting reelected mayor. I don't know about Coach Ridley and Dixie. The vicar always keeps an open mind. How does Al feel?"

Janet lifted one almost-bare shoulder. "Al doesn't give a rat's ass. What he'd really like to see is a new nursing home, with some residents from outside of Alpine. These Lutherans here in Alpine come from hardy Scandinavian stock that lives forever. No wonder business is bad. If I didn't work part-time at the travel agency, we'd be close to broke."

Given that Driggers' Mortuary was the only game in town when it came to death, I tended to be skeptical. But I wasn't going to argue with Janet. There was never any point—I knew that from playing bridge with her. Instead of continuing the discussion, I sunk to uncharted depths by grabbing Ed Bronksy and cutting loose.

"Nice party," I said noncommittally, wincing as Ed popped a puff pastry square into his mouth and let a dribble of mushroom cream sauce trickle down his chin. Or chins, in Ed's case.

"Inferior wine," Ed remarked, still chewing, still dribbling. "I've read up lately. Not that I like wine all that much, but I feel it's my place to know what to buy when Shirley and I entertain."

Never having been to a Bronsky party that didn't feature wienies on a stick and beer out of a can, I let Ed's pompous statement pass. "I have no palate," I admitted, my gaze wandering away from Ed, who was finally using a wrinkled napkin to cleanse himself. Across the room, near the closed flowered drapes that I guessed had come with the house, Scott Melville appeared to be arguing with Cal Vickers and Rip Ridley. The Texaco owner and the football coach both seemed heated; the architect retained his cool demeanor.

"You have to acquire a taste, as well as knowledge," Ed said in a confidential tone. "I'm thinking of buying by the case. Not that I need to worry about saving money, but practicing economy is a habit that dies hard."

The practice had been a necessity before Ed inherited his fortune. One of his saving ways had been to send the Bronsky Christmas cards through the office mail. He'd also stocked up on home office supplies at my expense. I'd finally called him on the carpet for charging six gallons of paint to *The Advocate*. Ed had insisted that his residential work space should be a business expenditure. For me. But since Ed didn't work very hard when he was on the job, I doubted that he ever put in much extra time at home.

"Dirt cheap," Ed was saying, even as my mind wandered down memory lane and over to the contentious trio by the drapes. "Ask Fuzzy."

Obviously, I'd lost the train of Ed's conversation. "Fuzzy? Ask him what?"

Ed looked exasperated. "Emma, have you been drinking too much cheap wine? *You're* fuzzy." He chuckled heartily at his own joke. "I'm talking about Melville's quote for this stupid resort deal. Fuzzy Baugh gets to see all the bids for building projects. Fuzzy and I have gotten kind of tight lately." Ed paused, puffing out his chest, his stomach, and his cummerbund. "You know, movers and shakers have to hang together. We played golf today. Fuzzy said that Melville's quote came in dirt cheap."

Now Ed had my full attention. "Really? Who else bid on it?"

Ed's chubby face grew grave. "Gee, Emma, I shouldn't leak this kind of information. You don't intend to publish it, do you?"

I forced a reassuring smile. "Of course not. We've already run the story about Scott Melville getting the job. There's no news value in who didn't, especially since he's the only architect in Alpine. The others were outsiders, I take it?"

Ed nodded. "Everett. Seattle. Even somebody from Skagit County—Mount Vernon, I think. But Melville won, fair and square. He had to, with a bid so much lower than the rest."

"How much lower?" Maybe there was more news value here than I'd thought.

Now Ed turned canny. "Considerable. Like . . ." He closed one eye in what passed for a discreet wink. "Like fifty percent."

"Hmmm." I sounded sage, but in truth I didn't know whether the bid would be fifty percent of a thousand or a hundred thousand dollars.

Nor did I get a chance to ask. At that moment, Cal Vickers took a swing at Scott Melville, missed, and caught Rip Ridley with a glancing blow to the cheek. The football coach reeled, then dived at Cal, knocking him against the drape-covered window. The glass shattered, flying all over Rip, Cal, Scott, and the vicar's wife, whose first name I suddenly remembered was Edith. Darlene Adcock and Irene Baugh both screamed. Janet Driggers jumped on top of Scott Melville, to what purpose, I didn't want to guess.

"Omigod!" Ed shouted, hopping from one foot to the other. "Help! Stop them!"

Leo Walsh was trying to do just that. My ad manager had leaped into the fray and was pulling Cal away from Scott. In alarm, Fuzzy Baugh glanced around the room, looking to a higher authority. Apparently, he felt that only God could pull rank on the mayor, and grasped at Regis Bartleby's sleeve. The vicar frowned, dabbed at his thin lips with a cocktail napkin, and nudged Cal Vickers with his foot.

"Gentlemen!" Bartleby called out in his familiar refined and often soporific voice, which both soothed and lulled his congregation. "Please! Where are your good manners?"

Scott Melville's religious preferences were unknown to me, but Cal was a Methodist and Rip was Presbyterian. According to my Episcopalian friend Mavis, other sects were in complete ignorance of good manners. It seemed that she was right. With blood trickling from his balding head, Cal was kicking at Leo Walsh and Rip Ridley, who were either trying to help or hinder. My eyes were riveted on Scott, who still had Janet Driggers clinging to his back.

Trying to avoid the combatants, I reached Edith Bartleby's side. She was in a state of shock, but seemingly unhurt by the flying glass. Charlene Vickers pushed both of us aside in an effort to reach her husband, Cal. In the process, she stepped on Shirley Bronsky's green satin pumps. Shirley squealed like a pig and grabbed a chunk of Darlene's pageboy bob. The two women faced off, screeching like harpies. They hit the floor just as Milo Dodge burst into the room, holding his King Cobra Magnum in both hands.

Everybody screamed, including me.

Chapter Five

"FREEZE, DAMMIT!" MILO ordered, raising his usually low-pitched voice. "What the hell's going on here?"

Everybody obeyed, more or less. At first Cal couldn't seem to quit flailing with his feet, and Janet wasn't about to release her arms and legs from Scott's torso. Leo had backed Coach Ridley into a corner. Finally, amid much angry muttering and embarrassed expressions, the room grew quiet and everybody assumed an upright position.

Mayor Baugh tugged at his shirt collar, then decided to take on the responsibility of spokesperson: "It seems there was . . . ah . . . some sort of . . . um . . . ruckus," he said, the vestiges of his original Louisiana accent never more apparent. "Friendly fire, as it were, Sheriff."

Milo was wearing a dubious expression along with his best sports coat and slacks. It flashed through my mind that he was either coming from or going to a date with his main squeeze, Honoria Whitman.

"Anybody hurt?" Milo asked, lowering the gun.

Cal rubbed his head, Coach Ridley touched his cheek, and Scott flexed his muscles. Shirley and Darlene stood like statues, with their backs to one another.

"I believe," the vicar said softly, "it was more sound than fury, Sheriff."

"Then how'd the window get broken?" Milo demanded, gesturing with the magnum toward the fluttering drapes. "I saw the glass flying as I drove by."

Fuzzy Baugh was fingering his chin. A tall, heavyset man in his sixties, he often assumed a ponderous stance, which he hoped the electorate took for wisdom. "Well now, Sheriff," he began, crinkling his small green eyes at Milo, "let's say that there are times when everybody can't agree on everything. If I comprehend all this correctly, what we have here is simply a matter of some people who don't see eye-to-eye about local development." His glance took in Scott Melville and Cal Vickers. "By mere chance, Coach Ridley got caught in the middle. It happens to those of us who are basically peacemakers."

As I've often told myself, Milo isn't as stupid as he sometimes looks. Milo, in fact, is very shrewd. Sticking his gun in its shoulder holster, he approached Scott.

"Maybe you ought to announce that the party's over," said Milo.

Scott's eyes narrowed at the sheriff, then he shrugged. Milo, after all, was a current client. "Maybe it is. Most of the appetizers are gone." His glance strayed to Ed and Shirley Bronsky, who were now appropriately reunited next to the buffet table.

Harvey and Darlene Adcock were the first to go for their wraps. The Bartlebys and the Bronskys went next, followed by a grim-faced Al Driggers and a reluctant Janet. Judging from her smoldering glance at Scott Melville, Janet Driggers had some unfinished business.

So did Rip Ridley. Clutching Dixie's wrist, he glared at Scott Melville. "This is a hell of a way to break into Alpine's social life, Melville. If it were up to me, I'd penalize you fifteen yards and the loss of a down." With that sally, the Ridleys also departed.

Regis and Edith Bartleby had taken it upon themselves to herd the still-fuming Cal Vickers and Charlene out the door.

Over his shoulder, Cal glowered at Scott. "The truce won't last. We've just begun to fight." Cal stomped down the carpeted stairs while Charlene tried to calm him.

Scott laughed, a bit uncomfortably. "Why me?" he asked of no one in particular. "I'm just the hired gun." He turned to Milo, who was standing with his arms folded across his chest. "I work for you, I work for VineFan. I have to put food on the table, too." For the first time, a trace of humanity emerged in Scott Melville's mien.

"Cal's feisty," Milo said, resuming his usual laconic manner. "So's Rip Ridley. Football coaches have to be aggressive."

Ever the gentleman, Fuzzy Baugh was helping Irene with her coat. "I should hope so," the mayor drawled. "But you'd think the man would have better than a seventy-two and sixty-four record overall. Plus eight ties. Sometimes I wonder if ol' Rip knows how to motivate. Now when I was a young'un, LSU had—"

Irene Baugh, who in her own way was as accomplished a politician as her husband, put two fingers over Fuzzy's lips. "Come on, honey, let's leave these nice people alone so they can clean up this place. It's drafty in here."

Leo and I were left with Milo and the Melvilles. "Okay," said Milo, "what *really* happened?"

Once again wearing his air of detachment, Scott shrugged. "I was talking to Vickers and the football coach. They both started in about so-called California carpetbaggers coming here and ruining the environment. I wanted to keep out of it, but they made some pretty outrageous statements. Narrow-mindedness—and ignorance—bother me. I tried to set them straight—politely—but they got even angrier. The next thing I knew, Vickers took a swing at me, but hit Ridley instead. I guess the coach had a knee-jerk reaction, and knocked the Texaco guy into the window." Scott shrugged again.

Beverly Melville, who had been silent for as long as I could remember, now spoke with fervor: "Small town, small minds. If these people want to make a living, why don't they do something about it instead of just griping when newcomers take action? They're all inbred, I'll bet, and that's why they act like idiots."

Beverly's previous assertion that she wanted to blend in seemed to be forgotten. Not that I blamed her much. In an effort to avoid further argument, I pushed Leo forward.

"Here's one newcomer who tried to break up the fight," I said, patting my ad manager's arm. "It could have been worse if he hadn't intervened."

"Bull," Leo said, but his face flushed slightly. "I wasn't even sure who was hitting who."

Milo regarded Leo with a lifted eyebrow. "Our hero," he said, but didn't sound completely sincere. "Okay, I guess that does it. I was heading home when I saw the glass break. I decided to get my side arm before I came in." He patted the holster under his sports coat. "Maybe I overreacted, but you never know. All of us law enforcement types are being warned about the dangers of domestic violence."

"Hardly that," Beverly sniffed.

Scott steered Milo toward the door. "Just the same, thanks for your concern, Sheriff. I'll drop by Monday morning with those blueprints for the revised storage space."

Milo left. Beverly was looking worried as she saw

Leo and me out. "This doesn't have to go in the newspaper, does it?" she asked, her forehead furrowing beneath the smooth center part of her hair.

"No," I assured her. "Not as long as charges aren't filed." I didn't add that if we reported every Alpine party that turned ugly, *The Advocate* wouldn't have space for other news.

"Good," Beverly replied with a sigh of relief. "Then we can forget about it. Maybe we should forget about giving parties at all. These people don't seem to be able to handle hospitality."

I didn't say anything; neither did Leo. The exterior view of the jagged window spoke for itself. It was no wonder that the Melvilles didn't bother to wave goodbye.

Father Dennis Kelly understood the problems of blending into Alpine better than most. A Tacoma native, he had spent the past fifteen years as a priest in the San Francisco Bay Area. Thus, he was considered a City Boy. As a Catholic clergyman in a basically Lutheran community, he was in the minority. And as an African-American, he was definitely an Alpine oddity.

Thus, he spoke from experience when he delivered his Sunday homily on acceptance. Naturally, Father Den didn't mention the Californians by name—or state. But his message was clear: The strangers among us were all children of God, and our brethren. Some of my fellow parishioners exchanged looks indicating they firmly believed that God hadn't made people from L.A.

The rest of the day passed uneventfully, which allowed me to finish getting caught up around the house. I did what I could to prepare for Adam and Ben's arrival, which was now less than two weeks away. In the evening, I tried to call Ben at the rectory in Tuba City, but he was out. I didn't leave a message.

Around ten o'clock I was thinking about a long soak in the tub when the phone rang. Ben, perhaps, sensing that his sister had him on her mind. But it was Tom Cavanaugh, and he sounded unusually vexed.

"I've moved into my club," he announced in a beleaguered tone. "Sandra and Zorro have taken over the house."

"That's not fair," I said, indignation rising. "Sandra was the one who moved out. You should have held your ground."

"I hate scenes," Tom replied. He, like most men, also hated confrontations. "I'd never met Zorro before and I was afraid I'd pop him one. Besides being twenty-five and built of brick with a brain to match, he's got an attitude. If I'd hit him, he probably would have killed me."

Tom is no small thing, but at almost fifty, the odds were definitely not in his favor. "Oh, dear." My comment was inadequate. "So what happens next?"

"The lawyers fight it out. At my expense, of course." Now Tom sounded rueful. "What's worse is that the kids will be home from college in a few days. I don't like the idea of them staying with Sandra and Zorro, but there isn't anywhere else for them to go. And it is their home."

I'd never met Tom's two legitimate children, nor had Adam. The elder, Graham, was a senior at USC, studying cinema. The daughter, Kelsey, attended Mills, but I didn't know her major. I'd often wondered if either of them had inherited any of their mother's goofy genes. Certainly the environment in which they'd been raised had been unstable enough to make them both a little wacky.

"Why," I inquired, trying to be helpful, "don't you take the kids away for a few weeks? A vacation to Europe or Canada or someplace."

Tom snorted. "I don't dare leave the lawyers for more than twenty-four hours at a time. They don't do anything if you don't keep prodding them. And when they finally act, it may not be in your best interest. I feel like a watchdog."

"Are you able to keep up with business?" I hoped Tom could sense the sympathy in my voice. For now, it was all I could offer.

"At a distance. No road trips, though. I might as well be in jail."

Seldom had I heard Tom so discouraged. Despite having suffered his share of life's traumas, he was basically an optimist. Desperately, I searched for some way to comfort him.

"Do you want me to fly down this coming weekend?" I could hardly believe my own audacity. Never had I offered to visit Tom.

I heard his intake of breath; I sat in motionless suspense. "Would you?" Tom sounded eager. "My treat. I'll book a room at the Fairmont. Or would you rather be out at Fisherman's Wharf?"

I didn't care if I had to pitch a tent on the Embarcadero. "The Fairmont's fine. But I can pay for the flight. I'll call the travel agency in the morning."

"Friday night, right?" Tom's voice had definitely lightened. "Don't eat on the plane. As soon as I know what time you're getting in, I'll make a dinner reservation."

I was excited, my heart racing madly, stupidly. "Where can I reach you tomorrow?"

"Here, at the club." He gave me the number. "If I'm not in, leave a message. I'll get back to you as soon as I can."

After mutual exchanges of abiding love, we hung up. For almost ten minutes I wandered around my living room, smiling to myself. I'd be seeing Tom in just five days. I'd be lying in his arms in an elegant suite at the

Fairmont Hotel. I'd be stuffing myself on delicacies in exotic San Francisco restaurants. I'd be in heaven, or as close as I'd ever get, considering my disregard for a couple of the major commandments.

At last, I took my bath and went to bed. Hugging the pillow, I hoped to dream of delicious nights on Nob Hill.

Instead, Ed and Shirley Bronsky dressed up as parrots and tap-danced in satin shoes. My subconscious might have a sense of humor but it sure didn't want me to have any fun.

Vida wasn't wearing satin shoes, but she was certainly tapping her foot. Every five minutes she looked up, obviously waiting for Ginny to arrive with the mail. It wasn't yet nine o'clock, and if the office routine followed its usual course, it would be another hour before delivery time.

"I still think the Melville party could go into 'Scene Around Town,' " Vida asserted in a pettish voice. "At least the part about the broken window."

"I told them we'd sit on it," I said, losing track of how often I'd repeated myself.

"Maybe," Vida murmured, "Rip Ridley will file charges."

"Against who? Cal Vickers? Cal hit him by mistake. He was going for Scott Melville." Now I was beginning to sound cross, too.

Carla looked up from her word processor. "It's too stupid. Why can't people in Alpine act civilized? I haven't heard anything so silly since I used to go to frat keggers at the UDub."

Carla's reference to her days at the University of Washington always made me wince. I'd never yet figured out how she'd gotten away with a diploma. Maybe she'd stolen it. Judging from some of her journalistic attempts, she sure as hell hadn't earned it.

Leo Walsh finished filling his coffee mug and poked Carla in the upper arm. "Hey, kid, lighten up. That was just a skirmish the other night. I hear some of the local preachers have got a bunch of bees up their butts. A couple of them came down pretty hard on the California contingent yesterday. What did your Presbyterian reverend have to say for himself, Duchess?"

As usual, Vida bridled at the nickname. "Pastor Purebeck doesn't indulge in smear tactics," Vida huffed. "His sermon was on vanity."

Leo raised his eyebrows. "It was? Why? I've seen some of your Presbyterians, and if there was ever a sin they didn't have any reason to commit, it's that one. How about self-delusion?"

Vida was close to an explosion. She stopped tapping her foot, made her hands into tight fists and glared at Leo. "Don't be so rude, Leo. What do you know about religion? You never go to church."

"That's because thanks to a Jesuit education, I do know a lot about religion," Leo retorted, grinning at Vida as he sat down behind his desk. "It taught me to think for myself. Spending an hour on my dead butt every week won't make me a better person. It's all show, not to mention hypocrisy. I'd rather do *The New York Times* crossword puzzle and stretch my brain."

Vida threw Leo a haughty look. "You're a humbug. Don't talk to me anymore this morning. I might have to do something I'd regret."

Puzzled, Leo turned away, sipping his coffee and studying a mock-up for Barton's Bootery. I sidled over to his desk.

"Did those preachers really speak out against the spa project?" I asked, knowing that lowering my voice wouldn't prevent Vida from hearing.

Leo nodded. "That's what Norm Carlson at Blue Sky Dairy told me. He's Lutheran, and his pastor—Nielsen, right?—wasn't one of them, but it seems that the fundamentalist guys got pretty worked up. Satan in our midst and all that."

The last thing we needed in Alpine was for church leaders to incite their congregations. I wondered if there was another story brewing. Maybe it would be better to editorialize. Emma Lord, the Voice of Reason. I could already hear the clichés bouncing off the back of my brain.

I could also hear the phone ringing in my office. I ran in to catch it before it trunked back to Ginny. Skye Piersall's faintly reedy voice was on the other end.

"I'd like to come in this morning to give you CATE's official point of view," she said. "I understand you have a Tuesday deadline."

I told her that was so. We agreed on ten-thirty. Noting that it was now exactly nine-thirty, I took a chance that Sky Travel was open. Before I placed the call, I closed my office door. There was no need for my staff to hear about my weekend plans. Not yet.

Janet Driggers answered on the second ring. "Hey, sweetie, how about that Scott Melville? Wouldn't you like to take a two-week tour of his anatomy?"

I had to confess that Scott's body wasn't on my agenda. Trying not to sound like a prude, I told Janet what I wanted. The cost of the round-trip fare made me wish I'd taken Tom up on his offer to pay for it. My second bank card would just barely accommodate the total.

"Do you need lodging?" Janet asked. I could almost see the leer on her face.

"I'm staying with friends," I replied a bit stiffly. "Newspaper types," I added, feeling a need to amplify.

"Business, huh?" Janet sounded disappointed. "Too

bad. San Francisco is made for sin. You can feel it the minute you cross the Oakland Bay Bridge."

"I'll be coming up from the airport," I reminded her. "No bridges."

"It's better with bridges," she insisted. "But what the hey, maybe you'll have time to sneak off with some visiting foreign hunk. The only problem with San Francisco is that so many of the local guys are gay. What a waste! Don't they ever think about what we're missing?"

"They know what we're missing," I noted dryly. "That's why they prefer each other."

Janet erupted into laughter. "Too true, Emma! Oh, well, to each his—or her—own. Your tickets will be ready this afternoon."

Thanking Janet, I rang off and quickly dialed Tom's number at his club. He wasn't in, but I left a message giving the arrival time of my Friday flight. Damping down my renewed giddiness, I put myself to work.

The front page was shaping up, with Windy Mountain again the lead story. I planned to give almost as much space to the latest news from the timber wars. The two items were linked, of course. There were also shorter articles on the sheriff's renovations, the inspirational speaker for the high school graduation ceremonies, and a traffic fatality on Highway 2 near Index. The victim was from eastern Washington, which earned him only two and a half inches of copy.

Since my door was still closed, Vida had to knock. She entered almost defiantly. "I thought you were in conference," she said, knowing that I wasn't. "What's wrong?"

It was pointless to keep secrets from Vida. I indicated that she should close the door again. Then I leveled with her about Tom's dilemma and my proposed trip to San Francisco. No one in Alpine except Vida and Carla knew about my relationship with Tom. As far as I knew, both had kept the secret. Milo had an inkling, but he never pried. And despite Tom's visit a couple of years earlier, he and I had not given cause for gossip. But if Tom—and Adam—were to spend more time in Alpine, somebody would notice the strong resemblance and put the pieces together. Maybe it would be Leo Walsh who'd first jump to conclusions. He'd worked for Tom in California, but he didn't know how well we knew each other.

Vida's reaction was magnanimous. "How very grand," she declared after I'd revealed my plans. "You and Tommy deserve a getaway. It's quite remarkable how you've maintained such closeness after all these years apart."

It was also quite remarkable that Vida, who could be so critical of more trivial trespasses, made no moral judgments when it came to Tom and me. She had that rare ability to cut through the excuses and deceptions that star-crossed lovers use to justify their actions. Under that prickly exterior, Vida had romance in her soul.

"Enduring love," she had once said, "especially in the face of obstacles and separations, is very unusual. You can't make it happen and you can't make it go away. It simply is."

Now, perhaps, it was Vida's turn. Ginny knocked timorously on the door. When I told her to come in, her shoulders were bowed with the weight of the morning mail. A quick glance at her left hand showed that the ring finger was still bare. Either Rick Erlandson hadn't yet popped the question, or Ginny had turned him down. The latter seemed unlikely.

"Here, Vida," Ginny said in a breathless voice, "your stack is under Emma's. You might as well grab it now."

Vida did. Without expression she sorted through the wedding announcements, bridal showers, end-of-school activities, and Father's Day items. Now unburdened, Ginny scooted back toward the front office. Vida reached the bottom of the pile, cradling a business-size envelope in her hands. "It's got the P.O. box for the return address. Who do you suppose it is?"

Naturally, I couldn't guess. But Vida was having trouble hiding her eagerness. "Open it and find out," I urged.

She closed the door again. The rest of the staff must have been wondering what was going on. Vida took the single sheet of white stationery out of the envelope and scanned it with her practiced eye.

"This is typed, with no mistakes. He's keeping his anonymity," she said in a voice that was both disappointed and intrigued. "Maybe that's wise. I admire caution."

I leaned forward in my chair, which had developed an annoying creak. "What does he say?"

Vida cleared her throat. " 'Dear Madame X.' I like that. It lends an air of mystery. He has imagination." She paused, then continued reading. " 'Your enthusiasm for books, culture, travel, and people shows that we have much in common. It also sounds as if you are relatively unencumbered by family responsibilities. For the most part, so am I. I, too, believe that grown children should stand on their own and lead independent lives. If you could tell me more about your background, I'd be grateful. Common life experiences are often the best foundation for lasting friendships. I'm a Puget Sound native, and I truly believe that we live in God's country. Let me know if you share my philosophy. If so, perhaps we can meet soon for coffee or whatever beverage of your choice. Sincerely yours, Mr. Ree.' " Vida tried not to smile too widely. "Mr. Ree! I think that's rather clever, don't you?"

I didn't, but I merely smiled back. "It's a well-composed letter. You know everybody in the area, Vida. Surely you must have some idea who he is. Especially if he's in your peer group."

But for once Vida appeared stumped. "He's originally from the Puget Sound vicinity," she said, pushing the envelope across my desk. "That takes in a great deal of territory. The ads are available to anyone in Skykomish, Snohomish, and parts of King and Chelan counties. But the postmark is Everett. I certainly don't know everybody who lives there. It's grown so much in recent years. Of course he might have been passing through and mailed it from there."

Everett is fifty miles away in Snohomish County, but as the nearest city of any size, it's a common destination for Alpine residents. Personally, I prefer to drive the extra thirty miles into my hometown of Seattle.

"You're going to reply?" I asked.

Vida ruffled her tangled curls. "I'm curious. It can't hurt to correspond, can it? Or have coffee. Though I'd prefer tea."

Vida's effort at nonchalance didn't fool me, but I pretended otherwise. Briefly, we speculated on Ginny's lack of an engagement ring. Vida figured that Rick's Saturday birthday celebration might not have allowed him the appropriate moment to ask for Ginny's hand. I wondered if he'd been able to get the ring out of layaway. Vida didn't know, but assured me she'd check with her niece, Lynette, at Tonga Gems.

After my House & Home editor left, I concentrated on the timber story. A great many numbers were involved, including board feet, cutback percentages, truckloads, and actual jobs. I've always been weak when it comes to figures, so I had to cudgel my brain to make sense of the accumulated statistics. It was after eleven o'clock when I finished the rough draft. I realized that Skye Piersall was late for her appointment.

Taking a break from writing, I checked the mail. A dozen letters criticized the Windy Mountain project, while two progressive thinkers endorsed the idea. We'd need extra space on the editorial page to fit in the written responses.

Half an hour later I wondered if Skye Piersall had forgotten our meeting. She didn't seem like the careless type. It occurred to me that there was no way to check, because I didn't know where she was staying.

Shortly after noon I wandered out into the news office. Carla and Ginny had already left for lunch, Leo was attending the monthly Kiwanis meeting, and Vida was munching carrot sticks. Usually she could be persuaded to abandon her diet for a vat of grease at the Venison Inn or the Burger Barn. But not today: Vida regarded me as if I'd suggested a roll in the hay with the high school football team.

"Heavens! Don't even try to tempt me! I'm determined to lose ten pounds before . . . Independence Day."

I turned away so that Vida couldn't see my smile. The goal, I guessed, was before she met Mr. Ree. "Okay," I said, heading for the door. "I'll shanghai Milo."

Stepping out under overcast skies, I started down Front Street for the sheriff's office. I got as far as the corner when one of the green and white Skykomish County vehicles whipped into traffic. The flashing lights went on and the siren screamed.

I couldn't see who was in the car, but it was headed out of town. Naturally, I kept walking. Emergency runs were always news, even if they involved only minor traffic accidents or a suspected prowler. In Alpine, that was often the case.

But not this time.

Chapter Six

DEPUTY BILL BLATT, who was also Vida's nephew, was on duty behind the counter in the sheriff's reception area. So far, the preliminary remodeling work was taking place in the rear of the building. I made a mental note for Carla to get a picture for our current edition.

Bill was on the phone, anxiously trying to rid himself of a long-winded caller. At last he hung up and turned his boyish face in my direction. His blue eyes registered shock or excitement or both. "Ms. Lord! Have you heard?"

"Heard what?" Behind the door that led to Milo's office, the evidence room, and the interrogation area, I could hear men shouting. "What's happened?"

"Mr. Levine—the tall, bald one—he's been shot!" Bill Blatt's Adam's apple bobbed up and down. After four years on the job, he still wasn't used to violence.

Neither was I. Clutching the counter, I reeled a bit. "Is he . . . dead?" I asked, vaguely aware that my tongue had grown thick.

In agitation, Bill waved his hands. "I don't know. Sheriff Dodge and Dustin Fong have gone up there to see what's going on."

"Up where?"

"To the hot springs." Nervously, Bill fidgeted with

some paperwork. "That's where it happened. Leonard Hollenberg found him. I think."

I stared at Bill. "Leonard hiked up to the hot springs? He's too old!"

"He's tough, though," Bill said, getting himself under control. The phone rang, but Bill made no move to answer it this time. "Toni can pick it up," he explained. "Toni Andreas. She's been hired part-time."

I recalled Toni Andreas, a pretty but dim young woman my son had dated once or twice. Still leaning against the counter, I tried to piece Bill's report together. Stan Levine had been shot up at the hot springs. He may or may not be dead. Leonard Hollenberg had found him and apparently called the sheriff. It would take Milo and his new deputy at least forty minutes to hike up the trail. There probably would be no confirmation until one o'clock, assuming Milo could use his new cellular phone at such an altitude.

"It's really awful," Bill Blatt was saying as the phone rang again. "If only Mr. Levine and Mr. Fannucci had come to us sooner. We might have been able to prevent this."

"What?" I felt as if I'd missed a beat.

"The threats. They've been getting threats, mostly on the phone. Mr. Fannucci came in this morning to tell Sheriff Dodge about them. He was here when the call came from Mr. Hollenberg about the shooting."

I blinked several times at Bill. "Where is he now?"

Bill Blatt didn't have to answer. Blake Fannucci, accompanied by Jack Mullins, came through the rear door. He looked as if he were about to collapse. Indeed, he got as far as the swinging door in the counter and passed out cold.

I was tempted to join him.

* * *

Bill Blatt convinced Jack Mullins that they should follow standard first aid procedure in reviving Blake Fannucci. But before they could decide who'd do what, Blake began to moan. Jack, who was the burlier of the two deputies, held Blake in place while Bill searched for a blanket.

"Shock," Jack said, his curly red head bent over the distraught Blake Fannucci. "He wanted to ride up with Sheriff Dodge."

At the door behind the counter, Toni Andreas peeked out. I remembered her from various places she'd worked around town, including Videos-to-Go and Itsa Bitsa Pizza. Her dark eyes were wide and her spiky hair stood on end.

"Is he dead, too?" she asked in a tiny voice.

Jack barely glanced up. "Nobody's dead for sure, Toni. Stick with the phones, okay?"

Toni disappeared just as Bill brought a striped Pendleton blanket to toss over Blake. The stricken man seemed fully conscious, though still overwrought. "Not Stan!" he cried. "Stan wouldn't hurt a fly! What's wrong with these backwoods bastards? Guns! They should be outlawed!" Thrashing under the blanket, Blake seemed on the verge of tears.

I turned to Jack Mullins, who was now standing up again. "Should we get Doc Dewey or Dr. Flake over here?" I asked.

Before Jack could answer, Blake broke in: "I don't need a doctor! I need a drink! Have you yokels got any decent Scotch?"

As much as Milo Dodge enjoyed his whiskey, I'd never known him to keep a bottle at work. Bill Blatt volunteered to go to the liquor store, then realized he shouldn't leave his post. I said I'd go instead.

The state-owned liquor store is at the far end of

Railroad Avenue, tucked behind Buddy Bayard's Photography Studio and across from the Burlington Northern tracks. According to Vida, the store is removed from the main commercial area because Alpiners don't want to be seen coming out with their brown paper bags, or in some cases, entire cartons of booze. Consequently, I had to hurry back to the newspaper, jump in my car, and drive down Front Street until I turned left on Seventh. I was so rattled that I could hardly maneuver the Jag into a diagonal parking place.

As usual, the liquor store had its share of customers. Among them were Henry Bardeen and Charlene Vickers. I was grabbing a pint of Dewar's White Label when Charlene sidled up to me. She had a shopping cart loaded with vodka, bourbon, vermouth, and cognac.

"We're having out-of-town company this weekend," she explained, avoiding my gaze. "I like getting a head start on my shopping."

"How's Cal?" I inquired, ignoring what I assumed was a fib.

"Cal?" Charlene seemed startled, as if she hadn't heard of her husband lately. "Oh, he's fine! So's Rip. They had a good laugh about the dustup at the Melvilles'. Rip knew Cal would never intentionally punch *him*."

"Good," I said, wanting to be on my way. "See you Wednesday at bridge club."

Henry Bardeen was already getting checked out at the register. He glanced over his shoulder and seemed to shrink into himself. "Ah—Emma," Henry said out of the side of his mouth. "I'm always amazed at the special requests from some of our guests at the ski lodge." He gestured diffidently at the four bottles of white wine and the half gallon of Old Grand-Dad.

"You'd think our bar would have an adequate supply, wouldn't you?"

I was sure they did. "People are peculiar," I murmured, and meant it. At the rear of the store I could just make out Charlene shuffling around in the rum section.

"Say," Henry said, patting his toupee as the clerk rang up his total, "did you hear those sirens a few minutes ago? I thought I saw a sheriff's car hightailing it toward the bridge. Has there been another accident on the highway?"

The only rumors I'm responsible for go into print. It was too soon to say anything about Stan Levine. "I'm checking on it," I replied.

Henry's tab came to almost sixty dollars, which necessitated the writing of a check. Suppressing a smirk, I noticed it was on his personal account at the Bank of Alpine. Scribbling furiously in a virtually illegible hand, Henry gave the clerk a thin smile.

"Back to work," he said in what passed for his most jocular tone. "By the way, Emma, will you be at the Chamber meeting tomorrow? We're going to take a vote on the hot springs project."

I stared at Henry. "Whatever for?"

Henry's expression turned dour. "Why, to get a sense of how the local merchants feel about the plan. These California fellows ought to know what kind of support they might get—or not get—from Alpine's businessmen. And women," he added, in his customary style which always made the female sex an afterthought.

I kept my lips clamped shut. I would attend the Chamber meeting, along with Ginny. But a vote on the resort construction was useless. It seemed to me that somebody had already cast a ballot. With a gun.

* * *

Blake Fannucci was sitting in Milo's office when I returned. He was still shaken, but had gotten himself under control. The Scotch was gratefully accepted.

"Do you mind?" he said, pushing the pint back at me. "This damned thumb—it's hell to open a bottle."

There was no ice, and the only decent receptacle was what seemed to be a clean coffee mug. I poured out a measure of whiskey and added twice as much water. Blake drank deeply, then asked if I cared to join him. I didn't.

"Tell me about the threats," I said, sitting in the other visitor's chair and taking a notepad out of my purse. "Bill Blatt told me most of them were made by phone."

"Right." Blake rubbed the back of his head. "We've been getting them ever since we arrived. They call both of us—we have separate but adjoining rooms—and some may be repeats. Offhand, though, I'd guess that maybe a dozen different people have called, including a couple of women. No names, of course, just various crazy warnings about what happens to interlopers."

"Warnings—or threats?"

"Both." Blake took another sip of his drink and sighed. "Last night I got a real zinger. It was a man, I'm pretty sure of that. The voice was hoarse, as if it were disguised. He said that if we went ahead with the project, we'd be sorry. Alpiners have a way of dealing with our likes. It wouldn't, the caller said, be the first time that somebody mistook a man for a bear."

It sounded like something a local would say. I frowned, wondering who would make such calls. And who might actually carry out the threat. "What happened this morning? Did Stan go up alone?"

Blake held his head. "It was pleasure, not business. He went bird-watching. Frankly, I've made that hike so many times that I'm sick of it. But Stan enjoys every inch of the way. He's a real nature lover."

"So I gathered." It seemed ironic that Stan was also a developer whose calling often resulted in the destruction of the very environment that brought him joy. As I'd said to Henry Bardeen, people are peculiar.

"When did he leave?" I asked, discreetly checking my watch. It was ten to one, still too early to hear from Milo.

Blake managed to pour himself another dollop of Scotch. "I came down for breakfast in the coffee shop around nine. He was just finishing. I suppose he left the ski lodge about nine-fifteen, maybe a little later."

I thought of Skye Piersall and the ten-thirty appointment she hadn't kept. "You're sure he went alone?"

"That was the plan." Blake eyed me curiously. The liquor had calmed him; he seemed to be back on track. "Why do you ask?"

"No reason, really." It was the truth. Except for my rampant imagination, there was nothing to indicate that Skye had gone with Stan. She probably had a credible excuse for not coming by the office.

Blake stood up and went to the door. The reception area seemed unnaturally calm, with Bill Blatt and Jack Mullins going about their business. A question popped into my mind. I moved past Blake and joined Bill behind the counter.

"Where's Leonard Hollenberg? How did he contact Milo?"

Bill glanced at Blake, apparently to make sure he was recovering. "Leonard's got a CB in his truck. Sheriff Dodge told him to stay put in the parking area by the trail. He might still be there." The young deputy's face turned slightly pink. "Maybe I shouldn't mention it, but I *think* Sheriff Dodge said Mr. Hollenberg heard the shot when he was coming up the trail."

My mouth dropped open. "You mean that whoever shot at Stan might be hiding in the woods?"

"Could be." Bill looked chagrined. "Of course by now whoever it was could have come out by a different route."

A vision of the steep climb traversed through my mind. Following unmarked routes in the Cascades isn't easy. An occasional glimpse of some landmark such as Windy Mountain can be deceiving. Even experienced hikers who got off the beaten path often ended up hopelessly lost.

"I don't suppose Leonard mentioned any cars parked in the lot," I said doubtfully.

Jack Mullins looked up from the official log. "Leonard was pretty incoherent. He probably wouldn't have noticed an elephant tied to a tree."

Blake, having again freshened his drink, now joined us. "It's one o'clock. How much longer before we hear?"

Jack shrugged; Bill grimaced. I considered my options: I could stay to get official word, or I could grab a camera and drive up to the parking area. Better yet, I could send Carla. That way, if Milo called in from the hot springs, I'd be able to hear the pronouncement firsthand. Carla could take a picture of Milo and Dustin Fong as they came out at the bottom of the trail.

Getting permission to use the phone, I called *The Advocate*. Ginny put me through to Carla. I began by asking her to take a picture, but before I could tell her of what, she interrupted:

"I'm tied up right now, Emma. Where are you? Skye Piersall is here and I'm interviewing her because you're not. Here, I mean."

I winced. Sometimes Carla talked the way she wrote. Or vice versa. I wondered if the University of Washington offered a course in Contemporary Colloquialism. "Where's Vida?" I asked, cutting to the crux. Hopefully, Skye Piersall could convey her organization's philosophy in simple, lucid terms.

"What's wrong?" Carla demanded, then dropped her voice to a hissing whisper. "Don't you trust me to fill in for you with an interview? You're poking big holes in my self-esteem. Why do you have to talk to Vida instead of me?"

"Because you're busy," I retorted, losing patience. "If I didn't trust you, why do I keep you employed?"

"You trust me with little stuff," Carla shot back. "I never get the big stuff. Hold on, I'll transfer you to *Vida*." Carla made my House & Home editor's name sound like a disease.

After several annoying clicks I heard Vida's voice. As succinctly as possible I explained what had happened—as far as I knew—and asked her to drive up to the hot springs parking lot.

Vida was aghast. "Well! Doesn't that beat all! Do you think that old fool Leonard shot Stan Levine?"

The idea hadn't occurred to me. Yet. "Why would he report it?"

"Maybe it was an accident. Or maybe Leonard's smarter than he looks. That's unlikely, though not impossible." Vida paused. "Very well. I'll head out in a few minutes. It's going to take Milo and that new fellow some time to get down the mountain. Has an ambulance been sent?"

I'd neglected to ask. As usual, Vida was taking a broader view. I posed the question to Jack Mullins.

"We've got a helicopter from Chelan County stand ing by. Even with the bond issue passage, we can't afford anything fancy like that," Jack explained.

Having relayed the information to Vida, I hung up. Blake Fannucci was now pacing the area behind the reception counter. It was obvious that he was getting in the way. Jack Mullins started to say something just as Grace Grundle tottered into the office.

Grace is a retired schoolteacher of seventy-odd with a chronic inner ear problem that makes her look as if she's half juiced. Since she was carrying an open umbrella, she also resembled a tipsy Mary Poppins.

"I wish to report a crime," she announced, teetering in front of the counter. "It's raining."

"That's not a crime, Ms. Grundle," said Jack Mullins, who, along with Bill Blatt and most Alpine residents over sixteen years of age, probably had been taught by Grace.

"I know that," she snapped, closing her umbrella. "But it just started a few minutes ago and I didn't think you'd noticed. You've never been very good at noticing things, Jackie. You stargaze, especially out of windows."

"I've tried to overcome that since fifth grade," Jack replied, keeping a straight face.

Grace's sparse eyebrows shot up. "I should think so. Paying attention to your surroundings is very important. That's why I was so worried about Toofy."

"Toofy?" Jack leaned on the counter. "Who's Toofy?"

Grace Grundle scowled at the deputy. "My cat. He has an extra tooth, so I call him Toofy, for Toofum-Pegs. This morning, he went berserk. Fortunately, he's all right now. But just as I was finishing my lunch, I saw Crazy Eights Neffel in my backyard. I want him arrested."

Jack sighed. "Crazy Eights is always wandering around people's yards, Ms. Grundle. You know that. He's nuts. He's also—usually—harmless."

Grace pursed her thin lips. "Not this time. His intentions were, at best, suspect. At worst, criminal." She took a deep breath, blushed, and focused her faded blue eyes on the smooth countertop. "When I saw him just fifteen minutes ago, he was . . . in the altogether."

Jack had to turn away to keep Grace Grundle from seeing his grin. Bill Blatt ducked under the counter. Even Blake Fannucci looked amused.

"Well now," Jack finally said in a semigulp. "That sounds . . . serious. Do you have any idea where Mr. Neffel went?"

Grace lifted her head. "I do not. Do you think I'd stand there at my kitchen window and watch him parade around in such a state? I waited until I thought he was gone and then drove straight down here. I hardly wanted to discuss such a thing over the phone."

The phone, in fact, had just rung. Apparently, Toni Andreas had picked it up. Before Jack could respond to Grace Grundle, it rang again, a different, buzzing sound. Apparently, this was the signal for the deputies to answer. Bill grabbed the receiver, listened, and turned pale.

"Oh, shoot!" he exclaimed after a long pause. "That's . . . awful!" He listened some more. "Sure, okay, right. Thanks, Sheriff." Bill hung up, then turned to Blake Fannucci. "Sir, I'm very sorry. That was Sheriff Dodge. Stan Levine is dead. The bullet wound was fatal. He was shot through the head and died instantly."

Blake Fannucci didn't collapse this time. Instead he stared blankly at Bill for a long moment, then slowly, painfully, turned around and walked back into Milo

Dodge's office. He quietly closed the door behind him. I guessed that he was searching for the Scotch.

I didn't blame him.

Chapter Seven

GRACE GRUNDLE HAD never heard of Stan Levine. She was shocked that a man had been killed, but pointed out that at least he wasn't a local. Did the sheriff's deputies intend to investigate Crazy Eights Neffel's lewd behavior or not?

Jack Mullins hastily assured Grace that they would act as soon as they could. For now, perhaps she'd like to fill out a complaint form? Grace would, as long as she didn't have to write anything that might be, as she quaintly put it, *suggestive*. Before setting pen to paper, she reminded Bill Blatt to stand up straight.

"How many times must I chide you about your posture, Billy?" Grace huffed.

Dutifully, Bill Blatt squared his shoulders as he checked with the Chelan County sheriff's office. He was informed that the helicopter had been requested by Sheriff Dodge to pick up the body, Milo, and Dustin Fong. They would land in Old Mill Park, which was about the only place in Alpine that could accommodate a helicopter.

I called Vida at once. Luckily, she hadn't left the office yet. After expressing appropriate, if objective, surprise, she agreed to meet me at the park.

Five minutes later I pulled the Jag into a slot next to Vida's big Buick. She was standing by her car, trying to tame a blue vinyl sou'wester.

"Goodness!" she exclaimed, keeping her camera tucked under one arm. "Who do you suppose was idiotic enough to shoot that poor man?"

"Your call," I replied dryly. "You know the local population better than I do."

Vida gazed at me from behind rain-spattered glasses. "I'm beginning to wish I didn't. Killing a man over a resort project is utterly wanton. Why can't people use *sense*?"

I had no answer for Vida. We stood in silence for a few minutes, watching the empty playground gear, the forlorn picnic tables, and the life-sized statue of Carl Clemans. Alpine's founder had been a handsome man, and the Everett sculptor who had been commissioned to cast the work had also captured his subject's innate dignity and kindness. At the moment, Clemans seemed a little melancholy.

While we waited, I told Vida about Blake Fannucci's reaction and that Leonard Hollenberg—maybe—had heard the shot on the trail. I also mentioned Grace Grundle's complaint.

Vida scoffed. "Grace's eyes are going. Macular, nothing to be done, according to my niece, Marje." Marje Blatt, who worked as Doctors Dewey and Flake's receptionist, was a primary source for Vida. If Marje knew anything about patient confidentiality, she also knew that informing her aunt didn't count as an ethical violation. Nobody could keep a secret from Vida. It was a good thing the CIA wasn't headquartered in Alpine. Or maybe it wasn't so good. Vida might be able to give them some sensible advice.

"Crazy Eights was probably wearing long underwear," Vida said, making a face into the rain. "He often does after the weather warms up in mid-May."

Again we stopped talking. I didn't want to ask Vida any more questions about Crazy Eights Neffel's underwear. We were both scanning the gray skies for the helicopter when the honk of a horn caught our attention.

Cal Vickers had stopped his tow truck next to the Jag and the Buick. The older model car that dangled from a heavy hook seemed familiar. No doubt I'd seen it around town. I put it out of my mind as Cal rolled down his window.

"What's this? A press conference?" Cal's usual jocular manner was back in place.

"In a way," Vida replied evasively.

At that moment I heard the noisy whirr of approaching rotors. Then the copter itself appeared, easing in over the treetops.

"Holy Oley," Cal cried. "What's going on?"

Keeping one eye on the descending copter, I moved closer to Cal's truck. There was no point in secrecy now. The copter's arrival would bring half of Alpine scurrying to Old Mill Park.

"Stan Levine's been shot to death," I said in a hushed voice.

Cal's broad face grew stunned. Then, to my horror, he broke into a grin. "You don't say? Who gets the medal?"

There was no suitable reply for Cal. I gave a little shake of my head before turning away to watch the helicopter land neatly on the tennis courts. As I rejoined Vida I heard Cal drive off.

"Cal's gloating," I muttered.

"As will much of Alpine," Vida retorted. She sounded glum.

Milo got out of the copter first. He was wet, weary, and, judging from the look on his face, angry. "Where's the goddamned ambulance?" he shouted, as if I ought to know.

His manner irked me. "Go get Cal. Maybe you can use his tow truck to haul the body."

"Don't be a smartass, Emma," Milo warned. He was now standing in front of me, pulling off his gloves. "I told Bill to have the ambulance meet us. Are he and Jack asleep on their feet?"

The rhetorical question still hung on the air as the ambulance came down Alpine Way. There was no siren and the lights were off. Milo might be in a hurry, but Stan Levine wasn't.

Predictably, the helicopter's arrival was beginning to draw a crowd. Vida resettled her sou'wester and started taking pictures. When the ambulance backed into a parking place next to the tennis courts, she came in closer. A moment later a covered gurney was lowered from the copter.

"Ugh," I groaned. Involuntarily, I turned to Milo, but he had moved off to oversee the transport of Stan Levine's body. Mustering my composure, I collared Dustin Fong. Judging from his stricken expression, this was his first encounter with violent death.

"Can you give me some details?" I asked, pulling out my notepad.

Dustin, who was about the same age as Bill Blatt, was close to six feet tall, very slim, with sharp cheekbones and straight black hair that came to a widow's peak. His dark eyes were touchingly sad, especially when he tried to be businesslike.

"The victim, Mr. Levine, was shot at close range through the head. The right eye, to be exact." Dustin paused, swallowing hard. I tried to hide my own dismay. "He's been dead somewhere between two and four hours. He probably died instantly, but the autopsy will tell us more."

It was now 1:35. If Stan hadn't left the ski lodge until close to nine-thirty, he couldn't have arrived at the hot springs much before ten-thirty. That meant he could have been killed as soon as he got there. Was his killer waiting for him? Had Stan hiked up the trail with his assailant? Or had he been followed?

"Where's Leonard Hollenberg?" I asked.

Dustin's gaze was fixed on the ambulance, whose rear doors were being closed. Milo was nowhere in sight. I assumed he'd gotten into the ambulance.

"Mr. Hollenberg?" Dustin echoed, wrenching himself back to my question. "We think he's still at the parking area. I'm going to get a car and drive back up there with one of the other deputies. We had to leave our other vehicle because Sheriff Dodge and I came out in the helicopter."

"I can save the county some mileage," I said. "I'll drive you and the other deputy. I'd like to talk to Leonard."

The new hire obviously didn't know the protocol with the local press. Having been raised in the city, he was another outsider who must have found small-town ways very different.

"I guess so," Dustin finally said in a diffident manner. "Does Sheriff Dodge usually let you . . . participate?" He winced at his own choice of words.

"We call it news-gathering." I gave Dustin a friendly smile. "I won't interfere. But I should talk to Leonard Hollenberg while his recollections are still fresh."

Fifteen minutes later I was driving Dustin Fong and Bill Blatt up Highway 2. They were only a few years older than Adam, and I felt as if I were carpooling. We would have gotten away sooner, but Vida had corralled her nephew, apparently to remind him where his duty lay when it came to revealing information.

The rain had dwindled to a drizzle by the time we parked under the power lines off the main highway. Leonard Hollenberg was sitting inside his aged pickup, half asleep. It took him a few moments to orient himself. Indeed, he stared at Dustin Fong in puzzlement.

"What . . . ? Oh! You're the Chinaman! I forgot, we keep getting integrated around here. Hell's bells, what time is it?" He fumbled inside his plaid jacket and pulled out a big railroad watch on a long chain. "Jesus! Two o'clock! I been here since before noon!"

"Yes, sir," Dustin Fong said politely. "We'd like you to come back to the sheriff's office and give a statement."

Leonard Hollenberg frowned. "What for? I already told Dodge what happened. I want to go home and have some lunch."

"It won't take long," Bill Blatt soothed. "We have to get everything in writing."

Leonard cursed under his breath. Then he glanced at me, realized that he had an image to preserve, and grinned in a cockeyed manner. "What're you doing here, Edna? Getting a big scoop?"

"Emma," I murmured, wondering if Leonard also confused the names of other voters. "Just a couple of questions, Leonard. Where were you when you heard the shot?"

Leonard's frown puckered his forehead all the way to the top of his bald skull. "You know that big cedar that got hit by lightning at about the one-point-eight mark?" I didn't remember the cedar. Leonard nodded sympathetically. "That's okay, Edna. It's just before the trail starts to go downhill instead of up. Hell, I thought the noise *was* lightning, maybe hitting the power lines. On the other hand, I know a shot when I hear it. I was pretty careful the rest of the way, just in case there was somebody practice-shooting. Wouldn't be the first time that people used the parking area to plug a few empty beer cans."

For a man in a hurry, Leonard was taking his time. But of course he loved an audience. "Still, the noise'd seemed closer. But the rain and the wind can trick you.

So I finally got to the hot springs, and there he was. I thought he'd fallen and hurt himself. 'Stan,' I says, 'what's wrong? You had an accident?' Then I got right next to him, and God Almighty, he's got this hole in his head, right through his damned eye! It's a wonder I didn't have a heart attack!"

The two deputies and I paused respectfully. Leonard didn't need any prodding: "So there I was with this stiff—excuse me, I knew the poor guy, after all—and the rain had started to come down in buckets. Levine was beyond help, so I headed back down the trail to call Dodge on my CB." Leaning on the steering wheel, Leonard let out an enormous sigh. "That's about it, Edna. I would've made record time on the trail if it hadn't been so rainy. Hell's bells, there was fog up at the springs. Lousy weather for June, if you ask me. Typical, though, around here." He sighed again.

I had one more question for Leonard. "Did you see any other cars parked in the lot?"

Leonard scratched his bald head. "Sure. That fancy whatdayacallit over there." He gestured at the black Range Rover, which stood a few yards away. In the veil of light rain, the vehicle looked lonely.

"That was it?"

Leonard nodded. "Who else? Levine and that other guy, Gagucci or whoever, posted a sign to warn people off."

Dustin Fong was standing by the pickup's hood. "But somebody else *was* here. The person who shot Mr. Levine."

"Well, I didn't see him." Leonard's manner indicated that the killer must have been a phantom. He immediately realized the implication, and leaned out of the truck's cab. "Hey! *I* didn't shoot the poor bastard! Search me, I'm not carrying a gun!"

Bill Blatt nodded deferentially. "Yes, sir. We aren't

accusing you of anything. If you'll follow us into town, we'll be off now."

The two deputies headed for their own car, which Milo had left parked in a haphazard manner. I waited until the others had pulled out before getting into the Jag. I was halfway to the highway when Cal Vickers came bumping along in his tow truck.

There wasn't room to pass on the rough dirt road. Through the windshield, Cal made a helpless gesture. Obviously, it would be easier for me to reverse. I did just that, then waited for Cal to arrive.

I was still vexed about his callous attitude toward Stan's death. But when Cal climbed out of his truck, he looked subdued.

"You must think I'm one mean S.O.B.," he said, walking over to my car. "Look, Emma, try to forget what I said at Old Mill Park. I can't help but get steamed up when I see these adventurers move into town and try to make a fast buck off of the rest of us. You weren't here during the Burl Creek Little Theatre fiasco."

I admitted as much. In fact, I'd only garnered snatches about the abortive plan to turn a dilapidated barn into a showplace for summer stock. Some twenty years ago a group of theatrical people from San Francisco had come to Alpine and made big promises about bringing musicals to town. Their plans hadn't worked out, and they'd ended up burning down the barn to recoup their financial losses. Naturally, the ill-fated venture had left a sour taste in the mouths of local residents.

"Hippies, that's what they were," Cal was saying. "Nothing but drugs and sex and incense. They plea-bargained their way out of an insurance fraud conviction. I'll bet that wouldn't have happened if we'd had Milo as sheriff back then."

I smiled a bit thinly at Cal. "I won't quote you in the paper. We've all got our prejudices."

Cal looked as if he were about to argue that he wasn't prejudiced, merely sensible. But he shrugged and went to check out the Range Rover, which I presumed he'd been asked to tow into town.

Cal seemed to read my mind. "Milo asked me to bring this thing in so he can go over it. I suppose the keys are on Levine."

Watching Cal prepare to tow the Range Rover reminded me of something. I leaned out the open car window and asked whose vehicle he had been towing when Vida and I had seen him at Old Mill Park.

Cal was about to climb back in the cab of his tow truck. "That Eighty-one Honda Accord? It's registered to an out-of-towner. I towed it in from across the highway, just the other side of Icicle Creek. It belongs to some woman with a weird name. Moon or Sun or Sky. Her parents were hippies or beatniks, I'll bet. But she was clean."

Maybe Skye Piersall had been a hippie in her youth. Now she was a woman with a cause. Smiling again at Cal Vickers, I turned on the ignition. I was anxious to get back to *The Advocate*, and more than a little curious to hear what Carla had learned from Skye Piersall.

When I reached the office, Carla was on the phone. Leo was out checking with our advertisers, and Vida had taken her roll of film to Buddy Bayard's studio. A glum-faced Ginny was distributing phone messages.

"I suppose," she said as I stepped over the threshold, "this means we won't be going to the Chamber meeting tomorrow to talk about the Summer Solstice."

Given the shock of Stan Levine's death, I had indeed forgotten our date with the Chamber. But I pretended otherwise. "No, Ginny, not necessarily. Although I expect the members won't want to talk of much else. Even before Stan was shot, Henry Bardeen said they planned on discussing the spa project and taking a vote of support. Or nonsupport, as the case may be."

"That's dumb," Ginny sniffed. "Maybe the whole thing will fall through. I mean, the sale couldn't be final this fast, could it?"

I'd neglected to ask Leonard that very important question. "The financing hasn't been secured. Stan and Blake were flying back to L.A. tomorrow to raise the money. My guess is that the deal's up in the air."

"It sure is," Carla chimed in, putting the phone down. "Skye Piersall and her group are asking for an environmental impact study. She says that will take months. I was just talking to the state agency in Olympia. They haven't been notified yet by CATE."

I sat on the edge of Carla's desk while Ginny slouched from the news office. "Why didn't Skye show for our ten-thirty?"

"She had car trouble." Carla was unperturbed; her own car was always having trouble.

I wasn't as easily satisfied. Not that I doubted Skye's word about her car. I'd seen it being towed with my own eyes. Cal Vickers had mentioned that the Honda had been across the highway, which indicated she was coming from the direction of the hot springs. I couldn't help but wonder why Skye had been driving west on Highway 2, perhaps about the same time she was supposed to be in my office.

"Skye was two and a half hours late," I pointed out.

Carla flipped her long black hair over her shoulders. "So? Cars are a pain. Give her a break, Emma. She was here when you called about Stan Levine. When Skye found out he'd been shot, she went to pieces. I had to drive her to the Tall Timber Inn."

"Really?" I was shaken by Skye's reaction. Apparently, I hadn't been completely wrong about Skye and Stan having more than an adversarial interest in each other. "What did she say?"

"Say?" Carla's expression was blank. "Not much. She just started to cry and beat her fists on my desk."

"She didn't know he was dead."

"She did when you called the second time. Vida hadn't said anything about it to us when you talked to her a few minutes earlier. Sometimes," Carla added with a grimace, "Vida can be a pill."

Vida tended to spout off about everybody and everything at the drop of a name. But she could also be close-mouthed. That was one of the reasons people confided in her. Having no comeback for Carla, I checked the phone messages at my desk. As yet, there was nothing urgent. I'd give Milo another half hour to get back to the office and collect himself. In the meantime, I started a rough draft of the shooting story. It seemed we now had a new lead.

Five hundred words into the piece, I decided to phone Skye Piersall at the Tall Timber Inn. Alma Eriks, who has owned the motel for thirty years along with her late husband, Gus, answered.

"Who?" Alma demanded in her sharp voice.

I repeated Skye's name carefully, then spelled it for Alma. She was in her seventies and perhaps was going deaf.

"That's a peculiar name, if I ever heard one," Alma declared. "Why can't parents call their children by proper names, like Hazel and Myrtle and June?"

"Don't ask me, Alma," I said, masking my impatience with breezy camaraderie. "I went way back and called my son Adam."

"That's back, all right. Sorry, Emma, no such person is registered here."

I frowned into the receiver. "You mean she checked out already?"

"She never checked in," Alma retorted. "I looked through a whole week. You must have us mixed up with the Lumberjack Motel."

Maybe, for reasons involving environmental espionage, Skye had used another name. As a last resort I described her to Alma.

"Nobody like that," Alma said firmly. "No single women at all in the last few days. All men or couples and families. Like I said, try the Lumberjack."

I did, but drew a blank there, too. Going to the door, I asked Carla if there was a possibility she'd made a mistake.

"Honestly," she said in an exasperated voice, "do you think I'm *stupid*? I know which is the Tall Timber and which isn't. The inn's just three blocks from my apartment."

That was true. Carla probably wasn't mistaken. For once. Thwarted, I decided to head for the sheriff's office.

The rain was coming down harder again. For some reason, June is often a wet month in western Washington. I have childhood memories of getting out of school on damp, gray days that often continued until the Fourth of July. Oddly, May is usually sunny and occasionally downright hot. Living in the shadow of the Cascades and in the path of the Japanese current creates peculiar weather patterns, including Februarys that feel like June.

Scorning an umbrella, I allowed my hair to get damp by the time I entered the sheriff's headquarters. Once again Jack Mullins and Bill Blatt were behind the counter. I inquired after Milo.

Jack gave me his puckish grin. "He's behind closed

doors, probably drinking some of Fannucci's Scotch. If there's any left, that is."

"Can he be disturbed or shall I wait until he passes out?"

Jack chuckled. "It'd take more than what was left in that bottle to put Dodge on his ear. But he's busy, consoling the bereaved partner. Blake Fannucci's asking for police protection." Jack rolled his eyes.

So far, I'd only considered Blake's personal feelings about losing Stan. Despite Jack's contempt for Blake's fear, I understood the Californian's point.

"Come on, Jack," I chided. "This is no joke. Half the team's dead. Who says the shooter won't go for the surviving player?"

Jack's eyes hardened. "Who says it was intentional? In the course of a year, we get a shitload of complaints about people firing guns in the woods. Some of them are practically in town. Take a look at the road signs along the highway. How many are riddled with bullet holes? My guess is that some half-tanked character hiked up the trail and tried to pick off a spotted owl. Instead he shot Levine."

"At close range?" I scowled at Jack. "Stan didn't look that much like a bird. Besides, it's not hunting season."

Jack was turning mulish. "It is for coyotes. They're unclassified wildlife. They can be taken year-round, except for some specific areas, and there's no bag limit." He shot me a superior look.

Jack could argue all day, but he wasn't going to convince me that Stan Levine had been mistaken for an owl or a coyote. Up close, Stan had looked very much like a human being.

"If I were you, I'd humor Blake Fannucci," I said. "Is he still flying back to L.A. tomorrow?"

Bill Blatt, who had made a pretense of not eavesdropping, edged closer to Jack. "He's postponed the trip until after the autopsy. The body probably won't be released until Wednesday. Dustin Fong is accompanying it over to the Snohomish County medical examiner in Everett. Even after the remodeling, we won't be able to do our own postmortems."

Rubbing at my wet hair, I tried to think of an appropriate question for the deputies. I was still leaning on one foot and then the other when Milo and Blake came out of the inner office. The sheriff was wearing an aggravated expression and his companion looked belligerent. I judged that the two men had reached some sort of stalemate.

"It's my best offer," Milo said to Blake's back. "The Peabody brothers are strong as oxes. Call them when you get back to the ski lodge."

The Peabody brothers were a pair of out-of-work loggers who made extra money by digging graves at the local cemetery. As Janet Driggers had pointed out, the undertaking business was bad. Having Stan Levine get killed wouldn't help if he were going to be buried in L.A.

Blake Fannucci gave me a brief nod as he exited the sheriff's office. "Bodyguards?" I asked after the door had closed.

Milo nodded once. "Right. We don't have the manpower to keep somebody on him. The Peabody brothers can handle it. They might not like Californians, but they've got a mercenary mentality."

My request to interview Milo was rebuffed. "It's after three," he said in an edgy voice. "I haven't had lunch. Back off, Emma. I'll talk to you tomorrow. You've got plenty of time before your deadline."

"I haven't had lunch, either," I announced, trotting behind the sheriff. "Where are we going?"

Milo sighed in surrender. Two minutes later we were

in a booth across the street at the Burger Barn. The restaurant was busy, especially with take-out requests. Alpine High had just been dismissed for the day.

"Okay," I said after we'd ordered. "What do I need to know?"

Milo shook a cigarette out of an almost-full packet. "You're up to speed, as far as I can tell." His mood was still grumpy.

"Has the crime scene been secured?"

Milo scowled at me through a cloud of smoke. "Get real. The rain was coming down in buckets up at the springs. Visibility was limited because the clouds settle in at that altitude. If there were any footprints or sign of a struggle, I didn't see them. We had to get the body out as fast as we could or we might not have been able to use the Chelan County copter. As it was, the damned thing had to hover until there was a break in the fog, and then the landing was dicey as hell. It's a wonder the rotors didn't hit the trees."

Wearing my most sympathetic expression, I steered Milo back to the original query. "So no man at the scene, right?"

"Right. Even with an extra deputy, I can't use somebody to watch the site." Setting the cigarette down in a black plastic ashtray, Milo rubbed his forehead in a careworn manner. "Go ahead, tell me this isn't a textbook investigation. But not many people get themselves shot on terrain that's only fit for mountain goats."

Having been to the springs, I understood Milo's dilemma. I also understood why he was upset. The conditions for seeking evidence were definitely unfavorable.

"No sign of the gun?" Weakening, I also lighted a cigarette, my first since breakfast.

Milo shook his head. "I'm guessing it was a handgun. The autopsy will give us some details." He didn't sound optimistic.

"What about the threats?" I asked. "Any idea who made them?"

Milo stubbed out his cigarette as his cheeseburger and my hamburger arrived with our fries. "Hell, no." He waited until the waitress had departed. "It could be anybody. Probably more than one person. When Dwight Gould comes on duty at five, I'm sending him over to the ski lodge to ask if the staff who took calls for Levine and Fannucci recognized any of the voices. It's a long shot, though."

"Have you checked out the Range Rover?" I asked, adding extra salt to my fries. Vaguely, it occurred to me that I was cruising in unhealthy waters. Maybe it was time to reassess my lifestyle. Maybe it wasn't. I was going to meet Tom in San Francisco. That in itself was an enormous change.

"We've only checked the rental vehicle in a cursory way so far," Milo said around a mouthful of cheeseburger. "Nothing obvious. I okayed some overtime for Jack so he could meet Dwight Gould at the lodge. They can go through Levine's belongings. I don't expect to find anything, but if Fannucci sees them hanging around, it might make him feel better."

"Are you ruling out an accident?"

Milo gave me an ironic look. "At that close range, even Durwood Parker couldn't mistake Stan Levine for a bear. The weather wasn't bad this morning, so visibility was probably good. But don't quote me. Wait for the M.E.'s report."

Swallowing a fat french fry, I asked a reluctant question. "I hate to say this while we're eating, but I'm bothered about Stan being shot through the eye." I swallowed again, even though my fry was long gone. "Stan was fairly tall, at least six feet. Wouldn't the killer have to be that tall or taller?"

Milo, whose stomach was stronger than mine, devoured a slice of dill pickle. "Not on that rocky ground. No matter where you stand, you're automatically several inches taller or shorter than whoever you're with."

I deep-sixed my quibble, wrenched my mind away from gruesome details, and bravely tackled my burger. I couldn't conjure up any more pertinent questions for the sheriff. Milo's disposition was improving in a direct relation to his consumption of food, coffee, and nicotine. I decided to help him along by changing the subject:

"Even if you can't do autopsies in Alpine, you'll be able to handle more of the lab work when the renovations are done," I said, raising my voice to be heard above the noisy arrival of a half-dozen teenagers. "What did Scott Melville say this morning about your storage space?"

Milo's long face was momentarily puzzled. "Scott? Oh, he had to cancel. He'll drop by tomorrow."

I stared at Milo. "He canceled? When was he due?"

The sheriff was now looking relaxed and munching three fries at once. "He called around ten. I'm not sure we had a set time. It was no big deal, just a decision about how many drawers versus how much shelving. Why?"

Feeling foolish, I told Milo about Skye Piersall and her no-show at *The Advocate*. I also relayed Carla's description of Skye's reaction to the news of Stan's death.

"You probably think I'm on a trip down Imagination Lane," I admitted, "but isn't it odd that both Scott and Skye skipped their morning appointments? They knew Stan quite well. I'm inclined to think Skye knew him extremely well. And Cal Vickers towed her westbound car from the highway."

Never one to jump to conclusions, Milo stuffed the last chunk of cheeseburger in his mouth and chewed thoughtfully. "I never heard of this Skye woman until now," he finally said. "You went up to the springs with the three of them Saturday? What did Skye and Stan do, stop to grope each other on the trail?"

"Hardly," I said, sounding a bit prudish. "It was the way they each reacted to the mention of the other's name."

"Oh, well, that clinches it!" Milo held out his coffee mug to the waitress for a refill. "I get it, women's intuition. Maybe I should collar her right now."

Milo's attitude annoyed me. "If you can find her. She's not at the Tall Timber, where she had Carla drive her."

Milo remained unruffled. "So? Did she *say* she was staying there? Or did Carla make an assumption? Your star reporter isn't always accurate."

I hardly needed the reminder. "Okay, so skip it. But I'd be interested in knowing where Skye was staying, if not the Tall Timber or the Lumberjack. There's always the ski lodge, of course."

The waitress, who knew Milo and me well enough to leave separate checks, did just that. Milo unwound his long legs from under the table. "Dwight and Jack can ask while they're there."

After crossing Front Street, Milo and I went our separate ways. We usually did. While I considered Milo a close friend, our socializing was limited to lunches and an occasional dinner. If there was a spark between us, we were sitting on it. In many ways.

However, sparks were flying in the news office when I returned. Vida and Leo were having one of their frequent arguments, this one over Blue Sky Dairy's full-page ad celebrating the company's fiftieth anniversary.

"I don't care what that ninny Norm Carlson told you," Vida declared, whipping off her glasses and rubbing frantically at her eyes. "Norm's father, Victor, started the dairy in Forty-five, not long after V-E Day. It was the end of my freshman year in high school. I remember, because I had a crush on Seth Cooper, who was a senior, and he went to work driving truck for the Carlsons after he graduated. He ran over our dog."

Apparently, Leo had not yet learned that there was no arguing with Vida when it came to Alpine's history. "Come on, Duchess, Norm's got to know when the family business was started. He's almost as old as you are."

"Norm's fifty-eight," Vida snapped, "and is lucky to remember his own name. His mother, Sophie, had all the brains. She actually ran the business and kept the books."

I waved a hand at my warring staff members. "Hold it—do we lose the full-page ad if it turns out this is only forty-nine years for Blue Sky?"

Leo all but smirked. "Probably. A full page costs—"

"I know what it costs," I interrupted. "That's the problem. Leo, check the archives. If Vida's right, let's offer a discount, but run the full page. It's still a milestone."

Reluctantly, Leo went over to check the bound volumes. Vida, who hadn't yet put her glasses back on, was glaring at me.

"Since when did you stop taking my word for things?" she grumbled.

I gave her a helpless look. "Leo needs to see it in black and white, if only to convince Norm he's wrong."

"Norm's usually wrong," Vida muttered, finally resettling her glasses on her nose. "What's Milo doing? Being obtuse?"

It was after four. I wanted to finish the draft of my story on Stan's death and also check with the local ministers to see if any of them had indeed been inciting their congregations. Not that I expected them to admit as much in so many words, but at least they'd have to reveal the topic of their Sunday sermons.

I leaned on Vida's desk. "Want to drive up to the ski lodge after work?"

"Whatever for?" Vida's expression was severe.

"To see what Milo's deputies have learned."

"Very little, I should imagine." But Vida's face relaxed a bit. "I won't eat there."

"Neither will I. I just had lunch at the Burger Barn."

"Well." Vida eyed Leo's back as he flipped through the old volumes of *The Advocate*. "It won't hurt to keep the deputies on their toes. We do have a deadline tomorrow."

Leo closed one of the volumes with a loud bang and a cloud of dust. "Damn!" He turned to grin at Vida. "You're right, Duchess. Blue Sky started up in Forty-five."

Vida narrowed her eyes at Leo. "Of course it did. I don't know why you felt the need to argue."

Carrying the January–June 1945 volume under his arm, Leo headed for the door. "Because someday, Duchess," he asserted over his shoulder, "I'm going to be right." Leo closed the door firmly behind him.

"No, he's not." With a sniff, Vida returned to her typewriter.

Chapter Eight

THE SUN DECIDED to favor us that evening, appearing shortly after five o'clock. It would likely be a pleasant interlude, until the clouds rolled in again before dawn. Vida and I arrived at the ski lodge just after five-thirty. A sheriff's car parked in the lot indicated that the deputies were already on site.

Henry Bardeen wasn't pleased to see us. "The summer tourist season is just starting," he said, standing stiffly on the lobby's flagstone floor and regarding Vida with apprehension. "We're sixty percent capacity tonight. What must our guests think, with deputies and reporters skulking around?"

Vida, who had exchanged her sou'wester for what looked like a crown of orange rinds, drew herself up to Henry's eye level. "I never skulk, Henry. Never. Let's chat in your office."

Unwillingly, Henry led the way. His office was finished in bleached knotty pine, with furniture to match. The centerpiece was a large aquarium with exotic tropical fish.

Vida sat forward on her cushioned pine chair. "Is Skye Piersall a guest at the lodge?"

Henry frowned. "I think not. The name isn't familiar. But let me check with Heather. She's still on duty because she's waiting to go home with me."

Heather was Henry's daughter. She had worked at the

lodge since graduating from high school seven or eight years ago. Heather was pretty in an unremarkable way, but she saved all her charm for the job. I could tell her shift was officially over by the sullen manner in which she entered her father's office.

"Those deputies act like *I'm* a suspect," she declared, banging the door behind her. "Who do Jack and Dwight think they are anyway?"

"It's their job, Heather." Henry showed remarkable patience. "Did you check on this Piersall woman?"

"She's not in the computer," Heather replied in a testy tone. "If she's been staying here, somebody sneaked her in."

It was a thought, apparently one that Vida shared, because she gave me a quick glance. I, however, changed the subject:

"Jack and Dwight must have asked you about the phone calls Fannucci and Levine received. Do you remember who any of them were from?"

Heather didn't deign to sit down. She was pacing around the aquarium, fussing with the lapels of her regulation blazer. "Some. The architect, Scott Whatsisname, called several times. So did Scott's wife, but not as often. That windbag of a county commissioner, Hollenberg. People from L.A., including a woman who kept giggling. Somebody from Phoenix." Heather shrugged. "There were more, but I don't know who they were. Chaz might remember."

Chaz was Chaz Phipps, a contemporary of Heather's who also worked behind the desk at the lodge. Vida pursed her lips. "Surely," she said in her most denigrating voice, "you must remember *someone* sounding suspicious."

"I don't know what you mean," Heather replied in a manner that was just short of insulting. Or so I thought until it dawned on me that maybe she really didn't know what Vida was talking about. The deputies might not have enlightened Heather Bardeen.

"There were anonymous threats," I interjected. "Phoned in to both Fannucci and Levine. Do you remember putting through people who might have had mischief on their minds?"

"Mischief?" Heather wrinkled her upturned nose, as if amused by the word as well as the concept. "There *were* some people who sounded sort of odd. But I just figured they were from L.A."

"No one you recognized?" I asked.

Heather considered. Like her father, she was cautious. "I'd hate to be wrong," she finally said with a wary look.

Henry was quick to intervene. "Of course you would, Heather. You might be accusing someone unjustly. That would be . . . terrible." Henry shuddered, as if he could see a long line of lawyers forming in the lobby.

Heather took the cue. "Then I won't try to guess." Suddenly, her composure fled. "What's going on here? Does the sheriff think that whoever made phone threats shot Mr. Levine? That's crazy!"

Making a soothing gesture in his daughter's direction, Henry spoke quietly. "I don't think anybody knows anything just yet. It could have been an accident. But as I said, the deputies have to do their job. Routine, you know."

Heather didn't appear convinced. "Is that all?" she asked in a tense voice.

It wasn't, as far as Vida was concerned. "One last thing, Heather," my House & Home editor said with a wag of her finger. "This may sound indiscreet, but it must be asked. Did women call on Mr. Fannucci or Mr. Levine?"

While her father looked vaguely offended, Heather had been in the hostelry business long enough not to be shocked by the query. "Not really. But I'm on the day shift. Except for Sunday night, when I filled in for Chaz." Again Heather took her time to answer. "There was a woman at the elevators I didn't recognize, around ten P.M. Not that I always know every guest by sight, but she was wearing big sunglasses and a scarf. It struck me as strange, especially the sunglasses after dark."

Vida arched her eyebrows. "Young? Pretty?"

"Fairly young. Pretty, maybe. It was hard to see much of her. She had a light raincoat thrown over her shoulders. I never saw her again, at least that I know of." Heather still seemed apprehensive.

Her father was toying with a silver ballpoint pen. "She certainly wasn't a prostitute. We've never allowed that sort of thing at the lodge."

She didn't sound like a prostitute to me, at least not the amateur Alpine variety, who usually weighed about three hundred pounds, had a few missing teeth, and were raising a couple of kids on welfare.

Vida and I had no more questions for Heather. She left, with an anxious glance at her father. It appeared she was eager to go home. So was Henry, but he was duty-bound to remain until the deputies had finished. When Vida asked their whereabouts, Henry informed her that as far as he knew, they were searching Mr. Levine's room. Vida announced that we would seek them out.

We were alone in the elevator. With her back pressed against the pine paneling, Vida spoke in a conspiratorial tone: "Heather's overly cautious. I'm certain she recognized one of the callers."

"I agree. But she's being candid about the woman with the dark glasses. Skye Piersall, maybe?"

"Maybe."

The elevator stopped at the third floor. Henry Bardeen had condescended to tell us that Stan Levine had been staying in the Tonga Suite, while Blake Fannucci was in the adjoining Tyee Suite. Even if Vida didn't know the ski lodge like the back of her hand, she would have been able to find the rooms. The Peabody brothers were standing outside of the Tyee Suite, looking like a couple of aspiring thugs from an old gangster movie.

Never having known their first names, and assuming they must be called something like Hunk and Beefy Boy, I was surprised when Vida addressed them as Purvis and Myron. I was also surprised that they had thin, high-pitched voices.

"We just got here about half an hour ago," said Purvis, who looked to be the elder, if the shorter, of the two. "This guy pays good. How come he's so chickenshit?"

Vida frowned at Purvis. "Mind your language. It's probably because his business partner may have been deliberately shot to death this morning. Surely he explained that to you?"

Purvis and Myron both looked dubious. "He didn't explain much," Myron said, flexing his impressive muscles. "He wants us to watch his . . . backside. At least until he takes off in a couple of days."

"You do that," Vida urged with a flinty smile. "Are the sheriff's deputies in the Tonga Suite?"

Purvis glanced in the direction of the next doorway. "Dwight and Jack? Yeah, they came up about fifteen minutes ago. Hey, Mrs. Runkel, is this really *serious*?"

"Very likely," Vida replied primly. "We're going to see the deputies now." She nodded her orange rinds at the Peabody brothers, who made no objections. I had the feeling that if Vida had told them she was going to call on Blake Fannucci with an AK-47, they would have nimbly stepped aside.

Dwight Gould was somewhat less welcoming. "Hey, we're in the middle of an investigation," he protested. "You can't come in here."

"We are in here," Vida replied calmly. "Surely you've already dusted for prints or done whatever it is that we might disturb."

From the door to the bedroom Jack Mullins grinned at Vida. "We don't know what we're doing. Have a seat on the sofa. If we find any hot clues, you'll be the first to know. As usual."

The Tonga Suite looked like most of the other rooms in the ski lodge, only larger. The walls were finished in knotty pine, the furniture was rugged but comfortable, and the colors were mostly dark blue, deep green, and rich red. The sofa on which Vida and I seated ourselves was covered in a plaid that featured all of the above shades, as well as a bit of white and yellow.

"You *have* checked for fingerprints?" Vida said, her gray eyes darting about the suite, as if committing the details to memory.

"Sure," Dwight replied. "We just finished. But Levine wasn't shot here."

Vida regarded Dwight with mild disdain. "Naturally not. But he must have had visitors. Mr. Fannucci would know, I assume."

Jack had returned to the living room, carrying a shaving kit. "Sheriff Dodge asked all those questions this afternoon. Check with him." He paused, rummaging inside the kit. "Boy, this guy went first-class. Fancy labels, expensive clothes and shoes, hotshot luggage. He was a health nut, too. Lots of pills and vitamins and stuff."

Like Vida, I was taking my own inventory of the suite. "What about letters?" I asked.

Dwight gestured at a hand-tooled briefcase next to an end table. "We're taking that with us. There are some letters, but they're all business. Hey, ladies, there's nothing here for you. Or for us, as far as we can tell."

Vida waved at the briefcase. "Was that locked?"

Briefly, Dwight stared at Vida. "No. Why do you ask?"

"What else is in there?" Vida's manner was brisk.

Dwight sighed. "Just . . . stuff. Mostly about the resort plans. Levine kept a journal, but there wasn't much in it, just what you'd expect about how the project was coming along and how enthusiastic he was about it."

"May we see it?" Vida rubbed her fingers together, as if she were already turning pages.

But Dwight grew stubborn. "No, you may not. Dang, Mrs. Runkel, we have to check in first with Sheriff Dodge. If it were anybody but you"—his glance passed right over me—"I'd have tossed you out at the door. Come on, trust us. There's nothing here of interest."

To my surprise, Vida obliged. "Certainly. Emma and I must go next door to commiserate with Mr. Fannucci. Is that the adjoining entrance?" The orange rinds were inclined toward a place in the wall where only a wrought-iron handle on the pine panels showed evidence of the well-matched doorway.

"You got it." Jack Mullins sprang over to knock on the wall. Getting a muffled response, the deputy opened the latch for us.

Blake was lying on another plaid sofa, watching the news. He eyed us warily, and I hastily introduced Vida.

"What are those deputies doing next door?" he asked, pulling himself into a sitting position and using the remote control to turn off the TV.

"Investigating," Vida replied, easing herself into an armchair that was a cross between Danish modern and Santa Fe. "I'm sorry for your loss, Mr. Fannucci. I assume you and Mr. Levine were friends as well as partners."

Blake seemed somewhat startled by Vida's remark. "Yes, of course we were. Friends, I mean. My God, Stan and I go way back, to UCLA, in fact. I don't know what I'll do without him."

A rap at the suite's front door caused all three of us to turn. One of the Peabody brothers—Purvis, I thought—asked if Blake was all right. Blake assured them he was.

"Dodge gave good advice," Blake said to Vida and me. "I think those two good ol' boys are okay."

"Solid," Vida remarked. "In many ways."

I leaned forward in the matching plaid armchair that was threatening to swallow me. "What will you do without Stan? Is the project still on?"

Blake made circular motions with his head. "Jesus—I hope so! As long as Hollenberg doesn't back out and I can secure financing. Yes, I intend to move ahead, though I'll admit, I haven't thought much about business in these last few hours."

"Of course not," Vida said with a show of sympathy. "I take it Mr. Levine's participation wasn't essential to your success?"

Blake bridled. "You bet it was. Stan had a way with money people. They trusted him. I've always been the concept man. I work better at the other end, selling ideas to the public." He stared down at an empty highball glass on the coffee table. "I guess I didn't do so well with the locals, though."

"No," Vida agreed candidly. "But they're what you might call . . . difficult."

The expression Blake turned on Vida was rueful, even bitter. "That's an understatement, Mrs. Runkel. My failure may have gotten Stan killed."

For once, Vida said nothing.

Vida held firm to her resolve not to eat dinner. She was sticking to her diet, and that was that. I didn't try to dissuade her, since after my late lunch, I still wasn't hungry. We had each driven our own cars up to the ski lodge, so after concluding the interview with Blake, we went our separate ways.

After arriving home, I tried to put Stan's death out of my mind. I had to concentrate on my trip to San Francisco. In the excitement over the shooting, I'd forgotten to pick up my airline ticket from Sky Travel. I could hardly believe the oversight. Where were my priorities? Not wanting to get into lengthy explanations with Janet on the phone at home, I called her office and left a message on the machine, saying I'd be in as soon as they opened in the morning. Then I went to my closet and surveyed my wardrobe.

I wasn't pleased by what I saw. The only new clothes I'd purchased had been for last summer's meeting with Tom at Lake Chelan. A shopping spree was in order, but I had neither time nor money to spare.

Discouraged, I wandered out into the kitchen and poured a glass of Pepsi. Maybe I shouldn't go to San Francisco, I thought. The plane fare had gobbled up my remaining charge card credit. I'd have to rely on Tom not only for lodging, but food as well. All my years of fierce independence were going down the drain in one weekend. Were two days of grand passion worth it?

But passion wasn't the point. Tom needed me, and not just in bed. I doubted that he confided in anyone else. The man was too private. And his situation was downright embarrassing. Tom's innate dignity wouldn't allow him to blab about his troubles.

If Mavis had called in crisis, would I have rushed off to Tigard, Oregon? Of course I would. I could hardly do any less for Tom. Even with a potential murder investigation breaking in *The Advocate*, I could leave town for two and a half days. Vida would make sure we didn't miss anything.

Having cleared my conscience, I returned to my closet.

I still didn't have a thing to wear.

Francine Wells was sympathetic. "Don't worry about maxing out your credit cards," said the owner of Francine's Fine Apparel the next morning. "Either we'll get them to raise your limit or I'll do an override."

In my career, I have faced down civic leaders, presidential candidates, star-studded celebrities, business tycoons, and unrepentant murderers. On the whole, I've acquitted myself quite well. But put me in the hands of a savvy saleswoman such as Francine Wells, and I become a simpering ninny.

So it was that one navy linen suit, three cotton blouses, two pairs of tailored slacks, a white pleated skirt, and $685 later I was holding my breath while Francine processed the charge. Naturally, a code came up. Francine dialed the requisite number. After a brief exchange, she handed the receiver to me. I had to stop holding my breath so that I could talk.

Increasing my credit limit by twenty-five hundred dollars was far too easy. I didn't know whether to be relieved or disturbed. Francine, however, proved reassuring.

"You got a real deal on the suit and the tan slacks," she pointed out, winding a thick rubber band around the plastic hangers that held my latest adventure into debt. "Everything works with everything else. Versatility is so important for today's professional woman."

"Nnnyah," I replied. At least that's what it sounded like in my own ears. Trying to recover my aplomb, as well as my credit card, I fumbled with my purse. The airline ticket I'd picked up at Sky Travel peeked out provocatively.

Francine lifted her carefully plucked eyebrows. "Emma! You didn't tell me you were going away! Where? When?"

She hadn't asked why, so I hedged. "This weekend, to San Francisco. I'm meeting with a weekly newspaper consultant." It was true, in a way.

Francine paused in the act of covering my extravagance with a plastic bag. "You aren't thinking of selling out, are you?"

"Heavens, no!" I laughed shrilly. "But I am thinking about restoring the back shop. We could do our own presswork, plus job printing. You know, the way it was in the old days, when Marius Vandeventer owned the paper."

Francine rolled her eyes. "Marius! He was quite a character. I wonder how he would have reacted to this hot springs project." She finished her task and handed over my purchase. "Are you coming to the Chamber meeting today?"

I nodded. "I'm bringing Ginny. We want to talk about the Summer Solstice idea."

"I like it," Francine said, now thoughtful. "But you won't get it on the agenda. The rest of them will be all agog about that Levine getting shot and what to do next. I hear Ed Bronsky's talking about sanctions."

"Sanctions?" I wrinkled my nose. "What do you mean?"

Francine shrugged her designer-covered shoulders. "Who knows with that bunch? I'll be frank, I wasn't for the project originally, but now that one of the Californians is dead, I feel sorry for them. I mean, they're human, too."

I tried not to look dismayed. "Yes, they are," I said carefully.

"Besides," Francine went on as Doc Dewey's wife, Nancy, strolled into the store, "a spa would be good for business." Francine lowered her voice while Nancy Dewey inspected a rack of new arrivals near the door. "Guests are bound to come into town, and what else is there for women to do except shop? Where else but here? If they're losing weight or toning up, they'll feel good about themselves. And they'll want to *buy*. Why should I vote to cut off my nose to spite my face?" Stepping out from behind the counter, Francine spoke in her normal tone: "Hi, Nancy. Don't tell me it's time for the annual AMA convention. Where is it this year?"

In something of a daze, I left Francine's Fine Apparel. It was almost eleven, and I'd used up over an hour between the clothing store and the travel agency. Feeling guilty, I raced past Harvey's Hardware, Videos-to-Go, and the Whistling Marmot Movie Theatre, then crossed Front Street and stashed my purchases in the Jaguar. I didn't want to answer any awkward questions from my staff.

My staff, however, wasn't there. The phone was ringing as I entered the news office. It was Milo, trying to reach me.

"Jeez," he said in an exasperated voice, "where were you? This is the third time I've called in the last ten minutes. I thought you had a deadline today. Don't you want the M.E.'s report or are you going to let Carla make it up?"

I had snatched up Vida's phone. Clumsily, I sat down in her chair, which had the same kind of beaded backrest that she used in her car. "Go ahead, Milo. We've all been out, running around." Hopefully, I was the only real truant.

"Okay. We said Levine was shot at close range, but it was more like intermediate—four to six inches. There was very little soot, but some tattooing from the gunpowder particles embedded in the skin. Remember, this is a little trickier to figure because the bullet entered his right eye and exited through his skull."

Writing furiously, I blanched. "Ugh. Okay, go on."

"We think this was a .357 caliber bullet, full-metal jacket. No, we don't have the damned slug, but the M.E. can tell certain things by comparing the small entrance wound with the much larger one exiting the skull."

I gulped. My appetite for the Chamber luncheon was evaporating. Why did I envision creamed something on toast?

"The bullet must be at the hot springs," I said, trying instead to picture rocks, trees, and gentle waters. "Are you going back up there?"

"Bill and Dustin headed out first thing," Milo replied. "It's cloudy, but we haven't had any more rain."

"Did the M.E. rule this a homicide?"

Milo's chuckle lacked mirth. "What else would you call it? There was no gun, so it sure as hell wasn't suicide. If it was an accident, nobody's coming forward to admit they got close enough to Stan Levine to shoot him in the head from four inches away."

I tried to think of other pertinent questions. "No sign of a struggle?"

"No. It looked to me as if Levine got shot and fell backward. The M.E. confirms there were no other bruises or evidence of a fight."

"Is there anything else I should know?" Like, I wanted to say, why the scenario didn't sound quite right?

"I'm not sure." Milo's voice dropped a notch. "We got a call this morning from Henry Bardeen. Somebody tried to break into Blake Fannucci's room last night."

As ever, I was amazed at what other people didn't think was news. "Good grief, Milo, what happened? Is Blake all right? Where were the Peabody brothers?"

"They were sacked out in the Tonga Suite, next door. Myron—or was it Purvis?—I forget—was supposed to stay on the couch in the Tyee Suite, but Fannucci told them both to get a good sleep because he figured nobody'd try to come after him at the ski lodge during the night."

I was running out of room on Vida's memo pad. Frantically, I dug in my purse for my notebook. "So how did they get in? Who was on duty at the desk?"

I had to wait for the answer. Milo was distracted by somebody, probably Toni Andreas, since I heard a woman's voice. The respite gave me time to find a blank page in my notebook.

"What? Oh," Milo said into the phone, apparently regaining his narrative, "whoever it was didn't come in through the lobby. Henry said the bedroom window had been tampered with. It's just off the fire escape."

I pictured the lodge's exterior, with its dormer windows on the top story. This was the section with the more modest rooms. Before the remodeling some two years earlier, the fourth floor accommodations were strictly dormitory-style. The Tonga and Tyee suites were below them, and featured double small-paned windows that swung outward. I hadn't noticed, but apparently the fire escape from the roof passed by Fannucci's rooms.

"Can you reach the fire escape from the ground or does it have to be lowered?" I asked Milo.

"Usually it has to be let down," he answered, "but Henry said they were painting it before the big rush of tourists after school gets out. You know how everything rusts in this climate."

"What about Blake? Did he see anybody?"

"I guess not. He thought he heard a noise around three A.M., so he got up and looked around. Nothing. He decided he was dreaming."

No wonder. I expected Blake Fannucci would have nightmares for a long time. "Nobody else noticed anything?"

"Not according to Henry. They keep a skeleton staff after the bar closes at two. One custodian, somebody in the kitchen, the shoeshine boy who acts as security if needed, a waiter who usually spends most of his shift cleaning up after the late diners and drinkers. One of the Gustavson kids was working the desk. Hey, Emma, are you going to print this?"

"Did Henry officially report it?" If he did, it would be in the sheriff's log, and therefore public knowledge.

"Yeah." Milo sounded glum.

I didn't blame him. The hot springs story was becoming more depressing by the minute. "I'll check with Henry. He'll be at the Chamber meeting. Where's Blake now?"

"He and the Peabodys went over to Everett. The M.E.'s done, so Fannucci can take the body to L.A. today if he can make arrangements with the airlines."

I couldn't resist the question: "Is he taking the Peabody brothers with him?"

"God, I hope not. Can you imagine them in L.A.?"

I could. That was the problem.

Chapter Nine

"THIS," GINNY BURMEISTER declared with a toss of her red hair, "is totally stupid."

The three dozen faces at the five cloth-covered tables stared in bewilderment. Though Ginny's cheeks turned pink, she stuck to her guns. "Why would anybody *care* who brings new business to Alpine, as long as people have jobs? Can't we stop talking about the hot springs and discuss something more important? Important, I mean, to this group. What's the point of Loggerama anyway? It's totally *old*."

After twenty-five minutes, Ginny had grown sick and tired of listening to harangues about the California-sponsored resort project. When Ed Bronsky finally shut up and sat down, Ginny had sprung to her feet and demanded the floor. Luckily, Harvey Adcock was chairing the meeting. Harvey had prejudices of his own, but he was basically kind and fair-minded. He had recognized Ginny and allowed her to speak her piece.

"What's wrong with *old*?" inquired Mayor Fuzzy Baugh. "I'm kind of old myself." The self-deprecating remark evoked laughter as well as denials, both of which Fuzzy had expected.

Francine was the first to make a cohesive statement. "Ginny's right. It's time to deep-six Loggerama." She waved away a burst of protests. "No, not this year—it's too late, the plans are made. But next summer we can move into the modern world. Admit it—change is everywhere. Why should Alpine cling to the past?"

Ginny gave Francine a grateful, if diffident, smile. I secretly applauded her, too, though I wondered if she'd have been less eloquent if I hadn't just dropped over six hundred bucks in her shop.

To my surprise, Cal Vickers also spoke up on Ginny's behalf. "Maybe we should be more realistic, folks. It wouldn't hurt to look at new ideas. What if we had a Scandinavian theme for this solstice thing? Isn't it some kind of old-world deal anyway?"

Norm Carlson might not remember when his family's dairy was founded, but he knew his traditions. "That's right, Cal," he said with an enthusiastic nod. "I think it has something to do with the Vikings."

"Gods and goddesses," cried Janet Driggers. "Fertility rites! Think what we could do on those floats!"

The next ten minutes were spent in a lively discussion of the possibilities. I sat back, toying with my raspberry sherbet and marveling at the herd mentality. The tables were being cleared when Harvey Adcock asked for a formal motion to consider the Summer Solstice Festival and vote on it at the next meeting. Ginny, urged on by Francine and Janet, nervously stated her case. I seconded, and it was passed, twenty-nine to four, with three abstentions. The meeting was adjourned.

Ginny was jubilant, or as close to it as she ever gets. Placing a hand on my arm, she beamed and sparkled. "I can't believe it! Why did they do such a turnaround?"

"People aren't unreasonable," I began, then saw Ed Bronsky plant himself next to Ginny and wondered if I should amend the statement.

But Ed also surprised me. "No room for fuddy-duddy ideas, eh, ladies?" He put an arm around each of us. Ed smelled like a cross between Drakkar Noir and tuna fish. "This solstice festival could be a class act. Janet's right about those gods and goddesses. We could have a grand marshal, like the Rose Bowl parade, only he'd be dressed up like . . . what's his name?"

"Odin," I supplied.

"Right, Odin. He'd have to be a civic leader, active, well-off, imposing. You know, to exemplify the forward-looking theme of the new celebration." Ed smiled coyly.

My perverse nature wouldn't let me play up to Ed. "It sounds like a natural for Fuzzy Baugh."

Ed's smiled faded. "Not Fuzzy! As mayor, he ought to disqualify himself. He'll have plenty of other things to do." Somehow, Ed had disengaged himself from Ginny, which was fine with her since Francine, Harvey, and Cal had drawn her off to one side. "Listen, Emma," Ed went on, edging me up against a long banquet table at the end of the room, "what's happening with the resort? Is it on hold or what?"

I was trying to listen to Ed while keeping track of Henry Bardeen. I hadn't yet had an opportunity to ask him about the break-in at the ski lodge.

"I gather Blake Fannucci intends to move ahead." My tone was vague as I saw Henry in a little knot of people that included Clancy Barton, Ione Erdahl, and Buddy Bayard.

Ed nodded eagerly. "Good, good. But he's used to working with a partner, right? And what's been his big problem? No local involvement. Maybe that's why Stan Levine got shot. Now Fannucci has his big chance—he can bring in an Alpiner. That ought to assure him of smooth sailing, huh?"

I let Henry out of my sight long enough to stare at Ed. "What? You're suggesting that Blake pair up with somebody from here?" Enlightenment dawned. Ed was referring to himself.

Apparently, a busboy had left a basket with two

uneaten rolls on the banquet table. Ed grabbed one and began gobbling it up. "You got it," he said, sputtering crumbs in my direction. "I could give Fannucci credibility. How about it, Emma? You know him. Can you make the introductions?"

Surely I'd heard of worse ideas; I just couldn't remember when. "Gosh, Ed, the poor guy is on his way to L.A. with his partner's body. I don't know when he's coming back. By the time he does, everything may be in place. Or it may be scrapped."

Ed snatched up the last roll. "That's why Fannucci should know he's got local support. He can use that in L.A. when he goes after the financing."

Henry was drifting away with Buddy Bayard. I tried to get around Ed, which was difficult in more ways than one. "Skip it for now, Ed. Besides, I thought you and most of the Chamber were dead set against the project. Or did I hear wrong about a half hour ago in this very room?"

"Letting off steam," Ed said, dogging my footsteps. "That was my plan, to go along with the criticism so that I could refute it after I got involved. These folks know I'm one of them, Alpine through and through. Come on, Emma—can't you get hold of Fannucci before he leaves for L.A.?"

Ed's persistence was making me cranky. "No, I can't. The last I heard, he was on his way to Everett to claim the body. See if Henry has an L.A. number for him, then call tomorrow. I'm not your business agent, Ed. I've got to run—Tuesday is deadline day, remember?"

If Ed did remember, he obviously didn't care. His sour expression brightened, however, when his cellular phone rang into his well-padded ribs. "Bronsky here . . . What? Listen, Shirley, you knew we were out of toilet paper when I left this morning. I'm not an errand boy . . ."

Ed had turned away, which was the perfect cue for my exit. I didn't catch up with Henry Bardeen until he was entering his office.

Henry was about as happy to have me pester him as I was to put up with Ed. "Emma, this is a bad time. I should have ducked out on the Chamber meeting early. Everything's gone wrong around here in the last twenty-four hours."

"Like the break-in?" I said, trying to sound both sympathetic and astute.

"Nobody broke into the lodge," Henry declared with a scowl. "A window latch was forced and some dirt got on the floor. But Mr. Fannucci didn't see anything suspicious. It might have been a raccoon. You know what nuisances they can be. They're around all the time, trying to get at the garbage. The guests think they're cute, so they feed them, which is a huge mistake. They can be vicious."

I knew all about raccoons. *The Advocate* featured at least one photo of the annoying little darlings every year. I had mixed emotions about feeding anything but seed to the birds who frequented my backyard. The raccoons devoured bread crusts, then boldly marched up to the back door and demanded another course.

Still, I was having qualms about raccoons climbing fire escapes and opening latched windows. "But you reported the incident to Sheriff Dodge, didn't you?" I persisted.

Henry was blocking the door to his office in an effort to discourage me. "Yes, and I wish I hadn't. Mr. Fannucci overreacted—not that I blame him—so I did, too. Later, when we talked it out, we both realized there was no real cause for concern. The air-conditioning, the laundry facilities, the fruit and produce deliveries, are more important to making this place run smoothly. I don't have time for errant wildlife or broken hair dryers or missing wing tips or a misspelled word on the dinner specials menu. If you don't mind, I'd appreciate it if you wouldn't blow this window thing out of proportion. The lodge's reputation will get enough negative publicity just because Mr. Levine stayed here."

Henry dismissed me with an abrupt nod that threatened to dislodge his toupee. My patience began to slip away, then I reminded myself that there was a deadline to meet. I couldn't indulge my temper.

By the time I got back to the office, I was willing to placate Henry Bardeen. I gave Vida the item about the window latch, asking her to include it in "Scene."

"Make it cute," I suggested, "but add a caution about people in general egging on the raccoons. Henry's afraid one of them will bite a guest."

"They will," Vida replied. "When Roger was only about six and didn't know any better, he got nipped badly. The poor little fellow was trying to put one in a grass skirt. His parents had just gotten back from Hawaii."

While wondering if Roger had taken the first bite, I really didn't want to hear any more grandmotherly anecdotes. "Henry's a wreck," I remarked, changing the subject.

Vida shrugged. "He always is. No doubt that's why his hair fell out when he was so young. Now what is this idiocy about Ed?"

The question caught Leo's attention. "So Ed wants in," his successor mused after I had finished recapitulating. "You know, it's not as nutty as it sounds. Putting a local name on the project just might give it the seal of approval. Are you sure Fannucci's left for L.A.?"

I nodded. "On my way out of the lodge, I asked Heather Bardeen if Blake was coming back today. She said he'd called from Everett and was headed for Sea-Tac. He asked her to store his things—and Stan's—until he returned. He didn't know when that would be. And no," I added for Vida's benefit, "the Peabody brothers didn't go with him."

Despite constant telephone interruptions from people asking for confirmation of the homicide rumor, I finally finished the front page. I'd left six inches for coverage of that evening's city council meeting, which I'd decided to let Carla attend. The agenda was short, and while I usually sat in on the monthly meetings, I figured the assignment might boost my reporter's self-confidence. Her story on Skye Piersall was predictable, with quotes along environmental party lines. I felt Skye had more to offer, but Carla had only skimmed the surface. What I wanted to know most, however, was Skye's whereabouts. Since hearing of Stan's death, she seemed to have fallen off the edge of the earth.

By four-fifteen we were waiting on a couple of ad corrections and Carla's inside picture feature on Dutch Bamberg's pet skunk. With the rare luxury of time on my hands, I decided to stroll down to the sheriff's office. Maybe Milo had some late-breaking information.

Jack Mullins was alone on duty. He looked up from his computer screen with a sheepish smile. "Hi, Ms. Lord. Boy, these things are tricky! I'm not looking forward to learning the upgraded system we've got on order."

"You'll manage," I said with a reassuring smile. "Where's Milo?"

Jack all but pressed his face into the screen. "He's out. Say, do you know anything about speadsheets?"

"Absolutely not." With growing suspicion, I watched Jack ply the keyboard as if he were playing Chopin. "Where did Milo go?"

Jack was biting his lip, shaking his head, apparently wrapped up in concentration. "Heck, I lost something here. Maybe if I hit Insert, it'll come up again."

The phone rang, and Jack grabbed it as if it were a life preserver. "Yes? . . . I've got it, Toni . . . Hi, Mrs. Barton . . . You don't say . . . Kids, probably . . . No respect for private property . . . Hold on, how do spell *zinnia*?" He glanced up, gave me a helpless shrug, then buried himself in the receiver again. "Two *n*'s? . . . Okay. What else did they pick?" Jack was scribbling away; I knew when to quit.

But only temporarily. It was four-thirty, and if the sheriff had a secret, I needed to know before *The Advocate* closed shop. Crossing Front Street, I entered The Upper Crust Bakery and ordered coffee and a twister. I positioned myself at one of the tiny tables closest to the window opposite the Skykomish County Sheriff's headquarters. There was still no sign of Milo when I finished my snack.

Brushing off my skirt, I glimpsed Beverly Melville entering the bakery. She recognized me and smiled wanly.

"I'm beginning to think we made a big mistake," she said, lowering her voice. "This town is turning into a disaster. What next, terrorists?"

"There's no escaping real life," I pointed out, then nodded in the direction of the bakery owners who were conferring behind the counter. "Gail and Brenda are from California. Riverside. They seem to like it here." I didn't add that they had gained grudging acceptance after a mere three years because the locals couldn't resist stuffing themselves on The Upper Crust's confections.

Beverly regarded Gail and Brenda with skepticism. "Good for them. I wish I were as lucky." To my amazement, Beverly's eyes filled with tears. She turned away quickly and left the shop.

It would have been presumptuous to follow her. On the other hand, I was leaving anyway. But by the time I got outside, Beverly Melville was slipping into the bucket seat of her blue Mazda Miata. She pulled out into traffic just as Milo Dodge swung into his reserved parking space across the street.

I caught up with Milo as he reached the double doors. Despite the cool, overcast weather, he looked hot as well as tired. The sheriff glowered at me when I attempted a smile.

"Not now, Emma. Call me in the morning." His elbows barred me from the door.

"Hold it—it's deadline." I actually leaned into him. "What's going on? Jack's a lousy actor."

Angrily, Milo banged the door, but allowed me to enter. "I don't want any crap on this," he shouted, causing Jack to jump in his chair. "We can only do so much, goddamn it! Don't even think of speculating!"

More confused than annoyed, I followed Milo inside the counter area. "Facts would help. What are you talking about?"

Whipping off his regulation hat, Milo tossed it across the room. Then he unzipped his jacket with a furious motion, ran a big hand through his sandy hair, and took a deep breath. "Okay." He paused to scowl at Jack, for no apparent reason. "Bill and Dustin went up to the springs this morning. They called in around eleven-thirty to say the place had been trashed. Teenagers, they guessed. I went up there right away. Sure enough, the place was a mess. Beer cans, condoms, general junk. They got the pools all dirty and ripped one of the plastic liners. They knocked over the birdhouse and burned part of it in a campfire. If we hadn't had so much rain lately, they might have set the woods off, too. I'd like to kill the little bastards. Every year it's the same thing—school's letting out and the kids go nuts!"

I tried to arrange the revisions in my head: The vandalism story would have to go in a box on page one. Maybe I could jump the Chamber piece to the inside and redo Carla's skunk layout. But I still needed more information.

"When did it happen?" I asked.

"Who knows? Last night, I suppose." Milo reached for a cigarette, remembered the NO SMOKING sign he himself had posted in the outer office, and got out a roll of mints instead. "The fire was cold. It doesn't get dark until almost nine this time of year, so they probably went up when it was still light. Coming down is easier, especially if you're stoned. It would've served them right if somebody'd broken a leg."

"Have you told Leonard Hollenberg?"

"Hell, no! I just got here!" Milo swung around, kicking at a wastebasket. "Bill and Dustin are on their way back, but I'm asking the Forest Service for help tonight. I don't want a repeat."

Jack seemed to feel left out. "Sheriff, I'll bet we can bust some of those kids. We're getting other complaints, about trampled gardens and stolen flowers and broken windows."

Milo sneered. "That's middle school stuff. Hell, these days it's probably first graders. These kids had to be older. They wouldn't walk all the way to the hot springs turnoff. They're too damned lazy."

Jack was still wearing an eager expression. "That's what I mean—we pretty much know the troublemakers from the high school. Not to mention the dropouts. I'll start checking on them."

Milo's shoulders sagged. "Okay. But they'll lie, and their lame-assed parents won't know where they were because they're more wasted than the kids. What we need is a witness who saw a bunch of teenagers heading for the hot springs trail."

A brief silence filled the office. Milo retrieved his hat, while Jack began going through files, presumably of Alpine's most wanted adolescents.

Given Milo's mood, I hated to ask my next question: "Did you find the bullet?" I cringed inwardly, expecting a volatile reaction.

But Milo gave me a lopsided smile. "Not even my luck is all bad." He felt inside his jacket and produced a plastic bag. "It's a .357 full-metal jacket, just like the M.E. figured. It appears to have gone through Levine, then hit a tree. It was embedded in the bark of a noble fir. I suppose we missed seeing it earlier because those nobles have kind of unusual bark."

I was familiar with the tree's small rectangular blocks of dark gray. "What about foot- or fingerprints?" I asked.

"We'll do our damnedest." Milo's back was turned as he tried to pour himself a cup of coffee. The pot was empty, and he swore. "Jack, can't you keep this cocksucker going? What have you been doing all afternoon, playing NFL football on your frigging computer?"

"Hey," Jack replied, looking put-upon, "I've been running checks on people. Levine. Fannucci. Melville. We may turn up a lead or two."

Milo snorted. "We may turn up with egg on our faces. Who benefits from Levine's death? That's always the big question. I'll admit, it's probably some broad in Beverly Hills who's out walking her Chihuahua."

Jack's expression grew puckish. "Maybe she sent a hit man."

"Maybe you ought to get off your ass and figure out where this bullet came from." Not waiting for Jack's agreement, Milo whirled on me. "You heard me, Emma—keep to the bare bones. I don't want the voters saying I botched this investigation after they approved a bond issue to beef up this department. What the public doesn't realize is that in law enforcement, it's always too little too late."

"Too true," I said, but my sympathy was wasted on Milo.

Leo and Carla and Ginny had gone home by the time I got back to *The Advocate* at five after five. Vida remained, looking worried.

"It's not like you to wander off on a Tuesday," she said in faint reproach.

Delegating the layout problems to her, I explained as I worked on the vandalism story. Vida was less appalled than I'd expected.

"Nothing's sacred to young people these days," she declared. "A murder site would merely titillate them. It's all this TV violence. When Roger stays with me, I insist that he watches only wholesome programs."

Knowing that Roger's favorite show was *NYPD Blue*, which he called "Butts and Guts," I made no comment. "Word will get out," I said. "If there were girls at the springs, they'll talk. And the boys will brag."

For some minutes we worked in silence. Then Vida spoke almost in a murmur. "He hasn't resubmitted."

"Huh? Who?" I was proofing my completed sidebar and thought I'd missed something.

"Mr. Ree. Ginny said the ad wasn't resubmitted." Vida looked pleased.

"Ah!" Disposing of the corrected vandalism piece, I smiled at Vida. "That means he must have gotten your response and doesn't feel a need for further fishing. Maybe you'll hear something tomorrow or Thursday."

Vida was now making an effort at nonchalance. "Perhaps." She leaned forward in her chair, rummaging through her in-basket. "Wouldn't it be nice to have someplace to go in Alpine?"

I assumed Vida was talking about the teenagers with time on their hands and mischief on their minds.

"Besides a murder site two miles up Spark Plug Mountain?"

"No, no." She tugged at a piece of paper, freeing it from the stack of what I knew to be mostly publicity handouts. "I mean for adults. Did you get this news release from the state about a study of new community college sites?"

Vaguely, I remembered such a thing from a month or so ago. "That's an annual announcement, isn't it?"

Vida nodded, scanning the sheet of paper. "But this one includes prospective areas other than the I-5 corridor. It doesn't specifically mention Skykomish County, but it proposes a study of potential sites within a hundred miles of Seattle and Tacoma. That *could* mean Alpine, couldn't it? Think what a two-year college could offer us!"

I agreed. Such an institution would bring a great deal to the county. I suspected, however, that Vida was thinking in more personal terms, such as going to a college choir concert with Mr. Ree.

"We don't have the population base to support a state-funded college," I reluctantly pointed out. "If local kids go on to college, they usually head over the pass to Wenatchee J.C. or into Everett."

Naturally, Vida knew as much—or more—about such things than I did. Still, she was loath to surrender the concept. "Geographically, this would be a good site. It would draw on the Highway 2 corridor and parts of Snohomish, King, and Chelan counties. I feel like writing a letter to our state senator."

"Why not?" I studied the finished front page. It was crowded, and our only photos were of the moribund hot springs parking lot and the helicopter landing. Unfortunately, no head shot of Stan Levine had been available. The pictures we'd taken of him and Blake for our previous editions had been too cheerful and informal.

"More of our young people would be motivated to attend college if we had a campus here," Vida said, standing up and reaching for her coat. "Let's be honest—young people today are lazy."

I thought of Adam. "Yes, they are. Unless they're really interested in something." To be fair, my son had worked very hard on the Anasazi dig.

"Which," Vida continued, as if I hadn't spoken, "makes me wonder about the vandalism at the hot springs."

Now my full attention was riveted on Vida. "What do you mean?"

Vida shrugged her shoulders into her coat, then adjusted her turquoise bowler. "Would your average troublemaking teenager—who is making said trouble because he or she is lazy as well as bored—bother hiking two miles uphill carrying party goods?"

I gazed at Vida with interest. "Good point. Why not trash Old Mill Park or the Icicle Creek Campground? Are you suggesting these weren't kids?"

Vida stroked her upper lip. "I'm not sure what I'm saying. It simply doesn't fit."

Somewhere in the back of my mind the same thought had registered. Indeed, Milo had remarked that the culprits must have driven to the turnoff because they wouldn't want to walk. Why, then, would they want to hike?

Swiftly, I reread my sidebar story: "While the sheriff allowed that juveniles may have caused the damage," I had written, "his department's investigation of the vandalism is being carried out separately from the homicide inquiry." That was safe enough. Anyone reading the article would come to the same conclusion—it was probably kids.

The knee-jerk reaction made me wonder if that's what we were meant to think.

* * *

I'd already changed into my bathrobe when the phone rang a little after eight o'clock. At first I didn't recognize the low, faintly reedy voice at the other end.

"Can I trust you?" There was a tremulous quality to the question, and I wondered if I had one of the local lunatics breathing in my ear. "I have to trust somebody," the voice said with more verve.

I recognized Skye Piersall. "Where are you? We're running your interview," I added quickly, lest she think me a personal as well as a professional snoop.

"I'm staying with a friend," Skye answered. "I can drive up to Alpine or maybe you could meet me here."

I glanced at my bare toes, sticking comfortably out of a pair of worn red mules. Even the most diligent journalist has lapses when it comes to pursuing a story. "Where's *here*?"

"It's . . ." There was a pause. I could hear another voice which sounded oddly familiar. "It's down the highway near Startup. You know the place," Skye went on, almost eagerly. "My friend's house is just off the main highway. Her name is Honoria Whitman."

Chapter Ten

IT MADE PERFECT sense. Honoria Whitman, Milo Dodge's girlfriend, was from California, and she had a genuine concern for the environment. Her rustic dwelling place was also her pottery studio, which I had visited on various occasions.

Having dressed, I called Vida at the last minute. She and Honoria knew each other fairly well. It occurred to me that I should ask my House & Home editor to come along.

But Vida was out. I recalled that this was the monthly meeting of her so-called Cat Club, a group of women who convened to exchange gossip and invent more. If they couldn't cram enough scandal, along with gooey desserts, into one evening, they spent much of the following day on the telephone telling tales about each other. Ironically, Vida never passed along any of the titillating tidbits for publication in *The Advocate.*

It was almost dark by the time I turned onto the dirt road that led to Honoria's converted summer cabin. Warm lights glowed from the windows she'd enlarged, and a big black and white cat greeted me on the porch that spanned the front of the house. The cat was new. Milo had proudly, if somewhat diffidently, told me the animal had been named Dodger in his honor.

It was a dubious honor, I thought, as Dodger wedged his round furry body in front of me and clawed the screen door. He then sat on the welcome mat, green eyes hostile, with his long tail swishing back and forth like a pendulum.

It took a few moments for Honoria to respond. Her lack of haste was caused not by languor, but by the wheelchair to which she'd been confined since her late husband had thrown her down a flight of stairs. Crime had paid for no one, since Honoria's brother had fatally shot Mr. Whitman for mishandling his sister. As I waited it occurred to me that I didn't know if Honoria's spouse had actually been Mr. Whitman, or if she had regained her maiden name. It wasn't the sort of question that tripped readily off the tongue.

"I feel like a spy," Honoria declared in her throaty voice as she let me in. "Emma, it's so good to see you. But you must think me Machiavellian. Milo has no idea that Skye is staying here."

Skye Piersall was sitting in a wire and wicker chair that must have been an original, perhaps made by one of Honoria's fellow craftsmen. The design reminded me of antique wheelchairs, and I suspected that the irony amused Honoria.

Skye, however, wasn't looking particularly amused or even at ease. She was holding a frosted glass that was decorated with a slice of lime, a sprig of mint, and a clear straw.

"Hello, Ms. Lord," she said, and her tone was dry. "You've got me pegged as a fraud, I imagine."

"A fraud?" With a shake of my head, I sat down on the black leather couch. "Not that—just secretive. I thought you were staying at a local motel."

"The Tall Timber Inn is across the street from the Texaco station," Skye said. Her tight little smile indicated that I was a dunce for not figuring it out sooner. "I didn't feel up to telling your reporter about my car troubles. They seemed trivial after I heard of Stan's death."

I accepted Skye's explanation for what it was worth, which I couldn't quite figure at the moment. "Carla said you were very upset," I temporized.

Skye put a hand to her forehead. "Violence! It's all tied into our attitude toward our surroundings. That's what makes us so uncivilized. The Japanese have a far greater understanding of humanity's bond with nature."

Honoria, always the gracious hostess, offered me a drink. I requested ice water, then watched my hostess glide away to the kitchen. I knew better than to offer my help. Honoria and I shared at least one trait—we cherished our independence.

I turned to Skye, hoping that my expression was sympathetic. "You said on the phone you had to trust someone. I assume you trust Honoria. So why me?"

Skye pushed a strand of strawberry-blonde hair over her left ear. "I've dealt with the media on many occasions over the years. As a rule, journalists know when to keep a secret. Certainly they know how to guard their sources." She gave me an appraising look, as if she wasn't quite sure that a small-town editor-publisher met any of the aforementioned guidelines. "You understand what I'm saying, don't you?"

I didn't deign to offer verbal confirmation. Instead I gave Skye what I trusted was an ironic, even mocking little smile. "Go on," I said, chucking sympathy for brass. "Try me. Or would you like to see pictures of my newswriting awards?"

Skye had the grace to allow a tinge of color to creep over her freckled face. "I didn't mean to patronize you. But this is serious. And," she added, deliberately looking away and biting her lip, "it could be dangerous."

Honoria had come back into the living room. She

handed me my ice water and asked if we preferred to be alone. Skye urged her to stay.

"You know this already," she said to Honoria. "You're the one who told me to call Ms. Lord instead of the sheriff."

Honoria inclined her head with its pale halo of fine hair. "Subtlety isn't Milo's strong suit," she said in a wry tone. "You understand him very well, Emma."

Maybe. But I did understand what Honoria was trying to say. Milo had neither the patience nor the aptitude for sorting through human emotions. Furthermore, he refused to take into consideration anything but hard evidence. If it wouldn't fit into a plastic bag or go onto a timetable, Milo didn't want to know. Circumstantial evidence might be admissible in court, but the sheriff preferred things he could see and feel. Human nature was too ephemeral for Milo Dodge.

"All right." Skye had put down the glass and clasped her hands around one knee. "This is by way of hearsay. But somebody should know about it. As I mentioned, I've come up against Stan and Blake several times over the years. That also means that I've run into Scott Melville as well. Scott's been involved in a couple of other projects that Stan and Blake promoted. To my knowledge, he did good work for them. But not every building Scott has designed turned out so well. There may be other reasons why he retreated to the Cascade foothills." Skye retrieved her glass, took a long sip, and regarded me with a meaningful look.

The meaning seemed clear. "Scott built *junk*?" I said, for want of a better word.

"What he did," Skye explained carefully, "was draw plans for homes that didn't stand up to the last big L.A. quake. I don't know if his designs required expensive materials which weren't actually used or what happened. I do know that at least four Melville-inspired houses collapsed over in Northridge."

As a journalist, I, too, am skeptical of hearsay. "How do you know this?"

Skye smirked at me. "This isn't just a rumor. My brother lives three doors away from one of the houses that fell down. He doesn't know the owners well, but he heard they sued Melville, the developers, the subcontractors, and the real estate agent."

Skye's report was still hearsay. "You're suggesting that Scott and Beverly Melville moved here because his reputation as an architect was ruined?"

"What would you think?" Skye simpered, though I figured she was trying to be congenial. "It's not exactly a coincidence that Stan and Blake came along in their wake." Another tight little smile played around Skye's mouth. "Scott's connection isn't just business. Beverly is Blake Fannucci's sister."

The relationship helped explain Beverly Melville's tearful reaction to Stan Levine's death. No doubt she was also afraid for her brother's life. But, I asked Skye Piersall, why keep the family connection a secret?

It was Honoria who offered illumination. "Nepotism. The people of Skykomish County were already opposed to Californians moving in with new projects. If they knew Beverly and Blake were related, Scott's low bid would be suspect. All of them wanted to avoid further cause for criticism."

As usual, Honoria was making perfect sense. "Does Milo know any of this?" I asked.

Honoria shook her head. "I don't think so. I didn't know it until Skye showed up this weekend." My hostess smiled at her other guest. "Several years ago, I worked with CATE in Big Sur. That's how Skye and I met. She had a friend with a gallery in Sausalito. The friend showed some of my first pottery efforts. And," she continued, her smile widening, "Skye bought several pieces."

I smiled, too, though it seemed to me that the charming Honoria and the pretentious Skye weren't particularly well matched. But then, I'd had close friends who liked me but couldn't stand each other. I had the feeling that I'd yet to meet the real Skye Piersall.

For a few moments the room was quiet, as each of us presumably entertained our separate thoughts. In this small space, which somehow didn't feel cramped, there was a sense of unreality. Maybe it was the spirit of creativity that was evident in Honoria's jars and vases and pots. Perhaps it was the collection of ethnic art, which ranged from pre-Columbian figures to African tribal masks. Or it could have been the scent of jasmine mingled with cinnamon and a touch of thyme.

I was growing whimsical. What was really bothering me was Skye Piersall. "Why are you dumping this stuff now?" I asked, breaking the dreamy silence.

Skye's eyes widened. "Background, of course. This is a big story for your paper, isn't it?"

"Do you expect me to expose Beverly and Blake as brother and sister?" I asked. "It's not exactly a crime."

Skye's lips tightened. "I said it was background. Stan's killer should be caught and punished. Honoria told me that sometimes you help Milo in his investigations."

The modesty I exhibited wasn't completely feigned. "It's not uncommon for journalists to conduct their own inquiries. Milo and I've been known to . . . dovetail." I winced at the phrase and avoided Honoria's gaze.

Skye lifted her hands in a helpless gesture. "That's all there is. But I felt it needed to be told."

Honoria favored me with a warm smile. "Skye

believes in candor. She comes across so much deception in her crusade."

"Right." I smiled back, but felt it wasn't a worthy effort. "Okay, I'll file this away for future reference." Getting to my feet, I rummaged for my car keys. "By the way," I asked of Skye, "what happened to your car the other day? Did Cal Vickers get it fixed?"

I might have imagined the change in Skye's placid expression. I was, after all, feeling somewhat fanciful. "Yes," she answered evenly. "It was some silly thing. I know nothing about cars, which is why mine breaks down every now and then. I ignore the warning signs, I suppose. The Honda's parked behind Honoria's car. One of the young men who works at the station brought it down here this afternoon."

"Good." I was still smiling, still feeling artificial. "I imagine you heard that Blake Fannucci flew back to L.A. today with Stan's body?"

This time I did not imagine the change that came over Skye's face. She paled, and the hand that had been toying with the strawberry-blonde hair suddenly trailed down her neck and fell into her lap like a dead bird.

"Oh!" she cried, then tried to look natural. "I hadn't heard. How could I?" Skye glanced briefly at Honoria, almost in reproach.

"You couldn't," Honoria said easily. She propelled her wheelchair alongside me. "You have to read everything in *The Advocate*. Isn't that so, Emma?"

I allowed that it was. Most of the time.

When I returned home a few minutes after ten, Leo Walsh was sitting on my front porch. As soon as I pulled the Jag into the carport, he jumped up and hurried over to meet me.

"What's wrong?" I asked in alarm as I struggled to get out of the car.

"You are," Leo replied. "Where the hell have you been?"

Not being in the habit of answering to anyone about my comings and goings, I bristled at Leo. "What difference does it make? Maybe I was at the Icicle Creek Tavern, picking up loggers."

"No, you weren't," Leo said, waiting for me to unlock the front door. "I was there with Delphine until after nine-thirty. I stopped by to ask you what was going on with the Duchess and her pen pal. There's not much chance to find out at the office without raising suspicion. I got here five minutes ago to find you weren't home, so I figured you'd been kidnapped."

Under the porch light, I tried to see if Leo was kidding. He looked serious. With a sigh, I let us both in.

"Gosh, Leo, since when did you get appointed my guardian angel?" Somewhat clumsily, I pulled off my linen jacket and tossed it on the sofa. "Do you want a drink or have you already had a couple of dozen beers with Delphine?"

"I had two," Leo replied defensively. "You know I've cut way down on my drinking."

To Leo's credit, he had. Or so it appeared. At least he hadn't shown up drunk at work since before the holidays. To prove his temperance, Leo asked for a diet soda.

"Well?" he inquired, making himself comfortable on my sofa. "Did the Duchess go for it?"

The question made me suddenly suspicious. "Leo—did you set Vida up?"

But Leo's weathered face showed genuine surprise. "What? Hell, no! I wouldn't pull a stunt like that!"

"I guess it just seems too good to be true," I allowed. "And yes, she's . . . intrigued." If Vida could keep my secrets, I could guard hers as well.

Leo, however, was still looking affronted. "I may give the Duchess a bad time now and then, but I wouldn't sucker her. I ought to be offended that you'd think I might." He got up from the sofa and began to roam around the room. This wasn't the first time that Leo had been inside my house, though I didn't recall him taking much interest in the decor until now. He paused by the desk where I kept my telephone. "What's with your male relatives working on a chain gang?"

I leaned forward in the armchair. Leo was studying the photograph of Adam and Ben. "They were on a dig," I said, almost mumbling. "You met them over the holidays."

"So I did. Ben's an okay guy—for a priest." Leo turned, eyeing me curiously. "Was I blitzed the whole time they were here?"

"Pretty much." It was an exaggeration. I'd hosted Leo for Thanksgiving and Christmas dinner. Liquor had flowed freely on both occasions. Leo might have been sober when he arrived, but he was definitely feeling no pain by the time he left. "Why?" I girded myself for what was coming next.

Once again he was scrutinizing the photograph. "Your kid—he reminds me of someone." Leo straightened up, then wandered back to the sofa. "He looks kind of like my son. Maybe it's a peer group thing. These kids all run to type."

I sucked in my sigh of relief. "Have you heard from your children lately?" Leo's offspring were a sore spot; rightly or wrongly, they tended to blame their father for the breakup with their mother.

Sitting back down on the sofa, Leo lighted a cigarette. "As a matter of fact, I did. Now that Liza's remarried, all three of them are running up white flags. I don't know if it's because they think she's better off without me, or that they finally figured out she was screwing the guy while we were still married. Kids are weird. They won't concede that their parents have feelings, especially amorous ones. Egocentric little bastards. I expect they don't grow up until they've got children of their own."

"Could be." But I was glad for Leo. I wondered if the tenuous reconciliation with his son and daughters had helped curb his drinking. "Have you thought about inviting them up to visit?"

Leo made a face. "They'd hate it here. No beach, for one thing. And who wants more Californians in Alpine, even as tourists?"

"Tourists are fine," I said, giving in and lighting myself a cigarette. "The locals only grumble if they think the tourists want to return on a permanent basis."

"Yeah, right." Leo drank his soda and puffed away. "Speaking of which, what's with Hollenberg?"

I wasn't making the transition from tourism to the county commissioner. "Leonard? What do you mean? Are you talking about the vandalism up at the hot springs?"

But Leo didn't know about the trashing of the murder site. He'd left the office before I returned with the story. "I went to the commissioners' office Monday morning to get whichever one of the old boys was around to okay their 'Congratulations, Alpine High Grads' ad. George Engebretsen and Whatshisname—Alfred? Al?—Cobb were there, but not Hollenberg. I kidded around with George and Al, which is not an easy thing to do since George hasn't laughed for about forty years, and Al's deaf as a doorknob. Then one of them mentioned Leonard—Len, they call him. They said he'd changed his mind about selling out to the Californians."

I stared at Leo. "Why didn't you tell me this sooner? This puts a different spin on everything!"

"Because," Leo replied in a reasonable voice, "I saw Hollenberg later at the Texaco station. He must have just come from the hot springs after finding Levine. He was all shook up, but I asked if he was going back on the deal, especially now that Stan was dead. He looked at me as if I were crazy."

Briefly, I reflected on what Leo had just said. Engebretsen and Cobb weren't the sharpest saws in the mill, as the locals were wont to say. The two commissioners may have been confused. Or else Leonard was being coy with them. Of course there was always the possibility that Leonard had lied. But which statement was the truth?

"Why," I mused out loud, "did Leonard go up to the hot springs Monday morning? I never thought to ask him that. I wonder if Milo did."

Leo had put out his cigarette and finished his soda. He stood up, yawning. "There's a better question," he said, giving me a tired, quizzical look. "Besides Blake Fannucci, who else knew Levine was going up there?"

I admitted I didn't know. Leo bade me good night, and it was only after he had pulled away in his second-hand Toyota that I remembered what Heather Bardeen had said about the woman with the sunglasses. She had come to the ski lodge Sunday night. Maybe she had called on Stan. Or Blake. My initial reaction was that she was Skye Piersall. But after talking to Skye, I realized that the mystery guest could have been Beverly Melville.

Then again, it could have been anybody. It was eleven o'clock, and I was too weary to try out new hypotheses. That wasn't my job. For once, I'd let Milo do his duty. Switching off the kitchen and living room lights, I headed for the bathroom.

But Milo didn't know some of the facts, at least not

what Skye Piersall had told me this evening. As I brushed my teeth, it dawned on me that maybe *what* she had confided wasn't as important as *why*. Knowing that I would eventually leak the information to the sheriff, could Skye have been leading me down the garden path? Was I not seeing the forest for the trees? Was a bird in the hand . . . ?

Bird. As I undressed I saw clouds of birds fly across my mind's eye. Sparrows and starlings and crows and woodpeckers and swallows and blue jays and purple finches. They soared and circled and swooped, just as my brain seemed to reel, in chaos and confusion.

I was getting nowhere. Except to bed.

In the morning my first call of the day was to Leonard Hollenberg. But before I dialed his number, I asked Vida if he had a wife. Somehow, Mrs. Hollenberg's name had never come up in my dealings with the county commissioners.

Vida explained why: "Violet Hollenberg is precisely what her name implies—a shrinking sort. What other type of woman could stay married to that old windbag for almost sixty years?"

By coincidence, Violet Hollenberg answered the phone, her voice soft and timorous. Her husband had gone steelheading at first light. She had no idea when he'd return. Leonard was like that, unpredictable. Violet sighed wispily into my ear.

Wednesdays always feel a bit like limbo. We wait for the paper to be delivered in the early afternoon, but suffer from an obligation to get a jump on the next issue. There's no problem with inside features, but front-page news is often late-breaking. Ordinarily, the lead stories are rather tame. This week was different. We had a pending homicide investigation, and it was unlikely that we could write much copy in advance.

In consequence, I mulled over my editorial options. As sensational as the murder story was, it didn't lend itself to opinionating. Maybe I could coerce the Chamber members by beating the drums for the Summer Solstice Festival. Previously, I had shied away from the topic, since its biggest booster worked for me. But now that the motion had been formally introduced, the self-serving nature of the issue was defused.

I was still mulling in the news office when Vida announced that she was going out. Her expression was canny, which put me on my mettle.

"Where?" I asked.

"I'm treating my nephew Billy to coffee," she said, crushing her Edwardian velour hat onto her gray curls. "He's been working very hard."

Carla, who was also about to leave, stopped at the door. "Is Billy still going with that Bjornson girl?"

Vida regarded Carla with something akin to alarm. "My, no! That was over two months ago. But he isn't interested in dating just now. He's . . . recovering."

Shooting Vida a dirty look, Carla made her exit. "What are you up to, Vida?" I asked, narrowing my eyes.

"Protecting Billy," Vida snapped. "He'd be putty in Carla's hands. Besides, she'd drive him quite mad. Oh—did I tell you that Lynette says Rick Erlandson still hasn't picked up the engagement ring? That explains Ginny's occasional lapses into gloom."

"Vida . . ." As she dashed for the door, I nimbly sprinted in front of her. "What's up? You've got something on your mind besides being a kindly aunt."

Planting both feet flatly on the floor, Vida let out an exasperated sigh. "Very well. Come along, two heads are better than one."

"At what?" I asked, but had already raced into my

office to grab a jacket. It was cool again, with a bit of drizzle mixed with fog.

Vida's gaze flitted around the empty news office as if she expected someone to pop out of the filing cabinets. "Stan Levine's journal. Billy agreed to let me have a peek."

Like spies, we settled into a rear booth at the Burger Barn. Since the restaurant is catty-corner from the sheriff's office, the subterfuge seemed wasted. But Vida enjoys her little intrigues, and so, it seemed, does her nephew. It must be in the genes.

"You won't find anything very interesting," Bill Blatt warned us. "If there were, I wouldn't dare remove the journal from the evidence locker."

Vida raised her eyebrows. "Then it *is* considered evidence?"

Bill gave a shake of his head. "Not really. We didn't know where else to put it."

The journal was book-size, with an imitation leather cover, the kind that's available in any stationery shop or drugstore. It began in mid-May; its entries were sporadic:

May 18—Lunch at Spago with Bernstein and Roux. Veiled interest in Baja concept. Roux has no money, Bernstein lacks imagination.

May 23—Flight from L.A. to Sea-Tac two hours late. Alpine is backward, economy still in toilet. Potential looks good. Scenery spectacular.

May 26—Hot springs site more rugged than we thought. Bids are all in, so met with Melville. Hollenburg (sp.?) is a tough old coot, but can be managed. Getting flack from locals, but that's to be expected. My enthusiasm high for project.

May 27—This is gorgeous country, great for

birdwatching. Wish I fished. Hollenburg (sp.?) beginning to bend. I can feel a rush, know we're going to move ahead. These people will thank us, eventually.

May 31—Deal with Hollenberg looking solid. Melville has some terrific ideas for coping with structural problems caused by terrain. Limitless possibilities opening up re facilities, marketing ploys, etc.

June 3—If we could get rid of the local residents, everything would be beautiful. Nasty bunch of narrow-minded provincial schmucks. But adversity adds excitement to the chase. On cusp of closing with Hollenberg. Californians 28, Alpine 3.

Then came the final entry, Sunday, June 5:

Everything except the weather is going our way. Usual environmentalist obstacles, but we can get around them. I can visualize the completed project, and it's wonderful. Financing should be no problem, once we get back to L.A. Saw a bluebird today, and feel it's on my shoulder. I'm sitting on top of the world at this altitude, in more ways than one.

So he was. I frowned as I handed the journal back to Vida. Stan had been so happy, so optimistic, so confident. I watched Vida's mouth turn down. She reread the last few lines, then returned the small bound volume to Bill Blatt.

"Plans!" she said in an uncertain voice. "They're so futile! It's no wonder so many people lead reckless, heedless lives."

Placing my hands around my coffee mug, I felt its reassuring warmth. If I could feel, I must be still alive. But Stan Levine wasn't. "I liked him," I said. "Obviously, he loved what he was doing. And he believed in it. If we ran those entries, would Alpiners understand?"

"You'd have to get permission," Vida said, speaking now with her usual crispness. "From Blake Fannucci, I suppose." She turned to Bill. "Were there survivors?"

"Jack checked this morning," Bill replied. "Stan had never married, but he has a sister in Encino. His father's dead, but his mother's in a nursing home. She has Alzheimer's."

"That's just as well." Vida adjusted her hat again. It seemed the velour wouldn't behave. "That is, she won't realize what's happened to her son. Poor woman."

We were all quiet for a moment, perhaps in homage to Stan. Then I remembered something, and abruptly broke the silence. "Bill, Stan had another journal. Well, not a journal exactly, but a notebook, with his bird-watching information. What happened to it?"

Bill looked blank. "It wasn't in the briefcase. Dwight never mentioned finding anything like that in Mr. Levine's room."

"Stan probably had it with him when he went up to the hot springs," I said. "Was it found on his body or at the murder site?" It was painful to think of Stan lying dead on the mountainside, with the small notebook falling at his side.

But Bill Blatt insisted that no notebook had been found, not on Stan, not in the rented Range Rover, not at the hot springs, not even along the trail. Vida frowned, then asked her nephew if there were any new developments in the case. With an anxious look around the restaurant, he lowered his voice and confided that the bullet was from a Ruger .357 Magnum.

"You can match the grooves from the bullet to a specific make of gun barrel," Bill explained in his conscientious manner. "But that doesn't tell us much. First, we have to find the weapon itself."

Vida didn't look entirely pleased, but she gave Bill a small smile of gratitude. "The weapon's incidental," she said, struggling with the calculation of a proper tip. Vida plunked down what looked like a dollar in coins. When Bill gave his aunt a questioning look, she scowled at him. "What you must do," she said, enunciating even more carefully than usual, "is find the person who fired it."

Chapter Eleven

I COULDN'T KEEP Skye Piersall's information to myself. I tried it out on Vida first, after we got back to the office. She grew thoughtful.

"What's Skye saying? That Blake gave his brother-in-law the job? Is that illegal?" Vida was speaking more to the air than to me. "Or that Scott Melville was afraid Blake and Stan would tell everyone he was responsible for faulty buildings, so he's killing them both off? That makes no sense. Why would they hire him in the first place?"

"I know it's odd," I said, sorting through the half-dozen phone messages that had accumulated in our twenty-minute absence. "I can't figure out why Skye told me this stuff in the first place."

Dispensing with her troublesome hat, Vida turned toward her typewriter. "You might as well tell Milo. I can't see that it does any harm."

I agreed, then decided to deliver the news in person. The phone messages were probably from people curious about the shooting, the mail still hadn't arrived, and inspiration hadn't yet struck for my editorial. Noting that the fog had lifted and the drizzle had stopped, I quickly covered the two blocks to the sheriff's office.

My arrival coincided with Leonard Hollenberg's noisome departure. He was blocking the entrance, still shouting over his shoulder. I waited for him to quiet down before I spoke.

"Emily!" he said in surprise, trying to regain his public image and my vote. "I didn't see you. Just letting off some steam—keeping Milo on his toes. We county officials have to row the boat together, eh?"

Swiftly, I took in Leonard's baggy suntan pants, suspenders, checkered shirt, and windbreaker. It was his usual attire, so I supposed he might have gone fishing. "I thought you were giving Milo a bad time because you caught a twenty-pounder. Any luck, Leonard?"

The county commissioner shook his bald head. "Naw. Not even a bump. Too cloudy. The river's off-color besides."

"It's a nice outing," I remarked, hoping my smile wasn't coy. "The way you get around amazes me. You must spend half your time outdoors."

"That's why I live here, Emily. I don't know how people stand it, stuck in the city. They have to drive and drive to get where you can drop a line or sight a deer. And noise! Ever stood on a street corner in downtown Seattle? Cars and horns and trucks and buses and jackhammers—no peace and quiet. What's the point of living if you can't listen to the wind in the trees or hear the ripple of a river?"

Leonard had a point, though I marveled that he ever shut up long enough to listen to anything. Maybe I wasn't doing the man justice. "Is that why you like to hike to the hot springs?" I asked in what I hoped was a casual tone. "To get away from it all?"

Leonard gave me a puzzled look. "I can get away from it all at my house on the river," he replied. "I go up to the hot springs to soak. Isn't that what they're for?"

"Is that why you went Monday morning?" Again I tried to sound conversational.

But Leonard wasn't as unobservant as I'd hoped. "Hey, Emily, why do you ask, eh? You sound like Dodge, trying to figure out if I shot poor Stan Levine. Now why would I do such a thing? I was doing business with him and his partner. Wouldn't I be pretty damned stupid to blow one of 'em away?"

That depended, of course. "You were happy with the bargain?"

Again Leonard surprised me. He turned away, gazing down Front Street. "I guess. It was a big decision. You always have to wonder if you did the right thing. It's like being commissioner—there's never any easy answers." He turned his fleshy face to me. "Yeah, I was happy. But now I don't know. With Levine dead, maybe it'll all fall through. Then I'll have to be happy with that, eh, Emily?"

A pragmatist, I thought. Or a politician. Both, of course. That's the way the system works. Before I could say anything more, Leonard thumped past me, heading for his old pickup truck. I went into the sheriff's office.

Milo was drinking his crummy coffee and eating a bear claw. He seemed unsurprised to see me.

"Hi, you want a cup?" He tapped his mug with the NRA logo. "Fresh pot."

The sheriff's coffee might be fresh, but it'd still taste like drain water. "No thanks. What's with Hollenberg? Is he giving you garbled accounts?"

"He's giving me crap," Milo replied, tugging at his left ear. "Every time I try to pin him down about *anything*, he waffles. Typical politician. Plus, he blames me for the vandalism at the hot springs. He says I should have kept a man up there." Milo's expression was rueful. "You know what? He's right. I screwed up. Most of all, Len's pissed about the birdhouse. He put it up for the spotted owls."

This time I beat Milo to the punch and lighted a

cigarette first. "I don't get it. Was Leonard making a statement?"

Milo nodded. "Sure. He loves the natural wonders, but he's willing to sell out for the sake of his constituents. The art of compromise—that's our county commissioner."

"Were the park rangers on duty last night?"

Milo evinced disgust. "Hell, no. They didn't have anybody available on such short notice. I promised Dwight triple overtime if he'd take a sleeping bag up there. He showed up at eight this morning, claiming he got fleas."

I asked Milo if he'd made any headway tracking down the vandals. He hadn't. They'd taken pictures, but didn't have the equipment to make casts of the footprint impressions. As for fingerprints, Milo wasn't holding out much hope.

"No decent surfaces," he explained. "Rocks, tree bark, underbrush. Nothing much that'd take a print."

I remained dubious. "What about the beer cans?"

"Smudged. We're still waiting on the paper stuff. There's one funny thing, though." Milo's expression turned bemused.

"What?" I exhaled lustily, relieved not to have Vida nagging me or Carla holding her nose.

"You have a son, you know kids," Milo said with an eloquent shrug. Being the father of three, he knew them, too. "When they're sixteen, seventeen, they buy cheap beer, by the half rack or those forty-ouncers. Convenience store beer, where their IDs won't be checked as closely. But these dozen cans—and they *were* cans—had good labels. Coors, Henry's, even a Molson's. Sam Heppner made the rounds, in town and along the highway. The clerks swear they haven't sold beer to any underage kids lately. Maybe they're lying, but if not, where did the good stuff come from? Did these kids raid their parents' stash?"

Milo had a point. There were only four places in Alpine that sold beer by the can: Safeway, the Grocery Basket, the 7-Eleven, and Marlow Whipp's small store by the high school. None of them, with the possible exception of Marlow, would knowingly sell to minors. And Marlow had had his own small brush with the law within the past year. I doubted that he was taking any chances these days.

"Another thing," Milo went on, lighting up and forcing me to share the glass ashtray that was balanced atop miniature elk antlers, "there were two empty condom boxes—but no condoms, used or otherwise. What do you make of that?"

"Ah . . . I'm not even going to guess."

"Seriously, Emma." Milo was very much the lawman, his long face earnest. "No joints, either. The rest of the junk was empty chips, beer nut, and pretzel bags. Now why did they need a campfire?"

I was trying to follow Milo's train of thought. "No hot dog wrappers? No marshmallow bags? No whittled twigs? Maybe they got cold after dark."

"Maybe." But Milo was clearly skeptical. "The only other debris was some metal scraps like key rings, or maybe beer can tabs. There were some bolts, probably from the birdhouse. Oh, and a bit of plastic, that could have been the handle to something. The rest of it had burned or melted away." The sheriff shook his head. "None of this plays for me."

It rang some discordant notes in my ears, too. We seemed to have come up against a brick wall. That was when I unloaded about Skye Piersall. Milo blew his stack.

"Goddamn it, why didn't Honoria tell me? This Piersall woman must have been staying there Saturday when I picked Honoria up for dinner. No wonder she wanted to make an early night of it!"

"I'm sure Skye asked Honoria to keep quiet," I soothed. "Skye strikes me as secretive."

"Skye strikes me as a pain in the ass," Milo seethed, bolting out of his faux leather chair. "What the hell kind of name is Skye anyway? I'm driving down to Startup right now. That's something that bugs me about Honoria—*she's* too damned private. I have to unload everything—'let my feelings out,' she calls it—but ask her one dumb question she doesn't feel like answering, and she shuts up like a clam. Screw it, I'm out of here."

So he was. I strolled into the reception area where Bill Blatt and Dustin Fong were staring in bewilderment at the still-swinging door their boss had left in his wake. They both swiveled to look at me, but I merely shrugged, caught the door on an inward swing and started back to *The Advocate.*

At the entrance, I happened to look down the block, toward the Venison Inn. Leonard Hollenberg and Ed Bronsky were ambling into the restaurant. They were in deep conversation, and Ed had one arm draped over Leonard's shoulders. I felt like following them inside and hiding in an adjoining booth. Vida would have done it, of course. But I didn't have the nerve. Instead I dutifully returned to work.

The mail had arrived. Vida's stack was still in her in-basket. I sensed that she had already perused it and found nothing of immediate interest. Or at least no message from Mr. Ree.

"Well?" she demanded, looking up from her typewriter. "What did you glean?"

Carla doubled up in her chair. "*Glean!* Where do you get these words, Vida? Out of a *dictionary*?"

Vida shot Carla a withering glance. "You might try it

yourself sometime, Carla. You'd be surprised. There might even be some words you already know."

Ignoring Carla's expression of delayed umbrage, Vida gave me a sweet smile. "So? Is there anything new from the sheriff?"

Succinctly, I recounted my visit. I remembered to include seeing Ed and Leonard going into the Venison Inn. Vida was intrigued by almost everything. But she offered no immediate enlightenment.

"The beer cans are very curious," she said, sipping at a mug of hot water. "So is the burned plastic. What did Milo think it was—a handle of some sort?"

"From a shopping bag, maybe," I suggested off the top of my head. "The kids carried the stuff up there in the bag. They'd bring a cooler for the beer, though."

Carla had recovered from Vida's effrontery. "How many cans?" she asked.

"A dozen, I think." I sat down on the edge of Leo's desk. He was out, beating the bushes for next week's advertising. There was never a letdown for the newspaper's business side.

Carla wrinkled her nose. "That's all? Two people could get blitzed on six beers apiece. But if you're talking orgy with a bunch of boys *and* girls, that sounds pretty tame."

It did. Carla's perceptiveness surprised me, as it always did on the occasions that it surfaced. "Okay, crack reporter," I said, swinging around on the desk to face her, "what do you make of this—condom boxes, but no condoms?"

Carla grinned. "No sex is better than safe sex, right?" She saw my face fall and frowned. "Wrong. I give up. What's the answer?"

But my expression had changed for a different reason. Carla's initial response had given me an idea.

"Actually, you're right. They didn't have sex. They just had empty boxes."

"Good grief," Vida muttered. "Don't tell me—they're collectors' items? Like trophies, or marking your shield for the number of kills in battle?"

"No," I said hastily, "not that. It's much simpler. Somebody is trying to fool somebody. The question is Who and Why."

Carla, who usually wasn't one to join in the deductive process, seemed fascinated. Perhaps it was the element of sex, or the concept of partying. "You mean, like the boys showing off the boxes to the girls and pretending they'd used them all up?"

I paused before answering. "Sort of. Except not quite." Frustrated, I shook my head. "Is it a coincidence that the murder site was vandalized less than twenty-four hours after Stan was shot? Another full day has gone by—how come nobody's heard about those kids going up to the springs? That's not like Alpine—tales breed around this town like mosquitoes in a pond."

Vida's chin was resting on her hand. "They do indeed. You think the murderer returned to the scene of the crime, don't you, Emma?"

I jumped, almost losing my balance on the desk. The thought had been in labor; Vida had just completed its successful delivery.

"That must be it," I said in a whisper of wonder. "Should we tell Milo?"

Vida rubbed the plain gold wedding band against her cheek. "No," she finally replied. "Let him figure it out for himself. It sounds to me as if he's almost there." She gave me that sweet smile again. "You made it, didn't you?"

I smiled back, but not so sweetly. Sometimes I wondered if Vida thought Milo and I were both a couple of dumb clucks. I already knew what she thought about everybody else.

In my cubbyhole I did some thinking of my own. Who were the actual suspects? Leonard Hollenberg loomed largest, if only because he'd supposedly found the body. But why announce the fact if he had shot Stan? Why shoot him in the first place? If Leonard had second thoughts about the sale, why not simply bow out? Even if a contract had been signed, a good lawyer could extricate him. As far as I knew, no money had passed hands, because Stan and Blake hadn't yet secured their financing.

Scratch Leonard, at least temporarily. The Melvilles came to mind next, mainly because Scott was involved in the project. He had canceled his Monday morning appointment with Milo. Had the sheriff asked him why? Where was Beverly Fannucci Melville at the time of the murder? But I still could find no motive for Scott, and certainly not for Beverly.

Then there was Skye Piersall. As the perpetrator, Skye showed promise. She'd skipped our interview, her car had broken down between Alpine and the hot springs turnoff, and she might have more than one motive. Professionally, Stan and Blake constituted The Enemy. I doubted, however, that CATE's mission statement or whatever they called it recommended homicide as an acceptable method of keeping Mother Nature intact. I preferred a personal motive, such as revenge or jealousy. But a romantic link between Skye and Stan was mere guesswork. I wondered if Honoria would know. And if she did, would she tell Milo or me?

I put Skye at the top of my imaginary list. Somebody had to be there. With a sigh, I realized that most of Alpine could compete with her: Henry Bardeen, Cal Vickers, Rip Ridley, even Ed Bronsky, before he switched sides in the resort controversy.

There were too many suspects—that was the problem. No wonder Milo was out of sorts. He had been presented with a homicide in isolated, rugged terrain, and five miles away there were over four thousand suspects.

"Could you kill anyone?" I asked Leo as he stepped into my office.

"Sure," he answered, setting a trio of ad dummies next to one of the vacant visitor's chairs. "I tried to strangle Liza's lawyer, but we both fell into a freaking potted palm."

"Be serious."

"I am."

"I'm talking premeditation."

"Hmmmm." Leo sat down in the other visitor's chair. "Maybe. It would depend on who had done or was about to do what to whom."

I sighed. "You are serious. You're saying that under certain circumstances, anyone is capable of murder."

Leo raised his thick eyebrows. "Hey—why else would we have armies? Soldiers are trained to kill in combat. If they can't do it, then they're conscientious objectors. But most men—and now women, I suppose—are capable of pulling the trigger. Transfer that to civilian life, throw in a blackmailer or a cheating spouse or the one person who stands in your way to achieving your heart's desire. It happens all the time. Read the newspaper." Leo almost managed to keep a straight face.

But I knew that underneath, he was deadly serious. So was I, which made me a glum luncheon companion for Vida. She was keeping to her diet, and refused to eat out. I had gotten a burger dip and fries from the Venison Inn. By the time I arrived to pick up my order, there was no sign of Leonard or Ed.

"I'll bet Ed's sucking up to Leonard in case he manages to talk Blake into a partnership," I said over the crunch of Vida's celery.

"That will never take place," Vida asserted. "After what's happened to Stan, Blake will renege on the resort project. He's a very frightened man, and I can scarcely blame him. If you ask me, we'll never see Blake Fannucci again."

As usual, Vida would be proved right.

Chapter Twelve

AFTER LUNCH I wrote a draft of the Summer Solstice editorial, even daring to suggest that it be held the third weekend of June. While that would move Alpine's annual celebration ahead by almost two months, the earlier date might encourage families who wanted a quick getaway as soon as school was dismissed.

Having completed that task, as well as having taken care of several minor matters including the morning's phone calls, I grew restless. There was an hour to kill before the papers returned from the printer in Monroe. At one-thirty I got into the Jag and drove over to the Icicle Creek Development.

Beverly Melville greeted me with more warmth than I probably deserved. "You must have thought I was an idiot the other morning at the bakery," she said, her wide smile displaying orthodontically perfect white teeth. "How about a glass of wine?"

While I'm not particularly fond of wine, I was trying to be an agreeable guest. A few minutes later Beverly and I were seated in the living room, surrounded by catalogues filled with fabric swatches.

"Decor plans for the remodeling," she said, moving what looked like carpet samples. "If we stay."

"More qualms?" I asked, noting that the broken window had been replaced.

"I can't help it." Beverly swirled the wine in her

glass. "It's all this rain and the gray skies. I thought I'd get used to it. But it's depressing. And then . . . *this.*" She made a slashing gesture with one hand, apparently taking in a multitude of sins.

"Stan?"

"Of course. Then there's the general hostility. The atmosphere is poisonous." Beverly stared into her glass. Maybe she thought I'd slipped in a toxic little something.

"Have you gotten ugly phone calls, too?" I remembered my own experiences as a new arrival. When my status as an unmarried mother had leaked out, the calls and letters had grown more malicious. Eventually they dribbled away. Either I had won the locals over or they had lost interest. The latter was more likely.

"We did at first," Beverly answered slowly. "They weren't threats—just a 'Californians, go home' sort of thing. As soon as Scott got the bid to design the sheriff's new offices, the calls stopped." She gave me an ironic little smile.

"I doubt there's a plan to systematically wipe out all California emigrés." I smiled back, hoping to lighten the mood.

Beverly ran a nervous hand through her long blonde hair. "Maybe not. Still, it's uncomfortable. Look at what a disaster our party was!" Her blue eyes strayed to the new windowpane.

There was no denying that the evening had turned out badly. I decided this was the moment to introduce my excuse for calling on Beverly Melville.

"How would you like to get better acquainted with some of the local women? Do you play bridge?"

Beverly looked at me as if I'd asked her to join in a game of piquet or pin-the-tail-on-the-donkey. "*Bridge?* Hey, I'm no cardplayer."

"Oh." I was mildly embarrassed. I'd hoped to get

Beverly to fill in for me at Edna Mae Dalrymple's get-together in the evening. Janet Driggers would be there, and I didn't want to face questions about my trip to San Francisco. The invitation had also seemed like a good pretext for leading up to other, more serious queries. "There'll be other opportunities. Have you been able to get involved with any groups or organizations yet?" I had the feeling that Beverly would find most of Alpine's activities as quaint as playing bridge.

"No, I haven't," she replied. "I keep busy here. This isn't just a hobby." Her fingers flicked at the nearest catalogue. "I'm an interior decorator by trade. I still consult with clients in L.A. When I finish figuring out our own decor, I intend to market myself on a regional basis. Alpine itself probably wouldn't keep me going."

"You're right," I agreed, taking in the present eclectic furnishings, which spanned three centuries and five times as many countries. "Do you go into Seattle often?"

"At least once a week. I was there Monday." Beverly gazed at me steadily over the rim of her glass. "All day."

I pretended she hadn't said anything important. "Lucky you. I don't get into the city more than once every three months. When you remodel, will Scott have his office here or keep the rented space in the Clemans Building?"

"He'll keep it," Beverly said, pretending I wasn't pretending. "He believes in separating work from home. I feel differently. I can integrate both without one taking away from the other."

"It's easier for women," I said.

"We're more flexible."

"We've had to be."

"Yes." Beverly put her glass down on a small rosewood table that probably dated from early nineteenth-century England. "I liked Stan. If Blake was the heart of their partnership, Stan was the soul. He had substance, integrity, compassion. I wouldn't dream of harming him. Neither would Scott. And Blake is going to be lost without him."

I avoided Beverly's level gaze. "I'm not very subtle."

Beverly shrugged. "One of the deputies—a young Asian-American, very sweet, very earnest—already called on Scott and me. Monday morning Scott was here. He had to come home unexpectedly because the glazier was arriving at ten-thirty, and I'd already left for Seattle. Why don't people around here work on Sundays?"

I didn't try to justify small-town philosophies. It was time for me to leave. "Do you expect Blake to come back?" I asked at the door.

Beverly stared up at the mountains with their lingering pockets of snow. "I'm not sure. He'll have to find a new partner, no matter what he does next. Blake could never operate alone."

I thought about Ed, waiting in the wings. There were worse things than working alone. I also considered mentioning Beverly's relationship to Blake. But the visit had gone better than I'd hoped. I decided not to push my luck.

I just wished that Beverly played bridge.

"Why," Vida asked in exasperation, "didn't you tell me where you were going? Secrecy gets my goat. I'd have gone with you."

"That's why," I said reasonably. "The two of us would have overwhelmed Beverly Melville." More accurately, Vida would have overwhelmed her.

"She never told me she was an interior decorator when I interviewed her this winter. More secrecy. I'm putting that item in 'Scene.' "

That sounded harmless enough. "Use Harvey Adcock's new sign for the hardware store. He's a good advertiser."

Vida nodded abruptly, still smarting from being left out. " 'Scene' has been too dull lately. Names make news, and everyday occurrences catch people's attention in a small town, but there has to be *something* that piques interest. This week is worse than last week." She waved the newly arrived edition of *The Advocate*. "Darla Puckett dropping a dozen eggs at Safeway. Ione Erdahl having her car washed by the Rainbow Girls and the De Molays. Guests at the ski lodge getting the wrong shoes back from Boots. The Thordahl twins eating fresh strawberries at John Engstrom Park. Whistling Marmot patrons complaining about low fat popcorn. Dull, dull, dull! We need sprightly items. Is no one paying attention to Alpine's human foibles?"

I tried to humor Vida. "What about Crazy Eights Neffel in the buff?"

Vida shuddered. "You know my policy on Crazy Eights items. Unless he's doing something extremely unusual—for him—I refuse to write it up. Besides, the police log story included Grace's complaint about an intruder. It was just as well to name no names or mention his lack of attire. Otherwise, he might be encouraged to do it again."

Vida's guidelines for Crazy Eights Neffel were shared by the rest of the staff, especially Carla, who found the old nut utterly unamusing. She dismissed his antics as silly, but I sensed that deep down she felt sorry for him. Carla's brain might be suspect, but she had a good heart.

The paper looked pleasing, from a journalistic standpoint. A page one murder is definitely subjective. I, too, had liked Stan, and wished to heaven he hadn't been killed. But death always makes bigger headlines than birth or whatever happens in between. Feeling callous, I skipped to the sports page, which almost always centered on the Alpine High Buckers. The stories were submitted by Coach Ridley and edited by me. Occasionally, Carla would write a feature, but as she had absolutely no interest in sports, the stories tended to take on a nonathletic slant. This week's coverage was exceptionally thin, due to the end of the school year. Some twenty column inches were devoted to the annual sports banquet, which had been held the previous Friday night, and an accompanying photo showing Rip Ridley presenting a lanky lad named Grant Aadland with the Alpine Athlete of the Year award. Grant had distinguished himself in basketball, baseball, and track.

Such stories are generally innocuous, so I hadn't read Carla's account closely. I knew Vida had proofed it, because she'd made some biting remark about Grant's parents, neither of whom had finished high school, let alone excelled at much of anything except warming bar stools at Mugs Ahoy.

"It's too bad Grant didn't continue with football," Rip Ridley had said in Carla's direct quote. "With his sure hands, he would have made a great receiver. With the graduation of our starting quarterback and most of the offensive line, the Buckers may be in for a rough season this fall. I'm beginning to think we should start recruiting some of those big, fast kids out of southern California. If all those people from Los Angeles want to move someplace else, why not bring in somebody who can actually help Alpine instead of hurt it?"

I blanched. The awards banquet story wasn't the place for Coach Ridley's comments. I should have read the article before it was published, but there are times when I feel I have to trust Carla's judgment. And, of course, Vida's.

I stormed out into the newsroom. Vida was still

alone, studying wedding pictures. "Whatever is Candace Daley wearing on her head? It looks like a pineapple."

Since Vida had been wearing orange rinds earlier, I felt she had no right to criticize. "How come you let this quote from Rip Ridley pass?" I asked, pointing to the sports page.

Vida frowned at the article. "I didn't. Not the quote. After Carla laid out the page, she was an inch short so she added that later. I never saw it."

At that moment Carla came into the office. I confronted her at once. She gazed at me with wide, innocent eyes. "What's wrong with it? I spelled everything right. I didn't even have to use the dictionary." Over my shoulder she shot Vida an impertinent look.

"It isn't that," I said, now fairly calm. "Maybe I'm reading something into it that isn't there. But the next night Rip and Cal got into it with Scott Melville. And now that Stan Levine is dead, Rip's going to want to eat his words. But first he'll chew us out for printing them in the first place."

Carla seemed unconcerned. "Well, he said it. I've got notes." With a toss of her long hair she sauntered over to her desk.

"I know that," I said with a sigh. "But all the same, Ridley's going to be mad. People often say things they'd rather not see in black and white. You have to use some discretion."

"Oh, pooh!" Carla snatched up a bottle of mineral water. "It was a *banquet.* There were sixty people on hand. Rip didn't exactly whisper the quote to me in a dark alley."

Carla had a point, but so did I. It was a judgment call, and as the more experienced journalist, I felt I was right. I was also the boss. Neither factor seemed to impress my reporter.

Two minutes later Rip Ridley was on the phone, barking in my ear. I could picture him wedged into the swivel chair in his small, chaotic office at the high school. Rip's burly body had been honed on a wheat ranch in the Palouse, and the former Washington State University linebacker now carried an extra thirty pounds. But his crew cut was still cropped close, if beginning to gray.

"That was a *joke*," he asserted. "Why didn't that dim-witted broad of yours put in the one I told about the rabbi, the priest, and the mailman? It brought down the house. Now everybody in town is going to think I'm some kind of bigot!"

"Bigot?" It wasn't the word I would have chosen. "Look, Rip, Carla quoted what you said, right? It was supposed to be funny, so most readers will take it that way. How did the audience react?"

There was a short pause. "They clapped."

They would, of course. Rip's listeners had agreed with him. And with his tone, which wasn't jocular, but sarcastic. "You weren't misquoted," I went on, "you knew Carla was covering the banquet, and it was a public event. I think you're getting worked up for nothing."

"The hell I am," Rip muttered. "It's one thing to be talking in front of a crowd that's having a good time, but it's something else to see what you said in print. It makes everything look so . . . *serious*."

Rip Ridley was right, but I wouldn't admit it out loud. There are occasions when the power of the press is an embarrassment. Especially when you hold it in your hands and can't quite see through your fingers.

"Do you want to write a letter?" I asked. "You know I'll print anything that's signed."

Rip hesitated again. "I'll talk to Dixie when I get home. She already called as soon as the paper hit the box. She was mad as hell."

Great, I thought, mouthing more soothing words before putting the phone down. Dixie Ridley would be at bridge club. So would Cal Vickers's wife, Charlene, and his sister, Vivian Phipps. As the clock ticked on I was growing more apprehensive. Even if Vida hadn't despised playing bridge, I couldn't have asked her to sub for me—one of the other regular members was her sister-in-law, Mary Lou Blatt. The two women weren't on speaking terms, for reasons that were as old as they were obscure.

Edna Mae Dalrymple is the head librarian, and though she wasn't born in Alpine, she has lived in town for almost twenty years. Edna Mae is small and jittery, but conscientious in her personal as well as her professional life. Her house is only two blocks from mine, so I chose to walk. Like most of the recent evenings, the clouds had finally lifted to provide a glimmer of late springtime. As I headed downhill on Fifth Street to Spruce, I could smell the fragrant evergreens and the sweet hint of sawdust from Alpine's last remaining shingle mill. Beverly Melville was wrong—gray skies and endless rain were trifles compared to noxious gas fumes and pervasive smog.

The atmosphere inside Edna Mae's trim little bungalow was equivocal, however. I wasn't quite the last to arrive, but I sensed that the others had been talking about me before I came in. Despite Edna Mae's nervous aura, she sought to put me at ease by offering a glass of wine. It was a standard ritual at our get-togethers, and always involved the tight pulling of drapes, lest passersby glimpse Alpine womanhood engaging in such vices as playing cards and drinking spirits.

As usual, there were three tables. I began the evening with Mary Lou Blatt and the Dithers sisters. Connie and Judy owned a horse ranch on First Hill. They somehow looked ageless, though I knew them to be in their late forties. Both were pudgy and had long horse faces. After that, describing them became difficult, because they were so painfully plain. I doubted that they'd ever used cosmetics or seen the inside of a beauty parlor. They smelled of horse, or maybe hay, and except when they grew excited, the sisters spoke in abbreviated fragments that were hard to translate. Naturally, they wore jeans and shirts and ponytails. I had heard that at funerals they wore black jeans. At weddings they wore new jeans. I couldn't imagine either of them in a dress.

But their taciturn manner prevented any volatile comments. As for Mary Lou, she was always reserved in my company, no doubt because she thought I'd carry tales back to her dreaded sister-in-law, Vida.

Thus, the first hour passed without incident. The second started tranquilly, too. My partner was Vivian Vickers Phipps, whose daughter, Chaz, worked at the ski lodge. Our opponents were Edna Mae and Janet Driggers. Vivian enjoys chatting between hands, and Edna Mae is always anxious to please. Janet, of course, prefers to shock. For the most part we were all accustomed to her outrageous remarks.

Vivian had just made a successful three no-trump bid when Janet dropped her first bombshell. "You hear all the rumors, Emma," she said, shuffling the cards like a Las Vegas pro. "You must know the buzz around town regarding Stan Levine." She wriggled her overplucked eyebrows. "Outraged husband. Guess who?"

Edna Mae, as usual, looked shocked, though we all knew better. Vivian was annoyed. I was dubious. "Who?" I asked as Edna Mae dealt the cards with unsteady hands.

"*Who?*" Janet was miffed. "I don't know *who*. Isn't *why* enough?"

I shook my head. "Not for *The Advocate.* We don't print gossip."

"Yes, you do," Janet shot back. "Look at that 'Scene' thing. It's all gossip. I saw Darla Puckett this afternoon at Stella's Styling Salon, and she insists she didn't drop a dozen eggs at Safeway. It was a pint of cottage cheese. She was one shelf over, next to the eggs. So that makes it untrue and mere gossip." Janet tossed her freshly permed chestnut curls.

"Darla must have been spotted from a distance," I murmured. "Whoever saw her probably thought she was in eggs."

"It's gossip," Janet repeated firmly.

Edna Mae leaned into the table. "One club," she said in a timorous voice.

Vivian Phipps was smirking at Janet. "That would be an honest mistake." She looked at her cards, and then at me. "One heart. Partner, I hate to say this, but there was another error in 'Scene' this week. Chaz says the guests at the ski lodge didn't get the *wrong* shoes back, they got the *right* shoes. But Boots hadn't cleaned them. In fact, they were dirtier than when they'd been left outside their rooms. But don't go printing *that,* because it might get Chaz in trouble with Henry Bardeen. He's already threatened to fire Tony Patricelli for not doing his job. Tony insists he's not at fault, but we all know what the Patricellis are." Vivian gave the three of us a knowing look.

"Two diamonds," said Janet with a sharp glance at Vivian. "They're Italian, so what? The Patricellis had a bunch of kids and some of them got into trouble. Then those kids screwed like minks and had kids of their own. Including Tony, who seems okay to me. Cute, too, great butt. Hey, Emma, you're Catholic—do you use birth control? I bid two diamonds, by the way."

"I believe that individuals, including Catholics, can

answer only to their own consciences." I sounded as prim as any celibate nun teaching first grade in a parochial school. "Two hearts."

"Beating as one," Janet interjected, unfazed by my prudish response. "Which reminds me, are you sure you haven't lined up a hot date for your weekend in San Francisco? Why waste the plane fare if you're not going to spend half the time in the sack? I tell you, that city is made for sexual pleasures."

Edna Mae blinked at me from behind her glasses. "You're going to San Francisco? How nice! When?"

I sighed, but smiled at Edna Mae. "This weekend. I've got meetings scheduled with newspaper people." Okay, so Tom was a person, not a people. It was close enough to the truth. "I'm planning some changes for *The Advocate*, on the business side."

"Dear me!" Edna Mae exclaimed. "Changes for the better, I hope! I do hate change—especially for the sake of . . . *change*."

"This would be to bring in more revenue," I answered, still smiling, but sounding very businesslike. "As you may have noticed, we've been trying to take a more aggressive stance in the marketplace lately."

Janet chortled. "Like the match-and-mate ads? Look, you let people say things like *plush*, which means fat as a pregnant pig, and *bantamweight*, which means you could slip the guy into your purse, and *slender*, which translates as don't-bother-to-open-the-door-this-one-can-slide-under-it. How about using real measurements? That includes everything, especially for the guys." Janet leered, then panted a bit for emphasis before gazing at her partner. "Well, Edna Mae? Are you going to bid or sit there and dream about peckers?"

"Really, Janet!" Edna Mae blushed furiously. "I've quite lost track of the bidding." She turned to me. "Two spades? Oh—two hearts! I'll bid three peckers. No! No!

I mean *clubs*! That is . . . oh, dear!" Edna Mae's glasses fell off.

Somehow, we got through the rubber, though nobody dared mention the word, lest it set Janet off again. At the last table, I was partnered with Charlene Vickers, while Francine Wells and Dixie Ridley opposed us. I hadn't looked forward to facing Dixie, but she didn't bring up her husband's quote in the sports banquet article. On the other hand, she was very cool to me. It wasn't until we were leaving that Dixie took me aside.

"You must print a retraction," she said solemnly. "Rip and I discussed it over dinner tonight, and we feel he can't let that statement stand. Already he senses that people are looking at him in a strange way. Suspiciously, you know. That won't do for a public figure like a football coach."

In Alpine, Rip Ridley could be defined as a public figure. That was unarguable. But I thought he was imagining the suspicion. It was too much of a stretch to take his basically harmless remark about Californians and turn it into a motive for murder. Except, perhaps, in Alpine.

"Look, Dixie," I said, trying to be friendly as well as reasonable, "we can't retract the quote, because Rip said it. Sixty people heard him, including my reporter. It would be better if he wrote a letter as I suggested to him on the phone this afternoon. He could expand on his comments and make a real statement, maybe even talk about the direction he wants for the high school athletic program. There's a growing sense of dissatisfaction about education in general. I'm sure Rip has plenty of good ideas we could publish in *The Advocate*."

Dixie's heart-shaped face grew uncertain. "Well . . . Rip certainly has opinions. But we don't like being under scrutiny. Even tonight I felt certain persons were watching me as if I were married to a Mafia don or something." She let her eyes flicker over the Dithers sisters, who were putting on their denim jackets and saying goodbye to Edna Mae.

"Tell me about it," Charlene Vickers said under her breath. She had sidled up to the two of us and was shaking her head. "Cal says some of his regular customers have been avoiding him the last couple of days and going to Gas 'n Go at Icicle Creek instead."

"Exactly." Dixie nodded vigorously. "It's contagious. Did you see how Linda avoided me tonight?" She nodded in the direction of Linda Grant, the high school women's P.E. teacher. "She cut Rip dead in the parking lot this afternoon."

Though I don't know Linda well, she has always struck me as more broad-minded than most. But she does tend to be preoccupied. "Maybe she didn't see him," I said.

"Maybe she should mind her own business," Dixie snapped. "If Jack Mullins was nosing around yesterday to find out if any of Rip's students came to school with hangovers, he should have asked Linda the same question. And having Jack at the high school hasn't helped. Now everyone will think he really came to question Rip about the murder."

Charlene was also indignant. "Bill Blatt stopped in to see Cal today. Now if that isn't enough to scare customers away, I don't know what is."

"Did you see the way Francine Wells acted when we were partners?" Dixie asked in a whisper. "She hardly spoke to me, except to bid, and even then she passed at three spades when I opened with two. Now I'm glad I returned that Maggie London silk blouse. And to think she practically accused me of wearing it!"

I seemed to recall seeing Dixie in the red and black blouse at least twice, but it was best not to mention the fact. I had been slowly edging away, trying to reach

Edna Mae. "Urge Rip to write a letter," I said in a confidential tone to Dixie. "I promise to run it next week."

Dixie glared at me, and Charlene's expression was unusually aloof. It wasn't my fault that Stan Levine had gotten himself shot on Spark Plug Mountain. But as so often happens, the messenger got blamed for the message. I grabbed my jacket, thanked Edna Mae, and would have run all the way home if it hadn't been uphill.

At that, I was slightly winded when I arrived. I had to quit the damned cigarettes again. No one smokes at bridge club because Mary Lou Blatt and the Dithers sisters claim to be allergic. Thus, I hadn't been tempted during the course of the evening. Now I picked up the half-empty pack I'd left on the coffee table and started to crumple it. The telephone interrupted my virtuous intentions.

"Where've you been?" Milo sounded querulous. "I've left three messages on your damned machine."

I glanced at the glowing red number, which actually registered five. "I was out," I said abruptly. Suddenly my male acquaintances seemed far too interested in my whereabouts. "What do you want?"

"It's too bad you published today," Milo said, still sounding irascible. "You missed getting a big story."

"About what?" Suddenly I was excited. As I fumbled around to take out a slightly bent cigarette, I heard voices in the background. It was almost ten-thirty; Milo must have still been at work.

"We got a print off the Chee·tos bag," Milo said. "You know how we got prints from several leading citizens a few months ago to push our program with the schools?"

I remembered. Skykomish County had launched a campaign to fingerprint all children fifteen and under. The goal wasn't to nail future delinquents, but to help in case the youngsters were kidnapped, especially by parents involved in custody battles.

"So?" I clicked the lighter, managing to miss the cigarette on the first try.

"The print on the bag matched Henry Bardeen's," Milo said, now downright unhappy. "We've brought him in for questioning."

Chapter Thirteen

HENRY BARDEEN STRUCK me as an unlikely suspect. Milo agreed, but insisted that Henry had to be considered "a person of interest." Not only were his prints on the discarded bag at the murder site, but he had the most clear-cut of motives. The hot springs would definitely compete with the ski lodge.

"What about an alibi for Monday morning?" I asked Milo.

"Henry swears he was in his office, going over the books. He usually does it the first of the month, but he got behind because of the three-day Memorial weekend." Milo emitted a weary sigh. "I don't like this one damned bit. But I have to follow procedure. If Henry can come up with a witness who saw him Monday at intervals of an hour, I'd let him go right now."

"Can't he? What about Heather?" I was now half-lying on the sofa, my shoes off, the cigarette down to the filter. "Or the rest of the staff. They must have seen him come and go."

"But they didn't," Milo replied doggedly. "He asked not to be disturbed. So he wasn't. Not even phone calls. Heather collected the messages."

"How is he?" I tried to envision the dour ski lodge manager in custody. If Henry were innocent, he'd be outraged. He was a man who stood on his dignity and his reputation. The toupee enhanced neither, but was evidence of concern for his image, as well as a certain amount of vanity.

". . . than flabbergasted," Milo was saying. Consumed by my own thoughts, I'd missed the first part of the sheriff's response. "Look, Emma, I've got to go. But I didn't want you to hear about this secondhand and come in tomorrow morning ready to clobber me with a baseball bat. Okay?"

It wasn't okay, but I hung up anyway. Then I called Vida. She usually stayed up until around eleven. I wasn't surprised that she already knew about Henry's detention.

"Billy phoned me and then I tried to reach you," she said, sounding agitated. "I called twice, but you weren't home yet from Edna Mae's."

That accounted for the other two phone messages on the machine. "What do you think?" I asked, wishing my brain wasn't falling asleep ahead of my body.

"Oooooh," groaned Vida, and I could see her rubbing frantically at her eyes, "I think there's something very wrong here. Henry would never shoot anyone. He lacks gumption. But don't ask me how his prints got on that wrapper. The only explanation that comes to mind is that Henry didn't shoot Stan Levine, but he did go up to the hot springs that night to destroy incriminating evidence."

I sat up on the sofa. "You mean he's covering for someone?"

"That would have to be it." Vida's tone became fretful. "The only person I could imagine him doing such a thing for is Heather."

Henry's wife had died of leukemia shortly before I arrived in Alpine. If Henry had courted any women since becoming a widower, Vida didn't know about it. Which, I figured, meant he practiced abstinence.

"Heather," I said slowly. "Do you honestly see her going up to the springs and shooting Stan Levine?"

"Well, no." Vida hesitated, then lowered her voice. Maybe she thought her canary, Cupcake, was eavesdropping. "There are just the two of them since Doris died. Henry was raised in Everett, and there was an older brother, but he was a career man in the Air Force. For all I know, they've lost touch over the years. Henry's not what I'd call a very warm sort of man. But he dotes on Heather, and it seems that the feeling is mutual. It's amazing what people will do for one another when they feel isolated from the rest of the world."

Briefly, I thought of my own situation. Adam and I had been on our own for over twenty years. Would I have killed for him? Maybe. Would he have killed for me? I was doubtful.

I was also tired. There was nothing more that Vida and I could do as far as *The Advocate* was concerned. Milo's questioning of Henry would be a week old by the time we published our next edition. Heaven only knew what might transpire in the murder investigation before deadline rolled around again.

The urgency of the case was beginning to bear down on me. As I prepared for bed, the first doubts about my proposed trip began to rise. I'd be gone only a little over forty-eight hours; surely Vida could cover any new developments.

But that wasn't Vida's job. She was my House & Home editor. This was a front page story, complete with screaming headlines. If I delegated my authority, it should be to Carla. The bald fact was that I didn't trust her to handle such tricky coverage. Carla had been right in accusing me of a lack of confidence.

But I couldn't back out on Tom now. It was possible, even probable, that he was looking forward to our weekend together with as much anticipation as I was. If

I asked Carla *and* Vida to keep on top of the story, difficulties might be avoided. Carla could save face, and Vida would relish being in on the chase.

Or so my foggy reasoning went. I couldn't cram anything more into my brain. When I fell asleep, I dreamed first of bridge club, meeting at the Top of the Mart in San Francisco. The Dithers sisters arrived on horseback, and Dixie Ridley came in a suit of armor. Janet Driggers was in rare form, tossing back shots of tequila and making lewd remarks about the TransAmerica Pyramid as a phallic symbol. Francine Wells kept changing from one designer outfit into another, and Edna Mae Dalrymple changed from Vivian Phipps to Charlene Vickers to Vida Runkel. I stayed the same, oddly passive, with my eye on the door. I was waiting for Tom. Janet kept pointing to the Transamerica Pyramid. I kept waiting for Tom.

Even in my dreams nothing ever changed.

In the morning, I went directly to the sheriff's office. Henry Bardeen had been sent home before midnight.

"I felt like a creep," Milo confessed, pressing his puny coffee on me. "I know I'm an evidence man, I have to be. But fingerprints or not, I can't see Henry shooting Stan Levine. And except for admitting that Chee-tos are his secret vice, he doesn't act like a guilty suspect."

"What about the footprints?" I asked, trying not to blanch as I sipped from a mug bearing the Toronto Blue Jay logo. The team symbol gave me a little jolt, but I didn't know why. I certainly wasn't getting a jolt from Milo's weak brew. Maybe I was worried about the impending baseball strike.

The sheriff was studying some paperwork on his desk. "That's really strange," he said. "It's another reason why I wonder about Henry. Have you ever seen him wear tennis shoes?"

I couldn't recall, but usually when I ran into the lodge manager, he was wearing a suit, a shirt, and a tie. I supposed he always wore dress shoes with them. "Henry's fairly formal, by Alpine standards," I said.

"That he is," Milo agreed. "Which is why these footprints are so damned odd. Not one of them is from a tennis shoe or a hiking boot or any kind of outdoor wear. That might point to Henry. But most of the impressions are irregular. It's as if somebody with a bad limp had left them. That's the only way I can explain it. And yet they're not from the same pairs—at least four different kinds of shoes left prints at the springs."

I practically jumped out of my seat. "Milo—I've got a brainstorm!"

Milo leaned back in his own chair, regarding me with mild interest. "Yeah? What is it? A well-dressed centipede?"

"Don't be a wiseass." I composed myself and became brisk. "You haven't found any kids yet who might have trashed the murder site, correct?" I saw him nod, if reluctantly. "Maybe it wasn't kids after all. Vida and I were tossing this idea around yesterday." I ignored his open skepticism; I knew how little faith Milo put in what he considered female deductions. "Whoever went up to the site Monday night—maybe the murderer—was destroying evidence. Don't ask me what, I've no idea. But he—or she—took along some garbage and—now don't you dare laugh at me—extra shoes, to make it look like several people. This person knew that you, and everybody else, would conclude it was kids, raising hell at the end of the school year. Don't you see why this explains so much of what otherwise doesn't make sense?"

Milo put his head in both hands. "Jesus. Where do we keep the butterfly net?"

"Milo!" I was used to the sheriff's skepticism; I didn't expect anything better. I wished I'd brought Vida along for backup. "This isn't as goofy as it sounds. Have you heard about Boots?"

Milo deigned to favor me with a scowl. "Whose boots?"

"Boots the shoeshine kid at the ski lodge. Tony Patricelli. Did you read 'Scene' yesterday?"

"Hell, no. I haven't had time to look at *The Advocate*. I've been too busy working my butt off trying to solve a homicide case." Tardily, Milo tried to cover up the sports section of *The Seattle Post-Intelligencer* that lay open on his desk.

I explained about the item and its inaccuracy. "The guests' shoes were returned dirtier than when they were left out in the corridor," I said. "That's how Vivian Phipps put it, and she got the word straight from Chaz, who works at the lodge." Even in my own ears the tale sounded like a typical Alpine rumor.

But Milo was now looking thoughtful. "That plastic thing—it could have been a handle from a laundry bag. You know—the kind they use in hotels for their customers. Honoria and I got one of those when we stayed at—" Milo broke off, his face changing color. The sheriff and I shared a reserve about discussing our love lives.

"You're right," I said swiftly, wanting to save him embarrassment. "Whoever did this may have loaded garbage from the lodge and put it in the laundry bag. The beer cans, the wrappers, the condom boxes. Which explains why there were no condoms. It also tells us why the beers were better brands than what your average teenager guzzles."

For a long moment Milo said nothing. I kept quiet,

waiting for him to sort through the revelations. Vida had promised that the sheriff eventually would come to the same conclusion as we had. I'd just given him a huge nudge.

"It'd also explain Henry's fingerprints." Milo was looking both relieved and puzzled. "Damn. Now do we conclude that whoever did this was staying or working at the lodge?"

"Not necessarily. Everybody in town knows the lodge's routine. But it might explain why Blake Fannucci thought he heard a prowler. It might also explain the raccoons."

"What raccoons?" Milo was regarding me quizzically.

"Henry mentioned them," I said, trying to remember the details of our phone conversation. "He thought a raccoon had tried to get into the lodge. It wouldn't be the first time—you know how they'll chew their way into houses. But he also said something about the garbage. I assumed he was speaking in general terms. But maybe he wasn't. It might have been a human, gathering red herrings and putting them in a laundry bag."

Again Milo mulled. "Henry sure didn't put any of this together. I'll have to show him that piece of plastic handle. He ought to recognize it as one of theirs." Milo rubbed his face with both hands. "God, I feel like a prize jackass! It's a wonder Henry doesn't sue us!"

"You mean you agree?" I spoke too brightly, which obviously irked the sheriff.

"It's a viable theory," he said in a noncommittal tone. "But there are still a lot of unanswered questions. Why would anybody break into the lodge? They don't lock the main entrance at night. They've never had to. Maybe Fannucci did hear a raccoon. Or else the guy was so nervous he imagined the noise. Now we've got to find out who came to the lodge on Monday with an unauthorized garbage collection in mind. Not to mention those shoes—I wonder if any of the guests who complained are still around." Suddenly, Milo burst into action. "Go away, Emma. I've got work to do."

"Hold it—what about Skye Piersall? How did your visit to Startup go?"

Milo waved a big hand in dismissal. "A washout. Skye's car broke down on her way back from the summit. She was checking the Stevens Pass ski area, to make sure there hadn't been any recent violations of their agreement with CATE. If she had anything going with Stan Levine, she's not admitting it. So long, Emma." The sheriff was beginning to sound impatient.

I left, with mixed emotions. If we were right about the vandalism at the hot springs, the investigation was now headed in the proper direction. As Milo had pointed out, there were still a lot of puzzle pieces that didn't fit. But some of them were factual, and the sheriff's department would follow through. What didn't sit right was Milo's cavalier attitude toward Skye's alibi and her apparent denial of a romantic link with Stan Levine. Skye was Honoria's friend. I suspected that Milo had treated his lady love's house guest with kid gloves.

I had no such compunction. As soon as I reached the office, I dialed Honoria's number. She sounded vaguely bemused when I asked to talk to Skye.

I'm not really a morning person, and have been known to forsake tact before nine A.M. "Is it true that you and Stan Levine were lovers?"

To my dismay, Skye laughed in her rather pleasant manner. "What a question! Are you running a tabloid, Ms. Lord? What if we were? Do you think I came all the way to Alpine to shoot him?"

"I'm trying to fill in the background of the people involved in this investigation," I said in what was definitely not my most charming voice. "We don't publish everything we learn, you know. I'm trying to make connections."

This time the laughter had an edge. "Don't make them with me. I'm just a hard-working environmentalist. If you want to know about Stan's love life, ask Blake. He knows everything, especially when it comes to people. Ask him about breaking up. Don't just ask about Stan and me. Ask Blake about Stan and Blake."

"Blake's gone," I said tersely.

"And so am I, as of this afternoon. I've imposed on Honoria too long. Goodbye, Ms. Lord. It's been . . . terrible." There was a catch in Skye's voice as she hung up on me.

My mood wasn't improving. What was Skye implying? Or was she merely trying to divert me from her possible romance with Stan? Feeling confused, I ran my fingers through my shaggy hair. I needed real coffee, which Ginny was brewing in the office pot. She smiled shyly when I entered the newsroom.

"What did you think of the new personals?" she asked.

I'd only skimmed them to make sure they contained no prurient material. "We should double the space for next month," I said. "They seem popular."

Ginny stepped back as the coffee began to drip into the carafe. "Carla says she's going to answer three of them."

"Carla?" I was aghast. "What about Dr. Flake? They've been going together off and on for the past year."

Ginny gave me a pitying look. "Emma, you don't keep up. Carla and Peyts split three weeks ago."

The last time the pair had called it quits, my reporter had threatened several forms of suicide. She hadn't been serious, but her doldrums had sunk the office into deep gloom.

"Then how come she isn't rending her garments and howling at the moon?" I inquired, readying my mug for the first full measure of coffee.

Over her shoulder, Ginny glanced at the door. Presumably, she was afraid Carla would burst in and overhear us. "It's a very tricky situation," Ginny confided, keeping her voice down. "Peyts is dating Carla's roommate, Marilynn Lewis."

"Wow!" I didn't know whether to be glad or sad. Marilynn was also Peyton Flake's nurse. She was a couple of years older than Carla, extremely bright, and very beautiful. I had always wondered why Dr. Flake seemed immune to her charms. I'd chalked it up to professionalism. The fact that Marilynn was African-American wouldn't deter the liberal-minded doctor, not even in Alpine. Peyton Flake didn't just march to a different drummer—his whole outlook on life was atonal.

"Carla really likes Marilynn," Ginny continued. "She says it's easier to find a new boyfriend than a good roommate. Besides, I think Carla and Peyts had too many conflicts. Their personalities never really meshed."

That was certainly true. Indeed, I had always marveled at Carla's attraction for Dr. Flake. She was pretty and fun, but under his flamboyant exterior, Peyton Flake was a serious man. Marilynn Lewis, who had traveled some very rough pieces of road, possessed much more substance than Carla.

"I wish Peyts and Marilynn well," I remarked as Vida came into the office. I assumed she already knew about the romance. Marje Blatt would have reported it to her aunt as soon as she sniffed love in the air at the Alpine Medical Clinic.

But as I drank my coffee and got my brain into high gear, murder was uppermost in my mind. I summoned

Vida into my cubbyhole and relayed the latest from Milo and Skye Piersall.

Vida didn't look pleased at any of my news. "Henry must be wild," she remarked, taking off her navy straw cartwheel hat. "I suppose Milo can't think of any way to keep Skye in the area?"

"Probably not." I resisted the urge to light a cigarette. "Skye's an enigma. I can't see her shooting Stan, yet her alibi for Monday morning doesn't hold up very well. On the other hand, Honoria would have known if Skye had disappeared for a lengthy period of time Monday night. It appears she didn't, or Milo would have said so."

Vida held the big hat in front of her like a shield. "Why the ski lodge?"

"What?"

Vida twirled the hat on one finger. "Garbage is everywhere. Why would anyone bother going to collect it at the lodge?"

"It wasn't just the garbage," I countered. "It was the shoes. Where else would you get enough shoes to make it look like a crowd of vandals?"

"Why do that at all? The shoes, I mean?" Vida lost control; the hat flew onto my desk. "Drat," Vida murmured, retrieving her headgear. "It rained most mornings in the past week or so. If not in town, certainly at the level of the murder site. That's why Milo couldn't get any footprints Monday after Stan's body was found. It just happened that we had no rain on Tuesday, not even in the mountains."

I still didn't understand Vida. She saw my puzzlement and exuded a small sigh of impatience. "Perhaps it's a minute point. But I'm wondering if the murderer isn't an outsider. He or she wouldn't know our weather patterns."

"You're hoping it's not a local," I said. "So am I. But

if you're right, the field becomes very narrow. Skye Piersall. The Melvilles—though Scott and Beverly have been here several months."

"They haven't lived through our typical June," Vida argued, keeping the hat under control in her lap. "You left out Blake Fannucci."

I stared at Vida. "He was in Milo's office when Leonard Hollenberg called in the news. He couldn't have gotten from the hot springs to the sheriff's office in the time it took for Leonard to hear the shot, find the body, and report the murder."

"Couldn't he?" Vida's expression was inscrutable. "Think about it, Emma. How long had Blake been in Milo's office? Where was he between the coffee shop at the ski lodge and showing up at the sheriff's?"

Of course I didn't know. I—and no doubt Milo—had taken Blake's presence in town for granted. But I still didn't see how Blake could have returned to Alpine ahead of Leonard Hollenberg.

"Blake is much younger than Leonard," Vida said carefully. "He and Stan have been up to the hot springs several times. Blake may have discovered a faster route down the mountainside. He could have parked a borrowed car elsewhere, which is why Leonard didn't see any vehicle other than the Range Rover. He might even have gone with Stan and walked back into town. I think Milo ought to contact Blake in Los Angeles and see if he actually does have an alibi for all of Monday morning."

Vida's idea had shaken me. It might do the same to Milo. Certainly it would raise his hackles. "Why don't you talk to him?" I suggested. "He's busy right now, but if he won't see you, there's always your nephew, Bill."

Vida got to her feet. "Milo will see me. If he's in." She settled the cartwheel back on her head and tromped out of the office in her splayfooted manner. For some reason I thought of the Crusaders, marching to free Jerusalem from the Infidel.

The thought was blown away by Leo Walsh and Ed Bronsky, who entered, arguing. They looked more like Abbott and Costello. Ed tried to barge his way into my office first, but Leo neatly outstepped him.

"You tell him, babe," Leo said, gesturing in annoyance at Ed. "*The Advocate* doesn't do opinion polls, right?"

Emma Lord's *Advocate* didn't. But I knew from browsing through the bound volumes under Marius Vandeventer's regime that my predecessor had occasionally resorted to presidential election polls. If memory served, the results were often the exact opposite of how the rest of the country had voted.

"What kind of poll?" I asked with some trepidation.

Ed plopped down in the chair Vida had vacated. "I want a mandate. Len Hollenberg is waffling."

"On what?" My gaze darted from Ed to Leo and back again.

Ed shot Leo a dirty look. "On local involvement in the hot springs project. On me, namely. Will Alpiners go for the deal if I put my money—and my name—into the resort? I'm thinking Bronsky's Baths. How do you like them apples?" Ed wiggled his eyebrows at me.

I tried not to look appalled. The name suggested some sleazy Turkish steam room, tucked between a tavern and a pawnshop. "What's wrong with Windy Mountain?" I asked, avoiding a direct answer to Ed's question.

"It's not Windy Mountain," Ed asserted. "It's Spark Plug, which doesn't sing. Bronsky's Baths does. Either that, or Cal-Wash."

Leo flicked his lighter. "It sounds like Car Wash."

"It does not!" Ed pounded his fist. "It combines the

two states—California and Washington—like the Cal-Neva in Reno. Nobody ever makes fun of *that*, and it's just a casino."

Leo frowned as he took a drag on his cigarette. "Don't tell me you're going to have gambling? What are you doing, hooking up with one of the local tribes? I thought casinos had to be on an existing reservation."

"Of course we're not," Ed replied in exasperation, then brightened. "It's not an impossible idea, though." Obviously it had just occurred to Ed, thanks to Leo.

"Back up," I ordered. "Ed, have you spoken with Blake Fannucci?"

Once again Ed was looking smug. "Len should be tickled pink to do business with me. He's up in the air right now because the shooting scared him. He'll get over it if somebody—like me—can talk turkey to him. As for Blake, I called him from my car last night. He's in L.A., of course, and he's still kind of upset, but I could tell he was excited about my offer of a partnership."

If Leonard had made up his mind to sell, he might like Ed's offer. Leonard might have been already counting his money. But Blake was another matter—I couldn't imagine him being enthused over Ed as a partner.

"Stan was the money man," I noted. "Does Blake want you to come to L.A. to help secure financing?"

"We didn't get that far," Ed admitted. "Sometimes my phone cuts out because of the mountains. Blake said he'd get back to me after Stan's memorial service. I think it's tomorrow."

Leo and I exchanged quick glances. I could tell he was thinking along the same lines that I was. "I don't see why you need a poll," I finally said, returning to Ed's premise. "As a matter of fact," I went on, suddenly struck with an idea, "who would be better at conducting such a poll than you, Ed? You've known all the local merchants and"—I tried not to wince at Ed's own words—"movers and shakers for years. Talk to them, see what they think about your involvement in the resort. That way, you won't get just a yes or a no or an I-don't-care. You'll actually be able to use your old persuasive powers as an ad salesman." Which, as I vividly recalled, consisted mostly of Ed sitting on his big butt, trying to slough off any form of advertising that would require real work on his part.

Appealing to Ed's vanity worked better than he ever did. "That's a great idea, Emma. Maybe I should call an emergency meeting of the Chamber." With a grunt, he got to his feet. "I probably should fly down to L.A. The family and I didn't see much of it when we went to Disneyland. I'd like to try some of those hot restaurants, like Speedo."

"Spago," I said under my breath, but Ed was already bustling away.

Leo rolled his eyes. "God, babe, how did you ever put up with him?"

I held my head. "It was easier when he was gloomy. How are we doing for next week's advertising?"

"I'm still trying to finish the school's-out section," Leo replied, stubbing out his cigarette. "I thought I had a jump start on the bridal edition for the end of June, but Henry Bardeen wouldn't see me, and Cal Vickers doesn't think it's appropriate for the Texaco station."

"But you had that cute idea, with the shoes and cans tied to the car and the bride and groom standing by the highway, waiting for Cal's tow truck."

"Right." Leo sighed, fingering his broken nose. "Maybe Cal will change his mind. He was pretty grouchy this morning. In fact, this whole town seems grouchy. Do you think it's the murder?"

"Maybe." Dixie Ridley and Charlene Vickers danced

across my mind's eye. So did several other people who had made irate phone calls or written outraged letters. It was bad enough that someone had been killed in Alpine; it was even worse for the locals to suspect their neighbors.

It was shortly after the mail arrived that Vida sidled into my office, looking furtive. "Mukilteo, the coffee roasting place," she murmured. "Sunday noon. Mr. Ree."

Mukilteo is just south of Everett, on Puget Sound. At the edge of the small commercial district, the Whidbey Island ferry shuttles back and forth to Clinton. "You're going?" I asked, somehow surprised.

Vida leaned on one of the visitor chairs. "I don't know." The broad shoulders that so many had leaned upon suddenly slumped. "Emma, am I playing the fool?"

I let out a strangled little laugh. "How would I know? It's been my favorite part for years."

Vida seemed to mull over this self-deprecating statement. Somewhat to my chagrin, she didn't contradict me. "Are all women fools?"

This time the laugh was more akin to a snort. "I'm going to San Francisco. At least Mukilteo is closer."

The rejoinder seemed to stiffen Vida's spine. "So you are. Then I suppose I ought to go to Mukilteo." Now looking like a paradigm of resolution, Vida marched out of my office.

Mr. Ree, I thought. Who was he? What was he like? I envisioned a tall, distinguished man of seventy with a well-trimmed moustache and a walking stick. Reality was probably quite different.

Then I thought of Tom, who was literally tall, dark, and handsome. Of course he was going gray, and there were lines in his face, and life had added a certain grimness to the noble Roman profile. But to me, he was eternally twenty-eight. Maybe, to him, I was still the dewy college student with the soft brown eyes and vivacious smile. I sighed like a teenager and then grabbed the phone.

Stella Magruder answered on the second ring. I desperately needed a haircut, I told her. Did she have an opening almost immediately? She didn't, but could squeeze me in at four-thirty. Gratefully, obsequiously, I thanked her. Stella rang off, sounding a bit smug. Had Janet Driggers or someone else from the bridge club been spreading rumors?

I didn't have a chance to speculate. The phone rang under my hand. It was Blake Fannucci, calling from Los Angeles.

"Emma, what can you tell me about Ed Bronsky?"

What couldn't I? But I didn't want to be unkind. "Ed's eager—once he gets the bit in his teeth," I replied, measuring my words. "I assume you're talking about his proposal to get involved in the resort project?"

"You got it." Blake sounded tired, but otherwise more like himself. "I think he wants to come to L.A. You know, Mr. Smith Goes to Hollywood. I was trying not to look beyond Friday—tomorrow—when Stan's services are being held." He paused, and I thought I heard his voice break. "But in my business, you have to seize the moment. Nobody knew that better than Stan. Would you recommend Ed as a partner?"

I was on the spot. I certainly wouldn't recommend Ed as *my* partner. But Blake Fannucci was a savvy guy. Maybe he'd know how to handle Ed.

"Ed's heart is in the right place," I replied, though doubts galloped through my mind. "He wants the best for Alpine." No, he wanted the best for Ed. "He needs to be busy since he quit his job." Ed *had* been busy, driving the rest of us nuts. "He has quite a bit of money, but no real sense of purpose." At last, maybe I'd found the key.

"But not enough to bankroll the project." It wasn't a question, but a statement of fact. I sensed that Blake had done his homework.

"Not all by himself," I replied. "But his financial position is very secure, which might lend credibility." I didn't know how wisely the Bronskys had invested their windfall. Certainly they'd spent some of it on cars and fur coats and travel. But if Ed and Shirley had been prudent, his inheritance should last a long time.

"I like the idea of a local coming into the deal," Blake said. "That was lacking in the original proposal. What do you think, Emma?"

"It would short-circuit some of the criticism," I allowed. "I take it you're still interested in moving ahead?"

"I guess." Blake's soft laugh was bittersweet. "At first I didn't give a damn-all. But Stan wanted to do this, even more than I did. Now I'm thinking it's like a memorial. You know, his crowning achievement. Jesus, Emma, he died for it! How can I let go?"

Blake's words were painful in my ear. I wasn't about to discourage Blake in any way. I couldn't bring myself to knock Ed. And I certainly didn't intend to ask Blake where he was Monday morning. That was up to Milo.

"I can think of worse things you could do," I said. Well, I could, like removing his own gallbladder with a pickle fork. But the project had been given a green light, mainly by Leonard Hollenberg, and it wasn't up to me to play devil's advocate. Besides, I'd love to see the maitre d' at Spago when Ed showed up. "Why not? Ed's very enthusiastic."

"I was hoping you'd say that." Blake's voice was now warm, even animated. "I'll give him a call today instead of waiting until after the memorial service."

"That's fine," I said, suddenly feeling inadequate. Since I still couldn't quite swallow Vida's theory about how Blake could have shot his partner and returned to town to establish an alibi, my heart went out to him. "You take care of yourself, Blake. By the way, I had a nice chat yesterday with your sister."

The line grew so quiet that I thought it had gone dead. Or that Blake had hung up. At last he spoke, and his voice was ironic. "My *sister*? I don't have a sister. What are you talking about, Emma?"

I was glad Blake couldn't see me, because I could feel myself blushing. "Ah . . . Beverly? Beverly Melville? Somebody said she was . . . ah . . ." I dropped my ballpoint pen and had to scramble around under the chair to retrieve it.

Blake laughed, a bit stridently. "Whoever told you that is confused, Emma. Beverly isn't my sister. She's my ex-wife. Our marriage didn't last long. I always called it Briefs Encounter. Have a good one."

Blake hung up.

Chapter Fourteen

On this drizzly Thursday morning in June, Vida was spurning all manner of food, including cottage cheese, hardboiled eggs, and munchable fodder.

"Do you think I look thinner?" she asked in an uncharacteristically anxious voice. She turned around several times in an attempt at a pirouette.

In all honesty, I didn't think she looked a bit different. But for once I had to lie: "Trimmer," I said. "Vida, Mr. Ree is interested in other things. He's not out for a Playboy centerfold."

"I should think not!" Vida sat down at her desk and picked up a mug of hot water. "Still, I'd like him to find me . . . comely."

I was glad that Carla wasn't in the office. Even I had to suppress a smile at the old-fashioned word. "Mr. Ree will find you utterly delightful," I declared. "By the way, I'm leaving early today. I have a four-thirty appointment at Stella's Styling Salon."

Vida arched her eyebrows. "Well! You're as vain as I am. How comforting!"

I gave her a half smile. "You have to admit, I'm pretty shaggy. What did Milo have to say for himself?" I hadn't spoken to Vida since she'd left for the sheriff's office because she'd gone on to cover her Presbyterian church's spring rummage sale.

Vida pursed her lips. "Milo was out. Or so Billy

claimed. But I talked my nephew into checking Blake's alibi. The more I think about it, the more likely it seems to me that he did it."

It was then that I told Vida about Ed's visit and the call from Blake. She was appalled at Ed's involvement, unsettled by Blake's inquiry, and flabbergasted by the news of Beverly Melville being the former Mrs. Fannucci.

"Who told you she was his sister? That Skye person? I thought Jack Mullins checked out the background on all these people." Vida's expression was severe.

"He did, but I suppose when Beverly turned up as Beverly Fannucci Melville, Jack thought it was because she *was* his sister." I was sitting at Leo's desk, trying to ignore the overflowing ashtray. I hadn't had a cigarette since arriving at *The Advocate*. "What I wonder is if Skye intentionally lied, or didn't know any better."

"She's unstable," Vida asserted. "You should have seen her when she found out that Stan was dead. She practically swooned."

"She didn't deny a romantic link with Stan," I said, glancing through Leo's mock-up for the end-of-school insert. "I'm going to call Honoria later today, after Skye's gone. Maybe she'll open up."

Vida sipped her hot water. "Don't count on it. Honoria is the sort of person who keeps confidences. It's a fine trait, unless you want to know something."

I didn't argue with Vida. While I kept busy for the rest of the afternoon, I half expected to hear from Ed, saying that he was now a full-fledged partner with Blake Fannucci. But by three o'clock he hadn't called. Instead, Milo Dodge phoned.

"What's this bee Vida has in her bonnet about Fannucci?" he asked in a vexed tone. "Will that woman ever realize I know how to do my job?"

"Okay," I said, "so where was Blake Monday morning?"

"At the ski lodge, putting the package together for the money lenders. He ordered from room service and Heather Bardeen saw him when he left to come see me."

"What did he order?" I couldn't resist pestering Milo.

The sheriff sighed in annoyance. "Juice. Grapefruit juice, the large size. The kid who delivered the order saw Blake because he had to sign for it. The ski lodge receipts are all time-dated, stamped right on the bottom. Blake's alibi is unbreakable. He and Stan drank a lot of juice."

"Maybe he was drinking juice when I talked to him just now," I said in a casual voice.

There was a slight pause, presumably while the import of my words dawned on Milo. "Fannucci? Why were you talking to him?"

"He called me." I was still being blasé.

"What for?"

Repenting, I told Milo about Blake and Ed. I also mentioned that Beverly Melville wasn't Blake's sister, but his ex-wife.

"Damn!" Milo breathed. "I wish Jack would learn how to use the computer. What's the point of having access to information if your personnel can't interpret it?"

"Don't ask me. I've got Carla."

"Does it matter?"

"What? Carla? Or Jack?"

"The relationship between Blake and Beverly."

"Oh." I reconsidered the question and came to the same conclusion I'd reached earlier. "Probably not to them. Maybe to Scott."

"It doesn't wash." Milo obviously didn't find the point of much interest. "If Blake had been killed, or even Scott, then we'd have a triangle. But Stan wasn't part of that equation."

I had a sudden thought. "What if Blake were the intended victim?" Hearing Milo groan, I kept talking. "Maybe this is all backward. The killer wants us to think that the motive is the resort project. But the intention was to kill Stan first, so when Blake got murdered, it would look as if both men had to die. It could be that the killer thought Stan *and* Blake were going up to the springs Monday morning. Have you looked at this line of inquiry?"

"No." Milo's voice had no inflection. "I haven't looked at Crazy Eights Neffel as the possible perp, or Durwood Parker resorting to a gun because he's bored with using his car as a lethal weapon. I don't look at anything that isn't evidence, because harebrained theories don't convict criminals. Goodbye, Emma, I'm going to lunch."

Despite Milo's disparaging tone, I liked my idea. After relaying Blake's alibi, I trotted it out for Vida. She was lukewarm.

"It's possible," she allowed. "But I don't quite understand the motive. Are you saying Scott Melville shot Stan Levine because he was jealous of Blake Fannucci? Scott is married to Beverly. Wouldn't it be more likely for Blake to shoot Scott?"

Unfortunately for my theory, Vida made sense. "Don't confuse me," I mumbled. "I keep trying to find a motive that doesn't involve an irate Alpiner hiding behind the rocks at the hot springs."

"Yes, yes," Vida agreed, somewhat impatiently. "So do I. I'm very disappointed that Blake can account for his time Monday morning."

I slipped off the edge of Vida's desk. "Blake would be very convenient," I admitted. "But what's *his* motive?"

Vida grimaced. "I haven't quite figured that out yet. Something to do with their partnership, of course. Maybe he's been embezzling, or wanted all of the profits. Money." She brightened. "Yes, that's it—*money.* It's always an excellent motive. Blake wanted to be on his own."

"So why is he asking about Ed?"

Vida expelled a hiss of air through her teeth. "Really, I can't imagine. Given his motive. Or putative motive, at any rate. You're right, that doesn't make sense. Oh, dear." She turned to the half sheets of copy that reposed on her desk. "I'm sick of weddings. And bridal showers. Will June never end?"

"We're only a little over a week into it," I noted. "Maybe you'll be doing an engagement story on Ginny and Rick before the month is out."

The remark didn't cheer Vida. I returned to my office and worked steadily until four-twenty. On my way out I thought of asking Carla about the personals ads that had intrigued her. But she was bent over her word processor, giving a fine imitation of thinking. I left with only a brief word of farewell for my staff.

I also left with a vague feeling of guilt. I would have to make an early exit the following day as well. My flight to San Francisco departed Sea-Tac at five-forty. I'd have to leave Alpine around three. There would be Friday afternoon traffic to contend with, and the drive would take almost two hours under the best conditions.

Just thinking about the trip made my heart beat a little faster. I was slightly breathless when I reached Stella's Styling Salon two blocks away in the Clemans Building.

Stella Magruder was combing out a perm on Shirley Bronsky's newly acquired honey-blonde head. "Emma!" Shirley squealed. "How are you? I should have had this done before the Melvilles' party."

I sat down at the vacant station next to Shirley. She looked like an aging chorus girl who'd spent too long at the trough. "It's a real . . . *change*," I said with a bright smile. "How do you think Ed will react?"

Shirley giggled and looked up at Stella. "Ed won't notice until I put on my new nightie with the ecru lace. I got it in Seattle this week at that fancy place on Fifth Avenue."

I knew the place, where, if lingerie sold by the pound, it would have cost at least a grand to cover Shirley Bronsky. "Lovely," I murmured, glancing at the shampoo bowls where Stella's assistant, a pretty but insipid girl I knew only as Laurie, was working diligently on someone I couldn't see enough of to recognize. "Did you and Ed drive down for the day?"

Shirley took the hand mirror from Stella and admired herself from every angle. "What? Oh, Stella, it's wonderful! But will it stay this frizzy?"

"No, dear," Stella soothed, "it'll loosen up when you wash it. But don't shampoo for forty-eight hours, okay?"

"I know," Shirley said with a small sigh of pleasure. She twirled around in the chair again, then reluctantly handed the mirror back to Stella. "Now what did you say, Emma? About Ed?"

I repeated my question. Shirley giggled some more. "I *never* take Ed shopping! He gets so bored. And antsy. Betsy O'Toole and I drove down Monday. We spent the whole day, and had dinner at Benjamin's in Bellevue on the way back."

"How fun," I remarked, diverted by the surfacing of Laurie's client. It was Heather Bardeen. The salon smock had almost completely covered her ski lodge uniform. I waved; she smiled. Stella brushed stray hairs from Shirley's bouncing body.

"Go get 'em, Tiger Lady," said Stella, standing back

with her arms crossed over her own voluptuous bosom. Stella also colored her hair and carried extra poundage, but she knew how to use both to her advantage. If Shirley had been willowy, she still would have required work. But Ed didn't deserve better. Indeed, he wouldn't have appreciated it, and, come to think of it, who was I to judge? The Bronskys had been married for almost twenty years, there were five children, and even before they inherited money, the couple had seemed happy together. Or as happy as Ed had ever been in his premillionaire days. I tried to join in the general enthusiasm for Shirley's new look.

But Heather Bardeen held back. At least she wasn't smiling. Her gaze narrowed as it followed Shirley's progress to the dressing room.

"Way too frizzy," Heather murmured, her own wet hair plastered against her scalp. "Why do the Bronskys think they run the town just because some old lady left them money?"

Laurie, who seemed to change her coiffure's color and style every time I saw her, wore a puzzled expression. "Except for spending a lot on her hair and nails, Mrs. Bronsky acts the same. Only happier. Besides, she'll lose the frizzies. Totally."

As Laurie toweled off her client, Heather was looking unusually thoughtful. "Maybe," she said ambiguously, coming to sit at the station on my right. Heather seemed tense as Laurie rummaged through drawers, then finally headed for the supply cabinet out back. "You know the Bronskys," Heather said in a low voice, one eye on Stella, who was seeing Shirley to the door. "Maybe she's okay, but is he . . . weird?"

"Define weird," I said lightly.

But Heather was very serious. "I mean it in the real way. Like . . . *obsessed.* Is that the word?"

I frowned at Heather. "Obsessed with what?"

Heather's exposed forehead also wrinkled. "That's the trouble—I don't know how to put it. It's just that—" She broke off as both Stella and Laurie returned from opposite directions.

There wasn't another opportunity to speak with Heather alone. I'd wanted to ask her how her father was doing in the wake of his interrogation by Milo Dodge. But Stella had me out of the chair in thirty minutes, while Laurie was still snipping and combing Heather. The new me wasn't much different from the old me, except that my hair was shorter and straighter. I wasn't entirely pleased.

I was almost finished packing by eight o'clock when the phone rang. To my initial delight, it was Tom. But as soon as he got past "Hello, Emma" my spirits sank. There was anguish in his voice, and I knew the news wasn't good.

"Zorro left Sandra," he said in a tight, tense voice. "She's a mess. Emma, don't hate me—I have to cancel the weekend. I'll reimburse you for your flight and—"

"Stick it," I interrupted. Anger, disappointment, and pain exploded somewhere inside my breast. How typical of Tom to mention financial details first. No, that wasn't fair—he could do something about money. He couldn't do anything with Sandra or Zorro or me. "What's happened?" I asked, trying to steep my voice in sympathy. But the sympathy was mostly for me.

"It was over the movie deal," Tom replied, still sounding unlike himself. "Look, Emma, I'm at home, Sandra's lying down, but she could pick the phone up at any minute. I've got to make this quick. Anyway, he'd asked Sandra to put some money into a movie he was writing. I think I told you about it a while back."

Vaguely, I recalled Zorro's cinematic ambitions. "So what happened?" Now my sympathy was in full spate, washing over both Tom and me.

Tom emitted a truncated laugh. "For once, Sandra got a grip on herself. She said no. One of her girlfriends used to be married to a Hollywood producer, and she advised Sandra that you never put your own money into a movie. Sandra doesn't listen to me, but sometimes she pays attention to her friends. When Sandra closed her wallet, Zorro took a hike. He left in the middle of the night. Sandra was hysterical when she called me this morning. So here I am, playing nursemaid again."

"She's stopped being hysterical, I take it?" I was slumped at my desk, visualizing my crammed suitcase. Maybe I should get hysterical. It seemed to work for Sandra.

"Sandra wasn't hysterical when I got here," Tom said, and I could tell from his rapid speech that he was anxious to get off the phone. "That's what really worries me. She's like a zombie. God only knows what kind of pills she's been taking. Or worse. I know Zorro does coke, and he may do other drugs, too. *Damn!*" The sudden fierceness of the word told me more than I needed—or wanted—to know.

Tom's anxiety was contagious. "Hang up, we'll talk later. Don't worry. I'll be fine." The outrageous lie fell from my tongue like cold lead.

"Emma—goodbye." Tom clicked off.

It wasn't the first time Tom had canceled on me. He was supposed to come to Alpine after Christmas, but his son Graham had broken a leg skiing at Lake Tahoe. Sandra had refused to leave Zorro, Zorro hated hospitals, and Zorro wouldn't budge from Big Sur. Tom had had to rescue Graham and, as usual, play the dual roles of mother and father.

None of it was Tom's fault, of course. It was always Sandra. Sandra, Sandra, Sandra . . . Her name beat on my brain like a mallet. It *wasn't* all Sandra's fault. Tom allowed her to manipulate him and shackle him and keep us apart. Maybe that's what Tom wanted. He needed to have Sandra need him, needed her more than he needed me. I wandered from room to room in my little log house, taking no comfort from its snug pine walls.

But the terrible irony was that if Tom ever abandoned Sandra, I'd lose my respect for him. I might even stop loving him. It was his very selflessness that made him so appealing. If it also made him unattainable, that was my tragedy. Or maybe that's what *I* really wanted: a handsome, charming, intelligent, wealthy, noble, generous man I could never have. I was like a teenager with an imaginary boyfriend. I could talk about him, think about him, dream about him—and take no risks.

The thought was often with me, sitting at the back of my mind like the symptom of a dreaded disease. If you ignore it, maybe it'll go away. But it doesn't, and you can't quite face it, and you always fear the worst.

Almost an hour passed before I unpacked. I thought of calling the airline, but decided to wait until morning. I didn't like the prospect of dealing with Janet Driggers at the travel agency. Maybe it would be her day off. She only worked part-time.

I thought of calling Ben, but he had troubles of his own. I considered Vida, but somehow I wasn't up to it. She would still be dithering happily over her Sunday date with Mr. Ree. Assuming, of course, that she had decided to go. Maybe she, too, would prefer romancing a phantom.

Then the phone rang again, and like a fool, I thought it was Tom. It wasn't. Heather Bardeen was on the line, and she still sounded worried.

"I can't settle down this evening," she said in a fretful voice. "Things have been so . . . *strange* around here lately, especially last night."

I spoke into the pause that followed: "You mean with your dad? Is he okay?"

"He's fine," Heather said, but she didn't sound convinced. "He understands that the sheriff has a job to do. Still, he's . . . well, upset. I mean, he *was* upset. But I don't like to bother him with any more . . . *problems*."

I sat down on the bed next to my empty suitcase. Heather is fifteen years younger than I am, and we've never been particularly friendly. She's aloof, which may be part of her professional persona, but possibly a shield against further hurt. The loss of her mother must have left deep scars. I had lost both parents at about the same age, and I understood more about Heather Bardeen than she could imagine.

Or maybe she sensed some sort of bond, which was why she had called. "Remember that blonde woman in the sunglasses I saw Sunday night?"

I remembered Heather telling me about her. "Did you figure out who she was?"

"Not exactly," Heather said. "I just talked to Chaz. She's working the night shift. She said a woman like that came in about half an hour ago, acting strange. She hung around the lobby for quite a while, but when Chaz asked if she could help, the woman said no and disappeared. Chaz thought about seeing where she'd gone, but the fire alarm went off."

"Good grief!" I exclaimed. "Was there really a fire?" The Bardeens didn't need any more problems than they already had.

"No," Heather replied. "It was a false alarm. It happens every once in a while. By the time Chaz got back to the desk, the woman had gone."

"Chaz didn't recognize her?" I asked, not very hopefully.

"She thought she looked kind of familiar," Heather answered, still sounding ill at ease. "But let's face it,

Chaz doesn't recognize *anybody.* Sometimes it's a real problem with guests. She's really good with names, though."

I wasn't particularly gifted in recalling either one, so I couldn't blame Chaz. "This woman must know one of the current visitors," I suggested. "She was probably waiting for him—or her."

"I don't know. We don't have any holdovers this week, so she couldn't have been meeting whoever was here Sunday night. I just hope she's not some imported . . . well, you know." Heather's voice faded. The last thing the ski lodge and the Bardeens needed was a problem with hookers. "But that wasn't my real reason for calling." Heather was speaking again, though she still sounded anxious. "You must have thought I was pretty weird to criticize the Bronskys today at Stella's," she said, now speaking with more assurance. "The truth is, he bothers me."

Visions of Ed, in his newfound affluence, playing the part of ladykiller romped through my mind. It certainly wasn't impossible. Maybe Ed was going through mid-life crisis, just as goofy as anybody else, but with money to give him a false sense of confidence.

"What's he doing?" I inquired, keeping my question on a safe plane.

"I'm not sure," Heather answered. "That's why I'm worried."

I became more direct. "Is he . . . ah . . . flirting or something?"

"Flirting?" Now Heather sounded genuinely horrified. "Oh, no! Nothing like that! Oh, good Lord!"

I sympathized with Heather's reaction. "Well, what then?"

There was another pause. "You remember asking me about the phone calls to Mr. Fannucci and Mr. Levine?" I said that I did. A sudden cold feeling overcame me.

"Honestly," Heather continued, "I couldn't swear to it in court. But I think at least one of those voices belonged to Ed Bronsky."

Chapter Fifteen

"RUBBISH," SAID VIDA. "Ed's a terrible ninny, but he's not dangerous. Heather may be right. Ed was probably trying to horn in on the project even before Stan Levine was killed."

I didn't agree. "Ed was against it in the beginning. He only changed his mind later. I doubt that he would have called to talk business. Not then."

Vida sighed into the phone. After hanging up with Heather, I'd surrendered and dialed Vida's number. She had taken my news about Tom in stride. Her compassion was primarily for him, which annoyed me. But I was still too shaken about Ed to let indignation get the upper hand.

"No," Vida was saying, and I was wondering if she was arguing with herself as well as with me. "Ed isn't capable of such a thing. Really, can you imagine him hiking up that trail to the springs?"

I actually couldn't. Indeed, I was beginning to wonder if there wasn't some other way to reach the site. The Chelan County helicopter had gotten there. Was it possible that Milo and Vida and I were all overlooking something?

"Ed does have a motive," I pointed out. "Eliminating Stan opened the way for him to become a big wheel with L.A. connections. You've got to admit that he's excited over getting involved in the resort."

Vida sniffed with disdain. "Are you ascribing ambition as a motive for Ed? Really, Emma, you can't be serious!"

But I was. It seemed to me that Ed was genuinely interested in being part of Windy Mountain. Or Bronsky's Baths. Ambition wasn't one of Ed's qualities. But identity—or ego—was. Ed had been a borderline failure in his job as ad manager. Wealth had given him the patina of success. But it had been inherited money, not earned. Ed wasn't stupid; he must know the difference. Cosponsoring the resort project would give him a sense of accomplishment.

Still, I didn't blame Vida for disparaging my basic theory. Heaven only knew, I didn't want Ed to be a murderer. But I could see him making threatening phone calls to Stan and Blake. It was carrying out the threats that caused me to founder.

"You're unhinged," Vida said calmly. "The weekend fiasco has addled your brain, Emma. Don't even think about Ed. Or if you do, consider this—perhaps Heather is trying to create a diversion. If Milo or anybody else begins to suspect Ed, they'll forget about the sheriff's interest in Henry Bardeen."

That idea hadn't occurred to me. Henry seemed to have been cleared of suspicion. I knew that, so did Milo. But did the rest of Alpine? Rumors ran like rats.

"Okay, I'll take my broken heart to bed. Good night, Vida."

"Good night, Emma. Don't be too upset. Next weekend you'll have Adam and Ben here."

Vida's attempt to cheer me was somewhat out of character. I sensed that it came from her own optimistic outlook. Thus, I guessed that she had confirmed her date with Mr. Ree. Silently, I wished that her luck would be better than mine.

I woke up early Friday morning with that

overwhelming feeling of emptiness usually reserved for IRS audits or the loss of a loved one. Chastising myself, I showered, dressed, and tried to arrange my hair the way Stella had fixed it. The result was disheartening. I needed a body perm. Maybe it was just as well that I wasn't going to San Francisco after all. I looked terrible. I felt worse.

When I reached Front Street, it wasn't quite seven-thirty. The day was going to seem long enough without getting an early start at the office. I kept driving, right past *The Advocate*, and put on my right-turn signal for Alpine Way. Five minutes later I was slowing down on Highway 2, searching for Leonard Hollenberg's mailbox.

I found it standing next to the metal newspaper cylinders for *The Advocate* and *The Everett Herald*. Leonard's sprawling house was almost across the road from the U.S. Forest Service headquarters east of Skykomish. It appeared as if the one-story dwelling had started as a cabin and been added onto by whim rather than design. Each jutting addition showed the Hollenbergs' increasing affluence over the years. The place looked a bit like a rabbit warren.

But the surroundings intrigued me. Very little of the land had been actually cleared. Leonard—and presumably Mrs. Hollenberg—genuinely liked nature. There were some separate, slightly dilapidated outbuildings scattered between the road and the river. The narrow paths that led to them were well trod but lined with ferns, vine maples, berry bushes, and even a few stands of devil's club. There was no lawn as such, but clumps of grass interspersed with clover, dandelions, buttercups, and a network of wild strawberries. As I approached the house along a series of moss-dappled bricks, I could hear the river and smell the evergreens. At the door, the sound of a woodpecker caught my ear.

With my finger on the buzzer, I turned, gawking up into the trees. I couldn't see the bird who was seeking his breakfast, but I noticed several birdhouses, not only among the hemlock and fir branches, but on poles near one of the outbuildings. Whatever other interests Leonard had shared with Stan Levine, birds must have offered a common bond.

Violet Hollenberg, small and spare as a bird herself, answered the door. I couldn't tell if she was more amazed or frightened to see a stranger. Identifying myself seemed to reassure her. She hopped away through the kitchen, cheeping softly to her husband.

Leonard was wearing his reading glasses, khaki pants, and plaid suspenders over a white T-shirt. He seemed slightly disconcerted by my early morning visit.

"I've got an unusual query for you, Leonard," I said, feeling somewhat foolish. "Tell me how spotted owls nest."

"What's unusual about that, Emmy?" Leonard replied, pulling out two chairs from the kitchen table. "You want some coffee?" He didn't wait for my reply. "Violet—get this lady and your poor old husband some coffee. My mug's on the TV table."

Violet had disappeared after calling to Leonard. She resurfaced like a wraith, a coffee mug in one hand, an empty plate in the other. Leonard ignored her and turned back to me. "People need to know about wildlife. Guess what I've always wanted around here. A bird sanctuary, that's what. But we're a little too high up. It'd be better farther down the river, maybe close to Grotto. Think about it. Grotto. Perfect for birds, Emmy."

If the county commissioner was getting closer to my real name, he had strayed from the question. "Spotted owls?" I offered. "Nests?" I smiled at Violet as she placed a steaming mug in front of me.

"Oh, right, right," Leonard said, rocking back in his chair. "The western barred owl—that's the real name. They're a funny breed, when you think about it. They almost never build their own nests. Starting in March or April, they find some other bird's nest—one that's big enough, of course, like a crow or a hawk. If they can't do that, they look for a hollow in a tree. Now the problem with logging is that when the trees are cut, the owls have no place to nest. They like to go high up, way off the ground. That may be why they have to use other nests. You know, like renters, during a housing shortage."

"Is that why you built the birdhouse at the springs?" I asked, finding Leonard's explanation interesting, if typically long-winded.

"You bet. I've put up a bunch of houses for birds here at my place on the river. You see them?" He paused fractionally for my nod. "Every spring, I get some pretty fascinating characters. But not all birds build nests, you know. And not all of them want to use a birdhouse."

"Did you get a spotted owl this year?"

"No." Leonard's voice dropped in disappointment. "I even put an old nest inside, a big one I'd taken from a tree. But the damned owls didn't show up. You know how it is—they're getting scarce."

"Leonard," I began, unsure of my reason for asking the question, "do you know why anyone would pull down your birdhouse at the springs?"

Leonard looked disgusted. "Sure, I do. It's happened here, right outside my door. Violet and me went to Hawaii about the time of the first spotted owl legislation. Some damned fools came through here and shot the crap out of my birdhouses. Then, one Halloween, a bunch of kids knocked over two of them. Violet and me were in Alpine that night, at somebody's party. I had an idea who a couple of the kids were, so I gave their folks a good talking to. It didn't happen again." Leonard's full face turned hard. It was obvious that he savored his clout as a county commissioner.

He sipped his coffee; so did I. Leonard hadn't told me anything that helped indicate who killed Stan Levine. My eyes roamed around the kitchen, with its crocheted dish towels, salt and pepper shaker collection, and airy yellow curtains. I had come to the Hollenberg house on a fool's errand. I doubted very much if irate loggers or spaced-out teens had dumped Leonard's birdhouse into the campfire at the springs. Unless, it occurred to me, the act had been symbolic. Maybe I shouldn't dismiss the loggers so hastily.

But Leonard had moved on. Like nature, he couldn't tolerate a vacuum. ". . . environmentalists and such. It's not all bad, that's what folks have to understand. Outside money, fresh ideas, new blood—that's the future of Skykomish County."

I tried to pick up the conversational thread. "True, stagnation is a real threat to—"

But Leonard was still wound up: "Look at Sultan. They've got plans for new businesses, new stores, new housing. People want to live away from the hustle and bustle of the city. They'd rather drive further to work every day and come home to clean air and a low crime rate. This is God's country, Emmy. Heck, even the girls get better looking. Like you." He winked, then took another slurp of coffee.

"That's very kind, though I—"

"No, I mean it." Leonard was nodding emphatically. "Monday morning, before I headed up to the springs—" He stopped, frowned, and rubbed his bald head. "God Almighty, what a day! That's why I almost forgot about those two blondes at the Dutch Cup. Now in the old days, how often did you spot a couple of real honeys letting down their hair along Highway 2?" He wagged a finger at me. "You bet—about once a year, when some coeds going over to Central Washington or Washington State would stop for a break. But these two weren't still wet behind the ears. The next thing you know, you girls will be wearing high heels at the Grocery Basket."

Inwardly, I shuddered at the thought. Outwardly, I gave Leonard a curious look. "Two blondes? Did you recognize them?"

"Just the one, that architect's wife. Melville, that's the name. She's from California, she's pretty as a picture, and she's living in Alpine. Now who can fault that?" He sat back again, stubby thumbs entwined in his suspenders.

Amazingly, Leonard had remembered Beverly's last name. But that wasn't what most intrigued me: "When was that?" I asked, trying to sound casual.

"When?" Leonard started to scowl. "Monday, like I . . . oh, you mean what time? Just before eight-thirty. Once in a while I like to eat breakfast out. No hard feelings with Violet, mind, but it gives me a chance to shoot the breeze and hear what the voters have to say. Just for the heck of it, I had breakfast Monday at the Dutch Cup. Sultan may be in Snohomish County, but I've got some cronies there all the same."

I wondered how candid I could be with the county commissioner. It was worth a try. "Was the other woman about the same age as Ms. Melville, with freckles and strawberry-blonde curls?"

Leonard gave another emphatic nod. "That'd be her, all right. I never forget a face. But she's not from around here," he added with authority.

"No, she's not," I agreed in a somewhat distracted manner. "She was staying with a friend at Startup." Skye Piersall had gotten an early start Monday morning. I wondered if she had called me at nine-thirty from the Dutch Cup.

"Did they seem . . . friendly?" I put a smile into the question.

Leonard jabbed his chest with a thumb. "To me? Hey, I didn't pull any fast ones! Commissioner Hollenberg isn't one of those politicians who chases skirts!"

I made a rueful face. "Of course not. I meant friendly with each other."

Leonard took the implied apology well. He thought about the clarification for several seconds. "They were serious. Real serious. Head-to-head, confidential-like. Now that's one thing I don't like about you young women—you're all too serious these days. Take Violet—she's a giggler. At your age, she was full of fun, always chipper, couldn't stop giggling."

I tried to imagine Violet as effervescent. I failed. Either life had taken the steam out of Mrs. Hollenberg, or her husband's memory was worse than I'd thought.

I thanked Leonard for his information and the coffee. The brief drive back to Alpine was made under listless gray skies. I pondered his sighting of Beverly Melville and Skye Piersall in Sultan. What had prompted them to get together? Beverly would have been on her way to Seattle; Skye would have come from Honoria's house. Had the two women known each other in California? And if they had, so what?

It was exactly eight o'clock when I entered the newspaper office. The half-hour detour hadn't been very profitable. I still wasn't sure why I'd felt the need to call on the county commissioner and ask about spotted owls. Leonard had sounded straightforward; his recital had made perfect sense. So what was it about birds that bothered me? I couldn't seem to get them out of my head.

My forlorn state must have shown. Leo was already at work. He eyed me with sympathy.

"What happened, babe? You look like bird shit."

"Thanks, Leo. Watch your mouth. Vida will be here any minute. Let's not talk about birds. They're driving me nuts." Ignoring Leo's curious glance, I poured a cup of coffee. Seated at my desk, I called Honoria, who I knew was an early riser. I'd meant to phone her the previous night, but in my disappointment over the canceled trip, I'd forgotten. She didn't answer until the seventh ring. I imagined her maneuvering the wheelchair with that languid deliberation that I didn't quite understand. Unlike me, Honoria never seemed to be in a hurry.

My initial inquiry about Skye Piersall evoked a deep sigh. "I'm fond of her," Honoria said carefully. "Oh, I realize she puts people off sometimes. It's part of her armor against the world, specifically in dealing with her causes. It's not easy, always being in an adversarial position."

As a newspaper publisher, I understood Skye's plight. But I hoped that my own armor wasn't as obvious. "Skye told me something that wasn't accurate," I said, trying to be tactful. "Maybe she made a mistake. It was about the relationship between Blake Fannucci and Beverly Melville, the architect's wife." I explained the confusion in detail.

Honoria's tone turned musing. "Heavens, I've no idea. Skye finds Blake very difficult, almost impossible to deal with. Her tendency with such people is to pretend they don't exist. You're probably right, it was a mistake. I'd guess that Skye doesn't care if Blake has a string of ex-wives or a passel of sisters. She got on much better with Stan Levine."

"Was she in love with him?" I could remain tactful for only so long.

I mistook the silence at the other end of the line for

shock. But when Honoria finally spoke again, her voice conveyed its usual calm: "Love doesn't come lightly to Skye. Her passions are reserved for ideas, not people. Still, she was much intrigued by Stan. According to her, he was very complicated. Did you know they first met in the Peace Corps? Central America, as I recall."

I didn't, of course. "Stan was in the Peace Corps? Was Blake?"

Honoria laughed in her musical way. "Not that I know of. He's hardly the type. But then I suppose some people would think the same of Stan. That's what I mean—he was a complex person. Or so Skye told me."

Now it was my turn to be silent for a moment. "Didn't Stan and Blake meet in college?"

"I'm not sure," Honoria replied. "But Stan dropped out of school to go into the Peace Corps and then went back to get his degree. He and Skye lost track of each other until they met again over some environmental issue near Palm Springs. The romance—if you'd call it that—was off and on for years."

I reflected on the ill-fated pair. Stan had been in his early forties when he died; maybe Skye was only a couple of years younger. As far as I knew, neither had ever married. Vida had told me that Stan's death practically unhinged Skye. Maybe Honoria had misjudged her friend's capacity for love; maybe Honoria herself was too cool, too self-contained, to fathom the depths of another's emotions.

"Honoria, do you remember where Skye was headed Monday morning? She left your place early, I believe."

The faint laugh had an edge. "Really, Emma, I can't think why you're asking me such questions. Has Milo deputized you?" Honoria's tone verged on sarcasm.

I tried to make a joke of my inquiries. "It's the snoop in me. I keep trying to figure out why people do things. A murder investigation is like one of those kids' puzzles where you color only the spaces with the dots. A picture emerges, but you need the blanks to set if off."

"I don't recall those," Honoria replied in a dubious voice. I guessed that as a child she was already creating original work with molding clay. Clods like me labored over filling up those dots. "Skye left here before eight," she said, conceding the answer to my question. "She insisted that I didn't trouble to make breakfast. Her schedule was full, but naturally I didn't pry."

The rebuke stung only slightly. I let it pass as a new thought occurred to me. "When I first met Skye, she said she was from Seattle. 'More or less' was the way she put it. But she flew back to California. And what about her car?"

Honoria's laugh now seemed forced. "Really, Emma, I can't keep up with her. CATE is headquartered in San Jose, I believe. Skye had been staying with friends in Seattle. During the last few months, there had been various projects in the Puget Sound area. I think her plans were to drop the car off in town, go to the airport, fly to San Jose, and check in with her managers, or whatever they're called. She'd requested to be reassigned. I'm sure you can understand why."

I could. Maybe. Yet I was bothered by Skye's reaction. "Stan's death certainly affected her deeply," I remarked.

"The entire Alpine experience affected her adversely," Honoria said, now speaking in a firm voice. "She simply couldn't get a feel for the town's attitude. They resent outsiders, yet they're in dire need of jobs. They love the wilderness, but they're perfectly willing to hunt and fish and chop down trees. She found them utterly paradoxical. Frankly, I do, too."

Honoria's views weren't foreign to me. But as a native Pacific Northwesterner, I intuitively understood my fellow residents' outlook. It was not unlike that of the regional Native Americans, who respected the land but believed that its bounty was reserved strictly for them. If the indigenous tribes of the nineteenth century had resented the white man, a hundred years later the descendants of the original interlopers despised those who had the misfortune of being born in another state. The natives—of every color and creed—had enormous pride and hostility to match. Some might call it selfishness; Pacific northwesterners deemed it self-preservation.

The conversation with Honoria ran down, dwindling away in an exchange of innocuous philosophical clichés. The two of us would never agree. After all, Honoria was from California. The chasm between us was deeper than the Columbia River, wider than the state of Oregon.

It was, I concluded, the same sort of polarization that had thwarted the romance between Skye Piersall and Stan Levine. Their basic attitude toward life was so different that they couldn't meet on any common ground. Love, if that is what had existed between them, wasn't enough to bind them together.

Or was it? Twenty years ago they had both joined the Peace Corps. Their ideals must have been very similar then. What had happened, especially to Stan, that would make him change directions so radically?

That was the question I posed to Vida when she entered my office five minutes later. Naturally, she had no idea, and wasn't in the mood to speculate.

"You look dreadful," she announced, echoing Leo Walsh's words. "Maybe you should go away for the weekend after all. Have you considered visiting your friend Mavis in Oregon?"

I shook my head. "I wouldn't pull such a surprise on her. Mavis is incredibly flexible, but I don't do that kind of thing."

Vida, of course, wouldn't do it either. "Then concentrate on your brother and Adam. They'll be here a week from tomorrow. Just be thankful that you have family. I'm taking care of Roger until Saturday night. His parents are driving over to Spokane for a wedding. This should be an enjoyable weekend."

As usual, I couldn't quite manage to congratulate Vida on having Roger under her wing. She, however, positively glowed. Or perhaps she was thinking about her Sunday date with Mr. Ree. I felt a pang of envy.

"It's trying to rain again," I said, sounding unusually gloomy at the prospect. Hastily, I tried to make amends. "We shouldn't have to worry about drought this year."

"My garden is flourishing," Vida said. "All my perennials are coming along beautifully. I think I'll teach Roger about flowers tomorrow. He loves getting his little hands in the dirt. The contact with Nature, you know. He's so in tune with the elements."

So is Satan, I thought. But for Vida's sake, I smiled. "Honestly, I'm looking forward to Ben and Adam's arrival. It's time to talk to my son about his future. He's old enough to consider a career. Or at least declare a major."

Vida was now looking away, in the direction of my filing cabinets. I assumed she was considering Adam's quandary, or perhaps dreaming of Roger as a botanist or a landscape architect or a grave robber.

I was wrong. "Blake Fannucci," she said, her gray eyes again fixed on me. "That's what happened to Stan Levine. He met Blake in college and turned a very sharp corner."

I considered Vida's statement. "Yes," I said slowly, "that may be true. Blake is very convincing. As a young man he was probably full of ideas—concepts, he'd call them—and he convinced Stan they could build empires of their own. That would have appealed to Stan."

Vida nodded, her summer straw hat lurching dangerously. "Idealists come in all forms. It's how that idealism is channeled that determines the course of a person's life. Really, I don't see a great deal of difference between a young man who goes into the Peace Corps to help Third World countries and someone who wants to create a luxury resort. It's all *building*—if you know what I mean."

I did. But what I couldn't see was how the road from youthful idealism in Central America had led Stan Levine to his death on a mountainside near Alpine. It seemed to me that the trail in the homicide investigation had grown cold. Indeed, I had the feeling that Stan Levine's killer would never be caught.

My pessimism must have showed. Vida was regarding me with a troubled expression. "You almost looked normal for a few moments. What happened, Emma? You worry me."

My laugh was rickety. "I worry me, too. It's nothing, Vida. Just disappointment, frustration, and a sense of hopelessness."

"Oh." Vida stood up, a hand on her hat. "Is that all? That's life. Don't fret over it."

I made a disparaging noise. That was easy for Vida to say.

But, of course, it wasn't.

By mid-afternoon it appeared that life was becoming even more onerous. My worst nightmare was about to happen. Well, maybe it wasn't the absolute worst, since it didn't involve my son, my brother, or Tom Cavanaugh. Instead, it was Roger, arriving at *The Advocate* after school let out. He intended to stay until his grandmother went home from work.

In the first hour, from a few minutes after three until not quite four, Roger was relatively benign. He unplugged Carla's computer, broke Ginny's calculator, and drew all over one of Leo's advertising layouts. For Roger, that was mild. I controlled my glee when Leo called him an undisciplined little bastard and took a swipe at Roger's rump. Leo missed. Luckily, or unluckily, Vida was in the front office at the time. Roger raced off to seek sanctuary with his grandmother.

But ten minutes later, when the wretched little creep violated my cubbyhole and dumped God-only-knew-what from my word processing disk, I called a halt. Taking Roger by the collar of his rugby shirt, I marched him into the news office.

"Look, Vida," I said, trying to remain calm, "why don't the two of you call it a day? You've put in a good week, and I won't quibble if you want to take your grandson home so you can get an early start on your fun weekend."

Vida's expression was inscrutable. But she didn't argue. She had some items to pick up at Cascade Dry Cleaners next door and needed to make a stop at the Grocery Basket. In the handful of minutes that it took Vida to organize her work life, Roger raced outside, where he presumably waited peacefully for his grandmother. I waved off my House & Home editor with a frozen smile.

Leo was hunched over his desk, redoing the layout that Roger had defaced. "That kid's practicing to be a world-class prick," he muttered. "How does the Duchess put up with him?"

"Roger's her blind spot," I said with a shake of my head. "She's much more strict with her other grandchildren. But of course they don't live here."

"He's a real jerk," Carla chimed in, hoisting the strap of her handbag over her shoulder. "I'm off to Buddy

Bayard's and then I'll head home. Marilynn and I are going to the movies tonight."

I tried to keep from looking curious, but for once Carla was observant. "Peyts is on call this weekend." She gave me a faintly amused smile. "It's okay, Emma. You can mention his name. You can mention his name in the same sentence with Marilynn. You can mention their names *together*. Frankly, Peyts made me crazy. Marilynn can have him." Her smile now arch, Carla swished out of the office.

Leo snickered. "Sour grapes—or not?"

I shrugged. "Carla and Dr. Flake were never a good match. I like Marilynn's chances much better. She knows how to deal with impossible men."

Again Leo bent over his layout. I started for my cubbyhole. "What happened?" Leo called out after me as I crossed the threshold.

I turned to look at him over my shoulder. "About what? Carla and Peyts?"

Leo gazed up from his work. He was wearing a short-sleeve summer sports shirt with no tie. His bare arms looked muscular as he rested them on the desk. "No. Your weekend pass to wherever. San Francisco?"

I turned all the way around. "Who blabbed? Janet Driggers?"

Leo nodded. "I ran into her at Parker's Pharmacy this afternoon. She said you were very mysterious."

I didn't understand the sudden urge to spill everything on Leo. But I did it anyway, at least in part. "I got dumped," I said, forcing myself to look my ad manager straight in the eye. "My hot weekend didn't pan out. If you tell anyone, you're fired."

Leo arched his eyebrows at me, but his expression was sympathetic. "The guy must be an idiot. I suppose I can't ask what happened?"

"No." I'd already said too much. "It wasn't really his

fault." It was, though. Tom had put up with Sandra's nonsense for far too long. But Sandra was sick. The mind could be as diseased as any other part of the body. I gave myself a sharp shake. This was no time to bring up all the old, tired arguments.

Leo was giving me his crooked grin. "Let Dr. Walsh cheer you up, babe. How about dinner at King Olav's? I owe you, remember? Our Sonics bet?"

I had forgotten the wager we'd made last fall in the NBA season's early stages. In a rare moment of basketball insight, I'd predicted that the Seattle team wouldn't get to the finals in the playoffs. They hadn't, losing to Denver in the first round.

I started to demur, then managed an uncertain smile of my own. "Why not? You can admire the price tags on my San Francisco wardrobe."

"I can find plenty to admire without that," Leo said, and for just a moment he looked very serious. "Go home, soak in the tub, unwind. I'll hold down the fort here until five and pick you up just before seven."

There was no compelling reason to argue. I'd already planned my workload so that I could leave early to get to the airport. Three minutes later I was going through the front office, wishing Ginny a pleasant weekend.

"Rick's taking me to dinner on *The River Queen* in Everett." Ginny seemed tickled at the prospect.

"It sounds like fun," I said, recalling the announcement of the paddleboat's arrival a couple of years earlier. "The sun's coming out, so you should have a nice view. Enjoy yourselves." With a farewell smile, I pushed open the front door.

The sun was indeed out, which made the drenching flood of water all the more astonishing. I let out a shriek as the brief torrent soaked me to the skin. In the middle of Front Street a man in a pickup truck screeched to a stop, while a handful of pedestrians, including Pastor Purebeck from the Presbyterian church, paused to gape.

I probably wouldn't have sworn anyway, since I was more stunned than angry. Ginny came running outside to find me wiping water out of my eyes and peering up at the lintel over *The Advocate*'s entrance.

"Emma!" she cried in alarm. "What happened? You're all wet!"

Simultaneously, we spotted the galvanized bucket dangling from a piece of cord. Our eyes followed the cord down along the door to the outside knob. Ginny and I stared at each other.

"Somebody set this up," I said, still dripping and spluttering. "Somebody," I added, now sounding grim, "like that little rat, Roger."

Ginny's eyes grew even wider. She started to laugh, then quickly put a hand over her mouth. "Oh, no! Roger is so awful!" But Ginny couldn't stop giggling.

The pickup had driven away, but most of the pedestrians, including Pastor Purebeck, remained. "Are you all right, Ms. Lord?" he inquired in his grave voice.

I was trying to squeeze water out of my navy slacks. "I'm okay. I'm just glad it's a late Friday afternoon and we don't get much traffic at the office. I wouldn't want one of our subscribers to get doused. You might give your Sunday sermon on discipline." My gaze narrowed at Pastor Purebeck. "Especially for grandparents."

The clergyman's sculpted features sagged. He understood that I was referring to a member of his flock. "Well . . . ah . . . yes, discipline is considered old-fashioned, I'm afraid. But it's never really out of style. God bless you, my dear." He moved away with unseemly haste, lest I actually take Vida's name in vain.

It wasn't hard to remove the bucket and the cord. I didn't understand how Roger had gotten up there until

I noticed the ladder standing innocently in front of the dry cleaners next door. Apparently our neighbors had been putting up their striped summer awning. Roger had taken advantage of the opportunity while his grandmother was collecting her clean clothes.

The drive home wasn't comfortable, but at least the incident propelled me into following Leo's advice. The first thing I did after grabbing the mail and checking my answering machine was to soak in the tub. I was relaxing and trying to forget that I should be en route to San Francisco when I heard an odd pounding noise. Hastily, I got out of the tub, wrapped myself in a frayed summer robe, and went into the living room. Someone was knocking on my door.

"Your bell's broken," Milo said, giving it a poke. "See? Nothing. You want me to fix it?"

"Jeez, Milo, why not? I can stand here and shiver while you play Mr. Handyman. Come in, I'm going to get dressed."

When I emerged in dry sweats, Milo was in the kitchen, searching for beer. He managed to find a lone can at the rear of the refrigerator. I made a mental note to stock up before Adam and Ben arrived.

"I heard you had an accident," Milo said with a grin as we went back into the living room. "Roger gotcha, huh?"

While I knew that Milo shared my loathing of Vida's grandson, I didn't find his remark very funny. "He's amazing, really," I said, collapsing into my favorite armchair and taking a deep swig of Pepsi. "He can create mayhem even when he's not around. That's genius, Milo. The kid may have a future after all."

But Milo scoffed. "Not a chance. I'm going to stay in office until Roger's old enough so that I can arrest him and put him away for life. Speaking of which," he went on, resting his feet on my coffee table and causing me to wince, "we learned something interesting today regarding our current homicide investigation."

"Oh?" I tucked my bare feet under me in the soft chair. "Something you're actually going to share with the press?"

Milo grimaced, then lighted a cigarette. "If I don't, Bill Blatt will. He's the one who took the call from L.A. Vida will be all over him like a patchwork quilt."

"So what is it?" I decided I might as well smoke, too. I'd been such a trouper at work, never giving into my nicotine frenzy despite my personal disappointment. Certainly I wouldn't manage to survive Leo's dinner without surrendering to a cigarette.

The sheriff looked as relaxed as I'd seen him for a while. He was gazing up into the rafters of my ceiling, studying the chinks between the logs. It suddenly dawned on me that Milo felt at home. The thought jarred me.

"We had L.A. County check into VineFan, Inc.'s accounts. That's the name of their corporation, by the way. It's a combination of their last names."

I knew that; I'd used it in the original story on the hot springs project. Sometimes I wondered if Milo ever read *The Advocate*. "Go on," I encouraged, trying not to sound impatient.

Milo puffed and sipped, then chuckled. "Big spenders, my butt. Those guys had less than twenty grand in the bank between them. We should have known they were both just a lot of L.A. smog. Emma, old girl, I think my troubles are over."

Chapter Sixteen

MILO'S SELF-SATISFIED ATTITUDE bothered me. I drank more Pepsi and tried to figure out why. "Are you saying they were con artists?"

Milo shrugged. "Maybe. I don't know that they did anything illegal *here*. Except that Levine got himself killed. But their financial status could give us a fresh motive that leaves me off the hook."

I was puzzled. "How?"

Milo swung his feet onto the floor, then leaned over to lift the lid on my crystal candy dish. It was empty. I made another mental note. "Somebody they swindled in L.A. Or wherever. But not anybody local. As I said, so far as we know, they didn't break any laws in Alpine."

The sheriff's information still perturbed me. It simply didn't ring true. Skye Piersall had fought Blake and Stan on other projects. Presumably, she'd lost a few battles. "Are you talking about the corporate account or their individual, personal accounts?"

Milo put his feet back on the coffee table. "Corporate *and* personal. Levine's, that is. We have no reason to check into Fannucci's. Yet." He drained his beer can. "VineFan, Inc. has around fourteen grand in two separate banks. Levine's savings came to just under six grand. Hell, I'd have that much if I weren't still paying Mulehide for our kids' support. I should have it, too, since that jerk she married makes twice as much as I do."

I didn't want to get sidetracked by Milo's domestic problems. As with Leo, I'd heard it all before. "Did you—or Bill—check into the projects that VineFan supposedly promoted?"

Milo was gazing soulfully at his empty beer can. "Oh, yeah. They exist. But that doesn't mean Fannucci and Levine are responsible."

"You could find out," I said in a chiding tone.

"We could," Milo agreed with a condescending smile. "Have you ever tried to sort through who owns what and where the money comes from with a California company? It'd take some doing, and in this case I don't see how the payoff is going to help find Stan Levine's killer. What we've told L.A. County is to look for somebody who got screwed over by VineFan. An investor, I'd figure." Gently, Milo belched.

So Milo intended to dump the investigation in the L.A. County sheriff's lap. The idea wasn't worthy of him. I said so, using an unusually sharp tone. "What," I finally demanded, "are you thinking of? That some sucker came all the way to Alpine and climbed up Spark Plug Mountain to shoot Stan? What's next? Blake gets lured to the Salt Flats in Utah and somebody runs over him with a four-wheel drive? Milo, you can't be serious!"

But he was. "The scenario is perfect. Revenge is a queer thing, Emma. You don't know people like I do. They brood, they dwell on stuff, they become obsessed. Think about it—whoever got bilked wanted payback time more than anything. Not in money, because it was gone. So this guy—we'll say it was a guy, okay?—sits around, figuring out how to do in Levine and Fannucci. He can take his time. That's all he's got, maybe. He follows his victims to Alpine. He could camp out this time of year. He gets Stan alone and shoots him. Now he's got Blake scared spitless. He waits. Then Blake lets his guard down and goes off someplace and—whammo!" Milo gestured, as if pulling a trigger. "Revenge is complete. And sweet."

"Then why doesn't VineFan have a big cash reserve?" I countered. "Why haven't Stan and Blake been reported to the authorities in California or wherever they did this alleged scam? Where did they expect to get the money to pay off Leonard Hollenberg?"

My questions didn't make a dent on Milo. "Good point," he said, nettling me still further. "Because they were going back to L.A. to find another sap."

Immediately, I thought of Ed Bronsky. That was when I told Milo almost everything I knew or thought about the homicide investigation. In his present mellow mood, the sheriff listened patiently.

"I wouldn't worry about Ed," Milo said, stifling a yawn. "Even he's not dumb enough to pour his inheritance into a resort project."

One of the things I hadn't mentioned was Heather Bardeen's alleged recognition of Ed's voice on the ski lodge phone. "Ed could be conned," I asserted. "Ego, for one thing. Blake Fannucci could talk the birds out of the trees." I paused, frowning. There were those blasted birds again. "Damn it, Milo, this case is still in your jurisdiction."

Stretching, the sheriff stood up. "Don't sweat it, Emma. The perp's not here. I guarantee it. This one'll get wrapped up in L.A., where it all started." He reached out a hand and ruffled my hair, which had finally dried. "Thanks for the beer. I have to change and drive down to Honoria's. She's making some kind of Mexican stuff. It's supposed to go good with beer. That's why I didn't steal your Scotch."

"I only keep it for you and Ben," I said, sounding sulky.

Milo stopped outside of the front door. He fiddled with my bell, tried it again, still got no result, and straightened up. "It's the wiring. I'll stop by over the weekend to fix it. See you." The sheriff made his exit, whistling.

Milo's visit had cast yet another shadow over my already dark mood. If Vida hadn't been showing Roger a good time, I would have called her. I knew she would agree that the sheriff was off base. But I also knew that, like me, she probably wouldn't know why.

Leo had reserved our table for seven o'clock. On a Friday night in June, we discovered ourselves surrounded by Alpine's young set. It was prom night, which I had forgotten. Carla, I hoped, had not—somewhere during the course of the week I'd assigned her to take pictures at the Elks' Club, where the dance was traditionally held. Maybe she planned to shoot a couple of rolls after she and Marilynn got out of their movie.

"Jesus," Leo muttered after we'd put in our drink orders, "were we ever that young? I hope not."

I laughed, remembering my own high school prom at Blanchet in Seattle. I'd gone with a fellow senior whose name I'd forgotten but whose behavior was etched on my mind. Whoever he was, he, like me, had been one of the less popular students. He had shown why by bringing along a flask and getting skunk-drunk after only a few sips. One of my darkest recollections was of driving his car from the restaurant to his house while he hung out of the door, throwing up all over Greenwood Avenue North. We had never made it to the dance.

To my surprise, Leo showed no signs of wanting to follow in my long-ago date's disgusting footsteps. After two drinks he was ready to order. By the time our salads arrived, some of the teenagers were leaving. Out of the corner of my eye I saw Rip and Dixie Ridley checking out the dining room. No doubt they had been assigned to make sure that none of the celebrants caused a scene.

Since the Ridleys appeared to be looking in our direction, I waved. They ignored me. I sighed at Leo.

"I wonder if by the time I retire or move out or die there'll be anybody in this town still speaking to me."

"Count me in, babe," Leo said, adding more pepper to his salad. "Don't worry about Ridley. He's your typical jock, still hearing the roar of the crowd on fourth-and-goal. Mrs. R was probably a cheerleader."

I gave a halfhearted chuckle. If memory served, Dixie had been a cheerleader in Colfax or Walla Walla or wherever Rip had played high school sports. She had put him through college at Washington State University. Or was it Oregon State? After two bourbons, I wasn't sure.

The table next to us had been vacated by one of the Gustavsons and his date. I hadn't recognized her, which meant she was probably an outsider, from Sultan or even Monroe. Somewhat hazily, I reflected on the lack of credentials for those who didn't belong. They changed with age, it seemed. Surely, mature people like myself considered anyone born on the right side of the Cascades as acceptable. . . .

"Pssst, babe!" Leo was hissing at me. "Our gracious hosts from last weekend." He nodded at the table where young Gustavson and the Sultan princess had so recently dined.

With a little start I glanced discreetly to my left. Sure enough, Beverly and Scott Melville were being seated by the hostess. This time I'd wait to be acknowledged.

Surprisingly, it didn't take long. Beverly hadn't

picked up her menu before leaning halfway out of her chair to call my name. Scott also smiled and nodded; Leo joined in the etiquette frenzy.

"You see, babe," Leo said after we had finished our mutual greetings, "the Melvilles aren't snubbing you. Now do you want to tell Uncle Leo about the rat who ran away?"

At first I didn't know what Leo was talking about. Then I realized he was referring to my canceled weekend. Somehow, I never thought of Tom Cavanaugh as a rat.

"Leo," I began, resting my elbows on the table, "if I had another drink, I might tell you the whole long, sad story. But I don't want another drink, and you don't want to hear it."

"Why?" Leo asked, keeping stone-faced. "Wouldn't I respect you in the morning?"

I lowered my gaze, concentrating on the Danish flatware. "That's not the point."

"Let me guess." Leo paused as the waitress removed our salad plates. "You've known this guy for a long time. Maybe you met him years ago, when you worked on *The Oregonian.* He quit and moved away. Or you quit to escape him. But you couldn't get him out of your system. And vice versa. So the two of you meet now and then in Seattle or San Francisco or wherever it's convenient for a getaway. It goes without saying that he's married and won't get a divorce. A serious Catholic, like yourself. How am I doing?"

A quick estimate told me that Leo was shooting about eighty percent from the field. If the Sonics had done that well in the playoffs, I'd be picking up the tab instead of Leo.

"How do you figure all that?" I asked, somewhat amused and rather impressed.

"Easy. You don't play around. You're careful, but

you're not cold. I never see you hanging out with anybody around Alpine except that horse-faced sheriff, and I know he's got anther woman. So if you're meeting a guy in San Francisco, it has to be a big deal, and probably long-standing. Loyalty is one of your great virtues, babe. Hell, you'd still be tearing your hair over Ed Bronsky if he hadn't quit. Carla will retire before you get rid of her. And some publishers would have fired my ass the first couple of months when I was still drinking like a shit-faced sot."

"I'm glad you're not drinking so much," I said earnestly. "It's great that you're getting your life back on track."

Briefly, Leo's brown eyes were serious. Then he laughed. "Nice try. We were talking about your love life."

Luckily, our entrées arrived. Leo had selected the house specialty, Meatballs à la Olav; I played it safe with the menu's most unadorned salmon fillet. Before Leo could start needling me again, Ed and Shirley Bronsky passed by our table.

"Hey, hey!" Ed boomed, hovering over us and causing both Shirley and the hostess to stagger in a quick stop. "Look who's here! My former boss and my replacement! How can that be? Shirley and I couldn't afford to eat here on my salary at *The Advocate*. Now we come almost every Friday night."

Leo eyed Ed with something akin to distaste. "We saved up all winter. Next year we might be able to afford dinner in Everett."

Ed threw his head back and roared with laughter. Shirley simpered and the hostess looked bemused. "That's a good one!" Ed declared, slapping Leo on the shoulder. "Say," he said, mercifully lowering his voice as he leaned closer to me, "things are bubbling re the you-know-what-deal. I've got a call into you-know-who."

I didn't know. "Leonard?"

Ed's good humor faded. He regarded me as if I were the village idiot. "Not Leonard. You know—the L.A. connection."

"Oh." I gave Ed a quirky smile. "You mean B.F."

"Right!" He stood up, allowing me to watch his chins wobble. "I imagine he'll call back tonight, unless he took off for the weekend."

"Stan's services were today, I think." I couldn't come up with a more enlightened remark. Maybe I was hampered by Ed's stomach, which was buffeting the table.

Ed looked appropriately mournful. "Right, poor devil." He shook his head several times, then turned to Shirley and the hostess. "Got to run—I'm going to try the stuffed sole."

"He's already stuffed," Leo said under his breath as the beleaguered hostess led the Bronskys away. "What a jerk."

I was frowning in Ed's wake. "You know, I actually used to like him. In a way."

Leo's eyes roamed to the ceiling, with its flags from Norway, Sweden, Denmark, and Finland. "Sheesh," he said, and began to talk of other admen he had known in thirty years of newspaper work. Some of them sounded almost as annoying as Ed, but I was secretly grateful to the bumptious, self-important Mr. Bronsky: His intrusion had diverted Leo from the much touchier topic of my love life. Even Ed was a better conversational gambit than Tom Cavanaugh.

Especially on a night when I should have been dining with Tom instead of Leo Walsh.

Leo and I didn't end our evening alone, however. As we perused dessert menus, Beverly and Scott Melville approached. It appeared they hadn't started with cocktails, so had finished their entrées at about the same time we did. They offered to buy us an after-dinner drink in the bar. Since neither Leo nor I particularly wanted dessert, we agreed.

"You're a sport," Leo said after we had waited for the presentation of the bill. "I thought you'd turn the Melvilles down for fear of having me run amok in the brandy section."

"I trust you," I said in a nonchalant manner. Oddly enough, I did. But the real reason I'd accepted the invitation had nothing to do with Leo. I still felt a need to sort out Beverly's relationship to Blake Fannucci.

Admitting as much to Leo, I asked for his cooperation. "You talk to Scott while I go one-on-one with Beverly, okay?"

Leo gave a faint wag of his head. "Sure, but I don't see why you're so hung up on Fannucci and Beverly. What difference does it make as far as Levine's murder is concerned?"

We had wound our way among the tables to the bar's arched entrance. "Probably none," I said candidly. "What intrigues me most is whether or not Skye Piersall lied. And if so, why."

We scanned the darkened bar for the Melvilles. The long Scandinavian night was evoked by deep recesses in the granite walls and a high, rugged ceiling. Illumination was provided by a curtain of soft lights representing the aurora borealis, and fat little candles squatting on the tables. Leo spotted our companions on a banquette that lined three of the four walls.

"So how's the sheriff's project going?" Leo inquired, wearing his ad salesman's best smile.

Scott tugged at the open collar of his khaki shirt. It looked as if it were U.S. Army issue, but the effect probably had been achieved at considerable cost. "It's coming along. Dodge has some problems making up his mind."

Leo nodded in sympathy. "He's a slow mover." The brown eyes flickered in my direction. "Then again, he's had some diversions this last week."

"That's law enforcement," Scott said. "The sheriff has to expect crises, even in a place like Alpine. I tell Bev, we can't expect Paradise."

"Heck no," Leo agreed with a smile for the waitress who brought our cognacs and Kahluas. "Personally, I'm glad to be out of southern California. It wasn't the crime so much as the quakes. Not that they don't have them here in the Pacific Northwest, but like everything else, it's relative . . ."

Leo and Scott appeared to be safely launched. I leaned across the rough-hewn table, offering Beverly a long-suffering expression. "Men don't understand, do they? If there were a Nordstrom or a Saks in Alpine, it *would* be Paradise."

Beverly laughed, a rather nervous sound. "That would be terrific, but I'd still have to go to Seattle to see the interior design wholesalers."

I nodded. "Of course. Maybe you'll be able to order via computer one of these days."

Beverly made a face. "Some things. But not fabric, which includes carpet, upholstery, wall coverings—so much of what I do. You have to touch it, watch the light play on the surface, get the feel of what's right. I'll adjust to the drive eventually."

"So you've decided to stay?" I tried to keep my manner casual.

Beverly's forehead wrinkled under the smooth fall of blonde hair. "Scott was the one who wanted to move from California. He hasn't changed his mind. Maybe it's just as well." She avoided looking at me, instead fixating on the flickering flame of the candle in the wrought-iron holder.

Beneath what I hoped was my amiable exterior, my brain was jumping through hoops, trying to find an opening that would lead to Blake Fannucci. "There's the spa, of course," I remarked. "Naturally, Scott would have to stay here to work on that."

"He wouldn't, really." Beverly sipped at her Kahlua, the frown still in place. "Scott has often designed buildings that weren't anywhere near our previous home in Manhattan Beach."

"But," I pressed on, "this is different. I mean, with Scott wanting to live in Alpine, and the . . . um . . . kinship with—"

The clumsy words were cut short by the entrance of Ed and Shirley Bronsky. Annoyingly, Ed was talking on his cellular phone. Shirley saw us first and raised her hands in exaggerated surprise.

"Oh! We seem to be following you! How hilarious!" She leaned into our table, the small candle's light barely making a dent on her black and gold tapestry jacket. "And the Melvilles! Isn't Alpine getting to be a regular party place?"

My mind swiftly took in the rest of the town, where I knew most public revelry centered around Mugs Ahoy and the Icicle Creek Tavern. The rest occurred behind closed doors in small bungalows and mobile homes and aging apartments. The element of liquor might be basic to all, but the atmosphere was far different. Friday night in Alpine courted depression, with lack of jobs, broken homes, unruly children, and all manner of abuse hovering among the evergreens.

"This is a very nice restaurant," Beverly Melville allowed. "But aren't most of the people who eat here visitors?"

"We're not," Shirley replied promptly. "Tonight's the

prom, so quite a few kids are eating here, I gather. Next year our Cathy graduates. We're thinking of giving her a Ford Explorer if she keeps her grades above a C."

I felt like asking if the Bronskys would present a Rolls-Royce to any of their offspring who could manage to bring home an A. But even if I'd been so inclined to rudeness, the opportunity was gone: Ed had shut off his phone and was beaming at Scott Melville.

"I just saved your backside, buddy boy. That was Leonard Hollenberg. Since I'm probably Blake's new partner, our esteemed county commissioner has agreed to move ahead with the sale. Let me buy everybody a round."

Ed started to squeeze his way onto the banquette next to Scott, but the architect held up a hand which swiftly turned into a fist. "Butt out, fatso," Scott snarled. "Blake may be desperate, but he wouldn't take *you* on! He and Stan were used to dealing with Fortune 500 types!"

Even in the bar's dim light I could tell that Ed's face had turned crimson. He fairly jiggled with anger. "Why, you crummy little . . . *Californian*!" With amazing dexterity, Ed whipped his rear off the banquette and two-stepped away from the table. Shirley was at his side, pressing her brocade-covered bosom against her husband's arm.

Scott's face had also colored. "Don't talk to me again," he mumbled, aware that other customers in the bar were staring. "Leave it lay. Buzz off. *Please.*" He snatched up his cognac and downed it like soda pop.

I didn't know where to look, so I fixed my gaze on Leo. My ad manager was fingering his chin and frowning. "Thanks for the drink offer," he finally said to his predecessor. "We'll take a rain check." The light note in his voice didn't exactly ease tensions, but it helped save face. At least for Ed, who nodded abruptly, then grabbed Shirley by the arm and steered her out of the bar.

Beverly was thoroughly shaken. There were tears in her eyes as she gazed at Scott, then leaned across the table toward Leo and me. "Scott was very fond of Stan," she declared in an unsteady voice. "He doesn't like the idea of anybody being his stand-in."

"Bull," Scott interjected, though he put an arm around his wife's shoulders. "Blake can get a new partner from the neo-Nazis or a bunch of East L.A. drug lords, for all I care. I just don't want to work with that buffoon of a Bronsky."

Chicken that I am, I lamented aloud my lack of warning for Blake Fannucci. "I didn't want to bad-mouth a former employee," I said, to excuse my omission. "Then again, I figured Blake would spend most of his time in L.A. and Ed would be . . . here." One hand fell aimlessly to my side.

"That's true enough," Scott agreed, his ire fading. He signaled for another round, but to my surprise, Leo shook his head. I followed suit; Beverly shrugged in apparent agreement with her spouse. "But *I'd* have to be here, working shoulder-to-jowl with Bronsky. Forget it."

Having wiped her eyes with a cocktail napkin, Beverly was now looking pensive. "It's really up to Blake," she said, sounding uncommonly meek.

"I'm calling Blake tomorrow," Scott asserted. "If he insists on a local partner, there must be somebody else. What about Hollenberg?" Scott rested his gaze on me, then Leo.

I raised my eyebrows. "Maybe. It could be Leonard's legacy as a county commissioner. He hasn't done much else. None of the three commissioners has, when it comes to helping the local economy."

The waitress brought the Melvilles another cognac and Kahlua. I sensed that Leo was growing fidgety. So was I, since the original purpose of this meeting seemed to have gone by the wayside.

Beverly surrendered her first glass, then turned an anxious face to her husband. "Let Blake make his own decisions. Don't get mixed up in the partnership angle. You don't want to get on Blake's bad side."

I detected a warning note in Beverly's voice. But Scott dismissed his wife's words with an impatient gesture. "Stop fussing. You're overly protective when it comes to Blake. He's a big boy, he can take care of himself."

I took a deep breath, then offered Beverly my most sympathetic look. "It's hard to let go, isn't it?"

Beverly's expression grew puzzled. "Let go? How do you let go of family? I wish I knew," she added, sounding bitter. "Big brothers are forever."

It was the awkward moment I'd dreaded for the past two and a half hours. We had turned off Alpine Way in Leo's secondhand Toyota and were rolling along Fir Street toward my house. Should I ask Leo in? Would he presume upon my hospitality and make a pass? How would I fend him off? Did I really want to?

But even as I glanced surreptitiously at Leo's profile, another vehicle came to a stop approximately by my mailbox. "It's the sheriff," I murmured in surprise. "I thought he was in Startup."

Leo applied his own brakes, then turned into the driveway. "A late date? You should have warned me, babe."

I assumed Leo was kidding. "Milo has already been here," I said, somewhat distracted.

"Really." Motionless, Leo sat behind the wheel. "Did you ask him to come back?"

I fumbled with the car door and finally managed to

get it open. "Don't be an idiot, Leo. Come in if you want to. Just remember, we didn't want dessert."

I thought I heard Leo sigh, presumably with regret, but maybe with impatience. Milo was already in the middle of my walkway, pacing.

"You still got that Scotch?" he asked as Leo and I approached from the drive. "I feel like celebrating. Blake Fannucci's disappeared."

Chapter Seventeen

LEO INSISTED THAT I give him only a finger of whiskey. Milo poured his own. "That Mexican stuff all tastes alike," he grumbled. "What the hell is a fujeeta anyway? It sounds like a Japanese camera."

I didn't bother to correct Milo. It didn't matter if he couldn't tell a fajita from a footstool. Honoria's efforts to broaden her lover's experience rarely got beyond the end of his nose.

"Cut to the missing link," I said, sitting next to the sheriff on the sofa. "What's this about Blake?"

Milo let out a sort of moan. "Sam Heppner phoned me in Startup, just as Honoria and I were . . . settling in." He looked askance at Leo, who was lounging in one of the armchairs on the other side of the coffee table. "Toni, our receptionist, had gotten a call from Fannucci this afternoon. She forgot to give me the message." Milo shook his head in disgust. "Sam found the number after she went home, so he tried to reach Blake in L.A. A woman answered and said she was the manager of the condo where Fannucci lives. Mrs. Simon—the manager—hadn't seen him since this morning when he went out—apparently to Levine's memorial service—but that some suspicious-looking guy in a raincoat and a slouch hat had been hanging around the building. Mrs. Simon had a key so she began checking the units where nobody was home. She'd just gotten into Fannucci's place, and it looked to her as if there'd been a robbery. Sam told her to call the cops. Then he called me at Honoria's."

I was bewildered. "Have you talked to Mrs. Simon?"

Milo shook his head. "We're waiting for a call from Santa Monica. That's where Fannucci lives. I'm officially off duty, so Sam can handle it. God knows I've earned a break. It's a damned shame if anything's happened to Blake, but I wanted to let you know that I was on the right track after all." The sheriff wiggled his shaggy eyebrows at me. "You were pretty skeptical when I stopped by earlier."

For some reason, I remained skeptical. "Blake could be anywhere. He might have taken off for the weekend. How do you know this isn't just your average L.A. break-in? They do have quite a bit of crime, even in Santa Monica."

Milo savored his Scotch, all but smacking his lips. Out of the corner of my eye I saw Leo regarding the sheriff with a sardonic expression. "That's what we're waiting for—confirmation," Milo said complacently. "It's not hard to tell if a burglary is faked. We also have to find out how the perp got in. According to Mrs. Simon, the building's security isn't any great shakes. That's why she's so careful about checking things out."

"A snoop." Leo stuck a cigarette in his mouth, then talked around it. "The raincoat and the slouch hat sound like they walked off her TV set. Make sure she's not a publicity freak."

Milo shot Leo a look of disbelief. "That's crazy. Sam says Mrs. Simon is in her seventies. What does she care about publicity?"

Leo snorted. "You're talking L.A., Sheriff. Everybody wants to be a star."

I didn't bother to hide my yawn. "It's going on ten," I said, not discriminating between either of my guests.

"Come up with some credible theories or go home. I'm beat."

Milo took umbrage. "You've heard my theory. Somebody got screwed over by Fannucci and Levine. They wanted revenge. They got it. End of case, as far as SkyCo is concerned. Now it's all up to the folks in L.A. County."

It was useless to argue with Milo. I knew it, but Leo didn't. "Levine got whacked here, Sheriff. That still makes it your case. If the killer scurried back to California, so what? You let him—or her—get away."

Milo lifted one shoulder. "So we sent out an APB. Bond issue or not, we don't have the money or the jurisdiction to do anything else. Besides," he added smugly, "Sam and Dwight came up with some other good stuff today. Five years ago, VineFan put up a housing development on the edge of Northridge. Several of those houses collapsed in the last big quake. Luckily, nobody got killed, but you can bet your butt those owners got pretty mad."

I fairly jumped in my chair. "Wait—Scott Melville designed houses in Northridge that fell down. Skye Piersall told me about them. I wasn't sure she was telling the truth."

Leo and Milo both stared at me, with varying degrees of interest. My ad manager looked intrigued; the sheriff's long face was dubious. As usual.

"Look," I said, enthusiasm banishing weariness. "Skye may be kind of a drip, but she's been telling the truth. Blake *is* Beverly Melville's brother. Don't ask why he lied—maybe it's just part of his L.A. con artist persona. I'll bet she's right about Scott, too. He designed those houses for VineFan."

"So?" Milo was unimpressed. "What's any of that got to do with irate home owners? If Scott gets whacked, I'll start another investigation."

There were times when I wanted to grab Milo by the ears and beat his head against a concrete wall. This was one of them. But I wasn't sure why. Before I could field a righteous argument, the sheriff's cellular phone rang. It was far less annoying than Ed Bronsky's.

Leo and I exchanged expectant looks while Milo spoke into the phone. "Listen, Sam, I'm off . . . No, I'm not home . . . Yes, you're bugging me . . . Tell Henry to stop fussing, he's not a suspect . . . Hell, he's imagining . . . Okay, okay, I'll stop by his house on my way home. It's not far from here . . . Jeez, never mind where 'here' is, you jackass! Just do your job and stop driving me nuts!" Angrily, Milo clicked off.

I started to say something, but Milo was contemplating his empty glass. "Damn, I could use a refill." He stood up, all arms and legs and indignation. "But I won't. I've got to stop off at Bardeen's."

"How come?" I asked innocently.

Milo waved a big hand. "Sam Heppner is losing his grip. Why can't he hold down the night shift on his own? It's some dumbassed thing about missing bills at the ski lodge. Henry Bardeen is paranoid, but I'd better humor him so he doesn't sue the county for false arrest or public embarrassment or—"

"What kind of bills?" I queried, interrupting Milo's monologue.

The sheriff was at the door. "How the hell do I know? That ditzy daughter of his probably lost them."

"Heather's not ditzy," I murmured.

But Milo was on his way. Thoughtfully, I watched him lope to his Cherokee Chief. "He's self-destructing," I said, closing the door.

Leo was also on his feet. "Dodge has no peripheral vision. Otherwise, he's okay. You two ever done it?"

I also could possess a one-track mind. "What?" I turned a puzzled face to Leo.

Leo was grinning. "Never mind, babe." He leaned down and brushed my cheek with a quick kiss. "How about the Seahawks? You think they'll make the playoffs?"

"Not this season," I forced a smile. "Thanks, Leo. Dinner was great."

He was at the door, a hand on the knob. "Will the Seahawks *ever* make the playoffs? Will they ever score? Will Leo? Good night, Emma."

Leo was gone.

I was alone.

Oh, well.

Shortly before eleven I risked a call to Vida. At ten years of age, Roger ought to be in bed. If not, he was probably engrossed in watching television.

"One of the privileges of visiting Grams is getting to stay up past his regular bedtime," Vida informed me when my second guess proved correct. "We had quite a raucous evening of it, especially after Roger let Cupcake out of his cage. He's so excitable."

I didn't bother to ask if the reference was to Roger or the canary. Instead I filled Vida in on my own evening, specifically the incidents that related to our current homicide. As usual, Vida sifted through the information, then pounced on what she considered the most intriguing:

"Beverly Melville—you mentioned that she still seems upset. Now why is that?"

"Because she doesn't want anyone to know that her husband and brother have been building collapsible houses in the L.A. area? That could explain why Scott was so anxious to move out of California."

Vida, however, didn't concur. "No. All sorts of buildings fell down during that earthquake. We don't know if Scott's design was the cause or if it was faulty construction or just plain bad luck. Nothing's really earthquake-proof. What we do know is that Skye Piersall seems to want to blacken Scott Melville's reputation. Perhaps Blake Fannucci's as well. Yet Leonard Hollenberg saw Skye and Beverly having an amicable conversation. Not that Leonard is the most observant man on earth, but we'll have to give him credit for possessing certain political antennae when it comes to people."

"I'd like to ask Beverly why she and Skye were huddled together last Monday morning," I put in, sitting back in my chair and using the wastebasket as a footstool.

"Then ask," Vida said reasonably. "I wonder if I can't guess."

I evinced surprise. "What? Why?"

"The common bond between them," Vida replied calmly. "Stan Levine. Skye was in love with Stan. Stan was in partnership with Beverly's brother and working with Beverly's husband. If you're accurately retelling Leonard's account, it sounds like girl talk. That's almost always about men—or a man. Who else but Stan Levine?"

Vida had a very good point. Maybe CATE wasn't Skye's primary motive for coming to Alpine. Maybe she had somehow managed to use her environmentalist's credentials as an excuse for confronting Stan. Maybe she had given him an ultimatum about their romance.

"She could have been enlisting Beverly as an ally," I said, knowing that women often do such things in the cause of love.

"Very likely," Vida agreed. "There was no one else she could ask. Not in Alpine."

"Blake?" I suggested.

"I don't think so. Skye and Blake seem utterly at odds with each other."

That was the impression I'd gotten, too. But were the rest of us supposed to believe that animosity existed between Skye and Blake? I remembered my own clandestine romance of over twenty years ago. At *The Seattle Times*, Tom and I were very discreet, hiding our affair from our coworkers. Thus, I often criticized him roundly in front of others; he had probably done the same with me. It was possible that Skye was covering for something else, such as a romance with Blake Fannucci.

But they were an even more unlikely couple than Skye and Stan. "What do you think happened to Blake?" I asked, dismissing furtive love affairs, past and present.

Vida harrumphed. "Nothing, probably. Milo is jumping to conclusions. Blake's landlady or whatever she is sounds like a meddler. Really, Emma, I can't tolerate people who pry into other people's private lives." I let the remark pass. Before I could say anything, there was a clatter in the background, followed by a gasp from Vida. "Excuse me, I must run. Roger has knocked over his TV tray."

He probably overloaded it, I thought, but did not say so. I hung up. Now I was truly alone, cut off from Vida by her spoiled-rotten grandson. I should have mentioned his so-called prank with the bucket of water. But I wouldn't give Roger the satisfaction of knowing he'd doused me, nor would I disturb Vida's weekend festivities. Besides, the murder was uppermost in my mind.

Or so I told myself. In fact, I had to concentrate on Stan's death to keep other thoughts at bay. A glance from my kitchen window revealed stars and a half-moon. The same sky hung over San Francisco. But I mustn't dwell on that now. Resolutely, I marched back into the living room, grabbed a notebook, and sat down on the sofa.

There were links between Stan and Skye; Stan and Blake; Blake and Beverly; Beverly and Scott; Scott, Stan, and Blake. Leonard figured in there, too, with the last three names. So did Ed, if belatedly. Out on the fringe were Henry Bardeen, Cal Vickers, Rip Ridley, and the rest of Alpine.

So what? I was getting nowhere. Almost everybody had an alibi, of sorts. Blake had been at the ski lodge. So, presumably, had Henry Bardeen. Scott was at home, waiting for the glazier. Beverly had driven into Seattle, as had Shirley Bronsky. Which meant that Ed was home alone . . .

I gave myself a sharp shake. Ed had to be discarded as a suspect, if only because I couldn't see him exerting himself to hike up the hot springs trail. Leonard Hollenberg had done just that, and found Stan's body. At least that was what he claimed.

Then there was Skye, whose alibi was the shakiest of all the serious suspects. She had met Beverly in Sultan for coffee, then gone up to the summit. Her car had broken down on the return trip, making her miss our ten-thirty appointment. Cal had towed the vehicle back to town around two o'clock, just before the helicopter had landed with Stan's body. Skye had arrived at *The Advocate* earlier, around one. How had she gotten back to town? Where had she been in the meantime? Why, as they used to say in old gangster movies, wouldn't she come clean?

Clean. Cal Vickers had said that Skye was clean. He'd said it while towing her car down Alpine Way. At that point Skye had been back in town for at least an hour. He'd seen Skye somewhere else, maybe along the highway with her car. Had Cal given Skye a ride back to Alpine, then returned later to get her Honda? What was Cal doing along that stretch of road in the late morning or early noon hours?

His job, I told myself. There was nothing suspicious about Cal Vickers being on Highway 2 at any time of the day or night. He was in the towing business. It took him all over Skykomish County.

Then there was Coach Ridley. But he would have been at school, encouraging young boys to grow into their jockstraps and do other manly things . . . or would he, so close to year's end? Classes weren't on a regular schedule this week; the seniors had already been dismissed. . . .

My brain was getting fuzzy. Nothing made sense. That was good. I was too tired to think.

That was even better.

On Saturday morning, reality was scrubbing the kitchen floor, vacuuming the living room, and doing the laundry. I refused to fantasize about what might have been: strolling Fisherman's Wharf, riding a cable car, driving over to Sausalito.

The washing had piled up during the week. The clothes I'd worn when Roger's bucket had dumped its contents were still damp. I cursed the little creep anew, though I couldn't help but grudgingly admire his ability to wreak havoc when he wasn't on the scene.

Startling myself, I paused with my arms full of towels. In theory, Roger could claim innocence. He had been with his grandmother when the incident occurred. How could I prove he had put the bucket above the office door?

What if . . . ? Slowly, I stuffed the towels into the washer, then added detergent and turned the dial. Was it possible that Stan had been set up? Could someone have arranged for the gun to off without a human finger pulling the trigger? Might the bullet have been intended for Blake as well as for Stan?

Maybe I was crazy. Certainly Milo would scoff at my

latest fancy. As I sorted through the rest of the laundry, I tried to figure out how a murder in absentia could have been arranged. I hadn't gotten very far when I mindlessly checked the pockets of my old brown slacks. There was something in the right-hand side. Money? I extracted the folded paper, but it was only a note.

Stan's note. Or notes, from his binder. I felt sad as I gazed at his slanting handwriting, with its detailed notations about the goldfinch. Stan's gesture had been small, but thoughtful and generous. I recalled his journal, with its optimism and enthusiasm. People say life is hard, which it is. But death is more cruel, at least when it comes violently and too soon.

Leaving the second load on the floor by the washer, I went into the kitchen to pour a cup of coffee. It wasn't quite ten o'clock. Milo ought to be up and about. Maybe he'd had news of Blake Fannucci.

I took Stan's note with me when I went into the living room to dial the sheriff's home number. The wastebasket by the desk yawned up at me. It was pointless to keep the note, yet I couldn't bear to throw it away. Not yet. I was punching in the call to Milo when I realized that I knew who had killed Stan Levine.

I stopped dialing before I hit the last digit in Milo's number. If I wanted to make my theory stick with the sheriff, I needed more information. Milo despised theories, even when they were right.

Again the phone rang at least a half-dozen times before Honoria answered. Her patience was definitely tested when I asked for Skye Piersall's phone number.

"I can give you CATE's headquarters in California or the regional office in Seattle," Honoria said peevishly, "but it's not my place to hand out her personal number. Nor do I understand why you want it. If this is regarding your homicide coverage, why can't you wait until you hear something official from Milo?"

I decided to be candid with Honoria. "Because I never will. Not along this line of inquiry. Your boyfriend doesn't believe in coloring outside of the lines."

To my relief, the statement evoked a snicker. "You're right—Milo isn't a font of imagination. But I still don't like having Skye pestered."

"I don't like doing it," I admitted. "On the other hand, it's my job."

"Is it?" The irony in Honoria's husky voice has hard to miss. "Or are you doing Milo's job for him?"

"Maybe. He's washed his hands of the case. Or haven't you noticed?"

"I haven't noticed *that*," Honoria said, now verging on sarcasm. "If he's signed off, why did he go haring out from here last night when Sam Heppner called?"

The last thing I wanted was to get mixed up in Honoria and Milo's romantic relationship. "It was Sam's call that made Milo throw in the towel," I explained. "Look, Honoria, I can wait until Monday to call CATE, but in the meantime there's a killer on the loose. Skye may be able to tell me something that will help convince Milo that I know what I'm talking about."

With the greatest of reluctance and several cautions, Honoria finally surrendered Skye's number in San Mateo. I thanked her profusely, but my indebtedness rankled. The sheriff's light-o'-love was getting on my nerves.

Then, to make me feel not only nosy but futile, Skye didn't answer. I reached her voice mail, which informed me in a professional tone that "the party you are calling is unavailable. Please leave your name and number. . . ."

I didn't. There was no guarantee that Skye would call me back. I'd try her again later. Putting on something less disreputable than my old sweats, I drove down to the sheriff's office. I didn't expect to find Milo there, but I wanted to take another look at Stan's journal.

To my surprise, the sheriff was on the job. He didn't seem very pleased by my arrival. "Okay, okay, so maybe this Mrs. Simon jumped the gun. The Santa Monica cops didn't find any sign of a break-in. It looks to them as if Blake Fannucci left in a hurry. He probably wanted to get a head start on the weekend."

I began to speak, then stopped. I wasn't going to break my vow of silence until I'd nailed down some more facts. Milo, however, wasn't finished yet.

"Then, just to drive me nuts, Henry Bardeen swears somebody waltzed off with the folder that contained Blake and Stan's bills. They also deleted the information from the computer. Now who would do that? And why?"

Dustin Fong, who had been sitting at his own computer, gently cleared his throat. "Maybe it has something to do with Mr. Fannucci's alibi, sir. Aren't those receipts stamped with the time when the order is rung up?"

Milo started to glare at his deputy, then began to nod. "Could be. Yeah, it might be somebody who didn't want Blake Fannucci proving where he was last Monday morning. But how did they do it?"

Dustin's fingers hovered over the keyboard, but his dark eyes rested hopefully on his boss. "The easiest answer is that it was someone who works at the lodge. Like . . . ah . . . Mr. Bardeen. Or his daughter. But," the young man added quickly, "I realize you have no reason to suspect either of them."

I waited patiently while Dustin resumed his work on the computer and Milo mentally chewed over his deputy's words. "It can't be Henry," he breathed. "Or Heather."

My own doubts were surfacing. Almost diffidently, I asked Milo if I could see Stan's journal.

Grumbling, he ordered Dustin to get the item from the evidence locker. "You've got something on your mind," Milo said with a trace of reproach. "What is it now?"

"Just wait." I offered Milo what I hoped was a placating smile. "Tell me this—where's Stan's bird binder?"

"Huh?" Milo scowled at me. "What are you talking about?"

Briefly, I explained. Dustin handed me the journal. "The binder should have been with this," I said, flipping through the first three pages that contained the Alpine jottings. Grimly, I reread the short paragraphs. There, in the final entry, was the clincher. I set the journal down on the counter, then dug into my handbag.

"Two things," I said, handing Milo the piece of notepaper from Stan's binder. "Three, actually. Look at the handwriting. It slants and it's legible, but it's not the same as these notes about the goldfinch. Secondly, there's the mention of the bluebird. And third, why wasn't Stan's binder found along with the journal?" I folded my arms, allowing Milo's brain to work its lead-footed wonders.

"Bluebird, my butt!" Milo breathed. "We don't have bluebirds around here. We've got blue jays."

"Precisely," I said, sounding as primly smug as Vida. "You didn't notice that before?"

Milo stared again at the open pages. "No," he muttered, then looked up sharply. "When did you see this? Dwight Gould swore that nobody went through Levine's room at the lodge after the murder."

Not wanting to get Bill Blatt in trouble, I shook my head. "Never mind that. As for the bird notes, Stan had them at my house. He gave me that slip of paper. What do you make of it?"

Dustin Fong was watching us out of the corner of his eye. A twitch along his jawline indicated his intense curiosity.

"We'll have to get a handwriting expert on this," Milo said at last. "But you may be right. The similarities are pretty superficial." He handed the open journal and the notebook paper to his deputy. "You got an opinion, Dustman?"

With deference to his superior, Dustin backed me up. I felt a rush of encouragement. "Show me those bits and pieces from the campfire at the springs," I said to Milo.

With a sigh, Milo trudged off to the evidence locker. "Is there anything else you need?" he called from around the corner. "I'm just a county peon, trying to do a job."

"One step at a time," I said, controlling my mounting excitement.

Milo brought out the plastic bag with its charred remnants. We went into his office, where he put on surgical gloves and sifted through the items. I stopped him when he picked up a half-dozen bolts.

"Why so many?" I asked, sounding peremptory in my own ears.

Milo scowled. "To keep the birdhouse in place. That thing was pretty big. It had to be, if Hollenberg expected to get spotted owls."

I let the explanation pass, speaking only when the sheriff sorted through what he'd earlier identified as pull tabs from the beer cans.

"Look at those," I urged, leaning on the edge of Milo's desk. "They aren't from aluminum cans. They're too thick. Those are from Stan's binder. Somebody wanted it destroyed so that we wouldn't have a sample of his handwriting."

Milo swore under his breath. It seemed that he was beginning to see the light. "Then those bills at the ski lodge—they were stolen for the same reason?"

No longer on such firm ground, I grimaced. "Maybe. In a way."

"Well?" Milo drummed his latex-covered fingers on the desk.

My smile was now pretty thin. "We'd better go up to the hot springs."

But Milo wasn't about to take even the mildest of orders. "Oh, no! I'm not wasting two hours climbing Spark Plug! The only way I go back is in a copter, and I'm not requesting one from Chelan County again."

In all honesty, I couldn't blame Milo. "Okay," I said, sinking into one of the sheriff's visitor's chairs. "Then let me tell you how I think Stan Levine was shot when nobody else was there."

Chapter Eighteen

THE ITEMS FROM the campfire had been replaced in the evidence bag. Milo had removed his surgical gloves and discarded them in the wastebasket. We both had mugs of dreadful coffee and lighted cigarettes. Obviously, the sheriff had settled in for the long haul.

"The problem is," I began apologetically, "that I don't know much about firearms."

Milo grunted.

"But I think I know how the murder was committed so that the killer could have an almost perfect alibi."

Milo arched his eyebrows.

"It was the birdhouse. It was big enough to accommodate spotted owls. A handgun would fit inside. The trigger was cocked and attached to something so that when Stan went up to look inside—which would have been at about eye level for him—he tripped a wire or a cord so that it fired. That's why he was shot through the eye." I paused, flinching at the thought. Milo simply stared at me. "I don't know exactly what caused the gun to go off, but that's why the birdhouse had to be burned along with Stan's binder and the phony party stuff that was supposed to be left by teenagers. The birdhouse would have shown traces of gunpowder or whatever. As for the gun itself, it could be anywhere along the mountainside. If a piece of cord or string was tied to the trigger, it was probably burned in the fire."

Milo blew out a big cloud of smoke. I stopped talking, waiting for some kind of response. When it came, the sheriff's manner was matter-of-fact:

"That's pretty damned complicated. How could the killer know Stan would be the one looking in the birdhouse?"

"Who else? Stan loved birds. Leonard put the house up, but he's too short to see inside. It was just a matter of time until Stan took a peek." Again I stopped. My earnestness must have showed. Milo took a deep breath.

"It sounds crazy," he said, but his expression showed interest. "Once a Ruger .357 Magnum's trigger is cocked, it'll fire under the slightest pressure. But the gun would have to be held in place somehow. Like a vise." Milo's forehead creased as he concentrated on his own reconstruction of the crime. "The bolts—that's what they were for. Leonard wouldn't have needed more than a couple to anchor the birdhouse. But the vise would have to be bolted down. Now where is the damned thing? And the gun?"

I was flushed with excitement over Milo's willingness to take my theory seriously. "Would you have to be a gun expert to carry this out?" I asked.

Milo gave a snort of disgust. "Hell, no. You'd just have to ask the right questions. It'd take some time to set it up, but that wouldn't be a problem if it was done after Fannucci and Levine posted that sign at the trailhead. Leonard would be the only one likely to go up there, and you could hear him coming from a mile away." Milo fingered the half-dozen telltale bolts. "I should have guessed these were put in at separate times. Two of them are rusty. The other four are clean." His head jerked up and he gave me an ironic look. "Okay, maybe we know how. So who did it? Or have you figured that part out yet?"

I couldn't quite tell if there was sarcasm in Milo's

voice or not. Before I could answer, his phone rang. He gave a shrug, then picked up the receiver. His face fell almost at once.

"The hell you say . . ." Fumbling, he stubbed out his cigarette. "Yeah . . . No shit . . . Where? . . . No, I don't know the area . . . What? . . . Who? . . . Oh, right, yes, I know who she is . . . Sure, we can do that . . . Thanks . . . I'll get back to you." Milo got to his feet. "That was Santa Monica. An hour ago the California Highway Patrol pulled Blake Fannucci's body out of his Maserati. It went off SR1 just south of Big Sur. I've got to tell Beverly Melville. I guess she really is his sister. I'll get back to you, Emma."

Milo might not have known the treacherous piece of highway around Big Sur, but I did. Much of it was hairpin curves carved into cliffs high above the Pacific Ocean. "White-knuckle driving," Ben had called it after we'd taken a trip down the coast from San Francisco to Los Angeles when Adam was about ten. It seemed to us nervous native Pacific Northwesterners that every car with California plates had passed us going at least twenty miles an hour faster. We didn't know if they were more expert or more reckless. But what we were sure of was that this was no route for the fainthearted.

I didn't try to hang onto Milo or beg to come along. Instead I went out to my Jag and followed him at a discreet distance to Icicle Creek. He was already inside the Melville house when I arrived.

A stunned-looking Scott opened the door. Beverly and the sheriff were in the living room. I could hear her strained, shocked voice, making the usual self-protecting denials of a truth too terrible to bear.

"I'm sorry, Scott," I murmured. "I was with Sheriff Dodge when the news came in."

"I don't get it," Scott said, bewildered. "Was he

heading north? That's the inside lane on SR1. Blake shouldn't have gone off the road unless he was forced."

We had entered the living room. Beverly stared at us with wide, horrified eyes. Her face was ghastly pale. Then her gaze wavered for an instant before it riveted solely on Scott.

"He *was* forced," she said in a choked voice. "By me. It's my fault that Blake is dead. I did it." Her body sagged and she would have fallen if Milo hadn't been there to catch her.

Scott jumped over a stack of fabric samples. "What the hell are you talking about?" he shouted. Then, realizing the enormity of his words and his wife's fragile state, he helped the sheriff settle Beverly onto the sofa. "What's happening?" he asked in a small, miserable voice.

Beverly's eyelids fluttered open. "Oh, Scott," she moaned, reaching for his hand. "It's been so awful. . . . What can I say now that it's finished?"

Milo frowned at me over the Melvilles' heads. Nervously, I signaled for the sheriff to keep quiet. He made a face, but stepped back a couple of paces. Scott was smoothing the blonde hair off Beverly's forehead and offering calming words.

"Is there anything I can do?" Milo finally asked.

Scott turned slightly, then looked again at his wife. "A glass of water? Some wine?"

Beverly, however, was struggling to sit up. "No, I'm all right. Go ahead, Sheriff. Do whatever it is you have to do."

Milo's long face showed complete confusion. "Excuse me, ma'am," he said formally. "Are you making a confession?"

"I told you," Beverly replied in a hollow voice, "I killed Blake."

Milo and Scott were both looking jarred. The sheriff

cleared his throat. "I see. And Stan—did you kill him, too?"

Beverly didn't seem to hear the question. She was fixated on her husband's hovering face. "There's some brandy left from our party the other night," she said quietly. "Maybe I could have some of that."

Scott stood up, hurrying to wherever the Melvilles kept the liquor. My nerves were ragged. I couldn't hold my tongue another second:

"Beverly," I said in a harsh, overloud voice, "you didn't really kill your brother. You called to warn him, and he was scared. I don't know how or why his car went off SR1. But I do know that he murdered Stan Levine."

We were all drinking brandy, including the sheriff. After the first few sips, Beverly opened up. Yes, she had guessed from the beginning that Blake had somehow shot Stan. A rented helicopter, she'd figured at first. It would have suited her brother's imagination and flair. But the how wasn't as important to her as the why. There had been hints, innuendos, veiled fears from Blake that the partnership with Stan was coming to an end.

"I wasn't convinced until Monday morning when I met Skye Piersall for coffee in Startup," Beverly said, her color now partially restored. "Skye confided that although she and Stan hadn't seen much of each other lately in person, they'd been talking a lot on the phone. They'd decided to get married. Stan had been begging her to marry him for years, but she refused, because of the business he was in. She simply couldn't live with a developer and her conscience under the same roof—or so she put it."

As Beverly paused for breath, I nodded. "Stan's forged journal was full of enthusiasm for the spa project. If he'd actually kept a journal, it probably would have shown that he was saddled with doubts."

"Exactly," Beverly agreed. "Skye said that basically Stan was a builder. He wanted to make things for other people, to improve their lives. That's why he joined the Peace Corps. I saw that side of him, so did Scott. He was a visionary, and his projects with Blake fulfilled a need. But according to Skye, his heart was no longer in it. He was ready to walk away."

Over his brandy snifter, Milo was clearly puzzled. "So Blake killed him because he didn't want to break up the partnership? That doesn't make any sense."

"I think that was only a small part of it," I put in. "Blake was angry with Stan for what he considered a betrayal. They'd been together in VineFan for over twenty years. It was like a marriage. But to carry the analogy further, Blake was cheating on the side." I turned to Beverly. "This is a guess, but did Stan know you were Blake's sister?"

Beverly laughed, a painful, mirthless sound. "No. As close as the business partnership was, Blake and Stan rarely socialized. The first time I met Stan was about six years ago, when Scott started working for them. Blake introduced me as his ex-wife. I thought it was a joke. But he told me later not to let on to Stan that I was his sister. I could never figure out why, but then Blake was always doing inexplicable things. When we were children, I had to pretend to his friends that I was the next-door-neighbor kid. Fooling people was just part of being . . . Blake."

I shook my head. "Not in this case. It was part of a scam. I think Blake milked VineFan's accounts for his own purposes. He probably told Stan he had big alimony payments to make. Neither the corporation nor Stan had anywhere near the money they should have had." I glanced at Milo for confirmation.

"Right," the sheriff replied, somewhat reluctantly. "Now that Blake's dead"—Milo bowed his head, apparently in respect of Beverly's feelings—"we can check into his personal accounts. Maybe we'll find quite a chunk stashed away."

I gave Milo a smile of approval. "Stan wouldn't go on forever believing that VineFan's profits were being eaten up by an ex-wife. Coming to Alpine was risky with you two here." I nodded at both Melvilles. "I suspect it was Stan's idea, not Blake's. Everything was falling apart for Blake. His sister was on the scene, so was Skye Piersall, and Stan was about to end the partnership. For all I know, if Stan had insurance, one of his beneficiaries was Blake. Business partners often do that, as a hedge. Blake saw a chance to cut loose, to take his money and run."

Beverly hung her head. "He did mention Switzerland recently. I thought he was joking. He often did."

Scott set his empty brandy glass down with an indignant gesture. "It was those houses in Northridge. Part of it, anyway. Blake hired the contractors. They had a questionable reputation. There are at least three big lawsuits pending right now. I'm named in two of them, but I'll be damned if they'll find fault with my designs. The homes would have been completely safe if the builders hadn't used cut-rate materials and squirmed around the local codes."

Beverly put a hand on her husband's knee. "I know. It's made me crazy, thinking that my brother dragged you into all that. I doubt that Stan knew what went on with that project."

"Jeez." Shaking his head, Milo stood up in his less than graceful manner. I rose from the footstool where I'd been sitting and hurried to his side. To my surprise, the sheriff took my arm. "We'll be heading out now, folks. Again, I'm sorry. Is there anything else I should know? If not, we'll be in touch."

The Melvilles couldn't think of anything. They both still seemed rather dazed. Milo and I left them to mourn and mull and meditate on their losses.

Out in the street, Milo kept me in tow. "Come on," he said, loping along. "I'm three doors down. Let's have a serious drink."

As usual, Milo's living room looked as if he hadn't done any cleaning in weeks. The newspapers stacked next to the couch bore dates from late May. The beer cans and TV dinner packages were probably more recent, but less appealing aesthetically. I pushed aside several issues of *Sports Illustrated* and fishing magazines to make room on the couch. Milo settled into his favorite recliner, a patched navy number that creaked under his weight.

It wasn't yet noon, but the bourbon didn't seem like a violation of my code never to drink before lunch. I'd earned it, though the moment felt more like a wake than a celebration.

"Birds," Milo said, shaking his head in apparent disbelief. "You put this all together because of *birds*?"

"And Roger," I said, giving Milo my blandest look. "His stupid stunt with the bucket gave me the idea about the rigged-up gun. The birds were always there, flitting around in the back of my mind. I knew something didn't fit—it was the bluebird. A non-birdwatcher would make that kind of mistake. Stan never would.

"There was the birdhouse, too," I went on. "That actually was the kind of thing that drunken teenagers might do. They can be cruel at that age, especially kids whose parents have been put out of work because of the spotted owl. But once we figured out that the murder site had been trashed by someone else, it didn't make sense. Unless, of course, there was a reason to burn the birdhouse."

Milo held up a hand. "Hold it—did Blake go up there Monday night with all that trash from the lodge and march around in those extra pairs of shoes? Is that why he reported somebody trying to break in?"

I nodded. "Blake had to embellish everything. Maybe he thought that if he was seen sneaking around the lodge, somebody might get suspicious. If he reported a prowler, then there was someone else to blame. For all I know, he went in and out of his own window."

"Speaking of the ski lodge," Milo interjected, making room for his glass on the overcrowded table next to his chair, "what about those bills? Who pulled them?"

"It had to be Beverly. I'm sure she'll admit it now. She went to see Blake last Sunday night. Heather saw her, but didn't recognize her. The Melvilles haven't been in Alpine that long. Then Chaz was on duty Thursday night, and Beverly showed up again. The fire alarm went off—probably Beverly's doing, too—which took Chaz away from the front desk. I imagine Beverly wanted those bills to prove to herself that her brother couldn't have killed Stan. Or else at that point she knew he had and was trying to help him."

Milo snorted. "Some help! The bills gave Blake his alibi."

"That wasn't the point. Blake wanted the bills destroyed because he'd signed some of them, like the one for grapefruit juice. Blake had to sign for it to secure his alibi. But I remember now that he also signed for our lunch the previous week. He didn't want his handwriting compared with the journal. Nor did he want anyone to see Stan's, for the same reason. Meanwhile, he was giving out a tall tale about not being able to write because he'd injured his thumb. Blake wanted to leave as few samples as possible of his own penmanship, as well as Stan's. The forged journal was supposed to create the illusion that Stan was completely thrilled over the spa project. That was vital in hiding Blake's motive. It's not that hard to copy somebody else's signature, but writing several original paragraphs requires a master forger. Blake was a lot of things, but not that."

Sipping at his Scotch, Milo ruminated. "What put the wind up Blake when Beverly called, I wonder?"

My answer didn't come readily. "Her certainty, maybe. She might have begged Blake to turn himself in. She may have threatened to talk to you. Beverly's an honest person, unlike her brother. She's been a mess ever since Stan was killed. I doubt that she could have lived with the knowledge for very long."

Milo stretched and yawned. "I wonder if Blake went off the road on purpose. Maybe we'll never know. I'd better check back in with the California Highway Patrol. And Santa Monica and my own people." He slumped a bit in the recliner, his expression sheepish. "Hell, Emma, what do I say to them?"

"That you heard if from a birdbrain?" The flippancy didn't sit well with the sheriff. "Okay," I went on, somewhat irked. "Tell them whatever you want. The evidence is all circumstantial and the killer is dead. Just close the case so that everybody in Alpine can stop suspecting everybody else."

Milo's hazel eyes threw me a challenge. "And how can I do that without going to the local press?"

I was dumbfounded, not so much by Milo but by my own obtuseness. In the past two hours since I'd unraveled the mystery of Stan's death, I hadn't consciously thought of the solution as a hot story for *The Advocate*. Where was my nose for news? What had happened to my priorities? Why had I bothered, if not to break out the big black headlines?

There was Stan, of course, an intelligent, decent man whose idealism had contributed to his murder. There was Truth and there was Justice and there was plain old-fashioned curiosity. But most of all there was Milo, who had pigheadedly refused to veer off the beaten path. Or trail, in this case. I hadn't wanted to see him self-destruct.

"I forget," I said. "When's your birthday?"

Once again Milo was regarding me as if I were a candidate for the loony bin. "March first. You bought me a couple of drinks, remember?"

I did. "Three. We all but reeled out of the Venison Inn. Okay," I sighed, "it's too late for your birthday. Consider this a Father's Day present. It's coming up a week from tomorrow."

"What are you talking about?"

I took a deep breath. "This is a gift. I don't want credit for this. It would be inappropriate. For one thing, I'm doing some guessing and making quite a few surmises. You can use what evidence there is—the burned stuff from the fire, the personal and corporate bank accounts, the forged journal, Skye's statements, Beverly's testimony. If Blake had lived and gone on trial, he'd probably have been convicted. The only thing you don't have is the gun."

"Shit!" Milo had sprung to his feet, knocking over a small lamp in the process. He made a grab for it, missed, and left it lying on the floor. "I'll bet I know where that sucker is! Come on, Emma, we're going up to the hot springs!"

"But I thought you said—"

It was useless to argue. Milo was at his hall closet, putting on hiking boots. I was wearing sandals. There was no way I could manage that rugged trail in such flimsy footgear.

"You'll have to go without me," I said as Milo

straightened up. I wiggled a foot at him. "Look, Pa, no shoes."

"We'll swing by your place so you can change," Milo said, opening the front door.

I opened my mouth to agree, then shook my head. "No, Milo." I put my hands on his shoulders. "This is your case. You grab the glory. I'll write about it. When you find the gun, I'll be down in the parking lot with my camera. We'll put you all over page one."

Milo looked as if he was going to argue, but he didn't. Instead he put his hands over mine and leaned down to kiss me. It started as a friendly gesture, then grew into something else. Startled, I let the kiss deepen and was vaguely aware that Milo now had his arms around me. When we finally pulled apart, perhaps by mutual consent or a need to breathe, he chuckled and I giggled.

"Crazy, huh, Emma?" he said, his voice a little thick.

"Really crazy." I suppressed what felt like a hiccup. We exchanged sheepish looks. "We've been under a strain," I said in a lame voice.

"Murder can do that to you." Milo rummaged in his pocket for his car keys. "Maybe I'll have time to fix your doorbell later today."

"That'd be great." We began walking out to the street. "Do you want to come for dinner?"

Milo grimaced. "I can't. I'm taking Honoria to some artsy-craftsy party in Snohomish. Can I have a rain check?" Suddenly, he sounded boyishly eager.

"Sure. Tomorrow would be fine. My weekend's wide open." We were almost to the Melvilles' house, where we'd left our cars. I could feel the unaccustomed awkwardness between us, yet it wasn't entirely unpleasant. "In fact, wait and fix the doorbell then."

"Okay." Milo had reached his Cherokee Chief. "You

had other plans, originally." His tone only hinted at a question.

I let out a long sigh. "I sure did. I'll tell you about it tomorrow. Maybe."

Milo nodded, then gave me his lopsided grin. "See you in the parking lot." He started to duck inside the vehicle, then bobbed up like a cork. "Hey—pick up Vida on your way. If you don't, she'll be . . . what's the word she uses?—*wild*."

I made a face. "Vida's got Roger."

"So? If it hadn't been for that miserable little brat, you might never have figured out who killed Stan Levine. Then I'd still be wandering around in a fog, and the rest of Alpine would go on being at each other's throats."

I didn't say anything. I just stood there by my car and smiled. Milo climbed into his Cherokee Chief and drove off. I got into the Jag, but waited to start the engine. The Melville house looked deceptively quiet, with the noonday sun glinting off its new picture window. Inside, Beverly and Scott were probably agonizing over the dark side of Blake Fannucci. There wasn't much I could do about their personal tragedy. They were young and strong; they'd struggle to put the horror behind them. Someday they might even feel as if they belonged in Alpine.

I did, most of the time. Passing the tree-lined golf course, I saw the stands of evergreens, marching up the mountainside. There was still snow on Baldy's twin ridges, though the patches had shrunk since the previous Saturday. As I drove out of the Icicle Creek development, San Francisco seemed far away and not quite real. The City, as Bay Area residents called it, has always struck me as a magical place—part chic sophistication, part unbridled hedonism, part cultural mecca. And always hostage to its history—the missionaries, the

Barbary Coast, the earthquake, the fire, the phoenix rising from the steep hills.

Alpine had hills, and there the similarity ended. I hadn't been able to spend the weekend with Tom. My opportunity to console him had been wiped out by Sandra's capriciousness. Or Tom's cowardice. Was his bondage a personality flaw? Had Sandra long ago bought and paid for him? Maybe I'd never figure it out. Anger with Tom, delayed and unfamiliar, was setting in, along with a sense of revolt. Maybe I was being unfair, even irrational. Tom's dilemma was mine as well—as long as I allowed it to affect me. But of one thing I was certain—I might not have helped him through his most recent crisis. Instead I'd been there for Milo.

The thought didn't make me sad. Not at all.

To my delight, Milo had found the murder weapon where his brainstorm had directed him. It was under the plastic lining in one of the hot springs pools. So was the small vise that had been used to hold the gun. In a typical show of respect for nature, the sheriff and his men hadn't wanted to disturb the mineral waters by making a search.

"We considered draining the pools at one point," Milo had explained while I fiddled with my camera in the parking lot later that afternoon. "But that meant stopping the incoming flow. It didn't seem right."

No doubt Blake had guessed how the local law enforcement people would react. Or maybe he just got lucky. Given time, the sulfurous waters would have corroded the gun, making identification impossible. But six days had done no real harm. With the help of his California colleagues, Milo was hoping to trace the murder weapon back to Blake. As the sheriff all but swaggered off to his Cherokee Chief, I shot my final frame of film.

It wouldn't be usable in the paper, but I wanted it as a keepsake.

Strangely, I didn't mind eating dinner alone at home that night. I'd finished my domestic chores while Milo was hiking up and down the hot springs trail. After I returned from my photo shoot, I considered calling Leonard Hollenberg. And Ed Bronsky. Their reactions to the death of Blake Fannucci—and thus of VineFan—would be included in our homicide coverage. It appeared that the ambitious spa project was also dead.

But Milo hadn't made any official pronouncements about the case. Knowing him, he'd take his time, mulling over the evidence, filling out reports, checking and rechecking with his fellow law enforcement officials in California. That was good. The longer Milo waited, the better were my chances for an honest-to-God exclusive. I didn't want credit for solving the murder, but I sure as hell hoped to get the jump on the rest of the media. That would be ample reward.

Which, as it turned out, was the very first word I heard out of my son when he called around nine that night. "Reward: one lost GPA. Please return immediately to owner. Gee, Mom, I think I'm going to bomb my finals. Why do professors have to give these dumb essay tests?"

I didn't bother to ask Adam why he hadn't studied harder. I skipped explaining the rationale behind essays. I ignored the need to point out to the younger generation that the written word still had merit.

"Have you talked to your uncle this week?" I asked instead. "How's the war?"

"He's got things calmed down. Uncle Ben is cool. He held a barbecue and everybody came and made up. Sort of. I wish I'd been there. Mom, these Native Americans need help. They're really great people, with serious feelings about nature and all that stuff. I think I'd like to be a social worker and help them. It's not fair what the white man did, barging onto their land and taking everything away. Think about it—how would you like it if some Martians came down to Earth and stole everything?"

Californians weren't Martians, but some Pacific Northwesterners considered them just as foreign. As long as there was a frontier, the adventurous would explore it. Exploit it, too. That was human nature, under any guise. Greed, ambition, opportunity—the bold and the desperate clambered all over the pages of America's history books.

"The Native Americans are getting their revenge with all these new casinos," I pointed out. "What better way to fleece the rest of the folks while letting them think they're having a wonderful time?"

"That's not the point," Adam said, sounding unusually serious. Obviously, he thought his mother was being frivolous. "We can't give back what we never had a right to take in the first place. You know, like their dignity and their culture. That's why I want to work with them like Uncle Ben does—and help break the cycle of poverty and alcoholism and being torn between two worlds. You wouldn't believe how deep these people are, both the Navajo and the Hopi. Then you go way back, to the Anasazi, and you see how they built their civilization in a time and a place that would have ruined other ethnic groups. Can you imagine the French or the Germans carving entire cities from the sides of cliffs?"

There are occasions when a parent shouldn't argue, even for the sake of argument. I sensed that this was one of them. Consciously or otherwise, Ben was exerting a heady influence over his nephew. The greatest lack in Adam's life until recently had been the absence of a father figure. I'd keep my mouth shut and wait to see what my brother had wrought.

Adam's enthusiasm didn't wane until someone arrived at his dorm, presumably to join forces in an assault on the upcoming exams. I verified the Phoenix flight's estimated arrival time at Sea-Tac, wished my son luck on the tests, and bade him good night.

The phone rang again before I got more than three feet away. I was half expecting it to be Vida, who must have been liberated from Roger by now.

But it was Ginny Burmeister, with bubbles in her voice. "Oh, Emma! I tried to call a couple of times earlier but you weren't home and I didn't want to leave a message. Not this kind of message, anyway. Don't faint—but Rick and I are engaged!"

Clearly, Ginny was more surprised that I was. But I wouldn't spoil her announcement. "That's terrific," I enthused. "When's the wedding?"

"February," she replied promptly. "We're not sure which day yet because we haven't talked to Pastor Nielsen at the Lutheran church. We'll do that next week. I can't wait to show you the ring! It's absolutely gorgeous!"

"Have you told Vida?" I asked.

"Yes, I talked to her this afternoon. She was utterly dumbfounded!" Ginny chortled. "Isn't it fun to put something over on her? I mean, she *always* knows *everything*."

So she did. So she had. But Ginny didn't need to know about the anxious speculation that had been going 'round the office. As for me, I'd forgotten about her romantic evening with Rick on *The River Queen*.

After hanging up with Ginny, I dialed Vida's number. She hadn't answered when I'd called to ask her along to the hot springs parking lot. I assumed she and Roger were off on their merry rounds of pleasure. Milo was right—Vida would never forgive me if I didn't fill her in on what had happened in the murder investigation. But Vida wasn't home. I guessed that she had dropped Roger off at his parents' house and stayed on for a visit. I'd keep trying to reach her every ten minutes or so. I couldn't let her find out about Blake Fannucci from Bill Blatt or some other source.

Just before midnight I became uneasy. Vida didn't go to bed early, but on the other hand, she was no night owl. I thought of calling her daughter, then changed my mind. Amy and Ted Hibbert had put in a long drive from Spokane. They were probably in bed and asleep.

Of course, Vida might be calling on some of her other numerous kinfolk. Perhaps she was seeking moral support for her Sunday meeting with Mr. Ree. That was dubious, however: Vida didn't need emotional props. She was always the one to nurture. Vida had broad shoulders in more ways than one.

At precisely midnight I put on my clothes and drove over to Vida's tidy little bungalow on Tyee Street. The house was dark, except for a light on the back porch. The detached garage was open and empty. Vida was out somewhere, having a good time. I was not her keeper, only her boss. And friend.

I stood by my car, chewing my lower lip. A murderer was no longer loose in Alpine. At least not one that we knew of. Still, it didn't seem right for Vida to stay out so late the night before the big meeting with her would-be suitor. Knowing Vida, she'd want to get her "beauty sleep."

A car was coming along Tyee, but it was going too fast for a sudden stop. I glimpsed a quartet of teenagers, probably returning from year-end revels.

I was switching on the ignition when another vehicle came from the opposite direction. This time the car did slow down, with its turn signal flashing. It was Vida's big white Buick. I expelled a sigh of relief.

"Emma!" Vida whirled when she saw me hurrying up the drive. "Whatever are you doing here at this time of night?"

"I wanted to tell you about the murder," I panted. "Blake Fannucci is dead and Milo found the gun and Beverly told us that—"

"Yes, yes," Vida interrupted impatiently. "After I dropped Roger off, I took Billy out to dinner at King Olav's. My treat." She unlocked the back door, then flipped on the lights. "Roger and I had seen Milo hightailing it out of town when we were at the Burger Barn for lunch. I suspected something was up. Why didn't you tell me?"

"Well . . ." Wearily, I sat down in one of Vida's kitchen chairs. "You had Roger and I didn't want to bother—"

"Bother, indeed!" Vida scoffed. "Really, Emma, you'd think Roger was a duty, not a pleasure. I'm surprised at you. Would you care for tea?"

I shook my head. "Mostly, I was worried about you. I've been trying to call since ten o'clock."

Vida removed her veiled pillbox and also sat down. "Goodness, I can take care of myself. I've been doing it for over sixty years."

"I know, but still . . ."

"Mr. Ree is Henry Bardeen."

". . . when it gets so late and . . . *what*?" I all but rocketed out of the chair.

"You heard me." Vida was looking very tight-lipped. "Henry put that ad in the paper."

I was incredulous. "But . . . Henry's around fifty. Why would he want a woman in her sixties?"

"Henry's handwriting is atrocious. He wrote down *sexy-plus*, not *sixty-plus*. Or so he claims. Ginny misread it. Not that I blame her. Doesn't that beat all?" Vida made a disparaging face.

I tried to let the enormity of the mistake sink in. My eyes wandered around the kitchen, landing on Cupcake's covered cage. Again I thought of birds. "So Mr. Ree has flown the coop?" I murmured.

"Not exactly." Vida tugged at one earlobe. "It seems that Henry somehow figured out I was the one he was supposed to meet tomorrow in Everett. He simply couldn't face up to it, so while Billy and I were having dinner at King Olav's, Henry came over and poured his heart out. It's really rather pitiful, Emma. He's been very lonely since Doris died, but he just couldn't bring himself to ask a certain woman out. So he bought the personals ad, hoping she'd see it."

Confusion replaced astonishment. "*She?* You mean the ideal sexy-plus woman?"

"She being Francine Wells. Henry's had a crush on her for some time. *Sexy-plus* was a larger-sizes line she carried for a while, but it was too risqué for Alpine. The ads caused quite a controversy. But that was before your time. Now it appears that Francine didn't read Henry's ad. Or she ignored it. I suppose I'll have to play Cupid." Vida's eyes sparkled at the thought.

"But what about you? Your hot date is all washed up." My gaze was full of sympathy. Vida and I were in the same boat.

But Vida hardly seemed dismayed. "Where there's life, there's hope." Her expression was enigmatic. "Henry felt just terrible about . . . leading me on, so to speak. He wants to make amends. And of course he's terribly embarrassed, which is much better than having him angry with the paper for running the wrong wording in the ad. After all, I proofed it, even though Ginny was the one who typed it up. She can hardly be blamed for not deciphering Henry's handwriting."

I recalled watching Henry scribble out the check at the liquor store. "Yes, it's pretty bad," I acknowledged.

"So," Vida went on with a monumental heave of her bosom, "Henry is fixing me up with his brother."

Vaguely, I recalled some mention of another Bardeen. "I thought he and Henry didn't keep in touch."

"So did I," Vida agreed. "But that was a false impression. Ralph Bardeen is retired from the Air Force—a colonel, I believe—widowed, sixty-four years old, and has recently moved back to Everett." Deliberately, Vida opened her purse and searched among its contents. "Here's his picture. This was taken a year or so ago at Vandenberg Air Force Base in California. Ralph's nickname is Buck."

Ralph "Buck" Bardeen was tall, broad-shouldered, and his gray hair seemed to be his own. He was attired in slacks and a rather hideous tropical print shirt. But the smile was open and the gaze seemed appropriately keen.

"Very nice," I remarked, handing the photo back to Vida. "Is he interested in the same things as Henry? Music, theatre, travel?"

"Not travel," Vida said, snapping her purse shut. "He's been everywhere and wants to settle down."

"So you'll go out with him?"

Vida shrugged. "We may as well meet." She gestured at her full figure with one hand. "I haven't lost all this weight for nothing, you know."

As far as I could tell, Vida didn't look an ounce thinner. But the important thing was that she looked like Vida and she was in one piece. It was almost twelve-thirty. I stood up to go, then leaned down and gave my friend an impulsive hug.

"You scared me," I said. "What would we do without you? What would I do?"

A small huffing noise came out of Vida's mouth,

which I took as a prelude to a testy retort. But Vida merely patted my arm and smiled. I pretended that I didn't notice the glint of grateful tears in her eyes.

"Come to dinner tomorrow night," I said, the invitation popping out of my mouth. "I've already asked Milo."

"That sounds enjoyable," Vida replied. "Unless," she added, seeing me to the door, "you two want to be alone."

I stared. "No, of course not! I mean, it's Milo and me. Why would we want to be alone?"

Vida had blinked away the tears. She now looked very ingenuous. "Oh—let's say that a little bird told me."

I refused to rise to the bait. "I'll see you around five-thirty. Good night, Vida."

On Wednesday afternoon *The Alpine Advocate* broke its exclusive coverage of the Stan Levine homicide investigation. Milo Dodge was covered in righteous glory. I was covered with a sense of professional achievement. It's rare that a small-town weekly gets a jump on the rest of the media.

I had written all the copy myself, except for the cutlines. I let Carla do that, figuring she couldn't get us into any trouble. Of course I was wrong: She'd spelled Fannucci's first name as *Bleak*. Nobody on the staff had caught the mistake.

Ironically, Milo was the first to call. "Great job," he said trying to sound modest. "You make me sound like a hero. But somebody misspelled Blake."

That was when I reread the front-page cutline. "Damn," I breathed. "You're right. We're wrong."

"Not entirely," Milo said in his laconic manner. "In a way, it's accurate. Last week I was feeling pretty bleak myself."

"You were too willing to give up too soon," I noted, juggling the phone with one hand and the newspaper with the other. "You're usually more tenacious. Frankly, I was a little surprised at your attitude."

"Maybe it's because I didn't want the killer to be someone from Alpine. That could have really put this town on its ear. There's enough gloom and doom without setting a precedent for killing off anybody with new ideas."

"I can understand that part," I replied. "But this is a good lesson in perseverance."

"Perseverance." Milo's voice took on a strangely musing tone. "You mean in not giving up even when you think there's absolutely no hope?"

I couldn't quite figure out why Milo sounded so odd. "Right. Persistence."

"But once in a while something happens that's encouraging?"

"Right. That's when you get a new dose of hope."

"Even if you get invited to dinner and Vida Runkel shows up wearing a sombrero?"

"That wasn't a sombrero, it was a gaucho hat. Hey, wait a minute, Milo—what are you talking about?"

The sheriff chuckled. "Persistence. Perseverance. Hope. Got to go, Emma. Jack Mullins just got a report of a cougar prowling the golf course. See you."

I sat there staring at the phone for about three minutes. Surely Milo didn't mean what I thought he meant? When had he ever shown persistence or perseverance in advancing our relationship? Coming off of the Levine investigation, the sheriff was in a good mood. He must have been teasing.

Then again, there was always hope. Vida had said the same thing.

And when was Vida ever wrong?